The Son of Silence

BY THE SAME AUTHOR

The Superhumans
The Human Ant

The Son of Silence and Other Anarchist Fantasies

by
Han Ryner

Translated, annotated and introduced by
Brian Stableford

A Black Coat Press Book

ISBN 978-1-61227-549-9. First Printing. August 2016. Published by Black Coat Press, an imprint of Hollywood Comics.com, LLC, P.O. Box 17270, Encino, CA 91416. All rights reserved. Except for review purposes, no part of this book may be reproduced or transmitted in any form or by any means, electronic or mechanical, including photocopying, recording, or by any information storage and retrieval system, without permission in writing from the publisher. The stories and characters depicted in this novel are entirely fictional. Printed in the United States of America.

TABLE OF CONTENTS

Introduction

Le Fils du silence by Han Ryner, here translated as "The Son of Silence," was first published by Eugène Figuière et Cie. in 1911. *Les Paraboles cyniques*, here translated as "Cynic Parables," was published by the same publisher in 1913, and followed in its turn by *Les Pacifiques* (1914; tr. as "The Pacifists" in *The Human Ant and Other Stories*)[1] but it would be a mistake to assume that the works were necessarily written in that order; the internal evidence of the last-named text strongly suggests that it was written in 1905, and although there is no internal evidence of dates of composition in the two texts included in the present volume, they were probably composed in close association with it. It is possible that they were able to get into print belatedly because of the sudden and unprecedented success of Ryner's *Le Cinquième Évangile* [The Fifth Gospel] (1911), which went through several editions in the early months of 1911, and that the order in which the three volumes cited appeared reflects the degree to which they were dear to the author's heart rather than their order of composition.

Like *Les Pacifiques, Le Fils du Silence* contains a vision of an anarchist utopia, here attributed to the influence of legendary philosopher Pythagoras as a result of a fact-finding tour of the philosophical and religious doctrines of his era. Although the fictitious cynic philosopher Psychodorus, whose more phantasmagorical explorations of hypothetical possibility had earlier been described in *Les Voyages de Psychodore* (1903; tr. as "The Travels of Psychodorus, Cynic Philosopher" in *The Superhumans and Other Stories*),[2] sternly refuses to found any kind of community, he too is an individualistic an-

---

[1] Black Coat Press, ISBN 978-1-61227-323-5.
[2] Black Coat Press, ISBN 978-1-935558-77-4.

archist of exactly the same stripe as Ryner's Pythagoras and his Atlantean pacifists. As such he is another of the many rhetorical devices with which the author experimented for the purpose of elaborating and disseminating his own philosophical ideas, in the particular phase of his literary development that he had attained in the first decade of the twentieth century.

That experimental period was brought to an end by the Great War, whose durance inevitably transformed the author's attitude and method of procedure; it certainly did not weaken his commitment to individualistic anarchism and pacifism, nor did it put a complete end to his literary experimentation, but it did leave him metaphorically shell-shocked for a while, as it did the entire French nation and its literary culture. Both of the works included in the present volume, along with the others cited above, were reprinted once the war was over, and continued to generate new editions thereafter—the 1922 edition of *Les Paraboles cyniques* was the sixth, and the list of the authors works included therein advertised the current edition of *Le Fils du silence* was the fourth—so they probably sold more copies after the war than before it, but hindsight allows us to see now that they were products of an earlier and more adventurous period of his thought and sentiment.

Jacques Élie Henri Ambroise Ner was born at Nemours, in the French colony of Oran—which is now Ghazaouet, in Algeria—on 7 December 1861. He described himself in *Les Voyages de Psychodore, philosophe cynique* as "a hybrid barbarian, the son of a Norwegian father and a Catalan mother" but his first language was French, and when he set his sights firmly on a literary vocation, working as a schoolteacher while he struggled with the usual difficulties attendant on nursing such ambitions, he went to Paris to work as a journalist. After publishing *Chair vaincue, roman psychologique* [Vanquished Flesh, a Psychological Novel] (1889), he was introduced into the salon culture of literary Paris, making the acquaintance of Alphonse Daudet, Remy de Gourmont and Joseph-Henri Boëx, alias J.-H. Rosny.

Although Ner's early novels were in a Naturalistic vein akin to that favored by Daudet, he shared Gourmont's interest in symbolism and Rosny's interest in speculative fiction, subsequently developing both threads in his own work extensively, especially in the short fiction he produced in some quantity during the 1890s. Much of that short fiction appeared in political periodicals of a radical stripe, and frequently took exotic forms, but his early novels remained conventional in their themes and narrative method; *L'Humeur inquiète* [A Restless Temperament] (1894), described the tribulations of a man torn between two women and *La Folie de misère, roman d'histoire contemporaine* [The Madness of Poverty; A Contemporary Novel] (1895) offered an account of a mother driven by desperation to murder her children.

As Ner's activity as a political journalist increased in volume, it also increased in polemical fervor, and he achieved a degree of fame as an outspoken anarchist, albeit of an unusual stripe that ostensibly took its inspiration directly from Greek philosophy, especially the Cynic, Stoic and Epicurean philosophies that he considered to be the most important legacy of Socratic thought. He often referred to his brand of individualism as "harmonic individualism," in order to distinguish it from the "egoistic individualism" of more aggressive writers, associating it with the Pythagorean and Platonic notion of "the harmony of the spheres," albeit in an idiosyncratic fashion. *Le Fils du silence* represents his most elaborate analysis and interpretation of those ideative roots.

In 1898 Ner decided to adopt a new signature, retaining the pronunciation of his name but transforming its orthography, becoming "Han Ryner." In that new guise, he put his talents as a writer of fiction firmly under the domination of his political-philosophical convictions, soon producing the polemical *Le Crime d'obéir, roman d'histoire contemporaine* [The Crime of Obedience; a Novel of Contemporary History] (1900), whose protagonist rebels—in a strictly not-violent fashion—against the oppressions of contemporary society. *Petit manuel individualiste* [Little Individualist Handbook]

(1903) summarized his ideas succinctly in non-fictional form. His literary criticism, the first collection of which was uncompromisingly entitled *Prostitués, études critiques sur les gens des lettres d'aujourd'hui* [Prostitutes: Critical Studies of Today's Men of Letters] (1904) mostly consisted of scathing attacks on the supposed moral failures of his contemporaries, which rapidly isolated him within the literary society of Paris, although a few of his friends, including Rosny, remained steadfast.

In addition to works cited above, Ryner's other important extended *contes philosophiques* of the first decade of the century were *L'Homme-fourmi* (1901; tr. as "The Human Ant") and *Le Sphinx rouge, roman individualiste* [The Red Sphinx: An Individualist Novel] (1905). He did not abandon naturalistic fiction entirely, however, his further work in that vein including *Le Soupçon* [Suspicion] (1900), a novel about obsessive jealousy, and *La Fille manquée* [The Defective Girl] (1903), a study of homosexuality. Always closely associated with his political and philosophical convictions, Ner's *contes* were frequently didactic, often being explicitly framed as fables, parables or apologues. He made plans to issue a collection of *Contes prophétiques* [Prophetic Tales], whose imminent publication was announced in the periodical *Partisans* in 1900, but it never appeared, and most of the short fiction he wrote for radical periodicals remained unreprinted in his lifetime, in spite of his being unexpectedly voted the "Prince des Conteurs" [Prince of Storytellers] in a poll organized by the newspaper *L'Intransigeant*—by no means a periodical noted for its Anarchist or pacifist sympathies—in 1912.

After the War, Ryner published *La Tour des Peuples* [The Tower of the Nations] (1919), a novel recycling the story of the Tower of Babel, which bears a considerable resemblance to his pre-war work and was probably written then, but only a handful of works he published for the first time thereafter were cast in fictional form. The most interesting are *Le Père Diogène* [Father Diogenes] (1920), a comedy about a Quixotic individual who tries to live like the cynics of old in the modern era; *L'Autodidacte* [The Autodidact] (1926), in which the autobiography of a hypothetical inventor attempts to analyze the relationship between human beings and technology; *La Vie éternelle, roman du mystère* [Eternal Life; A Mystery Story] (1926), a romance of serial reincarnation; and the spectacularly phantasmagorical futuristic fantasy *Les Surhommes, roman prophétique* (1929; tr. as "The Superhumans" in *The Superhumans and Other Stories*). He died in Paris on 6 January 1938.

Les Paraboles cyniques is probably a more interesting work in terms of its narrative method than by virtue of its oblique development of ideas that are more cogently, coherently and imaginatively developed elsewhere, in both *Le Fils du silence* and *Les Pacifiques* as well as other works. As an experiment in the development and use of the parable as an art-form, however, it is both highly unusual and remarkable. Its preface calls useful attention to the fact that the method of teaching now associated with Jesus was not original at the time, although its previous uses in Greek philosophy have been largely effaced from the historical record, partly as a result of deliberate suppression by jealous Christians.

Where Cynic parables appear to have differed from those recorded in the gospels was their deliberate use of a narrative strategy that the Greeks called *spoudaiogeloion* [serio-comic], the oxymoron in question having apparently being coined by Aristophanes in *The Frogs*. It was a rhetorical tactic taken up by numerous philosophers, although it was not always recognized by their stubborn followers; Plato's attribution of his account of the hermaphrodites in the Symposium to Aristophanes could hardly be a clearer advertisement of its spoudaiogeloionic nature, but even Psychodorus, who surely ought to have known better, implies in one of Ryner's parables that Plato might actually have meant it. Psychodorus' own followers, however, often seems to be have difficulty coming to terms with his uses of spoudaiogeloion, and Ryner must have had the same experience in measuring the reader reaction to most of his own works in that vein. Its use does, however, lend itself to quotability, which is why so many Cynic philosophers are now known almost entirely through quotes attributed to them by other writers, plus the occasional scurrilous anecdote.

Not unnaturally, seriously as well as seriocomically—the two are not incompatible—Ryner belonged to the school of thought that credited Jesus with being an important pioneer of anarchist thought, which he promoted enthusiastically in *Le Cinquième Évangile*, but the parables he credits to the cynic Polydorus are more elaborate and more elliptical as well as more comical than the ones conventionally credited to Jesus, and it is a pity that the actual cynic parables that are known to have been produced are no longer available for comparison. Ryner shrewdly observes, however, that most of the surviving anecdotes concerning Antisthenes and Diogenes, the founders of the cynic philosophy, and many of their contemporaries in the fifth and fourth centuries B.C. probably originated as parables themselves rather than records of actual events. Indeed, the various accounts of the origin of the term "cynic" [literally dog-like], including those allegedly invented by the cynics as well as by their detractors, are probably best considered as parables too, although Polydorus does not add to their number.

By comparison, *Le Fils du silence* is particularly valuable as a succinct, albeit blatantly opinionated, summary of the philosophical and religious ideas supposedly current in the sixth century B.C. It is a striking exercise in the speculative sociology of religion, and although its elaborate accounts of the Samothracian and Eleusianian Mysteries, the supposed teachings of Zarathustra, etc., are fictitious they are nevertheless based in the few classical accounts that we do have, and carry a certain amount of conviction. The story's accounts of "Chaldean" and Egyptian religion are more obviously satirical and sarcastic, but they too have scholarly bases that, although they have been superseded by more recent research, were by no means inept for their time.

The narrative takes full advantage of the fact that relatively little is known about the historical Pythagoras, leaving a near-blank space in which the novelist can carry out considerable invention, improvising a character that probably does not resemble the historical Pythagoras very much, but is both interesting and engaging. His resemblance to Han Ryner must also be reckoned slight in some respects, however, especially in the sense that, while the hero of the novel justifies his nickname, the author was by no means given to silence, and rather tended to the garrulous.

Ryner was, of course fully aware of that irony, as evidenced by the fact that his account of Psychodorus includes a chapter, complete with supportive parable, arguing the virtue of never writing anything—although one can, of course, concede that arguments that might have held good in the fifth and sixth centuries B.C. could have lost their cultural currency two and a half millennia later. In any case, Ryner's construction of his fictional Pythagoras is both intriguing and ingenious, and telling his story represented a challenging literary experiment as well constituting one of the most original adventures in the field of anarchist utopianism.

The translation of *Le Fils du silence* was made from the copy of the 1911 Figuière edition reproduced on the Internet Archive website at *archive.org*. The translation of *Les Paraboles cyniques* was made from the copy of the 1922 Athena edition reproduced in the same website. The English and French languages differ in their habitual transcription of Greek names, and are by no means entirely consistent in so doing; Ryner's transcriptions are sometimes eccentric and often inconsistent; I have mostly followed a policy of substituting familiar English transcriptions where they are available and have sometimes transcribed Ryner's fictitious names in a similar fashion, but have been content to allow a few evident inconsistencies to stand.

Brian Stableford

THE SON OF SILENCE

Book One: PHERECYDES

For two days the island had been celebrating. All the inhabitants of the city of Samos, and those of the tiny Oinon and Dracomium, as well as those of the villages and countryside, even those of Narthekis and other small neighboring islands, were eating, drinking, dancing and sleeping around the temple of Hera. Some had raised light tents against the heat and the sun's violence, on the beach or in the clearings of the sacred forest, but the majority was content with the shade of the trees, the sea breeze or the serpentine freshness of the Imbrasos.

Today, the third day of the festival, it was most moving solemnity of all: the famous hierogamy renewing the marriage of Zeus of the broad brow and Hera with the large proud eyes.[3]

Those who were not taking part in the nuptial pomp watched piously as the meanders of prayer and glory unfurled along the route strewn with verdure. Like the first waters of a flood, the hundred oxen of the hecatomb advanced in the lead, heavily and hesitantly; each step they took shook the flowers that hid their horns like two plumes. Then came the young

---

[3] When the novel was published, the hierogamy of Hera and Zeus was well-known thanks to representations found during the excavations at Pompeii and widely publicized. Excavations of the Heraion, a large sanctuary to Hera on the island of Samos, the birthplace of Pythagoras, had been carried out in 1890-92, and a new series had begun in 1910, but this part of the story is set shortly before that monument was built.

men with sparkling weapons and flute-players joyfully modu-
lating the hierakion.

The chariot was surrounded by the most beautiful young
women; they wore crowns of *agnus castus*;[4] the same flower
made blue, gray or pink clusters tremble round harmonious
girdles and the slender nudity of their arms. Sometimes, the
flutes fell silent, the cortege stopped and the virgins turned
toward the goddess. Some raised their empty hands, agitating
florid bracelets over their heads. Meanwhile, they sang:

"O Glorious One, born beneath the *agnus castus* that
borders the Imbrasos."

Or:

"O Glorious One, become beneath the *agnus castus* of
the Imbrasos the spouse of Zeus of the broad brow."

Others took handfuls of petals, corollas and calices from
baskets, and threw those brightly colored delicate forms beneath the feet of the harnessed oxen and the wheels of the
chariot. The perfume flowed into the air, taut and crackling
like fiery metal.

In the chariot, the statue stood very tall. But the candor
of its marble disappeared beneath the bridal vestments. A
necklace of the richest gems descended over her bosom, and
her robe made its colors of gold and crimson burst forth in
radiance. Behind her, hair trailed or floated strangely in long,
broad the thick tresses. They were blonde, brunette or chest-
nut, rude or supple, fine or coarse, all reserved for the glory of
that day: the hair of maidens who had died in the course of the
year. A powerful circle of gold, descending over the forehead
and falling almost to the nape, encircled the composite tresses,
maintaining the spoils snatched from the tomb on the head of
the immortal. Narrower and lighter, a second crown, a bonnet
of flowers, occupied the summit of the head; the *agnus castus*

---

[4] The shrub named Vitex by Pliny the elder and nowadays
classified as *Vitex agnus-castus*, was familiarly known as the
"chastetree" because of its supposed anaphrodisiac properties

of the goddess intertwined its rebellious stems there with the supple herbs of Aphrodite, sesame and poppies.

At the rear of the chariot, four peacocks allowed their sumptuous colors to descend, all the way to the crushed flowers and verdure, like the trail of a royal mantle. Excited by the noise, the heat and the innumerable eyes of the crowd, one of them occasionally elevated the opulence of a quivering and concave tail; as if in adoration, it turned toward the goddess the gloriously vibrant vault, which, in its tremulous display, sowed a metallic murmur.

The cortege, a superb river with living banks, flowed initially, amid the restlessness of the crowd, from the temple to the Imbrasos. It reached the bend where the river hides its coolest and most modest waves between the swaying grass and the bushy trees. There a young Samian girl, on the morning of her marriage, often comes to take the symbolic bath; there she strives to wash away in indecisive emotions of an awakening heart, and all the memories that do not indicate the husband, in order that they might flow away in the current of the river and drown in the vastness of the sea.

The goddess, undressed by the virginal anthesphores,[5] was plunged into the purifying waters; then, piously, the hands of the young women wiped her aristocratic beauty and dressed it again.

They returned to the temple. All the way to the utmost profundities of the monument, the occidental sun precipitated a flood of light and flame through the wide-open doors. In the

---

[5] This term, which seems to be mistakenly applied here, is found in several 19th century French texts, notably P. N. Rolle's *Recherches sur le culte de Bacchus* [Research on the Worship of Bacchus] (1824), from which Ryner appears to have borrowed some of the details of his account of the Mysteries of Samothrace and Eleusis, although most of them are ultimately derived Charles François Dupuis's *Origine de tous les cultes ou religion universelle* [Origin of all Cults; or, Universal Religion (1795), which the author might also have used.

growing emotion of the multitude, the young men threw down their weapons noisily, and the virgins intoned the most sacred hymns.

On the perron, the high priest waited, enveloped in the splendors of Helios. He held a long branch of ivy before him, showing it to the people, a symbol of the bonds that Cronus could not wear away. Porters took the statue from the chariot and headed slowly toward him. Then, his imperious gesture and his solemn words, having caused all heads to incline, he placed the ivy in the hands of the goddess. Then, standing aside, he permitted the porters to take Hera into the glory of her new life.

The sacrificers immolated the victims. Broadly and slowly, in a sticky sheet, a river of blood flowed down the steps of the temple, seeming to bear the red bellows of agony toward the redness of the dying sun. Meanwhile, the priests leaned over to examine the entrails. Eventually, they straightened up again, and their chief, turning to the people, proclaimed by means of grave and ritual formulae that the heavens were favorable to the marriage.

In the depths of the sanctuary, willow branches formed the nuptial couch. Stripped of the crowns and rich fabrics, the goddess, solely enveloped in the tresses of the dead maidens, was laid down in the sacred bed.

"Favor the gods by your silence!" cried the high priest.

The temple emptied noiselessly. With tremulous precaution, the doors, the hinges of which had been oiled the previous day, were closed again, and everyone drew away respectfully, weighed down by mysterious thoughts.

But night was falling. The wood and the beach were illuminated by torches. In families or amicable groups, sitting on the grass or the sand, the Samians began the banquet.

All day long, two men had been isolated from the crowd. If a unanimous preoccupation had not made the gazes of the people prisoners of a single spectacle, they would have been perceived across thirty stadia of pure, raw light, silhouettes shrunk by distance but not blurred; they stood high on the promontory of Poseidon, white against the blue intensity of the sky, behind the blue intensity of the sea.

They were conversing. Sometimes, they looked at the city at their feet, like a courtesan lying alongside the waves with her negligent head raised to the north, in accordance with an idle rhythm, in order to cover with a scattered disorder the first effort of the mountain, still uncertain and almost falling back like a wave.

More often, beyond the houses, their gazes, radiant with intelligence and scorn, extended to the Imbrasos, to the trees, to the beach, to the temple and the tents, all the way to the vast landscape of which they usually loved the noble grace and the austere smile of solitude, but which was rendered ugly today by the stupidity of the crowd and the lies of conventional gestures.

One of the men was eighteen years old. His commencing strength and the imminent beauty of his serene and thoughtful visage were most often—as the banks of the river are blurred by a mist that caresses and disperses light—covered and blurred by a floating prettiness, a light, filleting grace that might have been puerile or feminine. Young men of his own age called him, for the eurhythmia of his being, Pythagoras son of Apollo, but when he smiled he resembled his mother, the gently pensive Parthenis.[6]

---

[6] The allegation that Pythagoras' mother was named Parthenis originates from the neo-Platonist philosopher Iamblichus, but he might well have intended the name, which means "virgin" symbolically. Many of the generally-accredited details of Pythagoras' "biography" come from neo-Platonist sources, a previous life of Pythagoras having been complied by Porphyry. Those details thus date from the third and fourth centuries A.D., some seven or eight hundred years later than the philosopher's death, all the sources that Porphyry and Iamblichus allegedly drew upon having been lost.

Already, at certain thoughtful moments, noble shadows surrounded him, behind which an indefinable beauty awoke, a profundity in which the generosity and impetus of centuries gathered powerfully, a vast basin simultaneously both source and receptacle, in which the past, before precipitating its heavy cataracts toward the future, came to purify itself and to swell with new waves. It was an unusual beauty, as different from that of luminous and superficial Olympians as that of imprecise children and smooth-browed women. The man who has penetrated as far as you, Human Beauty, scorns the animal ugliness to which the vulgar give your name—even the secret suppleness of the tiger or the priest, or the powerful brutality of the warrior, similar even in repose to russet beasts lying on the sand, whose taut springs always threaten to unwind.

Mnesarchus, the engraver of seals, who had become one of the richest and most influential citizens of Samos, said: "Eunomus, my eldest son, will be, like me, a good man who serves the city. Tyrrhenus, my youngest child, proud of an insufficiently virile beauty, causes me anxieties.[7] But their brother Pythagoras, even I, his father, only dare name with respect, and his words seem to me to descend from the heavens like the light, or rise up from Hades like fertility.

Pythagoras' interlocutor, a man of forty-five, with long features and a vast forehead, abundant thick black hair and a beard that was almost tawny, was his loving and beloved master. That great wanderer, that great restless individual, Pherecydes, had quit fertile Syros in order to travel the world, to understand it and sing it.[8] For three years, however, he had

---

[7] Pythagoras is credited with two brothers, Tyrrhenus and Eunostus, by Porpyhry, allegedly on the authority of the *Pythagorica* of Neanthes of Cyzicus, written in the fourth century B.C. but lost. Both brothers are, however, said by Porphyry to have been older than Pythagoras.

[8] Only a few fragments of the works of Pherecydes of Syros survive, and he is almost exclusively known from references crediting him with being the teacher of Pythagoras. He was

lingered in the narrow isle for the sole joy of giving his science to the marvelous young man he hoped to see surpass him.

Anacreon and Ibycus said: "He's not a poet, he's only a sage."[9]

Old Pittacus, to whom he had once listened religiously in Mytilene, proclaimed with an equal disdain: "He's not a sage, he's only a poet."[10]

As soon as he spoke or sang, everyone listened, simultaneously moved and wounded, the poets by a poetry more splendid than their own, but whose depth and directness irritated them, the sages by a sagacity in which enthusiasm was mingled like generous wine in the blood of a thinker or the palpitating and uplifting power of wings on the heaviness of a body.

When he went by people fell silent, fearful and hostile. Behind him, timid voices related prodigies. Had he not been seen in Caulonis to kill a viper by biting it? Did not maladies and wild beasts obey him, as a quivering herd in which ewes and heifers are confused obeys a herdsman? "But the man is wicked," added the murmurs. His prickly mockery rejected the pleas of the sick, and he had only demonstrated his power previously in order to deepen the despair of those whom he refused to help. In any case, it was prudent not to show that one

---

allegedly an important promoter of the idea of metempsychosis, the transmigration of souls.

[9] The lyric poet Anacreon, who died around 485 B.C., came to Samos as a refugee from the depredations of Cyrus the Great and was said by Herodotus to have become tutor to Polycrates, who was the island's tyrant from c538 to 522 B.C. Ibycus, remembered by ancient scholars as a composer of pederastic verses, was also known to be in Samos during Polycrates' reign,

[10] Pittacus of Mytilene (c640-558 B.C.) was hailed as one of the Seven Sages of Greece by virtue of the social reforms he brought about when elected to rule the city following the defeat of a Athenian army by forces under his command.

hated him and it was necessary not to attack him, even by surprise and from behind, for the raised arm of the assailant
would wither like a dead branch.

When night fell, and the torches dispersed in the woods,
along the Imbrasos and on the beach, indicating the end of the
religious ceremony and the commencement of the banquet,
Pythagoras and Pherecydes, descending from the promontory,
traversed the deserted city. Having avoided the people all day,
now they went toward them. Did the spontaneous stupidity
and lax brutality of the crowd seem to them more instructive
or less repugnant than its docility and the savant lies of the
priests?

They passed close to groups, sometimes stopping, but
without mingling with any of them. They looked at everything
and listened to everything, but did not share any of the abruptly changing passions. Amid pity and scorn, they likened the
human herd to the herd of Poseidon, blind waves that unknown forces lift up and drive, sometimes toward some facile
shore, sometimes toward the abrupt hardness of rocks on
which folly and momentum break, where impotence is irritated and turns to foam.

Thus they observed the vast and multiple agitation, noisy
with songs, cries and quarrels. Over the luminous and moving
beauty woven by the night rich in stars, the torches and the
wind, they gazed at the ugly shadows cast by men: here, the
incoherent gestures of drunkards; there, the abrupt release of
lusts that could no longer be contained; elsewhere, rising and
growing, the violence of long-secret hatreds, shaken by the
orders of the wine, as an army previously immobile and hidden in the perfidious coverts in the hills hears the summons of
strategy, quivers and rushes forth.

Couples are also gliding slyly.

"Zeus and Hera," murmured Pherecydes.

Sometimes, in the couple, there is no woman but an
ephebe with trailing feet, upon whom the virile arm leans is
infamous nonchalance.

"Zeus and Ganymede," said the sage, contemptuous of men and gods.

Nearby, almost brushing them, one of those more ignoble couples passed furtively. Pherecydes pretended not to see them. Pythagoras, blushing, following them with a long glance that hid, broke off and returned. It was the richest of Samians, the handsomest and strongest of men of thirty, Polycrates, son of the tyrant Aeaces, and, as pretty and shy as a thirteen-year-old courtesan, Tyrrhenus, Pythagoras' younger brother.

The noble son of Mnesarchus, ashamed, wondered how brothers can be so different.

No precise response surged forth within him, but like fragments of a commencing dream, images formed and were deformed, the uncertain lineaments of a future doctrine. With his mind's eye, he saw souls avid to live again and which—like the drunkards in the distance fighting over a cup—struggle around the gesture of amour. The initial problem is resolved into multiple questions: "Who was I before being called Pythagoras? Who was he before being called Tyrrhenus?"

Perhaps he was about to pose those redoubtable questions to his master; but the thought, still floating, was dispersed by an external event, and its fragments fell back into the unconscious depths, an ear of corn spilled into the blind earth but which would rise again in future, an enriched crop.

Pythagoras had felt a hand placed on his shoulder, and, turning round, recognized the priest Demas, a friend of the family.

The young man renounced following his train of thought, which became as sparse and ungraspable as a fleeing flock. He looked at Demas and Pherecydes, rapidly comparing the two men.

The priest was perhaps the more handsome for vulgar eyes; but his beauty did not reveal, like the silent Pherecydes, emotional and curious sincerity, or noble self-examination, or the anxious joy or a man groping in the might of existence in the dusk of his soul. Even less did it reveal, as the face of

Pherecydes did as soon as he spoke to his disciple, generous affection and the need to impart its treasures. By virtue of his powerful equilibrium, by the emphasis of a stride that never hesitates and the gesture that was always firm, by the heavy and disdainful determination in his eyes, the eloquent and masterful crease of his lips, Demas retained, even in the flickering light of torches, the implacable precision of a tyrant or a destiny. At certain moments, however one sensed the suppleness that hides and returns, something fleeting and obstinate, the coquetry of savant refusal that excites desire, or the false retreat that draws into an ambush; his eyes then became as searching as those of spies, as avid as those of courtesans.

"O son of pious Mnesarchus," he said, "where are you coming from at this hour, and where were you during the wedding of Hera?

His tone modulated both reproach and condescending affection, seeming to summon confession and repentance, already promising pardon.

Pythagoras smiled, like a disabused lover who knows the tricks of old mistress too well.

"I saw the ceremony," he replied. "I saw it from higher up than you."

"Arrogant!" cried the priest. "Has Ate the baleful blinded you to the extent that you believe that you can rise higher than the gods!"

With a negligent gesture, the young man cast remarks that were seemingly disconnected.

"With Hera's aid, Ate blinded Zeus to the extent of making him the persecutor of Heracles. A father persecutes a son worth more than him. A king persecutes virtue and courage. Zeus, who had had the trouble of being born and betraying his father, became the enemy of Heracles, the enemy of monsters. Heracles was the only virtuous god, because he was first, and for a long time, a man. If I don't show Ate the irresistible more force than Zeus, will Zeus dare to condemn me?"

"Zeus orders that he should be worshipped, and not judged."

"In that respect he resembles the tyrants, his sons. That's why he is, like tyrants, respected by trembling multitudes and scorned by the few free-thinking men."

"Who is your god, then, Child?"

"I'm looking for him."

"Fool, who is looking for what we have found a long time ago."

Pherecydes intervened: "Keep looking, my son...and since you sincerely want to find, search above all within yourself." Then he turned to Demas. "For myself, I love your Hera, and I think with emotion about her future glory."

"Why future?" interrogated the surprised priest. "Has she not yesterday and today, as much as tomorrow, the glory of being the spouse and almost the equal of Zeus?"

"Don't blaspheme the goddess any more than you are," mocked the sage. "She is greater than Zeus, and her grandeur is more durable. If I love her, it's because she will see that god, too favorable to tyrants, die."

"What are you saying, insensate? Zeus is immortal."

"Why, then, is Olympus anxious when Prometheus agitates like a threat the uncertain future? But, if it is natural that you, a traitor to your benefactor and a slave of his enemies, do not know the secret of Prometheus, you ought at least to know, O priest of Hera, what concerns Hera. And since you affirm that Zeus is immortal, you can doubtless explain to me the thought of Temenos,[11] who nourished and raised your goddess. In Stymphalos, as you know, he consecrated three temples, the first to Hera the child, the second to Hera the wife and the third to Hera the widow. How can she be a widow, if Zeus is immortal?"

---

[11] This reference to Hera being raised by Temenos of Arcadia near Stymphalos comes from Pausanias' *Description of Greece*, written in the second century A.D., where it is cited as a fable. It does not appear to have any other Classical warrant among surviving texts.

"Everything," said the priest, vaguely, "is subject to scandal for the impious. Only the man who puts his confidence in the gods can know the depths of things and the meaning of words. The Olympians dazzle those who look up. If you want to see Helios or Zeus and conserve your eyes, curb your head, incline toward the mirror of the waters or toward the lake of adoration. But you manifest pride and hostility to the truth; how can the truth deliver itself to you?"

And Demas withdrew, with his most scornful gait.

Meanwhile, Pythagoras, turning to Pherecydes, exclaimed: "Master, what joy you give me in telling me that Zeus, protector of tyrants and enemy of our father Prometheus is condemned to death. For, if I dare confess it, I experience a veritable hatred for that wicked god."

"It is necessary to hate him, my son, for the blindness with which he loves himself. And it is necessary to love him, my son, for the intelligence and justice with which he hates himself, for he is better than the gods before him; by virtue of everything that he has that is better, he engenders with a bitter joy the one that will succeed him, and aspires vertiginously to die."

The sage fell silent.

"Speak, Master," the young many implored, "say more."

As his plea obtained nothing but a shake of the head and a smile, he added, more urgently: "At least tell me the name of the one that is to come."

"You are asking me," Pherecydes objected, gravely, "what it is not my prerogative to tell you."

A silence separated them increasingly after those evasive words. Finally, Pythagoras, in an effort to recall Pherecydes, whose thoughts seemed distant and forgetful, said: "Master, beneath the contradictory lies of the priests, I sense a root of truth of which they are unaware. But beneath the verities that you speak, I sense other verities more precious, which you know and are hiding from me. Why, oh why?"

"You shall know everything," Pherecydes promised. He continued, in a suddenly saddened voice: "You shall know everything, but far from me, and from lips that are yet unknown to you."

A few days after the hierogamy, Pherecydes and Pythagoras, seeking a little freshness in that burning season, went out of the ramparts by the Gate of the She-Bear.[12] They walked to the limits of the torrid plain, along a meadow whose verdure rose up toward a high forest. They finally reached the entrance to a grotto and went into the delightful shade.

They were not now in a mediocre shelter but in a long tunnel that pierced the entire basal width of the mountains. In the middle, at a depth of twenty cubits, ran the waters that were to refresh the fountains of the city. To either side of them, a path extended, wide enough to permit three men to walk abreast.

Pherecydes's words were to the soul of Pythagoras the plowshare that opens the terrain and renders it avid for the next sowing.

"Priests," he explained, "will tell you the words that I am forbidden to pronounce, but you alone my son, can give yourself the veritable initiation. The ordinary priest is a skillful butcher, and his entire science consists of cutting the throats of his victims according to the rites. The priests of the Mysteries, even the dadoukhos[13] and the hierophant, know words that remain words for them. They speak a language that remains foreign to them, and they believe, naively, that the sounds themselves possess the power to purify and justify. They do not know that the word's value is the knowledge it contains, and that, sown in a noble being, knowledge is the seed of ac-

_____

[12] I have translated the French *Ourse* [She-Bear] literally, here and elsewhere, although it is always used metaphorically; the reference is to the constellations Ursa Major and Ursa Minor, and hence to the North.

[13] The *dadoukhos* [torch-bearer], which Ryner renders in French as *dadouque*, was one of the senior officiants in the Eleusinian Mysteries.

tion. They are not the living who vivify. They are the vessels of the dry ground, dead and infertile, in which seeds are contained. But our soul is a fertile Gaia; nothing falls into it except for resurrection; you will suffer from the anxious labor of all the roots, but you will enjoy all the growing verdure, all the flowers and all the fruits."

"Master," replied Pythagoras, "as soon as I have received the words, I shall return to you. I shall bring you faithfully the caskets to which I do not have the key, and you will open their treasure for me."

"No, my son. I can only heap other words around those words, as one heaps up sterile wheat in a granary. I am not you, noble terrain that cries out for sowing; I cannot flower and fructify for you."

Thus spoke the master and the disciple. And in the semi-darkness in which they believed themselves to be alone, they walked, each of them looking into his own soul and his companion's.

A voice awoke them from their double dream. It said, in a soft and sinuous voice: "I salute you, Pherecydes, son of Bados; I salute you, Pythagoras, son of Mnesarchus; and I proclaim you fortunate to a match for the encomion, the most beautiful of all songs, which reconciles the flute and the cithara, the grace of the ephebe and the strong beauty of the man; for you have come to the solitary darkness to enjoy a mutual love. But I, unfortunately, am a cithara that the flute no longer accompanies and can no longer make any but lugubrious sounds heard; my Bathyllus[14] has refused to follow me. That is why I weep, a source fled by young lips."

But Pherecydes replied: "I salute you, Anacreon of Teos. Most harmonious and most ingenious of poets, you make amours and chagrins by artifice, in order to sing them and charm us."

---

[14] Bathyllus, mentioned as an object of fervent desire in a surviving ode by Anacreon, was alleged by the Roman poet Horace also to have been Polycrates' lover.

"You calumniate me, son of Bados. I only sing with the breath of amour. I sing, or rather I groan, like the white poplar. Because it always resonates with the tremor of all its leaves, would you accuse it of creating the winds, O too ingenious and insulting sage? Is it my fault is Zeus has made me as sensitive and tremulous as numerous foliage? But I can leave interrupted the pedic hymn with which I hoped to touch the heart of my Bathyllus. On the most sonorous strings, Pherecydes, I proclaim your glory and your good fortune. What rhythms match the triumph of the man who is loved by Pythagoras? O Pythagoras, young Apollo, whom I prefer even to Aphrodite...."

"Your words speak truly, O harmonious one, and yet your mind deceives you. The beauty that I love in Pythagoras and the strength that he loves in me are not the beauty and strength that you think."

Anacreon's retorted, sarcastically: "You speak like a sage before an importunate individual—but I believe that you are sage enough, in fact, to enjoy solitude like a poet."

Without leaving time for a reply, he fled rapidly, sowing laughter behind him.

The amours of Polycrates and Tyrrhenus had become not only public but notorious. People were talking about them as much as the amours of Anacreon and Bathyllus. They talked about them more favorably, those who judge a rich man worthy of affection being more numerous than those who take an interest in a poet.

An emotional admiration rose toward the marvelous couple. What warrior gave a more energetic impression of virility than Polycrates? But what virginal body ever sang the hesitant and equivocal, ignorant and perverse, softly shrill melody as graciously as the forms of Tyrrhenus? A prelude to the double and twice incomplete impulse, a still ambiguous awakening of a balanced dream, a dawn and tremor whose cadences, scarcely dewy, is reminiscent of the imminent languor of Phoebe, shepherd of the stars....

Charm of a moment, which will disappear, not by fading but by blossoming, you are not yet the flower. The flower, naively, will have a stamen or pistil, and will sing, too colored and too precise, active or passive joy. The flower is already a choice. You are the bud in its green corselet, the mystery that will open tomorrow, alas, summoning with a loud voice the banal population of butterflies and bees, rejecting those who love your chilly withdrawal today.

Oh, those want neither the yes nor the no! They need, parted with the pretty smile that says both and says nothing, uncertain lips. The eventual precisions would wound them, as the affirmations of the crowd and the priest shock the dreamer. Every proximal song, every song whose words have a meaning, becomes indifferent and coarse to them, and ceases for them to be music. But you disturb them delightfully, subtle caress of a song that is not entirely sure of being heard over there on the far side of the hill, the other side of youth....

Polycrates' sentiment did not resemble the charmed uncertainty of those delicate individuals at all. Polycrates was the gluttonous brute who knew nothing of dreaming and who, wanting, as is peers put it "to know everything" is condemned to know all realities: the being without philosophy who judges happiness coarsely, imagines that disparate pieces can be constrained and increased by the same procedures as a miser's treasure; the hardened mud of the conqueror whose energy is admired by avid cowards. He loved Tyrrhenus as he would have loved a woman of celebrated beauty, as he demanded wines that were praised and meats that were declared flavorsome; as he pursued the gold adored by the vulgar and dreamed of the tyranny sung by the poets. He glorified himself twice over: because men were jealous of him and because ephebes were jealous of Tyrrhenus.

Only Pythagoras was severe on them. Certainly, the harmony that brings together virile vigor and puerile grace was not wounding to his mind, as to the mind of a barbarian—but he criticized his brother's choice. He was scornful of Polycrates' contradictory and banal character and tyrannical soul, a double folly that wants to take everything and squander everything, a blind avidity for which everything is good, an infamous prodigality that rejects as unnecessary after having soiled; of everything it touches it makes excrement and ordure, favoring the unworthy and finding in benefit not the joy of giving but the voluptuousness of being unjust and debasing. He becomes insatiable who, in order possess and dominate, would consent to the crawling of base ruses, the grossness of violence and the ugliness of bloodshed. How could a son of the honest Mnesarchus prostitute himself to the son of the tyrant Aeaces?

However, Pythagoras went to the feast that Polycrates gave in honor of Tyrrhenus. At first he had refused, but he learned that Pherecydes would be singing "The Lair with Seven Coverts." The disciple had heard the poem in the whispers of intimacy. He wanted the magnificent celebration of full-voiced rhythms and thoughts freely spreading the span of their wings.

Lying on the same crimson as his master, he had not joined in with the laughter of the numerous guests. Like Pherecydes, he had scorned the meats, and had only eaten, frugally, fruits and vegetables. No one was astonished; it was known that he was already leading the Orphic life. Only Anacreon, speaking to Bathyllus, had commented on the gesture with which the young sage refused the first meat:

"Once initiated, he'll catch up with omophagy."[15]

But Pherecydes had replied: "Among the Orphics, several have listened to me and have renounced eating the god grossly. I have taught them better symbols than raw flesh and

---

[15] Omophagy, the eating of raw flesh, was said to be an important element of the Orphic Mysteries—a development of the Eleusinian Mysteries—connected with the symbolic reenactment of the devouring of Zagreus by the Titans, although the versions of the Mysteries subsequently featured in this story gloss over that element, incorporating the modification here credited to Pherecydes.

more efficacious means of having the light in the lamp of Dionysus penetrate the heart.

The poet Ibycus had approved:

"The strength of the bull is more in the vine than the bull himself. Those who are not ignorant of the mysteries will understand me."

Pherecydes was dissatisfied with the interpretation. "The glutton, as well as the drunkard, can think himself an initiate. They're both mistaken, and also those who, in the phallus, worship the phallus."

Ibycus then became irritated. "Don't talk to me with so much arrogance. I heard the words of the hierophant and saw the gestures of the dadoukhos on the same day as you."

"Before numerous ears the same words become several words, and if multiple eyes gaze, the gesture made once nevertheless does not remain a unique spectacle. If you place Ibycus, Thales and also a donkey at the same point of the shore before a smooth sea, do you think that the donkey, Ibycus and Thales will all draw equal wealth from the same treasure? The donkey will take away, in drifting eyes, a vision too vague for you to find a name for it. Ibycus will take away in his charmed mind a dance rhythm. But do you know what a marvel the sea will given Thales? It will have explained the universe to him! Henceforth, he will know the world supported on humidity throughout the breadth of space and in all the depth of time."

Among ingenious words, the time had arrived when, hunger having disappeared, one only eats to excite oneself to drink. No more meat, not even fruits—but the cicadas and the cercopes fill the mouth with a dry dust that calls for wine as Gaia, under the ardors of torrid summer demands rain and the kiss of Zeus. Idle teeth slowly crush the thirst-creating powder of roasted chick-peas or, burning for the palate that will refresh itself deliciously, a salted olive, beetroot in vinegar and mustard. It is the comus:[16] large cups invade the table, crowned with roses like the guests; the conversation, like a tottering child fleeing and crouching down to make room for the rhythmic gliding of his big sister, whispers and then falls silent before the song; speech is no longer a marcher on the road but, under the sounds of the flute or cithara, bounds and laughs like a dancer on flagstones strewn with flowers.

Obedient to everyone's pleas, Anacreon is the first to get to his feet. A lyre is brought for him. He refuses it with a gesture.

"Rather give me a myrtle-branch," he says, and let a flute sing with me.

Carystus, the most famous of flute-players, is summoned.

"O singer," he asks, "in which mode shall I accompany you? Indicate by a brief prelude the direction of your song and the sentiment to express."

But the poet shakes his head. "It pleases me today to follow and not to guide. Play what you please. My improved words will unfurl over your rhythms, as supple and tight as ivy around an oak."

The astonished Carystus makes uncertain sounds heard, which drift.

Anacreon balances his words. "O flute, for me you are Bathyllus himself; where you go. O slender one, I shall follow. You grope, hesitantly…and I wait, anxiously, not knowing my route as long as I do not know yours."

The modulations continue to play without precise intention; and the light poem agitates like a trembling leaf in changing winds.

"Here I am at a crossroads, the blind man whom the guide consults. Decide, O my guide, if you want me to decide. Here I am, before the goddesses, the shepherd Paris before Aphrodite, promising him the beauty of Helen."

---

[16] Named for Comus, god of festivities and nocturnal dalliances, and cup-bearer to Bacchus.

The flute becomes abrupt, agile and tortuous, the flight of a child leaving laughter behind her. Anacreon continues:

"You flee, Bathyllus. To follow the cruel one, as rapid as youth, forget, my footfalls, the heaviness of the banquet, dispel the Dionisiac languor. Now I am as rapid as the stag dying of thirst, who knows where the spring is. Now I am as swift as the cavalier behind his enemy's wife; she is beautiful and he is about to seize her by the hair floating behind her. Is it faster than my song, the arrow shot from Eros' bow?"

But the flute slows down, wearily, and the poet: "Ah! Bathyllus already almost my Bathyllus, your course is weakening. I am less rapid myself than a while ago, and yet nearer. I advance toward you at rhythms that seem slow and which are soft. The wings of my hope flutter, supple and soundless."

The flute slows down, like a runner out of breath who wants to lie down on the grass.

"I hold you, Bathyllus, already my Bathyllus. Fall, fall, under the weight of my happiness."

The flute seems to modulate a balanced pause.

"O Bathyllus, trembling beneath my tremulous kiss...."

The music rises, strange and shrill, frail and fading, and a flame without fuel flickers before going out.

"Die, Bathyllus, under the joy of kisses. Die the death from which one awakes, alas. Let us die together of a voluptuousness as sow as the laughter of water beneath a fallen stone; it broadens, extends, spreads out, finally becomes invisible before it occupies, immensely, the vastness and profundity of the liquid."

The flute and the poet fall silent. The charm is so penetrating that the listeners remain motionless and mute for a long moment, still stretched toward the abolished sounds. Then applause bursts forth. And Bathyllus gets up, comes to Anacreon, throws his arms around the singer and gives him on the mouth, amid enthusiastic approval, the first kiss of amour.

There is, for a few moments, a tumultuous noise of conversations, kisses and laughter; but the doors open wide. A silence, as abrupt as an impact, is then prolonged, seeming to expand gently, like a hope.

Everyone awaits the chorus whose dances and songs that Ibycus, after having practiced them in jealous secrecy, will direct.

And here it is. Attention, seething with surprise, is stimulated. One chorus was expected; two make their entrance, one composed of ephebes, the other of young courtesans.

Ibycus summon Tyrrhenus. "Most handsome of young men," he says, "come here in order to be the immobile thymele around which the rhythms will turn."

The double chorus envelops the gloriously blushing youth. The cithara and the flute play a prelude, groping like lovers seeking one another in darkness. But the sounds gradually fall into accord in a fortunate harmony that brings them together in an intercourse into which two beings melt into one.

Meanwhile, the choruses, moving to the right, form an ardent garland around the living altar, which circles. And all the mouths, opening gracefully, sing, softly:

"In spring, irrigated by the water of streams, the Cydonian apple-trees decorate the garden of the Nymphs with fresh verdure. In spring, under the shade of vine-branches, the young grapes flourish placidly along the vine."

And, turning to the left, in a rhythm that quivers apprehensively: "Since my first season, Eros has pursued me: a Thracian tempest ablaze with lighting, he launches himself from the bosom of Kypris.[17] The burning furies of that summer storm curb and oppress my spring."

The double chorus stops in order to beg:

"Summer storm, why precipitate yourself upon me? Respect my fragile spring, summer storm."

And it is the second strophe. But the chorus of women turns silently. Only the ephebes sing, proudly:

---

[17] Kypris is the island of Cyprus, but the word is used here specifically to refer to Aphrodite Kypris, the goddess of the island.

"I am not the Cydonian apple-tree that summon freshness and the waters. In spite of my youth I shine in the aridity of the gymnasium and my limbs, streaming with oil and sunlight, marry strength with beauty."

In the silence of the young men, the courtesans match the antistrophe of pride:

"I am not the fragile cluster of grapes that hides in the cool shade. In spite of my youth, I do not dread eyes burning over the purity of my forms and my dancing grace. The athlete allows oil to flow over his limbs; I allow the fire of gazes and the gentle violence of kisses to flow all over me."

And the motionless epode reunites the two choruses in a vast and powerful aspiration:

"Summer storm, my spring is summoning you. My spring is strong, summer storm, it loves your ardor."

But the young women flee to the right, a harmonious flock of doves; and the ephebes pursue them, bold hawks. Does terror close the feminine mouths? Only the ephebes accompany their avid dance with song:

"I am the summer storm that you summoned. Why do you flee before me? A lie boasted your amorous ardor. Burning Eros frightens you, but your fragile spring loves the shade, peace and silence."

Then the antistrophe puts the silent ephebes to flight, pursued by the young women, whose song, in its turn, is reproach and irony:

"I am the summer storm that you summoned. Why do you flee my passionate ardor? Cowardly athlete, the combats of Eros frighten you, but your enervated weakness seeks peace and solitary shade."

The epode and immobility reunite the two choruses in a hesitation that astonishes and interrogates:

"The menacing storm that pursues me is not the benevolent tempest that I summoned. I am already strong but ignorant of life. What, then, am I summoning? What, then, am I fleeing?"

The response will come.

The flights and the pursuits recommence.

But now the pursuers are mute and it is the flight that sings.

The guests listen, curious and moved, to the rhythms of the young women:

"I flee the ignominy of vulgar amours; I flee the man whose kiss fecundates and makes ugly. I flee the man whose rough and unyielding strength does not harmonize with my supple grace."

Then they pursue, silent in their turn, while the young men, quick to avoid them, sing the antistrophe of refusal:

"I flee the ignominy of vulgar amours; I flee the woman that the kiss fecundates and makes ugly. I flee the woman whose suppleness slips and betrays, inharmonious with my sincere strength."

And the epode unites them in this invocation:

"O kiss, noble temple of Eros, for a life or for an hour, always be the monument, worthy of the god, which brings together equal columns."

The last strophe makes the desire of the ephebes precise:

"Men, let us come together, powerful columns of a fine Doric temple. Men, let us come together to make for the chariot of Eros a powerful and equal team. Curse the barbaric poet who mingles dialects; curse also the architect or the lover who mingles composite forms."

The women express themselves in the ultimate antistrophe:

"Beneath our tresses of gold or ebony, which twist in spirals, let us be in the temple of Aphrodite the beautiful Ionic columns. Doves attached to the chariot of Kypris, let us not mingle with the black crow."

All, finally, sing the epode:

"Let the eagle love the eaglet, let the dove love the dove. Summer storm, you know the desire of my spring. Come as my spring summons you, summer storm."

The guests do, indeed, feel stirred and nervous, as under the oppression of a storm. The hands that applaud and the cries that acclaim make the din of a tempest sound. The tumultuous lips of men seek the lips of ephebes. However, the puerile mouths tremble. So, in the wind, and in the yellow darkness that precedes the torrential cloudburst, its thick tissue rent by lightning, the vine or the Cydonian apple-tree shivers.

The choruses have gone out; the musicians have gone out. Ibycus, in triumphant isolation, contemplates the unleashing of amour, a satisfied god approving of his work.

Polycrates was one of those banal natures whom the wind of words agitates and carries away like leaves. What amour was ever more ardent than the amour of Polycrates in that feverish moment? He was proud of the passionate force that he sensed burning and crackling in his soul: a poor hearth cold by itself, where strange words and strange rhythms blazed, a poetry and folly brought in from outside.

He presses the abandoned Tyrrhenus against his breast, his lips weighing upon moaning lips; his eyes plunging into the bath of a gaze as fresh as a spring and likewise trembling beneath a victory of hot light.

But the avid and vain man feels an appeal within him toward something other than amour. It is as if a slave were tugging at the hem of his tunic to warn him of some negligence. He remembers, in the midst of his emotion, that a celebrated poet, much sought after but who rarely performs, is due to crown his feast. He pushes the astonished Tyrrhenus aside and says:

"O my guests, we are the soldiers of Eros and Samos, the combatants ever ready for the impetuous kiss that tips back the friend and the violent blow that casts down the adversary. Intimate and jealous voluptuousness will find us as vigorous in a little while and possess us without division. It remains to us to drink a common cup. The great Pherecydes, in whom sages respect a sage and poets salute a poet, will place in our midst the bowl and the intoxication.

"Ibycus, your poetry is the wine of Byblos fully charged with perfumes; as soon as you open one of your amphorae, the atmosphere is heavy with roses, violets, aromas and caresses.

Ibycus, beautiful on your own as the vastest of orgies, the hectic dance of bacchantes, a broad landscape of amour that stimulates, trembles and spins, I do not know words worthy to praise you. But the rhythms of Pherecydes are the wine of Rhodes: the bitterness of brine and thought relieve its sweetness, and one does not know whether that bittersweet wine appeases thirst or ignites it.

"Sing, then, Pherecydes. Like the skeleton at the feats of Egypt, your austere poem will incite us, whose sagacity is made of glad folly and the ardor of life, to throw ourselves more violently into joy, kisses and laughter. Luminous Pherecydes, burst in our sky like Helios at midday in order that, pursued by your strength and your glory, we shall precipitate more eagerly toward the sweetness of shadow, the coolness of murmurous springs."

Pherecydes only responded to that praise and irony with laughter, perhaps scornful, and, grasping a cithara with a strong hand, he began:

"Powerful Eros, vast Eros, I shall sing of you. Let my hymn avenge you against vulgar poets. Their adorations soil the vicinity of our temple when they crawl toward you, dogs soaked by the storm of passions. Streaming and malodorous dogs, your master does not know you and you shall not enter into the sanctuary.

"It is not you that they honor, vast Eros. As the rustic blinded by desire calls the female whose ugliness excites him in an ugly fashion Helen or Aphrodite, they salute by your name, vast Eros, I know not what ridiculous or infantile daemon.

"Vast Eros, the ignorant who seek in their songs see you diminished therein: a landscape reflected in the eye of a child. They see you deformed therein: a visage of light reflected in a poor pond that the hand of a herdsman troubles with ripples and mid.

"For the sage who, refusing the divine name to passive matter and the incoherence of blind forces, reserving glory to the creative energies of harmony, you are, vast Eros, the foremost of gods. Nothing existed before you save for Chaos and Chthon. Chthon, not yet Gaia but a dolorous and deformed tree, bore Chaos in the vague tempest of its branches. You came, and there was form. You came, and there was beauty. You came, and there was life.

"For Cronus had drawn wind and water from the seed of fire. But, in the breath of Ophion,[18] the disorder of the water, wind and fire was agitated, a storm of ugliness. Or rather a storm dispersed too far from form even to merit the name of ugliness. What would later be the world was a hectic battle, a melee devoid of strategy, in which, less stable than clouds, imprecise blind forces barked, bit one another and tore one another apart: a struggle of all against all and each element, not yet an element, against itself. Vertigoes and turbulences, abysmal flights, floating upheavals, howling impacts, crumblings of what was not, destructions of what would be. Cronus himself remained formless, eternity agitating and seeking without finding, not yet time, which orders the steps of being and the scale of the generations. Nothing was born, nothing died, nothing existed.

"But you came, Eros, as vast as space, as immortal as duration. You came, O visage of beings and design of things. You gave a form to Cronus, and weapons, and eyes that looked forward and eyes that looked backward. And in order that he could combat them effectively, you gave a rudiment of form to Ophion and the roars of the abyss. Thanks to you, Cronus vanquished Ophion and the roars of the abyss. The water of the seed of Cronus covered Ophion and his cohorts,

---

[18] The story of the Titan Ophion, or Ophioneus, was featured in Pherecydes' *Heptamychia*, of which only fragments survive, on the basis of which this passage is improvised. Ryner's *Antre aux sept replis*, which I have translated literally as "The Lair with Seven Coverts," is his somewhat fanciful translation of *Heptamychia* (*mychia* means "scratch"). Ophion is also mentioned in surviving fragments of Orphic poetry, presumably derived from the *Heptamychia*.

and over their ugliness and their barking there was the beauty of the singing sea.

"The wind of the seed of Cronus carried Ophion and his cohorts away and he filled the distant abysms with them, and there was a beginning and a past.

"The fire of the seed of Cronus burned Ophion and his cohorts. With their flaming darkness he made light. With their burning chill he made heat. And on your forehead, vast Eros, you bore, crowned with the radiance that warms, illuminates and signals, the sun. And there was day and there was night.

"The Cronus turned to you and he saw, beneath your crown of light, your visage, more radiant than your crown. And, bowing before you respectfully, he named you Zeus. And you replied to him: 'Zeus is one of my names and light one of my forms; but I am the god with a thousand names and a thousand forms. I am vast Eros, creator of all forms and dispenser of all names.'

"And Cronus said to you, his eyes full of love: 'O Zeus, my son!' And you replied to him: 'I am vast Eros and I am your father. Before me you had no form and your incoherent force was self-destructive. You were the river, not yet a river, that has neither a bed not a slope. I, the sole creator of forms, gave you your bed and your slope, O river from which I emerge, O river which is a river by virtue of me alone.'

"And Cronus said: 'O Zeus, O my son, create forms then, in order that I might pass through them the indifferent flow of matter. Create forms, in order that I can destroy and remake them.'

"And the god replied: 'I, vast Eros, emerged from you and yet your father, will create the forms with which you will play, dispersing them and assembling them anew, O infantile old man.'

"Eros wove an immense cloth, on which he embroidered the earth, and Oceanos, and the palaces of the earth, and the palaces of Oceanos. And he saw Chthon, the skeleton of the earth, floating in space, in the form of an oak borne by wings. Over the oak sustained by the agitation of wings he deployed

41

the immense embroidery. And since there then there have been forms, and since then there has been beauty, which passes and which recommences. And things flee as they did before time was time, but they flee between the banks of Eros and following the slope of Eros, leaving behind them daughters similar to themselves. And birth replicates death, and the shores of the river are always full, like a lake. And the universal movement equilibrates, with the result than one can imagine a stability that sings, laughs and shines. For there is no longer chaos, and the gestures of Cronus are no longer free and foolish, but guided by a law. Now that law is called, when one regards it in its energy, vast Eros; and that law is called, when one regards it in its works, Beauty, Order and Cosmos."

Momentarily, Pherecydes fell silent. They believed that he had finished, and yet they all listened, for they heard prolonged within themselves the multiple echo and the emotion of his canticle. But he suddenly proclaimed, while the cithara cried with scorn and pride between his fingers:

"Vulgar poets stammer a detail of the Cosmos and they believe that they are saying vast Eros in his entirety. I alone sing without diminishing him, the *Lair with Seven Coverts*; and in my verses alone, the seven roars of Ophion became the seven hymns of Eros."

Under the rude power of the song, all heads were bowed for some time like the culpable beneath a collapse of light. Then there was a murmurous hesitation, a hectic whispering of contrary sentiments that could not all be expressed. What mysterious god makes the choice between the emotions whose swarming agitates toward the light? Some sink into darkness more profound than silence; others rise up to the half-light of babble, as far as the daylight of speech, as far as the flash of exclamation. And some are surrounded with eloquence like a tunic of sunlight, and haloed with poetry and music.

Pherecydes was thoughtful, a smile of indifference on his lips. The shame of a crowd, ordinarily, is shaken off in the fashion of a wet dog, and quickly transformed into anger that howls insults and stands up with clenched fists; but in rare surprises it clamors praise and holds out tremulous palms to-ward the insulting thinker. Today, the crowd had a leader and, while the uncertain murmurous waves swayed, eyes turned to Polycrates, imploring a word or a sign, asking what it was necessary to think.

The one who had to speak for all finally spoke.

"O Pherecydes," he said, "The gods alone have the right to certain kinds of pride, but your thought and speech make a god of you."

A vast sigh of relief filled the hall, but stopped abruptly, ashamed of its insufficiency; and enthusiastic cries resounded. The guests ran toward Pherecydes to shake his hand, or at least to touch the hem of his chlamys or his forcefully harmonious cithara.

Doors and windows opened, the immense hall now seemed narrow and stuffy. A battle of emotions overpopulated it with breathlessness and storm. They went out to breathe in the gardens. Under the trees there were large cassolettes of perfumes, and in the gentle fluttering of the wings of the nocturnal breeze, they dispersed for amicable words and the gestures of amour.

Pythagoras, alone with Pherecydes, exclaimed: "Master, when I hear you after the priests or the poets, I always experience the same joy and the same disappointment. O priests and poets, your groping words seize indifferently lies or superficial truths; you, Master, are a god who lifts up a corner of the darkness, but refuse to tear it and draw out the darkness."

Pherecydes replied: "You alone, my son, can disperse your darkness, for there is only night in the eyes. One can do nothing for men who sleep or those of ill-will. Those who wake up and agitate toward the light can only be summoned to the mountain where the spectacle broadens out. It has been given to me to indicate to you the first upward-lading paths. Sacred promises forbid me to do more. Go find those who have the right to guide you higher, but never forget, O dearest of disciples, that it is the prerogative of every man to raise his own eyelids and walk with his own legs."

43

He fell silent, for several people were approaching. It was Polycrates, leaning on Tyrrhenus, and Anacreon poring over Bathyllus.

Polycrates said: "I like and admire you, Pherecydes, and I do not doubt the force of your thoughts, even though you are severe and true power manifests indulgence—but your bad sentiments sometimes deceive your mind. They prevent you from seeing that there is a dialectic of amour as there is a dialectic of knowledge. For myself, I hope that the beauty of Tyrrhenus will lead me to love the beauty of the Cosmos."

Anacreon launched winged words in his turn. "What does the mind matter; it is neither the point of departure nor the point of arrival; the road should be traveled, known and loved in its entirety. I have known the beauty of the Cosmos for a long time, and, drinking from the palm of my hand all the fleeting freshness of the stream, I enjoy the universe through Bathyllus."

But Polycrates' discourse recommenced, as sly and sinuous as a serpent that finally rears up and hisses: "I will not ask you, Pherecydes, for I am a discreet host, whether Pythagoras leads you to vast Eros or vast Eros leads you to Pythagoras."

Pherecydes replied, haughtily: "Pythagoras is not a Tyrrhenus or a Bathyllus, an empty beauty like a crimson fabric in a shop, and I am not an Anacreon or a Polycrates, superficial kisses that do not penetrate the realities of being."

Polycrates laughed loudly, and Anacreon began: "I congratulate you, Pherecydes, if you penetrate...."

But the sage stopped him. "Shut up, harmonious one, for you are about to speak vulgar words and translate into speech a laughter that is not yours. Know, however, that love links me, like a ray of light, to Pythagoras. Do you know what I was saying as you arrived?

"I would, if you would do me the favor of repeating it."

"I was ordering him to go far away from Samos and from me."

"If that is the case, you do not love him," affirmed Polycrates.

And Anacreon said: "If that is the case, when you name Eros you name a god that you do not know. You risk resembling the orphan whose birth was mortal to his mother but who boasts of her beauty."

Pherecydes replied, gravely: "I love Pythagoras, but is this child already Pythagoras? Amorous of the glory of the oak, I do not enclose the acorn in the moving sterility of my hand. I confide it to the earth, support and nurse. As for this young sage, he loves in Pherecydes a word of which Pherecydes can only pronounce the first syllable. That is why my love says to his love: 'Go into the lands of light where you may read the whole word.' You, Anacreon and Bathyllus, Polycrates and Tyrrhenus, will love one another for a time in your poverty. Pythagoras and I will love one another forever in our increasing wealth. Cherished son of my mind and my heart, go then to collect the portion of my riches that I cannot give you here. Go into the fortunate climes where you can realize and deploy the riches buried within you, of which you are unaware."

Book Two: THE MYSTERIES

The day came when Pythagoras, in order to obey his heart, had to rend his heart, and, in order to follow his master, had to quit his master. Pherecydes was with him on the dock. Also there, among the numerous troop of his friends and relatives, were Mnesarchus and Parthenis, Eunomus and Tyrrhenus.

A bird falling from the even warmth of the nest into capriciously changing and treacherous space, escaping from protective narrowness and an enclosed spectacle to enjoy the vast universe with his eyes and wings, he felt his heart trembling with regret for puerile peace, with desire for and fear of the multiform world that, before the boldest flights, always opens broadly the infinite and the unknown, and behind the most victorious flights always closes the hermeticism of the horizon and forgetfulness.

Surrounded by young people who shook his hands, embraced by the hugs of those dearest to him, enveloped in the mantle of the final recommendations of his beloved master, he saw the ship approaching the shore. In a dreamlike mist, the sailor directed the poop toward him. Some maintained the prow with long poles. Others suspended the anchors from the projections that curved like ears from both sides in the prow. Others hastened to dispose the ladders. A few, finally, hauled the cables and threw them to the shores, summoning the passengers.

Pythagoras and five other Samians grabbed the ropes and, lifting up their garments, went into the water, walked toward the vessel and climbed up the long dangling ladders.

For a long time they exchanged gestures of affection and farewell with those who were remaining. Alas, everything they loved shrank into the distance. A moment came when Pherecydes, was the size of an infant in the avid eyes of his disciple. Then, abruptly, he disappeared. The harbor wall loomed up between the ship and the city. The pensive Pythagoras felt a dolorous void within him, and tears rose to his eyes; but no tear spilled; an effort of courage drove them back.

And the young man affirmed, in a murmur: "It is appropriate that I rejoice, Pherecydes, when I quit you in order to find better."

He no longer saw anything but the white monotony of the harbor wall, which, struck by the sunlight, displayed negation and refusal, the dazzle of a rock built by men.

A little distance rendered the spectacle, not of the port, the city and the people, but of the charming and sturdy island. Against the water and the sky it thrust up, like a loving cry that recalls fugitives, the green stages of its robust mountains. It was like a mother who, descending toward Hades, extends increasingly distant and increasingly moving arms from the far side of death.

In order not to be vanquished in his heart, Pythagoras turned away toward the open sea.

Was not that slight movement, unperceived by anyone, the gesture of a hero? He did not want to hear the interior grinding of his energies, and proclaimed aloud the glad reason for his departure: "Pherecydes," he said, "is greater in my eyes."

Then, gazing at the vast dance of the violet sea, his thoughts on the flotation of the promising and fleeting future: "Pherecydes told me that Pherecydes is a word. I am going. O joy, to hear the entire speech, to embrace Pherecydes entirely."

The sway of the vessel and the sway of his mind caused him to seize a support. His hands clasped the rail that seemed to be moving away, and his thought grasped a memory. "While awaiting the end of the word, I'll repeat the syllable that I know."

And quietly, as one calms an infant taking too long to go to sleep, he intoned the poem confided to his faithful memory, the rude and mysterious poem in which the strangeness of origins is seen, where the Lair folds its seven creases into darkness, where, over Ophion crying the seven roars, Eros sings the seven canticles.

They were heading for Corinth, the city of false pleasures, the breathless forge where, for the stimulation of coarse beings, gold melts and evaporates in the breath of a kiss. Pythagoras hoped to find a ship there that would take him toward Athens crowned with violets and Eleusis crowned with narcissi.

Laboriously folded into himself, he applied himself to casting into the shadow the troop of regrets. With a heavy and clinging net, he strove to drag into the present sunlight the hopes of time and distance, which floated like vague sniggers. And he did not perceive the present as his eyes seemed to gaze upon it, nor the agitation of his companions, nor the darkening of a sector of the sky, nor the distant fury of the sea, which was howling and rushing, swelling as if with folly.

The ship fled at top speed, with its sails inflated and by means of the rhythmic force of its oars. The tempest ran faster. The sails were lowered. Pythagoras, inattentive to the maneuvers, suddenly noticed that the sun, previously blazing, had disappeared, and there was too much darkness for it to be night.

A hand touched his shoulder and he divined that words were being addressed to him, but the din of the tempest, similar to the cries of warriors, prevented human voices from being heard.

Pythagoras understood, and, with the curious energy of youth that summons all struggles and rejoices in everything unexpected, he said: "Here, with the hymns of Eros, are the roars of Ophion."

The wind and the lightning split the noisy darkness. The young sage knew who was beside him, a hand on his shoulder; but his first thought was not for his neighbor; his first thought, as rapid and vibrant as a cry, was for thought: "O lightning, brutal light as magnificent as death..."

Then his curiosity wanted to know the unheard words that he knew had been pronounced. He did not ask for them externally; he did not wait for a silence of Ophion to permit human voices to be heard; but, searching within himself, he found there what had been said to him.

The man who was touching his shoulder with a hand that was simultaneously trembling and protective was Syloson, the youngest son of the tyrant Aeaces.[19]

In the distant fold of himself to which, like a grain-loft, Pythagoras rejected and heaped up the men that he did not want to be, the possibilities he did not want to realize, and the seeds, the treasures of intelligence, that, in order to impoverish an earth reserved for nobler crops, he refused to let germinate, he encountered, folded up and asleep, a Syloson that his smiling effort woke up instantly and deployed.

From that interior mouth opened by his will, he heard words emerge:

"You have fled your brother Tyrrhenus and I have fled my brother Polycrates. But if we had known what the gods reserved for this vessel, we would still be with Tyrrhenus and Polycrates."

The storm died down. It seemed, however, that to the heavy darkness, blocks of darkness were added. It was, crushing and maddening, a moment of false respite, during which the enemy ceases his howls and blows because he is reforming, reinforcing his hideous cohorts with new troops. But sometimes, utilizing that unique opportunity, a skillful and bold leader can break the attack before it recommences, dispersing and driving back the suspended threat.

Syloson was, in the eyes of his companions, that skillful and bold leader.

---

[19] Syloson is mentioned as Polycrates' brother by Herodotus, although Herodotus' interest in him begins after he vanishes from the greater part of the present story, banished by Polycrates, and allies himself with the Persians, eventually reconquering his homeland with their aid.

"Friends," he shouted, "I am an initiate of Samothrace. Let us promise the helpful Cabiri[20] that we will all go the sacred island to pray and to learn the mysteries."

While the trumpets of the storm, indecisive and as if distant, seemed to be performing a prelude before sounding a new charge, he shouted again, louder than the first hostile noises:

"Promise, or we're doomed!"

A vast unanimous clamor replied to him, in which hope and dread trembled:

"We promise, we promise! Helpful Cabiri, save us! To Samothrace, we are going to Samothrace, O Cabiri!"

The tempest was upon the vessel, growling and formidable. Syloson, meanwhile, pronounced the mysterious names that the profane must not hear, and which alone can summon the four Saviors efficaciously. The great attack passed rapidly, fleeing, it seemed, rather than charging.

And now, in the atmosphere that slowly settled and brightened, amid the rout of the winds, the waves and the darkness, fires were seen balancing on the summits of the masts.

Syloson, with the triumphant strength of relief and gratitude, shouted, louder than the fleeing tumult: "The Cabiri! See with your own eyes their flaming presence. Hear with your grateful hearts their favorable crackling. They are saying: We grant your wish, O Ephemerae, and we accept your promise."

The sailors fell to their knees, but the initiate ordered: "Get up, get up! The Cabiri are not gods down below. Stand-

---

[20] The term Cabiri or Kabeiroi was applied to the "Great Gods" of the mysteries of Samothrace by Roman writers referring back to them from a much later period, and it was also Roman writers who grafted the mythology of Demeter, Persephone and Hades on to those mysteries, thus making them an alternative version of the Eleusinian Mysteries. Ryner accepts that in his own improvised rendering, although it is historically dubious.

ing, with palms turned to the divine flames, let us renew our promise.

While all the bodies came upright, all the heads tipped backward, and all eyes hands were extended toward the floating flames, Syloson pronounced with a joyful emphasis: "O beneficent Cabiri, who have driven the tempest and death away from us, receive our actions of grace."

He stopped. The meaning of his silence was understood, and his last words were repeated: "Receive our actions of grace, O Cabiri!"

He resumed, in the tone of a priest: "We shall go to renew them in the Sacred Isle. Accept our promise, O Cabiri."

Everyone repeated: "Accept our promise, O Cabiri."

"And we shall owe you even more for the future initiation than the benefit of today. You have saved our vulgar lives in order to permit us to attain a higher life. Twice we thank you, O Cabiri."

And the chorus improvised: "Twice we thank you, O Cabiri."

The fires disappeared, doubtless satisfied. In and around the ship, there was a great serenity, as mild as a convalescence, deeply emotional; after the jolts and the anguish, there was a free expansion of the heart.

Because, under the hand that had offered and requested amity in the disturbance of the peril, he had found Pythagoras tranquil, Syloson liked Pythagoras. It was him that he sought out among everyone; to him he confided that an initiate had the right to speak before the hierophant.

"Will the mysteries of the Cabiri teach me some important verity?" asked the young sage, anxiously. "Pherecydes knows them and he did not counsel them to me. Demeter and Isis are, according to him, the sole Initiators, Eleusis and Egypt the pure sources at which the thirst for knowledge drinks. 'The other mysteries,' he told me, are deformations of those.' And he went on, laughing, the Master who was ordinarily so grave: 'Have you noticed, Pythagoras, that the statue does not resemble the model as much as than the sculptor?

Does not the Hera that reigns by the bank of the Imbrasos bear in her insolent beauty the insolence and beauty of Similis? Thus, all the mysteries of which people boast translate the beauty of Eleusis and Egypt into sacerdotal ugliness. They are Muses sculpted by apes. They are poems sung by children devoid of intelligence and memory; they forget the most necessary words and their ignorant tongue deforms the others, removing from rhythms where were powerful all force and all significance.'"

"You will judge for yourself, man avid for futile knowledge. But as you have seen, initiation, the treasure of salvation, has a practical value. Even if you do not esteem it as science, acquire it as a weapon and a refuge. If I had not known the mysterious names of the Cabiri, the only names to which they respond, we would now be at the bottom of the sea, unfortunate prey of the mute fish."

Pythagoras did not reply aloud, but his mind, a vast and luminous smile, thought:

Is it not the rule of storms to have a beginning and an end? How many violent men have I seen calm down solely because their fury had expressed itself and agitated sufficiently? Is not the tempest, dangerous but brief, which exhausts itself of its own accord, a crisis of the folly of Zeus?

He also thought:

Pherecydes has warned me against the dementia that transforms and displaces the power of words. The word, when it speaks the truth, is a torch that illuminates my gesture; it can do nothing directly to things or to the gods. Neither things not the gods are in the number of those light moths that human enlightenment can attain.

The brother of Polycrates told the brother of Tyrrhenus the history of the isle for which they were headed. Its present name spoke simultaneously of its proximity to Thrace and the fugitive Samians who, several generations ago, had taken possession of it. A rock dazzling in its sterile nudity, they had initially called it Leucania, which is to say, "the White." Dwarf olives, rare fig-trees and vines with meager and desiccated grapes were its apparent wealth, but the names of the Cabiri saved numerous navigators who never believed that they could pay dearly enough for the benefits they received and those for which they hoped. That was why the infertile island was richer than the pleasant Arcadia. As the stone of Magnesia attracts iron, its gold brought the neighboring lands the pleasures and commodities of life.

I understand the utility of the Cabiri, Pythagoras thought.

"The inhabitants," Syloson added, "are not numerous. Many are attached to the service of the temple. Others, slaves of the priests, cultivate the land for them or go in small boats to seek in Thasos, Imbros, Thrace and Asia what the ingrate soil refuses them. King of men and favorite of the gods, the hierophant combines the wealth of the two desirable powers. As the grace of a capital spreads over the strength of a column, he bears on his head, the abode of inspired science, the golden crown."

The ancient Leucania soon appeared, a block of whiteness and poverty, its four thousand cubits dominated by Mount Saoce. On a promontory, a man in a crimson robe was observing the sea. He sent signs of welcome toward the ship. Then his gestures indicated the inlet in the rock that was the least inhospitable—for, Syloson explained, the island like science, was devoid of ports and difficult to land upon.

The man dressed in crimson was soon walking among the frozen tempest of the rocks. Sometimes he disappeared into a black hollow, and then reappeared on a crest as bright as the foam. He stopped at the place designated by his gestures. Already, the ship was dropping anchor. Sailors and passengers waded through the shallow water to the shore. The watchman, perceiving Syloson at closer range, opened his arms, and the brother of Polycrates exclaimed:

"O Philistion, holy priest, I recognize you and I see that you recognize me. My heart is a fountain that is overflowing with memory and joy. You were on watch when I came to this sacred land for the first time. Thrice blessed by the gods, since it is you again, my father, who welcomes me with the companions saved by the mysterious names that the hierophant taught me."

The priest, with a condescending gesture, extended his hand to Syloson and helped him to climb the rock. Then, he only said: "O my son." And, like a joyful merchant, he put his arms around the man who had brought him clients.

Philistion led the protégés of the Cabiri to his vast house. On the way, he spoke to some of them, enquiring benevolently as to the resources of each one. In his house, hasty slaves brought nourishment and refreshments.

Afterwards, the priest said: "The gifts of the gods are gratuitous, but gratitude is a virtue that they love and ingratitude a vice that they punish. In the temple of Samothrace, every initiate exercises freely his virtue or his vice, summoning to himself further benefits or the wrath of the Cabiri.

After a silence in which he seemed to be praying, he continued; "You are, O Cabiri, the most benevolent of gods. Elsewhere, the mysteries are rarely celebrated and the epochs inexorably fixed. Here, we renew them as frequently as our guests desire. We are obliged nevertheless to wait until the mystes[21] are numerous enough to support the expenses of a celebration. Do you desire, my sons, an initiation for yourselves alone, or would you prefer to wait on the hospitable island until other men come to share the expenses and advantages of the ceremony?"

Syloson replied: "Holy priest, I will make the contribution of which you speak and my companions will manifest, each in accordance with his fortune, their gratitude toward the gods and their host."

Philistion took responsibility for informing the high priest of the Samians' desire, and three days later, the mysteries were celebrated.

---

[21] I have left this term, referring to a candidate for initiation into mysteries, as Ryner renders it, as users of the English language do not appear to have invented a equivalent.

54

A slow procession unwound from the host's dwelling to the temple. At the head marches the benefactor Syloson, crowned with laurels. In two parallel lines, the priests followed him solemnly. Their hair was raised up above their bare heads by strips of white cloth; a long loose robe hung down along their bodied, but their feet were shod in crimson phaecasia. Flute players came next, and finally the mystes in the order determined by age. Under the guidance of the *hieroceryx*,[22] who, proud in a blue-tinted tunic embroidered in gold, bore a closed casket in his pious hands, the thirty sailors and passengers advanced in a single line, barefoot and dressed in while. Their foreheads bore a gilded plaque.

Before the closed door of the temple the *coes* and the *hydranos* were waiting for them. The hand of the latter held a laurel branch, and in front of his feet was a large basin full of lustral water. Everyone stooped beside the coes and, in a low voice, confessed his sins.

After having heard them the coes proclaimed: "This man is culpable, but he has not committed any inexpiable crime. Let the water purify him."

With his steeped branch, the hydranos sprinkled the myste and pronounced this invocation: "Water purified by the benevolence of the gods and by the power of words, purify this man."

When all of them had been subjected to the aspersion, the hieroceryx knocked on the door of the temple. They opened and the hierophant appeared, a tall old man with great attitudes, who, with a dominating hand, was leaning on the dadoukhos. Each was crowned with a diadem and clad in a long stola.

---

[22] This term for one of the officiants in the Eleusinian Mysteries is found in various nineteenth-century sources, seemingly popularized by a widely-read book first published in the 1820s by Heinrich Hase, whose English version was entitled *The Public and Private Life of the Ancient Greeks*.

The hierophant spoke the ritual words: "Why has the temple been opened?"

No one replied.

After a moment, the dadoukhos interrogated: "Did you not hear the words of the favorite of the gods? Why have the doors of the temple been opened?"

No response was forthcoming.

Then the hierophant said: "The doors have been opened in error; let them be closed."

At a sign from the hieroceryx, however, the priests and the mystes threw themselves to their knees, and all hands extended their supplication toward the two men standing regally on the perron.

Meanwhile, the hieroceryx implored: "Wait, O Master of the Sacred Sciences. I will give these mutes the book that will unbind their tongue a little, enough for them to stammer the commencement of a response.

Opening the casket that he was carrying in his hands, he took out of it a small book, which he deployed, and presented to Syloson, saying: "You, the least blind of these men, look, in order that you become the least mute, and say the words that they do not know how to read in their avid and obscure hearts. Respond. Why have the doors of the temple been opened?"

In a loud voice, Syloson read: "We have knocked, and they have been opened to us.

"Why have you knocked?" asked the hierophant.

Guided by the book, Syloson replied: "We are blind, and we want to see. We are deaf, and we want to hear."

"Are you mute?" interrogated the high priest.

"We are mute, since we do not know the words."

"When you know, will you remain mute?"

"We will remain mute, out of love and respect."

"Why will you still be mute?"

"There will be words within us too large for our mouth."

"By what do you promise not to speak?"

"By all the gods that we know, we promise not to speak. By the holy Cabiri that we hope to know, we promise not to speak."

"And if there is a perjurer among you?"

"May the Cabiri desiccate his tongue in his mouth!"

"If the Cabiri disdain to desiccate his tongue in his mouth, and he speaks?"

"Let me perjurer by put to death by the brothers he has betrayed!"

The hierophant addressed the hieroceryx: "Are these men pure?"

Turning toward the hydranos, the hieroceryx repeated the question.

The hydranos affirmed: "With the water over which the hierophant, representing the gods, has pronounced he powerful words and made the efficacious signs, I have purified these men. With the water into which the hierophant, the representative of the gods, had plunged the fuming brand, I have purified these men."

The hieroceryx repeated that response; but the hierophant, having heard it, proclaimed in a severe voice: These men are not pure enough for the Cabiri. Let the doors of the temple be closed again."

"O Master of the Sacred Sciences," implored the hieroceryx, "have pity on these men. They will be purified with the lightning-stone. Order therefore that the doors remain open before their footsteps and before their desires."

"The doors will open when one knocks on behalf of pure men."

"Have you orders to give, O Master of Sciences and Destinies.?"

"Let the first be the last, let the last be the first."

The doors of the temple closed again, loudly, in a hostile manner. Then, commencing with the youngest, in accordance with the hierophant's order, everyone passed before the hydranos again.

With the lightning-stone, the priest touched their two eyelids at length.

Meanwhile, to the rhythm of invocation, the hieroceryx and the chorus led by Syloson exchanged these responses:

"Stone which is of fire;

"Purify of all stain the eyes of the myste Pythagoras."

"Stone, which is spirit;

"Purify of all stain the eyes of the myste Pythagoras."

"Stone, gift of the heavens;

"Purify of all stain the eyes of the myste Pythagoras."

The same ceremony was repeated for the ears, the opening of the nostrils, the lips, the hands and the feet.

And that solemn slowness recommenced with each of the mystes.

When the thirty had been touched by the lightning-stone, the hieroceryx went back to knock on the door of the temple, which opened again.

The hierophant asked: "Why have the doors of the temple been opened?"

And the slow dialogue unfolded, as it had three hours before. Finally, however, the hierocryx affirmed that the men had been purified by water, fire and spirit.

Then the hierophant interrogated: Why are these men wearing the white vestment of those who know? Or, if they know, what do they want with me?"

"Do not be irritated, O Master of the Inspired Sciences. These men will put on again the tunic appropriate to their ignorance.

Thirty ewes were brought by thirty *necores*. Before each myste the *epibomion* placed a little portable altar. Then thirty priests, at the same moment, cut the throats of the thirty victims. With a rapid gesture, they were stripped of their fleeces. Meanwhile, the mystes, on the order of the hieroceryx, took off their clothes, and they were covered with the still-vital warmth of the black fleeces.

The hierophant proclaimed: "The ignorant individual who wears the vestments of man is an impostor, and before him the doors of the temple will remain closed. Since these ignorant individuals are sincere, let them enter the temple."

And the dadoukhos said: "The ignorant individual who puts on the skin of a beast is beginning to know himself. Since these ignorant individuals, lost in the initial darkness, have the strength to lift their eyelids and the will to open their eyes wide, let them enter into the light."

Priests and mystes penetrated into the temple, which was illuminated by countless torches; but, the doors having been closed behind them loudly, the lights all went out at once, and there was darkness, disturbing in its suddenness.

They heard, coming from a strange distance, the voice of the hierophant and the vice of the dadoukhos. They were singing a hymn whose words, poorly perceived, more often than not made no sense. Immobile, penetrated by a slow terror, the mystes waited.

When the hymn fell silent, the powerful voice of the hieroceryx interrogated:

"Where are you?"

The hydranos replied: "We are in the darkness of the vestibule."

"Who are you?"

"We are those who are not born."

"Where are you going?"

"We want to climb toward the light."

"What do you want to be?"

"We want to be those who are."

Abruptly distant, the voice of the hieroceryx cried: "Come! Come, then!"

The groping mystes headed toward the voice, which continued to call and the draw away.

"This way, this way," called the voice.

Beneath their feet, the groping mystes felt the ground lacking. They fell, one on top of another. They did not come to any harm, but they remained in a fearful immobility. Now, beneath their bodies they felt the ground slide, transporting them…where?

"Don't move!" recommended the distant voice. "Let the ignorant allow themselves to be carried, without any disturbance, by the gods and by the harmonious movement that the gods impart to things. Do not act, do not act in the darkness. But tell me, tell me, tell me what you are?"

The hydranos replied: "We are the metal that forms in the depths of the earth."

"What else are you?"

"We are the seed that toils in the earth."

"What else are you?"

"We are the child in his mother's womb."

Then with an authority and a force that increased with each command, the voice, which drew closer every time, said: "Be the metal liberated, which rises toward the daylight. Be the grain whose effort has pierced the soil. Be the child that springs forth into the light."

As if ignited by the final word, light burst forth, abrupt, multiple and blinding.

After the initial dazzlement, the mystes saw that they were in a vast subterrain, alone with the hieroceryx and the hydranos. Before their possibly-deceived eyes, however, the back of the subterrain slowly parted, a curtain of darkness that slid from right to let and from top to bottom. Soon they recognized, on a kind of elevated platform, the hierophant and the dadoukhos. Before the latter priest there was a basket, and to either side of the basket there were two crude statues.

A small roll of papyrus was distributed to each myste, which permitted him to follow certain details of the ceremony and to take part therein by means of his responses. Then, in two columns led by the hieroceryx and the hydranos, they went to the foot of the vast altar on which the gods stood, with the mysterious basket, the hierophant and the dadoukhos. All together, they bowed to the hierophant, who occupied the far right of that stage of sorts, and, addressing him, the hieroceryx commenced in a loud voice:

"O Demiurge...."

The hydranos continued: "You who created the body...."

On the indication of the little book, the thirty completed the invocation: "Create our soul, O Demiurge."

But the Demiurge, represented by the hierophant, did not pronounce any word or make any gesture.

Then, head bowed, in a humiliated fashion, they all headed toward the dadoukhos, who was standing in the middle of the altar.

The hieroceryx said: "O Helios...."

"And the hydranos: "You who give the body the first rudiment of the soul, heat...."

The hieroceryx continued: "You who pour forth light toward open eyes, toward closed eyes, toward beings devoid of eyes...."

"Enlighten our eyes! Enlighten our eyes!" implored the mystes.

But Helios, represented by the dadoukhos, remained motionless and silent.

The attitude of the mystes became more sorrowful, as if in despair. Before the mute hostility of the gods and their interpreters, their guide, the hieroceryx, abandoned them. He climbed up to the altar by means of a mobile staircase disposed at the left-hand extremity. Immediately, in order that no one could attempt to follow him, a temple servant took away the mobile staircase. It seemed that every link was broken between heaven and earth, between the men and the gods. The intercessor, doubtless a god himself, had returned to his dwelling.

No word, no gesture came from on high to diminish the anxiety of the abandoned, from whom the servants brutally snatched away the useless books.

They remained in that sad dejection for what seemed to them to be a long time. Their gazes went, bearing interrogations and implorations, from the hierophant to the dadoukhos and from the dadoukhos to the hieroceryx. Sometimes they seemed to be recklessly invoking the four unknown statues, or even wondering whether salvation might emerge, as a precise form or a floating cloud, from the mysterious basket.

On the altar—which is to say, in the heavens—everything remained motionless and mute, terrifying in silence and enigma.

Suddenly, the hydranos, as if impelled by an abrupt aspiration of mercy and courage, made a sign.

The servants arranged the mystes behind him in a single column and he headed toward the hieroceryx, before whom he bowed profoundly. Then the hydranos half-turned toward the first mystes:

"Let each one, one after another, repeat each of my prayers." Then he said: "O Hermes...."

Like a streak of fire, along the line of mystes, the murmur ran all the way to the depths of the temple.

"O Hermes...."

"Be the psychopomp," the hydranos went on.

Successive and prolonged, the murmur supplied: "Be the psychopomp, O Hermes!"

"Make souls rise into our bodies."

He had spoken the last words in a more elevated tone, as if a definitive appeal.

The accent of the mystes imitated his, and it was like a crackle that was repeated and multiplied: "Make souls rose into our bodies, O Hermes!"

Hermes did not reply, any more than the Demiurge or Helios—but he moved.

He arched toward the middle of the altar, occupied by the dadoukhos, and, before the dadoukhos, by the mysterious basket and, to either side of the basket, by the statues.

Everyone's attention followed him; and everyone remarked that the hierophant was also marching toward the central point.

When the three priests met up, the hierophant leaned toward the basket. Then, straightening up, he displayed the object that he had taken from it. It was banal: a piece of iron.

But the solemn voice of the high priest pronounced: "I, the Demiurge, made metal, and plunged it into the depths of the earth."

He handed the iron to the dadoukhos, who enclosed it piously between his hands and is breast, saying: "I, Helios, warmed the earth in its depths and caused the metal to mature."

He passed the fragment to the hieroceryx, who, agitating it up and down, declared: "I, Hermes, made a soul rise into the metal, in order that, as plowshare or sword, it would work for the welfare or woe of men."

Then he threw the fragment of iron to the hydranos, who transmitted to the first myste. The metal passed from hand to hand. A few had a smile that was beginning to understand but which still hesitated; one of the fine smiles, the most human, in which light and darkness mingle and play.

Retracing its route in reverse, the iron came back to the hieroceryx, who plunged it back into the sacred *kiste*.[23] Scarcely had he straightened up, however, than the hierophant bent down again. He pulled out a second object and displayed it, ostentatiously. It was an ear of corn.

Now the high priest, with the ear elevated between his two hands, affirmed: "I, the Demiurge, formed the seed and placed it in the earth, the universal matrix."

Then the ear passed to the dadoukhos, who placed it preciously against his breast, saying: "I, Helios, warmed the earth and warmed the seed."

But the hieroceryx took the wheat from him and making a slow upward gesture with it, said: "I, Hermes, made a soul rise into this seed. The valiant soul sprang forth from the earth, like a growing shoot, and then multiplied, like a fecund woman."

Like the metal before it, the ear passed from hand to hand. Now, there was no one who was not meditating, amid a

---

[23] Ryner appears to have fused two of the key reported aspects of the Eleusinian ritual here, the *kiste*, or chest, and he *kalathis*, or basket, although he separates them when he describes the Elusinian rite itself. Only initiates were allowed to know what they contained, so Ryner's account is guesswork.

broken silence, upon these various travels, for the hierophant sang: "All is dead, all is blind, all is deaf and mute. That is why I enclosed everything in the cold and tenebrous depths of the earth."

But the song of the dadoukhos protested: "My heat penetrates everywhere. My heat is already the desire for my light. Everything strives toward my light."

And the hieroceryx: "Everything is alive, everything is full of souls and full of gods. I make souls rise toward your light, O Helios."

Then the three priests took one another by the hand, and circled, singing: "I am you and you are me. Death is life and life is death. I rise and I descend, I descend and I rise. I am the departure, the road and the arrival; I am the arrival, the road and the departure. I am one and I am three; I am three and I am one. I am you and you are me; you are me and I am you."

When they had ceased the strange round-dance, when their hands had separated, the hieroceryx, receiving the mystical ear or corn from the hydranos, replaced it in the kiste.

And the hierophant asked: "Have all those who have ears heard?"

But the hieroceryx replied: "The ears of men are slow to hear. Some will hear."

"Have all those who have eyes seen?"

"The eyes of men are slow to see. Some will see."

A silence followed, long, broad and profound, full of emotion and thought.

Then the hierophant proclaimed: "Hear the divine names."

And the hieroceryx: "Never profane the treasure of the divine names."

The hydranos replied, and all the mystes after him:

"We are listening to the divine names.

"We will keep the treasure of the divine names.

"We will not profane the treasure of the divine names."

Then, designating each statue, the hierophant solemnly proclaimed the four inestimable names:

"Axieros!

"Axiokersos!

"Axiokersa!

"Cadmilos!"[24]

Then, placing his hand on the first image: "O Axieros, are you not Demeter? O Demeter, are you not Deo? O Deo-Demeter-Axieros! O Amour, need to rise, impetus of the earth toward the sun, O Amour, need to descend, impetus of the sun toward the earth! O heat that rises and descends, O light that descends and rises. O blond! O radiance! O Eros, Eros, Eros…."

Now the dadoukhos, arms raised, admired: "O marvel of the divine names! O power of the divine names!"

And the hieroceryx recommended: "Guard the treasure, men, guard the treasure!!

But already, the hierophant was placing his hand on the second statue.

"O Axiokersos," he said, "are you not Hades? Are you not Plutos? Are you not Chthonian Zeus? O ithyphallic, erect by the force of Eros, O male force, O impetuous desire, Man! O heat that wants to penetrate the cold, O Helios, amorous spirit of matter, O light that wants to penetrate the darkness! O Kersos, O Kersos, O Kersos…."

The dadoukhos and the hieroceryx cry, successively:

"O marvel of the divine names! O power of the divine names!"

"Guard the treasure, men, guard the treasure."

---

[24] These names for the Cabiri are slight variations of four names said to have been attributed to them by Mnaseas of Patara, a historian of the third century B.C., although only a few fragments of his works survive. The names are not Greek and probably derive, like the Great Gods themselves, from the Phrygian mainland; their identification with the Greek deities of the Eleusinian Mysteries might have been a Roman improvisation.

And the hierophant, touching the third statue: "O Axiokersa, are you not Persephone? Are you not Cora? Are you not Chthonian Hera? O Axiokersa, O Woman, O passion, O, avid passivity, desire that waits, that hopes, that appeals and sometimes seems to refuse! O closed door, O open door, O Matter amorous of Spirit! O Kersa, O Kersa, O Kersa...."

And the other two initiators:

"O marvel of the divine names! O power of the divine names!"

"Guard the treasure, men, guard the treasure."

The hierophant touches the final stature.

"O Cadmilos, are you not Hermes? O ithyphallic, O Son who wants to be a father. Son of Axiokersos and Axiokersa. O World, product of married forces. World that senses death eating it away and wants to live. O dying in order that you can create anew. O eaten away from below, launching toward on high; eaten away by yesterday, launching toward tomorrow! Today ithyphallic, today eternal. O Cadmilos, O Cadmilos, O Cadmilos...."

One last time, the dadoukhos admires:

"O marvel of the divine names! O power of the divine names!"

One last time, the hieroceryx recommences:

"Guard the treasure, men, guard the treasure."

Then the three initiators, approaching the statues, link them together with strips of cloth. They lift up the group in their hands and, turning with it from tight to left they sing:

"O Four who are One, O One who is Four. Venerable Eros who unites the venerable Kersos with the venerable Kersa. O Kersos, O Kersa, who, in the precarious unity of the kiss, reform the durable unity of Cadmilos. O Amour, O Father, O Mother, O child."

Then, turning from left to right, they add:

"I am you and you are me. I am one and I am several. I am one and I am all; I am all and I am one."

In the vessel that was sailing toward Corinth, everyone was joyful. Like misers who shut themselves in cellars to count and palpate their treasure, they descended into their own darkness in order to stir luminous gold, the memories of initiation. Several, moved to external solemnities, did not understand either the words, the symbolic gestures, or the thoughts with which the priests charged the iron and the ears of corn that so many hands and gazes touched stupidly, but they repeated in low voices the four divine names that had saved the ship. They felt that they were the depositories of a power that raised them above other men.

The smile of their lips and the vague gleam of their eyes revealed their dream: on a vessel occupied by the profane, they saw themselves during a tempest. They promised salvation, and then, while all gazes turned toward them, they pronounced the names that dissipate storms and put dangers to flight.

But Syloson affirmed: "The treasure that we possess has numerous virtues. It gives victory in various combats. Death is a strait where reefs lie in wait and engulfing whirlpools, where the violence of winds roar or waves, rearing up like mountains, fall back as abrupt and overwhelming as avalanches. He who, in the final torment, invokes the Cabiri by name, triumphs over the storm and comes safely to the port of delights called the Elysian Fields; but those who do not know the salutary names will be precipitated into the infernal depths; plunged into the noxious mud of a marsh, they will await, groaning, the distant hour of the new birth."

There were old men on the vessel to whom those words were a wine of strength and joy. The young loved the divine names for their power over irritated waters.

One day, the glad intoxication of the old men had an upsurge of ecstasy. Syloson had recounted: "Before the divine name, death sometimes recoils in fear. I know an initiate who has always been able to throw them, like victorious projectiles, in the face of Thanatos. Today, his bald head sustains the weight of a hundred and forty-nine years.

Pythagoras remained apart from this chatter. When Syloson reproached him for his voluntary isolation, the young man declared: "The grain of wheat makes no sound in the bosom of the earth. I bear in me a seed that is striving in the silence to rise up and to grow." He added: "Why would I speak, ignorance that has nothing to say? How many words I need to collect before becoming a Word. Words come from everywhere, accumulate and scour of all mud the lake of my silence!"

In Corinth, they all ran greedily toward gross pleasures; but Pythagoras went away into the country. Rolled in the folds of his cloak, he lay down on the edge of the harmonious sea, and he thought:

Corinth is not one of the sacred places where one has some chance of hearing. Cities that make so much noise are empty of words.

Soon, a vessel transported him toward Piraeus. He was desirous of hearing the sage Solon. He arrived to learn of his death and attend his funeral.[25]

There it is, said Pythagoras. *The word of this land is extinct. What remains for me to hope for here except the mysteries?*

He went to the Athenian Protogenes for whom Pherecydes had given him letters and was to serve him as a mystagogue.

Protogenes, a man of thirty, a priest of Orpheus and a disciple of Pherecydes, welcomed Pythagoras joyfully.

"O my brother, the father of our two minds writes to me about the power of your impetus toward knowledge. He asks me not only to be your intruder to the mysteries but also to

---

[25] Solon reportedly died in 558 B.C. or thereabouts, a date not consonant with the supposed age of Pythagoras at this point in the story, if the usual estimate of his birth-date as c570 B.C. is accepted, so Ryner is stretching his fictitious chronology somewhat in order to accommodate this detail,

open to you the secret meaning of words. Since you are an initiate of Samothrace, there are things I can tell you now.

"O my brother, Anthesterion[26] is about to begin, a month in which spring and the petty mysteries flourish. When the moon seven times renewed has brought Boedromion, we will celebrate the great mysteries. Here, as is often the case, the names are thoughtlessly taken for appearances; the petty mysteries will be fuller and more generous for you than the great.

"In Boedromion you will hear few sacred words. You will be shown the spectacle at which, without seeing it, you have been witnessing since birth. In order for you finally to perceive it, the life of a year and the life of a lifetime will be squeezed into a few days. That fortunate lie will reveal the truth to you, with the consequence that henceforth, you will no longer distinguish between the circular course of nature and the cycle of your soul.

"But at the petty mysteries, oh, how the words will flow, abundant and perfumed, toward the noble vase of your silence. In olden days, they already said something. They say everything since the divine Orpheus, renewing them like a spring, gave them a powerful life and a durable youth.

"The petty mysteries, as no one is unaware, are those of Persephone, but the great celebrate Demeter. Once, Hades was associated with Persephone. Orpheus has expelled Hades, the god of immobile and enclosed death, the god of the vast cavern that does not open. He has given his place to Dionysus, the master of the life that persists in all its forms and who, victorious, makes the circle of eternity turn. Hades, a liar like immobility and appearance, does not know that death is the rejuvenation of life; but Dionysus...."

Protogenes stopped, perhaps too emotional, or perhaps fearing to say what he ought to keep silent. Soon, he resumed, with the most enthusiastic tone of adoration.

---

[26] Anthesterion was the eighth month of the Athenian calendar, overlapping our February and March; Boedromion was the third, overlapping September and October,

"O Dionysus, vanquisher of the Hades below; thanks to you he is fallen, he who paralyzed subterranean life, transforming it into an apparently immortal death. O Dionysus, when will you be the vanquisher of the Hades above, the implacable Zeus who, by means of the tyranny of the tyrant or the tyranny of the Law, makes the city of tomb and the life of citizens a death?"

"O my brother," exclaimed Pythagores, "your voice, which I love, awakens and strips bare words that were dormant, mute and masked, in the depths of my silence. You are the radiance thanks to which some blind seed causes to spring forth before my eyes a plume of verdure that rejoices them. But if it is permitted, elucidate an obscurity that surrounds your light with its cloud. Orpheus, you say, introduced to the mysteries the cult of Dionysus. But I was told in childhood that Orpheus, a priest of Apollo and harmonious wisdom, was killed by the incoherent madness of bacchantes, priestesses of Dionysus."

"Orpheus, priest of Apollo, poet of appeasement and harmony, came, like a tamer among wild beasts, to soften and soothe the wild enthusiasm of dionysiacs. But Dionysus excited his eyes and his heart with a beauty of which they were as yet unaware. Henceforth amorous of emotion and Bacchus, he quit Apollo to dedicate himself to the new god. His lyre knew the surging harmony that, instead of coming from rules, emerges from the soul.

"For you, Apollo, are the calm and deceptive lyre of Zeus, protector of tyrants and laws; but you, Dionysus, lyre as vast as the four winds of the sky and as sonorous and various as the sea, are you not the multiple vigor of people and free gestures?"

"Why, then, did the Bacchantes tear Orpheus apart?"

"The Bacchantes adore the vulgar Dionysus. They believe that they are communing with the god when they drink wine and eat the raw meat of the bull. They are the blind enthusiasm that, bounding beyond harmony, falls into dementia.

"But the Orphean Dionysus…oh, my brother, in what a blossoming silence you will receive, in the mysteries, the revelation of his true name, and the marvels of his birth, and the mourning of his death, and the triumph of his resurrection. Oh, that one is not wine and the folly of the senses; he is the heart and his wisdom is higher than the wisdom of the brain.

"From an authoritarian wisdom, and a harmony constructed externally, Orpheus passed to free Wisdom, to the living Harmony that emerges from ourselves and deploys. He was torn apart by madwomen who denied all wisdom and all harmony."

Protogenes added, in a sudden melancholy: "For a long time yet the hands of the people and the incoherent thought of the people will tear you apart, heroic sages who attempt to liberate the people and give a voice to their unknown harmony."

Crowned with myrtle and clad in dyed animal-hide, the mystes gathered on the agora, uttering loud cries. The mystagogues in long robes of linen and wearing their hair elevated in topknots, held by golden rings, were no less noisy.

Suddenly, the tumultuous noise and laughter fell silent. The oldest of the mystagogues, his arms extended toward the setting sun, abruptly closed his hand, as if seizing a sunbeam. At the same time, the hieroceryx arrived, bearing an unlit torch. Turning toward him, the mystagogues invoked:

"Iacchus, O Iacchus!"[27]

"Divine child!"

"You whose light will guide us into the night;

"You who lead the chorus of the stars;

"You who preside over the nocturnal hymns…."

A demi-chorus of mystes implored:

"Light, light the flame."

---

[27] Iacchus was an epithet of Dionysus particularly associated with the Eleusinian Mysteries, where his name was attributed to the torch-bearer of the procession to Eleusis.

And the other demi-chorus:

"Guide us, guide us, guide us."

At the precise moment when the sun disappeared, the hieroceryx, who was playing the role of Dionysus in the first part of the ceremony and until the appearance of the hierophant, inclined the torch toward the fire of a small altar, and brought it back crowned with flames. The flute-players arranged themselves behind him, and, amid the enthusiasm of the crowd, which repeated a thousand times "Iacchus! Iacchus!" the procession set forth across the city.

As soon as it had surpassed the ramparts, it stopped momentarily. The priests cried: "Who is on the road? Who is on the road? Far from here, profanes!"

After that brief halt, the cortege resumed its march along the Ilissus toward the sacred mountain. At the foot of Mount Agra,[28] the purification took place, less solemn than that in Samothrace and with a completely different ritual. Between two columns, a heavy bouquet of flowers in the form of a phallus hung from a pine-branch.

Each myste leapt up three times to touch it with his head, and pronounced an invocation at each contact:

"Purify me, O phallus!"

"Purify me and enlighten me, O radiance!"

"Purify me and animate me, O Spirit!"

A few paces further on, next to a winnowing-basket suspended from laurel and myrtle branches, a priest stood. As soon as the purified myste presented himself, the officiant said:

"Mystical winnowing-basket;

"You who separate the good grain from the straw;

"You who distinguish the initiate from the profane;

---

[28] The district of Agra, or Agrai, where the petty mysteries were traditionally celebrated, is not a mountain; it is possible that Ryner is confusing it, accidentally or deliberately, with Mount Hymettos.

"What will you make of the man who is coming toward you?"

Three times, in silence, he agitated the winnowing-basket. Then he pronounced:

"Man, the air has taken away what there was within you of the impure and light. But you, man, the mystical winnowing-basket has not rejected. Go therefore in the joy of your heart and rejoin the sacred troop that follows Iacchus."

On the other side of the passage, tents were erected. The mystagogues led the mystes into them, calling them their sons. They explained to them what they had seen and heard thus far, and prepared them to comprehend what they would see and hear in the morning.

In the middle of the night, there was the silence of slumber and the silence of meditation at the foot of Mount Agra.

Scarcely an hour had been accorded to repose when resounding cymbals summoned the mystes outside the tents. In a vast meadow sloping gently toward the Illisos and rising gently toward Agra, they gathered, free of the animal-hides and dressed in white linen.

Choruses commenced by the light of torches. The mystes sang, while dancing:

"Iacchus, venerated god, respond to our voices. Iacchus, Iacchus, come to this meadow, your preferred abode; come to direct the choruses of your initiates. Let the myrtle branch charged with fruits, a thick crown, balance on your head. Let your bold foot figure the free and joyful dance, the dance inspired by the Charites, the religious and holy dance that reproduces, without knowing it, the choruses of the stars, the choruses of the seasons, he rhythm of day and night, of life and death; the dance that reproduces our choruses amid the shadows and incoherent gleams, but which, thanks to you, we shall continue in the unripped fabric of a victorious light. Wave the ardent torches, then, and revive their glare, brilliant star of our nocturnal mysteries, Iacchus, Iacchus. Revive the glare of torches and agitate their flames, you for whom the night becomes brighter than the day, death more alive than life, Iacchus, Iacchus!"

Obedient to those prayers, Iacchus—which is to say, the hieroceryx—seized a lighted torch, shook it, and began to climb the hill. Behind him, the mystes, taking possession of other torches, climbed slowly. Amid the hymns and the flutes they marched, agitating the flames to the noble rhythm that guided their feet and their voices.

At the summit of the Agra, the hieroceryx, extinguishing his torch, sat down on a stone. Everyone imitated both gestures. There was silence and darkness for a time.

Attention soon extended toward distant voices. They were coming from the abandoned meadow.

"O night," they sang, "who has told you, then, that you are not day? Child, who has told you, then, that you are not yet a man? Man, who has told you, then, that you are not a god? O Iacchus, child-man, O Iacchus, man-god!"

Other voices responded from the other side of the hill:

"No, night is not day. A child is not a man. A man is not a god. O Iacchus, tell us what you are, child, man or god, god, man or child."

But the first voices, with an increasing force, with which some irony as initially mingled, but which soon became firmer and exalted faith:

"Can you tell me where the night ends and the day begins? Can you tell me where the child ends and the man begins? Can you tell me where the man ends and the god begins? O Iacchus, who is Dionysus; O Dionysus who is the one whose name I must not say; O child who is a man, man who is a god, god who will vanquish the other gods; respond, respond for me to these ignorant individuals."

Then, in the quiver of emotions, the hierophant appeared, and he said:

"The Truth, the Truth, I shall proclaim to my beloved the whole Truth. I am a man because I am a child. I am a god because I am a man. I shall vanquish the other gods because, in being a god, I have not ceased to be a man, or, in becoming a man, to be a child. I have not lost yesterday in gaining today; I shall not lose today in gaining tomorrow. But when you are alone, my beloved, no longer call me Iacchus. No longer call me Dionysus. Zagreus, Zagreus, it is Zagreus alone that it is necessary to invoke."

From the unknown part of the hill, the voices that were affirming the night a little while before rose up, lamentably:

"Dionysus, Dionysus," they wept, "Iacchus, Iacchus, we are those who, ignorant of your true name, are ignorant of everything. We are the blind for whom night exists.

But from the sacred meadow an ardent and joyful chorus rose up:

"Zagreus, Zagreus, we are those who, knowing your name, know everything. We are those whose eyes you have opened and who march in the beauty of eternal day."

First light blanched the horizon. On the plateau that crowned the Agra, numerous priests came running from all directions. They were not wearing their customary vestments. By the costumes that covered them and the attributes they wore, each of them as similar to a different god. That strange living Olympus agitated in a strange representation. Before the eyes of the mystes, a dramatic fable unfurled. Sometimes, the songs of invisible choruses rose from both sides of the hill to comment on the actions of the gods; more often, the voice of the hierophant explained them.

First, the priest all cried in unison: "Pour rain, child!" And Zeus was seen to descend from Olympus and pursue Demeter. He caught up with her, and seized her for a kiss that she rejected. Then his irritated gesture threw into the bosom of the goddess an object that the mystes, too far away, could not distinguish, and then fled, sowing mocking laughter behind him.

The hierophant announced that Demeter had received in her bosom the organs of a ram. At the same time, he took a snake from the sacred basket, introduced it into the neck of his robe, and allowed it to slide along his body. Soon, the snake reappeared, coiled around his leg. And the high priest proclaimed, in a loud voice:

"The Venerable has given birth to the Venerable. The Strong has given birth to the Strong."

Emerging from the bosom of Demeter, they see Zagreus born.[29] Immediately, the Strong starts walking unaided.

But monstrous giants, the Titans, appeared. They conspire together. They call to the child, offering him a toy. Smiling, full of confidence, little Zagreus comes to them. They seize him and tear him apart. Amid the laughter of cruel triumph, they flee, devouring his limbs and throwing the bloody remnants behind them.

Pallas Athene has seen the crime. She runs to the heart, still palpitating; she collects it in her pious hands, carries it to the summit of Olympus, and presents it to Zeus.

O marvel! Under the emotional gaze of Zeus, around the heart, the Child is reconstituted n his entirety. And Zeus pronounces these words:

"O Zagreus, you are the one who, in my eternal designs, I have decided to engender. Because you were good and defenseless, the wicked wanted to kill you. Nothing is as deceptive as the actions of the wicked. See, they have dispersed far from you that which was not You; they separated from your heart that which as not Your Heart. Thought and will, if they persist for a long time, become better than themselves, freeing themselves from all poverty and impurity, eventually flowing down the slope of love. O my son, of god better than me, O god who is a Heart, is it not already You who are speaking through my mouth? Zagreus, are you not the one that I want to become? Are you not the one that Prometheus has promised me in all his threats? Are you not the one in the life of whom I must joyfully die, in order that you alone may live?"

But Zagreus, quitting Olympus and not pausing in the abode of the Ephemerae, went into the underworld. He en-

---

[29] According to some sources the mother of the Orphic Zagreus/Dionysus was nor Demeter but her daughter Persephone, and it was Persephone who played the symbolic role in the Orphic Mysteries credited here to Demeter.

chained Hades and espoused Cora. With her he rose up to the earth again. With each step they took, herbs grew, flowers rose, cheerfully perfumed and colored. The wheat was charged with ears, the vines swayed under the weight of clusters of grapes.

Meanwhile, on the heights of Olympus, the voice of Zeus implored: "Come and enchain me. Come and enchain me...."

On that spectacle of joy, with that hope of the complete triumph of the heart, the performance ended.

The hierophant proclaimed the solemn words: "*Conx ompax*," which, in an old lost language, signify: "Go, you have seen everything."

They retired in silence, slowly, listening to the chorus that rose from the sacred meadow:

"Zagreus, the Titans tore you apart and you disappeared from the world; Zagreus; fecundity henceforth spread throughout nature entire. Husband of Cora, your blood is the seed of beings; men are the issue of your blood. Men, limbs of Zagreus, O sons of the same father, O brothers; he who drinks the wine of Dionysius, he who eats the wheat of Cora, eats the god and drinks the god whose flesh and blood are everywhere. Men, eat the god fraternally and drink the god fraternally, in order that you might become gods."

The petty mysteries are annual, the great are only renewed every five years. Pherecydes had chosen a year of the great mysteries for Pythagoras' departure; before receiving the complement of initiation, the young sage had only to let the moon lose and regain its strength and its light seven times. He spent that time traveling.

He stayed in Crete for some time. He was initiated by the Curetes; he lived for thirty days in the lair of Mount Ida and saw the seat on which Zeus was born.

Impressed by his curiosity, the priests told him proudly about Epimenides, loved by the gods. They told a thousand strange and contradictory stories about him. According to some, he had already lived for a hundred and fifty-seven years, but others credited him with two hundred and ninety. He had spent fifty of them asleep in a grotto, and when he awoke, had begun prophesying. His mother was a nymph. He had never tasted the gross aliments of men; he nourished himself on a marvelous substance, a gift of the nymphs, which he carried contained in the foot of an ox.

Pythagoras remembered the popular tales that his dear Pherecydes dressed with eccentric strangeness. The man around whom the colored clouds of legend amassed appeared him to be a superior being, and he desired to make his acquaintance.

For several years, Epimenides, grimly solitary, had been wandering in the most deserted regions. After having searched for him for a long time, Pythagoras succeeded in encountering him.

Was the old man's name still appropriate to him? He appeared to have surpassed all the human ages. round the wrinkled parchment of his face, the hair and beard bristled stiffly white, like vegetables. He was lying on the ground, unmoving. The hair of his arms and legs was reminiscent of moss covering a felled tree.

"My father!" cried Pythagoras, "Are you still alive, or have I arrived too late?"

Epimenides lifted his upper body slightly and looked to see who was speaking.

"Who are you?" he asked.

"People call me Pythagoras, disciple of Pherecydes."

The old man's eyes were the eyes of a man looking into the extreme distance, toward the horizon of memory. Then his head nodded, and he said: "Pherecydes? I remember. The sages say: 'He's a poet," the poets say: 'He's a sage,' Rejoice in your heart, my son; you could not encounter a better master." He fell silent momentarily. Then he pronounced the single word: "However...."

Pythagoras trembled, as a vulgar man trembles in danger of death. Was he about to hear that venerable sage speak ill of his master?

A glimmer of pride quivered on the earthen face of Epimenides, and he continued: "However, I am worth more than him. The Son of the Nymph is not only the most profound of sages and the most sublime of poets; he is also the foremost of priests, the most powerful of purifiers, and the most farsighted of prophets. Learn, young man, that I am the one who breaks all horizons."

But he let himself fall back on the ground and he murmured: "I am…? No, I was. It is appropriate no longer to speak of Epimenides, as of yesterday's sun. The time has come when I ought to disappear. The nymphs have told me the name of Pythagoras, and that your coming would be the signal for my departure. Be proud: the glory of burying Epimenides is reserved for you."

After a pause, he resumed: "I would like to sing you the truth, but the strength is lacking and the time. Let the man who cannot give a cock give the egg from which the cock will emerge. Listen, hear and retain. Only the Air and the Night existed, but they engendered the Egg. From the Egg emerged the World. Everything comes from the Egg, even the gods—or rather, the gods first. Adore the Egg, and all the gods will be adored. Honor the Egg, and everything beautiful will be honored. Scorn the Egg, and you will have scorned all ugliness and all crime. But if you are able to distinguish the top and bottom of the Egg, the shell and the contents, the yolk and the white, then you will possess all science."

Exhausted by effort, breathless, he fell silent. Finally, when his breast was calm, he murmured these final words:

"It is in the sole company of the Nymphs, my relatives, far from everything that is perishable, that I want to render to the Egg my great fertile soul. So go away, man, without turning your head. But as soon as the sun has set in the vastness of the sea come back, and lay down in the narrowness of a tomb a man greater and more luminous than the sun."

Pythagoras obeyed piously. When darkness descended over the fields, he came back with two other men. He found that the old man, in whom a sage and a charlatan were mingled, was dead.

He buried him. And the tears flowed over his visage, because Epimenides was great, and because Epimenides was small. He thought, privately:

My Pherecydes is a thousand times more admirable, because he is pure, devoid of vanity and deception.

And he believed that Epimenides had held his breath in order to die at the hour he had predicted.

"The great mysteries to which I am leading you ought to be called the long mysteries. Certainly, they have not come to us as they were instituted; nothing can last except on the condition of being changed. Through the centuries, they have been ornamented by a thousand dramatic elements. But no one has come like Orpheus for the mysteries of Agra to enrich them with gnomic and fecund beauties. I compare them to a river that is increased and embellished by numerous streams. But the mysteries you know are the Nile in the season of floods; they are not only beautiful fleeting waters; they bear fertile soil; in whoever is worthy, they construct a delta that will be covered with flowers and joy, strength and wheat."

Protogenes fell silent. The two men arrived at the porticoes of the Eleusinion, where the assembly was taking place. As before the Petty Mysteries, there was great agitation there: popular gaiety, empty chatter, foolish cries and sonorous laughter. That day, the fifteenth of Boedromion, had nothing troubling about it. When the mystes fell silent, it was uniquely to hear the hierophant proclaim the conditions of admission and the order of the first ceremonies.

On the second day, the mystes went to the sea together, for ablutions and purifications. Then three days were employed in sacrifices and expiatory ceremonies.

Pythagoras found those exercises even emptier than Protogenes had announced to him. But the priest of Orpheus encouraged him, promising him that, afterwards, the Eleusinian part would bring interesting subjects of meditation.

On the twentieth of Boedromion, after solemn preludes to which Pythagoras had already been subject in his previous initiations, the procession set forth behind Iacchus. It went further—much further; it was more pompous, richer in color and music; one might have thought it a magnification of the procession of the Petty Mysteries. From the Eleusinion they headed for the Agora, which they traversed, as well as the Ceramic; they were purified for the last time in the salt-water of the Rheitoi and they arrived on the bridge of Cephise, where there was a tumultuous pause, exchanges of coarse words, absurd sallies and unbridled laughter. Then the march resumed solemnly along the sacred path. After several silent stations they reached Eleusis in the middle of the night.

Under the guidance of mystagogues and rhabdophores, the mystes returned to tents in order to rest until morning.

At first light, without explanation, the spectacle commenced, often mute. Sometimes, however, it was charged with prolix speeches in which the dramatic genius of Athens was already being tested.

First, among the chorus of the daughters of Oceanos, the young Persephone was seen playing in the Nysean meadow. She was picking flowers: saffron, violets, irises hyacinths. She perceived a narcissus. Its brightness seemed to her to triumph over all corollas and calices. She threw away her disdained crop and extended her hands to pick the new flower, but the earth opened up, and Hades appeared in his chariot. At the very moment when the young woman touched the narcissus, the cruel Aidoneus[30] abducted her and took her to his subterranean abode.

Pythagoras watched with his eyes and his mind. He said to himself:

---

[30] Aidoneus was a mythical king of the Molossians who was represented by the Roman historian and Christian polemicist Eusebius—for reasons that are unclear—as the husband of Persephone, and is thus identified here as Hades.

Persephone, a flower among flowers, has disappeared underground. That is in order that I think about the seeds that are the flowers of the meadow fallen into the bosom of Gaia. The continuation of the spectacle will doubtless sing the resurrection of the seed.

Then his interior voice said:

Narcissus, flower of the dead, symbol of the torpor that seizes us for the passage through the darkness, as soon as Cora has touched you, she is the prey of Hades. A day will come when, seduced by the enlightenments of death, I shall throw away the bouquet of life and extend my hand toward the bright and torpid narcissus. On that day, Hades will take possession of me. But the victories of Hades are apparent and precarious; after a time, I shall escape him, as, in the renewal, plants and Persephone escape him.

Then he silenced the voice of his soul in order to hear a strange voice, for the hierophant was singing a hymn:

"As long as the goddess perceived the earth and the starry sky, and the impetuous waves of the sea, she retained the hope of seeing her venerable mother appear, and the tribe of the immortal gods; for a long time, in spite of her dolor, that hope charmed her mind. O incomplete defeat that might perhaps be transformed into victory…gripping death-throes, but which abrupt help might relieve….

"Meanwhile, she called for help; the summits of the mountains and the abysms of the sea resounded to her immortal voice. Her august mother eventually heard her. Dolor, like a sharp dagger, penetrated the heart of Demeter. With her hands, she tore away the headbands that retained her hair. She threw a somber veil over her shoulders. As swift as a bird, she launched herself over the nourishing earth and the sterile waves in search of her child."

The lugubrious cries of the mystes welcomed the end of the hymn. The hieroceryx took them to the subterrains, where they were subjected to the ordeals of Persephone. For interminable hours, they were made to describe painful circuits in the darkness. A thousand crude artifices delivered them to terrors and anxieties. There was nothing but falls, impacts and cold, sticky, sliding contacts.

Sometimes, abruptly, the darkness brightened. Around them, for a second, they saw an agitation of serpents, lions and fantastic beasts, terrifying threats. Then, amid the hissing, the roars, the mewling, the grating and the most terrible cries of new and unknown creatures, the darkness closed over them again.

Human voices too are heard, sometimes growling powerfully like angry people; more often they are faint, moaning, fading away, extenuated and then resuming, shrilly, like the rhythms of dolor. They draw away only to approach again; they bruise the ears and then suddenly flee in all directions....

At the end of a long corridor, a glimmer of light similar to an indecisive first light summons the mystes. They go toward it. No joyful haste buoys up their tread. They have been deceived too many times; too many times, a hope and a light, as amiable as the mother who sees her child coming, makes a sign to then—"Come quickly!"—and, running toward the light and hope, they have fallen into some voracious pit of darkness and impotence.

This time, however, their hearts beat faster.

They soon stop in order to listen to the voice of the hieroceryx:

"Come, my beloved. Emerge from Tartarus where the profane will remain plunged until their next terrestrial life. Are you not those whom I have chosen? Come and hear the sacred discourse; come and contemplate the divine visions."

Alas, before them the corridor, like an anguish of agony, narrows and lowers. One after another, the mystes lie down on their bellies; through the strangled tunnel they slide painfully.

Finally! Here they are in the open air, among the verdure of a meadow, in the comforting freshness of the morning.

Their hearts rejoice. They are about to cry out their gladness; their feet, still immobile, shiver with a desire to dance.

A gesture from the hieroceryx stops them and troubles them. Then he speaks. The day, which is commencing so radiant in the heavens, will be a day of sadness and fasting for them. And he orders them to utter funereal howls.

All night long, through traps and menaces, in the mad terrors of a waking nightmare, they have marched without nourishment. Until the sun sets, they will still be deprived of all nourishment and any beverage. Several tremble with fever. They gaze, however, with avid curiosity. The holy tragedy recommences in which the drama of nature, by virtue of being humanized, is divined.

Demeter appears, a great veiled figure. Her dolor is not expressed by words or cries. Her hands agitate the flames of two unequal torches, raising one and lowering the other. Nine times she repeats the double movement. In the meantime she twists her arms, and her eyes and heads turn in all directions like someone searching, desperately.

"For nine days," laments the hierophant's hymn, "the Venerable wandered the earth. Entirely given over to her affliction, she did not taste any of the nourishment of gods or men, and did not plunge her body into a bath."

Thus, a naïve gesture and a few sung words express nine days of empty searching. The spectacle now recounts the tenth day.

Demeter encounters a strange figure. On a woman's body are three heads. Two are mild, with blonde hair and a virginal smile, the third is covered in thick black hair which sometimes hide it entirely and sometimes part like a stormy sky and allow glimpses, like lightning, of the flaming abruptness of the gaze. It is the Triple Goddess: as Artemis she launches the silver of her radiance over the forests; as Selene she leads the brilliant chorus of the stars in the havens; as Hecate, enveloped in vapors and clouds, she rips with sudden glimmers the dismal horror of nights and presides over magical operations at crossroads, amid the howling of dogs. Few secrets escape her. She penetrates hearts and darkness.

She divines the wordless dolor of Demeter and tells her what she knows. She has heard Cora's hectic cries, but she has not seen the abductor. Demeter listens, and dies not reply, but, accompanied by the Triple Goddess, she resumes her search.

Now, before them, is Helios crowned with golden radiance. Hecate interrogates him, who knows everything, and he turns to the dolorous mother.

"None of the immortals is the cause of your tears, except for Zeus, the supreme god, who has permitted his brother Aidoneus to take your daughter for his spouse. Console yourself, however, O Venerable, for the king of the underworld is not a son-in-law unworthy of you; is he not your daughter's uncle, and is not one of the three parts of the Cosmos obedient to his law?"

Demeter flees these vague consolations. Again, she is alone. She puts on the appearance of a wretched old woman, and travels the cities and the countryside.

She arrives in Eleusis. By the roadside, near the well of Parthenios, she sits down in the shade of an olive-tree, which covers her with its branches. Three young women, three sisters, come with bronze vessels to draw water from the well. Moved by her age and dolor, they interrogate her benevolently. The goddess replies to them with subtle words.[31]

"My name is Deo; that is what my venerable mother called me. Pirates abducted me from Crete, my homeland. They disembarked at Thorice and while they were taking their evening meal I succeeded in escaping. I have been wandering for a long time. I do not know where I am or what people inhabit this region. Dear children, take pity on me and find me some employment as a nurse or maidservant."

Callidice, the most beautiful of the three young women, shows her the dwelling of the sage Triptolemus, that of

---

[31] The passage that follows is quoted, save for a few abridgements and transcription errors, from Alfred Maury's *Histoire des religions de la Grèce antique* (1857). I have corrected some of the transcription errors but have not restored the full text of the original.

Diocles, that of Dolichus, that of the irreproachable Eumolpe and finally that of Celeos, her father, and says:

"The wives of these heroes watch carefully over their dwellings. When they see you, none will disdain you or reject you; you will find a welcome in all of them. For you seem to be, rather than a mortal, a goddess clad in false poverty and deceptive old age. If you wish, however, wait here. We will go to my father's palace; we shall report to Metanire, our mother, that we have seen you, and she will give you shelter. We have a young brother whom the gods have sent to our parents in their old days; you can serve as guardian and nurse."

Deo makes a sign of assent and the young women depart joyously toward the good deed like a white troop of doves toward a region covered with wheat.

Soon the maidens return at a run, like hinds in spring, sated on pasture, bounding through the grass. They have lifted up their gracious veils, and around their shoulders their hair floats, as soft as flowering crocuses. From a distance, their cries and their gestures summon the old woman, who stands up. All together, precipitately, they tell her the good news.

Behind their animated joy the goddess marches, sad at heart. Her head is enveloped in a somber veil, which descends along her body and winds around her immortal feet.

As she enters the palace of Celeos, she removes her veil. Through her mask of old age shines a mysterious gleam that illuminates the entire dwelling, for the gods cannot disguise themselves completely; through the mask of matter, their light reveals itself in the most humble as in the most magnificent of their works.

Gripped by respect, Metanire cedes her place to Deo. The goddess refuses with a gesture. Like mourning over a royal life she extends her veil over her face, and remains immobile and mute for a long time. But the young Iambe, all laughter and merry gestures, offers her a seat covered with a light sheepskin, and addresses words to her radiant with affection and good humor. The dolorous goddess sits down.

She refuses the cup and aliments that are offered to her. Then Iambe pours water, flour and mint into a vase; she carefully composes the *cyceon* that gives strength to couriers and health to the ailing.[32] The goddess refuses the beverage at first, but can she resist the tender persistence of Iambe for long?

"Drink," she says, "for I cannot drink for you, O Venerable. Drink, O Venerable, for I am not the one who has traveled the route that has made you weary. Drink, O Venerable, for it is not my throat that is on fire behind your closed mouth."

The amicable and delicate pleasantries obtain a slight smile from the goddess. Iambe utilizes that commencement of victory.

"Drink, then, Venerable, since your lips are already parted. Don't close them; you are not the maladroit who makes the effort twice instead of once."

Deo yields to the benevolence and subtle insistence. She drinks the cyceon.

Now the representation of that slow and multiple action has filled the entire day. Now the sun is enveloped in the bloody clouds of evening. The mystes get up, and they cry: "The goddess has drunk the cyceon; the time of the fast is over."

The priests bring the sacred baskets. Each myste takes therefrom a cup of cyceon and a morsel of bread. He eats and drinks silently. In another basket, he deposits the empty cup and a fragment of bread. Then he says:

"I have fasted, I have drunk the cyceon, I have taken the kiste and, after having eaten, I have deposited in the kalathis;

---

[32] Maury adds a footnote to the original version of this passage explaining that cyceon was a medicinal and magical beverage, from which Ryner's supplementary comment is derived. Other sources describe it as a suspension of partially-ground uncooked barley and pennyroyal. The passage in Maury then proceeds with an account of Metanire confiding her son Demophon to Demeter's care, which Ryner omits, although he refers to it subsequently as if he had included it.

tomorrow, I shall take up the kalathis again and place it in the kiste."

Then the hieroceryx asks: "O my beloved, has not Iambe, by her amicable pleasantries and the ingenuous youth of her laughter cheered up the goddess and enabled her to forget her dolor momentarily?"

The mystes respond:

"Young Iambe, by her amicable pleasantries and the ingenuousness of her laughter, has cheered up the goddess and enabled her to forget her dolor momentarily."

"Be, therefore, like the goddess; in memory of young Iambe, cheer up and rest until the next sunrise."

Like lax schoolboys after a long application, the mystes shake themselves and jostle one another, in joyful movements and broad laughter. But the games, the cheerful words and the agitation of limbs does not last long. None has slept for three times fourteen hours; they are not long delayed in going to their tents.

The next day, at daybreak, there is the continuation of the great spectacle.

Old Deo is carrying Demophon, the little child confided to her care, in her arms, and the hierophant's song informs:

"He is growing like a god. However, he is not nourished on bread and does not suckle milk. As soon as no one can see, Deo rubs him with ambrosia and blows on him softly. But what she does for him during the night, watch, my beloved."

The goddess approaches the hearth, stirs the fire, and hides Demophon, who shines like a firebrand, among the flames and embers."

Troubled by the strange behavior of the old nurse, Metanire is watching behind the door. She opens it and comes in, crying out, and raising her arms indignantly and desperately. Deo retrieves the child from the hearth and, turning toward the mother, pronounced words as irritated as thunder:

"Blind humans, you are incapable of distinguishing the good and evil that destiny reserves for you, but you call evil the proof that purifies. I wanted to free Demophon from old age and death. Your lack of confidence has cost your son immortality. You have not permitted me to purify him of the terrestrial elements that are in him. Let him remain, then, since his mother has wished it thus, a wretched mortal, superior to others only in the futile honor of having had a goddess for a nurse."

She falls silent momentarily. The old age is a fallen mask; the anger a mask that falls. The visage of the goddess appears now, an eternal beauty over which the spasms of a dissipating dolor pass, a great immortal light beneath a great wind that is calming down. And she says:

"I am the glorious Demeter, the joy and utility of gods and humans. Above the city and the high ramparts, on the lofty summit of the Kallikoros, let all the people build me a temple and an altar. I shall inform you myself of my mysteries, in order that in future, you will practice the sacred rites therein and appease my spirit."

She keeps her promise. As soon as the Eleusinians are initiated, she flees again. Wandering in the most solitary places she refuses her benefits to the gods and humans. Unknown to all she hides again beneath a deceptive old age and poverty. But Pan, who is roaming in Arcadia, recognizes her beneath her disguise. He runs to inform Zeus. The supreme master sends to Demeter the most eloquent and most powerful of goddesses, the Moirae, whom none can resist. Their voices, sometimes slow and penetrating, like reason, and sometimes violent, like the slope of a torrent, affirm that even the gods cannot triumph over necessity.

Demeter responds: "Dolor is grimmer and more inexorable than necessity. In my place, a mere mortal would die. I can only refuse to live, by which I mean to act."

Zeus yields to the will of the Great Goddess.

"Abstention," he cries, "of the weakest you make the strongest, and injuriously, you place above the gods themselves a small number of men; abstention, the liberty of sages, the sole victory over necessity."

And he dispatches Hermes in order to take Persephone from Aidoneus and return her to her mother.

Before letting Cora go, Aidoneus opens a pomegranate, whose numerous seeds symbolize fecundity. He makes his spouse eat a seed, a sacred pledge, like a first child, of a bond that nothing can undo.

At the sight of her daughter returning from the depths, Demeter launches herself like a maenad, through the somber forests, down the mountain. Amid the kisses and tears, she asks:

"Dear child, you have not eaten anything in the abode of the king of the dead? Speak, do not hide anything from me. If you have not touched aliments down below, you can henceforth, snatched from tenebrous Tartarus, live in Olympus with Zeus your father. But if you have taken some nourishment in the somber empire, then it will be necessary for you to return there. You will dwell with your husband for a third part of the year, and for the other two with me and the luminous gods. When spring gives birth to the odorous and varied flowers, you will return from the obscurity to be a great prodigy in the regard to the gods and humans."

Thus the marvelous drama reached its conclusion. And the hierophant sang these beautiful words, which testified, in spite of what Protogenes had said, to the earliest Orphic infiltrations:

"Henceforth the seasons will be regular. Demeter has vanquished her dolor, sure of seeing her daughter again in spring; the miser consents to sow, sure of the eventual crop; the initiate dies smiling, sure of living again. Deo has vanquished her dolor, and Deo has vanquished Rhea. Rhea is exiled to the arid lands and to the icy summits of the mountains.

"We adore you, Deo, better than Rhea, more divine for having been an old woman who weeps, for having known human dolors, human lacerations and the loss of dear ones. The grim Rhea is only a daughter of the gods, but you, Deo, are a daughter of gods and humans, a daughter of a daughter of men, a daughter of the plow: O Deo, so human and, by virtue of that, more divine than all the gods."

Once again, the mystes drank the cyceon and ate the sacred bread. Then they wrapped the symbols in a linen cloth, in order to preserve them piously: an ear of wheat, a morsel of bread, a pomegranate and also a top, which rotates like the sun and the seasons.

All together, with a profound emotion, they recited the formula:

"I have fasted, I have drunk the cyceon, I have taken the kiste and, after having eaten, I have deposited in the kalathis; tomorrow, I shall take up the kalathis again and place it in the kiste."

The hierophant added: "I have taken from the earth and, after having tasted it, have deposited in my granary; I have taken from the granary and replaced in the earth."

Then, in a very low tone, as if his voice were coming from a land of dream:

"I have taken from death and I have tasted life. In order that it should germinate more abundant and more glorious, I have confided my life to death, I have sown my life in Elysian and fecund death."

But he cried suddenly, in his loudest voice:

"*Conc ompax! Conx ompax!*"

And the initiates, some solitary and thoughtful, the majority in cheerful and talkative bands, returned to Athens by the sacred way.

Book Three: EGYPT

Pherecydes had said to Pythagoras:

"Like the voyager traveling toward the source of the river, as soon as you know the mysteries of Greece, embark in order to go among the Egyptians, the most ancient and the most knowledgeable of men. Amasis, their king, loves the Hellenes and I will give you letters for him.[33] He will recommend you to the best among the priests. Strive to make yourself loved by those guardians of the most ancient treasure of science. If you succeed in that, they will teach you the sacred language and will permit you to study the books of Hermes. Thanks to them, you will possess the most beautiful among the words that men say and those which are written with the figures of sounds or the figures of things. It will remain for you to descend, in accordance with your strength, into the depth of words; visiting each one as one visits a granary, you will abandon those which are empty but you will nourish yourself with the plenitude of others."

That is why Pythagoras was sailing toward Egypt. Sometimes he closed his eyes in order to see again, in its entire sequence, the spectacle of the mysteries and to penetrate further than the instruction of the hierophant. Often, however, he unrolled a book that Protogenes had given to him, and he read:

"Orpheus, son of Apollo, after he had quit his father for a better god, sang this poem in the assemblies of initiates. Sometimes, when he sang the poem, Orpheus called it *The Mixing-Bowl*, because wine and water, good and evil, Zagreus and the Titans are mingled therein as in the world. Sometimes, when he sang the poem, Orpheus called it *The Winding-Sheet*,

---

[33] The reference is to Amasis II, who reigned from 570 B.C. to 526 B.C., prior to the Persian conquest. Most of what is known about him is derived from Herodotus,

92

because the loom of the world weaves eternally a broad and uninterrupted procession of living beings.[34]

"The initiates, if they are good, comprehend this poem; the good comprehend the poem if they are initiates.

"In the beginning...but if you are one of those who comprehend you know that there was no beginning, there was a commencement for the speech that unfurls things; there was no commencement for the things that are unfurled. Things want to be said, and they make speech, as your body makes shadow. Things want, although said, to remain unheard by the profane and the wicked. That is why they prevent the shadow of speech from becoming full like them and alive like them.

"The shadow moves and the body moves, but the shadow does not have the plenitude of the body, and does not have the life of the body; it has another life that is deceptive, and it stretches or shrinks without the body stretching or shrinking.

"Things are the circle that always unfurls entirely; speech is the finger that follows the circle, and departs from a point of the circle.

"Or rather things, since they are living and since they are full, only form one unique circle; but their divine name is Sphere, because they intersect and unfurl in circles that no one can number.

"The living plenitude of space is a sphere. The living plenitude of time is a sphere. And there are not two spheres, but only one.

The shadow of the sphere is a circle. Even for initiates and for the good, speech is a tremulous finger pointing at the shadow of the sphere.

---

[34] *Le Cratère* [The Mixing-Bowl] and *Le Péplos* [The Winding-Sheet—referring to a garment rather than a shroud] were the French versions of the titles attributed to two Orphic poems, discussed in a passage that seems to be the inspiration for the present improvisation in a history of Greece by Karl Otfried Müller dating from the 1830s.

"At the commencement of speech, not at the commencement of things, there was water and there was mud. A dragon emerged therefrom; its shoulders bore wings and its visage was that of a god. But it had, around its divine visage, two other heads, the head of a lion and the head of a bull. Some call it Heracles because there is no force external to it. Some call it Cronus because it is always young, because it is always old, because there is the union of all the ages within it. But I call it Phanes, because it shines with all the future and all the past; because it shines sufficiently to dazzle even the most profound among initiates, those who know that everything is ever-present, and that there is no future and no past.[35]

"Now, Phanes was all things. Is not the lake the river that casts itself into the lake? Is it not the river that emerges from the lake? And Phanes was man and he was woman.

"He is united with inevitable and immense Adrastaea who penetrates the limitless world to its extreme limits. And she is woman and he is man.

"And Phanes has all forms and Adrastaea put on all forms. But the good know that Phanes and Adrastaea have no forms; and the initiates know that they have no bodies. It is speech that makes the river become the lake; it is speech that collapse in a form and life in a body. And the eyes also, because they want to see, arrest things. And your mind too, because it wants to understand, arrests things. But you can only understand, see and say things by reforming them. The sphere rotates, but the circle, which is the shadow of the sphere, seems to you to be motionless. You cannot see the sphere; and if you are not good or not an initiate, you cannot even see the circle.

---

[35] Phanes was a primordial deity of procreation introduced into Greek mythology by the followers of the Orphic tradition, coupled with Ananke or Adastraea—an incorporeal personification of fate—in the context expanded here, and idiosyncratically elaborated by Ryner to reflect his own notion of the necessary overthrow of Zeus and the tyranny he symbolizes.

"Phanes, whom you can call Cronus because he has all the ages, whom you can call Heracles because all force is within him, having united with inevitable and immense Adrastaea, there was an egg.

"And that egg having broken in the middle, there was a top and a bottom, there was the sky and the earth.

"God, who is the commencement, middle and end of all things, root of the earth and he sky. Both sun and moon, air and fire, man and woman, had a form, like speech. The sky was the head of God, the moon and sun were the eyes of God; the air was his chest, the earth his belly, the worlds that extend above the earth were his feet and the ether was the intelligence of God, which is never mistaken.

"God therefore had a form, as speech has a form. But if you know the languages of all peoples you will change the form of your speech without changing your speech. And the more you know of symbols the more you will change the form of God without changing God.

"Now Phanes desired to change his form, and no longer to be called Phanes. For he is more alive than all forms and vaster than all names. And he had two daughters that he called Echidna and Gaia, and a son that he called Uranus. But others have sung these things.

"Uranus had for a son Cronus—for the same name belongs to several, and is the same for the ear, but not for the mind. The first Cronus, whom some call Phanes, is absolutely measureless, but the second Cronus, son of Uranus, son of Planes, although surpassing all measure, nevertheless has measure. For the one has no parts, but the other has. And there are days and nights. But there will never be a last night or a last day. And speech, the creator of the commencement, the creator of deception, the creator of intelligence, is deceptive in order to be clear, when it is forced to speak of the first day and the first night.

"Cronus, son of Uranus, son of Phanes, had numerous sons, and one is named Zeus. And vulgar poems sing the story of Cronus and the story of Zeus. And what they say is not true.

However, listen. The stammering of a child is deceptive for a stranger, but his mother understands it and hears the truth. The stammering of the aede is a lie that deceives the vulgar, but the initiate knows the truth that is behind the deception. He knows that the light shines on the other side of the song that casts the shadow. But there are lights that are too high and cast no shadow, with the consequence that the aedes do not know what I am singing now.

"When Zeus had become king, Phanes said to him: 'Devour me, in order that I am no longer, and in order that I still am.'

"Then Zeus devoured Phanes. But Phanes is indigestible. And Zeus, containing all things, rejects all things, and produces the world that you see. And he is also the father of the latecomers among the gods.

"The last you encounter in following the circle from the point at which my speech departed and in the direction that my speech is following. But in the eternity of the circle, the shadow of the Sphere that rotates upon itself, there are no lasts, no firsts or any middle.

"And there were other sons of Cronus, the Titans. And there was the earth, which was then called Themis. For justice does not come from the sky, it comes from the earth. And there was Prometheus, the son of Themis and the brother of the Titans.

"But the Titans were wicked, and Zeus is wicked. However, Zeus, having intelligence, is less wicked than the Titans, who only had strength. And as he has a goal, one can anticipate the evil that he will do and can combat that evil.

"Themis and Prometheus persuaded the Titans not to do evil. But strength without intelligence has no ears for forethought and for justice, and the Titans still did evil, with the consequence Prometheus and Themis passed, weeping, to the side of Zeus.

"Forethought and justice, therefore, allied themselves with the new god because he is intelligent; but he who is not heart and justice is not all intelligence. Zeus is a tyrant who sees many things, but does not penetrate certain things. He is half intelligence, half violence. He had Strength for a servant, and Strength is a servant that commands its masters. And to see far, it is necessary to be a son of justice. That is why Prometheus knows the future, but Zeus is a tyrant, who knows the present but does not know the future.

"Themis wants all justice and all the future, but the tyrant wants to remain the master and he only wants the justice that helps him to remain the master. He does not want the justice that flows toward the future; he wants the continuation of the present and raises a dyke across the slope. He is intelligence, since the mud of the marsh is water, but in the water that run feely toward the sea and in the justice that runs freely toward the future you will not find any mud and you will not find any cunning.

"It requires water to make mud; it requires intelligence to make cunning and to make Zeus. But the water is lost in the mud and the intelligence is lost in the cunning of Zeus.

"But the enemy of the future is better than the Titans, who were ignorant and even ruined the future, and since he protects the present, is not the enemy of the future the father of the future?

"The initiate, if I interrogate him thus, will respond: 'Yes, for Zeus had a son better than him, and that son is named Zagreus. And all the initiates know his story, and the good, among the initiates, understand his story.

"The Titans, having torn Zagreus apart, devoured his body. But the heart was saved by Pallas Athene. The initiates know that the heart sufficed to reformulate the god, the good understand why the heart was sufficient to reformulate the god; and those who are worthy of hope, hope.

"Zeus destroyed the Titans, and they were consumed. Their ashes contained particles of the substance of Zagreus. And it is with those ashes that Prometheus modeled man, who is better than all the gods, Zagreus excepted.

"But beware; there are within you Titans that roar and which, if you listen to them, will make you more wicked than the gods. But there is also within you Zagreus, who palpitates.

"Make the Titans that howl within you shut up, in order that you can hear your heart. Nourish, detach and purify, in the midst of the evil substance, the Zagreus that is within you.

"If many do as you do, Zagreus will be stronger than Zeus and will devour him. And there will be happiness, instead of tyranny; and there will be justice, instead of law. And the happiness will summon love, and the justice will summon liberty.

"Then all will know and all will understand. Today, only the initiates and the good comprehend.

"I have finished singing the poem that is called *The Winding-Sheet* because the loom of the world weaves eternally a broad and uninterrupted procession of living beings. I have finished singing the poem that is called *The Mixing-Bowl*, because wine and water, good and evil, Zagreus and the Titans are mingled within you and within the world. Listen often to the poem in your memory, in order that it should aid you to listen to your heart. Your heart is the only aede that can sing you the whole truth."

King Amasis, having read Pherecydes's letters, said to Pythagoras:

"I do not share the error of my people, who scorn and detest foreigners. I welcome favorably those who come to me with benevolent intentions. Among them all, the Hellenes are my friends. They do not have the sublime science of the priests of Egypt; the little they know about the gods and the origins of the world they learned from us, but, turned toward the detail of human life, they know it more perfectly. Our science is the pure and high spring; the estuary, which is laden with impurities and runs lower down, spreads out more vastly and more richly. As for you, you bring me letters from Pherecydes, the wisest of Hellenes and the one I love above all others. Having read these missives, I know you; you are entirely worthy of love; you will become entirely worthy of admiration; over the generation of those who are young at this moment, you will shine as the light of a crown over the head of a queen. Tell me, then, what you desire, and if you only desire the possible, you shall obtain it. Do you want riches? Do you want honors? Speak, in order that I know and can satisfy you."

Pythagoras replied:

"O Amasis, life, health, strength, I do not desire riches or honors, but wisdom."

"Riches and honors depend on me, but Pherecydes has more wisdom and he can give you more of it. If you have received all that Pherecydes possesses, I must salute you as a sage."

"Amasis, life, health, strength, if I were speaking to a vulgar man or a priest I would say that wisdom belongs to the gods, not to humans, but before you I dare to tell the truth. I do not know whether the gods themselves are wise. I only hope that God will be wise one day. As for me, I can only love wisdom and aspire to it with all my strength. I want to climb to the highest summits, and I do not affirm that my hand touches or will touch the sky. That is why I refuse, in the present and in the future, the name of sage. If, therefore, for the surge of my heart, you want to give me a name of love and glory, rather call me philosopher."

"I am hearing a word new to my ears," said Amasis. "In order that your prudent words might enlighten me like a circle of lamps, I would like you to explain further."

"Amasis, life, health, strength, I am at the age of silence. I am at the age of open ears and a closed mouth. Nevertheless, since you order me to do so, I shall speak. The life of men appears to me to be similar to public games. Some come there to dispute the prizes, others to engage in commerce and gain wealth, and yet others to watch the spectacle and reform their mores. In the same way, some come into life in order to conquer glory, and others to love the riches they have and those they do not; but some seek the truth and strive to become better. Those I call philosophers."

"I call them sages."

"In the same way, Amasis, life, health, strength, I call you king; but you recognize no other king than Osiris, and to reign over a single country seems to you to be a small mater. The wisdom that I have acquired, oh, how small a matter it seems to me; but that which is before me summons me and attracts me irresistibly, and I know that there will always be more before me. That which I still lack, I still name wisdom; that which I shall lack, I shall call wisdom."

"I am entering, Pythagoras, into the noble subtlety of your thought. And I will say this: in the country of the mind, the sage is a peaceful and satisfied king, but the philosopher is an avid conqueror. Although young, you enrich men with a new anxiety. That is why I like you, young conqueror of the high regions. I will do for you what I can. I will give you letters for the priests, particularly for those of Heliopolis, who are the most knowledgeable. On my recommendation, perhaps they will open to you the country of thought and science in which their satisfied royalty strolls. Go, then, and make yourself loved by those men, in order that you might conquer their kingdom and add it to your domain."

With the letters from Amasis, Pythagoras went up the Nile toward Heliopolis. The waters were still low, dormant, troubled and muddy. Their ugliness was limited by a black mud that, cooked and recooked by the sun, extended in flat banks or rose up in abrupt masses. Beyond there was a gray sterility, all the way to the parallel dazzle of the Libyan mountains and the Arabic mountains. The dusty khamsin had ceased to blow, but the atmosphere remained blinding, inflamed and charged with sand. Some distance away, the trees, clad in dust, were confused with the monotony of the desert.

Pythagoras listened to the ardent prayer that a sailor addressed to the river:

"Rise, rise, O mighty one.

"In order that the earth might be filled with delight, rise.

"In order that every belly might rejoice, rise.

"In order that every tooth might chew and every living being receive nourishment, rise.

"Powerful Apis, I invoke you;

"Although the priests say that no one knows you save by your works;

"No one knows a road to go toward you;

"Neither service nor offering rise as far as the places you inhabit;

"You cannot be attracted in the mysteries and you cannot be found by way of the sacred books."

When the sailor's chant fell silent, Pythagoras came to him. "Instruct me," he said, "you who know. Where do the sources of the divine Nile flow?"

The man made a vague gesture. "The priests," he replied, "say that they descend from the sky. There is a Nile on high on which the boats of the gods float; the one you see comes from that celestial river."

In the eyes, the tone and on the lips of the sailor a hint of malice and doubt was smiling. Nevertheless, the philosopher did not dare ask the question that was burning his lips: "What do you think of what the priests say?" but asked instead: "Have you been very far up the river?"

"In my youth I was a soldier. In pursuing the Kushites, I went upriver for months. I always saw it as broad, a full and as strong. In order to leave us time to sow and time to reap, there are unequal seasons; it knows no other inequality. It is said of vulgar rivers that they receive tributaries and streams; this one receives nothing and gives everything. Perhaps it has no source."

In a low voice, he added:

"Listen to what my ancestor told me in my childhood. Sailors who render life, health and strength to Pharaoh's mines go so far up the Nile that they end up emerging into a sea up there, very high, in the land of Punt. Thus the Nile, which precipitates itself in order to combat and repel the wicked sea, the sea that is Typhon, comes from another sea that is as good as

Isis. In the source-sea there are numerous islands. Benevolent beings populate those lands, but no word can describe the form of those beings, nor their fashion of walking, nor the mystery of their language, nor their fantastic nourishment and the manner in which they eat. When you are in one of those islands, if you find it good, be careful not to leave it; you will never find it again. Perhaps you will think that you have come back to the place you left, but you will only encounter floating foam there."

Having arrived in Heliopolis, Pythagoras did not go to see the priests immediately. The spectacle of the Nile retained him. Now the Etesian winds were blowing forcefully all day long. To people and trees they brought a fresh joy. They freed the foliage from its layer of dust. The river was, however, rising slowly and its color was changing. It became a dull and viscous green, very similar, if had not been swollen and moving, to the brackish waters that lie dormant in marshes.

Clad in the Egyptian costume and lost among the people. Pythagoras gazed at the green Nile with astonishment, and listened. The chatter, often coarse, said that no filtration could strip the waters of the nauseating and unhealthy substance and that anyone who drank it would suffer intolerable pains.

The river gradually became troubled. After a few days it was a mass of opaque, rising blood, the red Nile. The people drank the bloody water and declared it very good.

The spectacle was nothing but joy. The current, majestically broadened, covered the thirsty sands again. Hour after hour, with a din drowned by applause, some muddy dyke collapsed. The river was the multiple victory that, amid the cortege of acclamations and exclamations of the voluptuousness of nature, and quivering expectation, penetrated channels triumphantly. Herds, children and men all frolicked in the water. The broad waves carried shoals of fish whose scales flashed silver in the sunlight. Birds with all hues of plumage assembled in loud and vertiginous flocks above the conquering march. Even before the arrival of the river, the sand, moist at its approach, became animated, swarming with millions of insects.

Among the fish that the Nile bore, one seemed particularly popular. Children did not perceive it without addressing amusing words to it: "Fahaka, fahaka, the waters will go down and you will be trapped." It is a slender fish but it has the faculty of inflating itself. In order to be lifted up by the waves it blows itself up like a bladder, to uh an extent that the weight of its back carries it away, so that it bobs and drifts, showing a belly sown with spines that makes it resemble a hedgehog. In four months, the waters that withdraw will abandon the grotesque monster on the muddy fields; it will be the prey of birds and men or—and even more deplorable fate—become the plaything of cruel children.[36]

In a group of spectators, before the overflow of the Nile and joy, a scribe said: "Let us bless the gods and our ancestors. The Nile is the greatest of gods, but people did not know at first how to make use of it. Once the old histories say, abandoned to itself, it changed its bed continually. The flood never reached certain parts of the valley and they remained unproductive. Elsewhere it remained persistently and transformed the ground into pestilential mire.

A man of the people remarked: "The Nile of that epoch was like the riches of today. Poorly distributed, they produce arid areas and rich marshes."

The group laughed heartily. Then the scribe resumed:

"The triangle of victory that the Nile hurls before the roars of Typhon was not yet our rich and magnificent Delta. One part was drowned beneath the river, one part lost beneath damp and sterile bitterness. It was a formless marsh cut by rare sandy islands, encumbered by papyrus, lotus and enormous reeds, through which the arms of the Nile agitated as if in despair and impotence. Our ancestors were valiant. They learned to regulate the course of the river, to build dykes and

---

[36] The reference is to the Fahaka puffer fish, or Nile puffer fish, *Tetraodon lineatus*.

hollow out channels that carried the flood and its benefits all the way to the mountains. The combat lasted myriads of years, and we enjoy its victory."

The scribe concluded:

"Misraim is a gift of the river; and yet Misraim is a conquest of our forefathers. The gods provide the materials; they want us to work them. The first seeds come from the gods; it is necessary to sow hem in order to have enough. Let us bless the gods and bless the men who came before us."

Pythagoras thought:

All that is good is the common work of men and the gods. My form and my thought come from those of old, gods and men. The form and thought of tomorrow's gods will come, to some slight extent, from me. It is necessary for me to imitate God and is progress in order that God imitates Pythagoras and his progress. It is necessary that I lend my aid to the external work that God sketches with difficulty and the effort God makes in becoming.

Then, unrolling the book that Protogenes had given him, he descended into the Orphic depths. Pythagoras spent a month watching the river and the joy that spread forth, listening to the words of the simple folk and their naïve plenitude.

Often, he asked himself: "Does not the ignorance of the people contain a quantity of wisdom as great as the errors and lies of priests?"

He thought about the worker who had compared riches to the once-maleficent Nile, and wished that they might eventually be distributed equally throughout the human valley, putting an end to the aridity of some and the marshy putrescence of others.

"Perhaps that man," he thought, "has given me a treasure as precious as the hierophant of the great mysteries."

His desire to know the various secrets that the priests hid from the vulgar was combated by a repugnance for the priests.

Zeus and the tyrants, he said to himself with the Orphic poem, *love the small measure of justice that serves at present for the continuation of the present. The priests love the small portion of the truth useful to maintain priests. But the tyrant names justice his will and his caprice, and the priest names truth the words of the priest.*

In the end, however, he took Amasis' tablets in hand and went with them to the dwelling of the high priest Menna.

"Amasis, life, health, strength," said the prophets, after having read them, "asks that we love you as his own son. We therefore grant you, young foreigner, that which we would accord to a son of Amasis, life, health, strength who is not Egyptian."

He smiled condescendingly and maliciously. Then he interrogated Pythagoras.

"Pharaoh, life, health, strength, praises your intelligence. You are not the first Hellene who has come here praised by a king. I knew your master Pherecydes, and my father often spoke to the Solon who later gave laws to one of your most illustrious cities. Are you, young Samian, a sage like Solon and Pherecydes?"

"God alone is sage," said Pythagoras. "As for me, I am a man who is striving toward God and toward wisdom."

"What do you desire of me?"

"I am, before you, a pauper requesting alms, but you can enrich me without impoverishing yourself. I am asking for the wealth that can be shared without diminishing it. I am asking you to give me what you have of wisdom."

"Wisdom has led many to riches, and you are asking a great deal."

"I am asking for more. My love of wisdom suffices to enable me to scorn riches. If, therefore, you give me wisdom, the only durable wealth, the one that no one can take from us, the one that never becomes an evil, what will be my disdain for perishable, precarious wealth, similar to slaves ever ready to revolt and turn against their master!"

"Wisdom has led many to power, and you are asking a great deal."

"I am asking for more. Wisdom is the only veritable beauty, the only veritable power. Whoever loves it scorns, with an ardent fidelity, everything else.

"You would refuse power, then, if men offered it to you?"

"I don't know yet. Wisdom will teach me what power is, and whether it is necessary to submit to it as a burden that relieves others or reject it as an evil with which no good is mingled. When I have heard the only voice to whose counsels I want to listen, I shall act in accordance with what it has said. If power permits rendering people happy and does not make the man who wields it bad, than I would consent, out of love of my brothers, to wield power. But if, as I fear, tyranny, in all its forms, only permits evil; if a crown always depresses the head, crushes thought and impedes momentum toward God and wisdom, then with all my strength, all my love for the welfare of others and for my own welfare, I would reject the deforming and malevolent charge."

"What will you give in exchange for what you ask?"

"I am asking for it because I have nothing. Nevertheless, I will give something."

"What can the man give who has nothing?"

"The pleasure of giving."

"Are you ready to pay us the sums we ask of you?"

"O master, spare me that vulgar proof. If you sold your wisdom for gold, it would then be poorer than gold, the poor thing that you call wisdom. The wisdom and love that are for sale are no longer love or wisdom, and are not worth being bought."

"Why do you ask for wisdom, you who possess it?"

"Wisdom is the caduceus around which virtue and knowledge are coiled. The love of knowledge might give me a commencement of strength and a stirring of virtue. Give me what you have of knowledge in order that I might make virtue of it."

"Sometimes you seem to believe that virtue is the road to knowledge, sometimes that knowledge is the road to virtue."

"A strong man works. His work produces his nourishment. His nourishment produces his strength, and his strength produces his work. Perhaps nothing in the world is like a straight line; perhaps all things are like circles." He added in a lower voice, as if speaking to himself: "The route and the effort are a spiral that rise into the light and into glory. But if I cease to strive, there is a burdensome weight within me and my route becomes a spiral descending toward darkness."

"You are worthy to enter," said Menna.

A vast joy illuminated Pythagoras' face—but a glint of malice scintillated in the eyes of the priest, who repeated: "You are worthy to enter; but the door is thick and you do not know the fashion in which it is appropriate to knock in order to be heard on the other side of the door. Go away, then, for you are worthy of everything, but you shall obtain nothing."

"Teach me the art of knocking."

"You know many things. That which you do not know, we cannot teach to foreigners."

"Am I a foreigner?"

"You come from Samos."

"I come from the gods and I am marching toward God. I am not Samian; I am a philosopher. I do not love any fatherland; I love the truth. If Heliopolis is, for me, the land of truth, Heliopolis becomes my fatherland and my love."

"You are knocking obstinately, but you do not know how to knock."

"Did you not instruct Solon?"

"We did instruct Solon."

"Was he not a foreigner, like me?"

"When we had instructed him, he was no longer a foreigner."

"Enable me, then, to become similar to him, and no longer be a foreigner."

"You are beginning to knock well. Now, go to the city, listen and look. Do not try to penetrate any temple or speak to any priest. Let a month pas thus. Afterwards, come back, and perhaps you will find me."

"I render you thanks, O Menna, for the future; but today I weep for not having found Menna."

The high priest subjected Pythagoras to other interrogations and other proofs. Finally, he ordered him: "Have yourself circumcised. Then you will be an Egyptian and it will be permissible to communicate the science of Egypt to you."

"Every road is good, O Menna, that leads to science."

After the circumcision, the prophet said to the philosopher: "Now you are one of us. Our temples are open to you, our words will be sincere and our books will deploy before you. Go make yourself loved by those who know the words and those who have the key to the books.

Pythagoras made himself the friend and disciple of several priests. They told him the successive doctrines that wrapped Isis with increasingly intimate veils. Then they taught him the sacred language. Then the prophet Oinuphis, who was particularly fond of him, opened to him the treasure of books and permitted him to study the writings of Thoth, whom the Hellenes call Hermes.[37]

Not only did Oinuphis open for Pythagoras the treasure of books, but he also took pleasure in explaining whatever the young man did not understand on his own. Now, Pythagoras had caused the guardian of the books to love him by a ruse, as a seducer makes a rich woman love him, but gradually, he came to love Oinuphis. He was not a priest like the others. Exempt from ambition and pride, he enclosed himself in study and the only joy he knew was the joy of learning. The hours that he did not spent reading he employed in reflection. He floated scattered in the light dreams that continued his reading, which ran in all directions beyond what the ancients had written. He encountered thoughts there beyond the words that the ancients consented to speak, fleeting and distant thoughts that disappeared and showed themselves at the elbows of inaccessible mountain paths. In a few generations, they might perhaps

---

[37] According to Plutarch, Pythagoras learned astronomy from an Egyptian priest in Heliopolis.

be graspable and expressible, but today, they excited in their friend an unknown dolorous joy, an appeal and disappointment, fuller nonetheless than the poverty of all precise joys. Around his voice they put a strange tremulous and hesitant half-light.

In the speech of Oinuphis, sometimes heavy with too much past, sometimes as breathless and unsteady as a child's first steps toward the future, often as eloquent and rapid as a chariot of light, Pythagoras loved the science of Egypt. And in the beauty of Oinuphis, the Hellene loved Egyptian beauty.

Like the finest of his race, the prophet was tall, thin and lanky. His broad, full shoulders, the bulging muscles of his torso and his sinewy arms gave the impression of strength. His long hands and sober hips, the stiff legs, where the calf and knee stood out sharply, and the slender and extended foot spoke of finesse. The Greek sculptors would have found his head too pronounced for his body. The square forehead, perhaps a trifle low, seemed the seat of thought, mildness and sadness. The gaze of the large and wide-open eyes, the smile of the thick but not slanting lips sang the nobility of his resignation, almost the grace of dolor.

Oh, the beautiful ideas that he sometimes seized in the basket of a symbol, empty or others or full of banality. Oh, the profound freshness of sentiments that, like the water of legend springing from the rock struck by the mystic staff, sprang forth from the aridity of old stories as soon as they were touched by Oinuphis!

On day, Pythagoras was disturbed by the folly of the men who, under the conduct of Cyrus, were beginning to threaten great wars.

"Listen, my beloved son," said the prophet. "You believe that you have read, in Homer, the story of Helen the Ionian; but Homer saw what a warrior saw, and he did not know the truth.

"Hera, irritated against Paris, abducted Helen and confided her to Hermes in order for him to transport her to our land of Misraim. Meanwhile, the goddess had assembled a phantom formed of air and wind, on which the son of Priam lavished the folly of his kisses. Achaeans and Trojans fought for ten years and for ten years enriched the kingdom of the underworld for the conquest of a phantom.

"O my son, men have only ever fought for phantoms. True beauty cannot be conquered by weapons. If you want to possess Helen and not the phantom, do not go to the land of combats and the world of vain exterior conquests, but descend within yourself to the kingdom of peace. Never be among the madmen who kill for a little wind."

Oinuphis, the prophet of the fine and somewhat discouraging words, was not, however, the equal of Pherecydes in the heart of Pythagoras. He remained a priest by his application to puerile practices. He would have thought that he was committing a crime if he had neglected to purify the air he breathed twice a day; but he would have considered it an abominable sacrilege to disrupt the fixed order and employ in that office myrrh in the morning or resin when the sun was at the zenith. Pythagoras had difficulty hiding his smile when he heard him address solemn recommendations to a slave:

"Carry the ardent torches before me and purify the air according to the sacred rotes. If some profane individual has soiled the ground on which I walk, let the lustral flame efface the imprint. Everywhere I go, spread the vapor of the burning resin. After having rendered homage to the gods with the prescribed ceremonies, bring the hearth of the sacred flame back to the temple."

He carried numerous amulets on his person. Written in archaic characters, the name of the divinity possessed, he affirmed, the power of averting all exterior dangers. Amid the forest of symbols or the haunted streets of old stories, he was not always the hunter who, in an abrupt chase or with an adroit and patient trap, seizes a new thought. Often he studied the *Collection of chapters of the divine rites conducted in the temple of Amon-Ra, the king of the gods, by the priest of service.*

It was him that his colleagues consulted when a hesitation tormented them with regard to some detail of ritual. With gravity, he recited the *Chapter on placing the measure of incense in the incense-burner*; then the profundity of his commentaries moved the young priests to admiration. He was incomparable for explaining the *Chapter on agitating the firebrand* and obtaining information as to how to stimulate, by shaking it, the flaming wick when the fire of sacrifice had to be taken. No gesture was as solemn as his for breaking, in the prescribed circumstances, the seal and the bond that fixed the bolt of the naos. While he trembled with mystical emotion as he advanced toward the statue of the god, as if he feared forgetting one of the innumerable genuflections, he recited internally the *Chapter on sniffing the ground, putting oneself on the belly and touching the ground with one's fingers.*

Pythagoras spent several years in Heliopolis reading and listening. He had sometimes, in the beginning, interrupted Oinuphis with a question or an objection. The prophet looked at him then with astonishment, and pronounced irritated words or, for several days, fell silent as one falls silent before a man devoid of intelligence. If he sometimes replied, Pythagoras sensed that his thought, deflected from its natural course, became difficult and turbulent, like a river encountering a dyke.

After a few experiments, the philosopher made it a rule no longer to interrupt; except that, if Oinuphis' discourse ended too soon, Pythagoras pronounced the words of avid admiration that stimulate orators.

One day, the young man made himself an amulet, exactly like a priest. On a papyrus that never quit him for a long time thereafter he wrote:

O Pythagoras, listen and do not interrupt. Your voice is the rock against which the tide of waves is irritated and foams, and the sea soon withdraws and leaves you poor and arid. But is not your silence the vase into which the waters precipitate joyfully in order to enrich you?

"O my son," the prophet said to him, "the finger over the mouth, never forget, is the hieroglyph that designates childhood. Do not forget either this law of life: the more perfect a creature becomes, the longer its childhood is prolonged. A dog

111

does not take long to become self-sufficient, but it requires years to make a man and far more to make a sage. As long as your ears fill with new knowledge, prolong your fortunate childhood and, like a seal placed over a treasure or the naos of the temple, place a finger over your closed mouth.

Then Pythagoras descended into profound meditations. *How many more centuries,* he wondered, *will the childhood of God last?*

But he rejected the drifting invasion of reverie and opened himself like a noble mixing-bowl to exterior speech.

Oinuphis proclaimed: "Since the commencement, was Teb-Temt, which is to say, the Envelope within the Envelope. And sometimes, when you speak of the Envelope, you are naming the Universe; and sometimes when you speak of the Envelope, you are naming God. Now the Envelope was initially humid, and, in that first state, we called it Nou, but the Hellenes call it Oceanos. Its uncertain flotations agitated the confused seeds of things—and that is why some people also call it Chaos.

"But try to understand, my beloved son, that when I speak of the commencement or the initial state, I am speaking deceptively and beyond a requirement of your mind, not a requirement of the real. Your body needs to be supported on something; your mind needs to be supported on the past. The seat on which you sit rests on the ground; and the past that sustains you reposes on a commencement. But do you believe that the earth needs to be supported on something else? Do you believe that time needs to be supported on a commencement? Outside your mind, time is called Eternity. It is that which sustains and has no need to be sustained.

"In the liquid periods when the elements were confused and the Formless floated shoeless and devoid of slope; in the harmonious periods when forms flowed over the slope of Amour, between the banks of Law; always, in the bosom of the Envelope. God engenders and gives birth to himself: God, the unique One, the one that exists by essence, the Only One that lives in substance, the only generator in the heavens and on earth that was not engendered by another, the Father of fathers, the Mother of mothers, his own Son.

"A Father solely by virtue of what he is, he engenders eternally without exhausting either his strength or eternity. He cannot be without engendering, and it is impossible for him not to be; that is why the world is as eternal as Him. The world, but not the present form of the world; the forms of the Envelope change, but He, the Envelope, does not change. The Envelope changes forms, but never disappears; and that is why one does not raise the veils of Isis.

"Throughout eternity God produces in himself another Self; Father, Mother, Son, he is eternity, he is immensity, he is independence, he is sovereign will, he is limitless bounty. He develops his virtues eternally, and he creates his own limbs and he produces the gods, but the gods are limbs; his limbs are his virtues, but his virtues are his virtue, and his virtue is his essence, and there is nothing but Him.

"And he has no name, and he has all names. All names name him, since everything is an envelope that, like the bubbles that children blow, would dissipate if the Envelope were not within to sustain it.

"And you are Him and He is you. And you hide Him, and you reveal Him. And when He engenders himself, he does not exhaust himself, and when you die, you do not annihilate him.

"For you are not uniquely your envelope either. You are a thing that the eyes can see, but you are three things that the eyes cannot see. And what the eyes can see will die like the eyes, but what the eyes cannot see is immortal, like light. Listen, then, my beloved son, to the truth that concerns you, you who are only Pythagoras, you who will become Osiris-Pythagoras.

"There is in you a double that survives your body. If you are buried in accordance with the rites and the necessary precautions, it will live immortal in the tomb. But your double is only a shadow, and there are beings more precious within you.

113

"A subtle matter is within you, by virtue of which you are properly human. And those who know name it bai, which is to say, bird. When you die your bai flies away toward the other earth, a hawk with a head and the arms of a man; and it can, according to its whim, renter the tomb or emerge therefrom.

"But you are not only your body, your double or your shadow, your bai or your human soul. There is within you a parcel of flame. And those who know name it khou, which is to say, the Luminous. Instruct your Luminous down here with all wisdom, equip yourself with all the talismans against the perils of the great voyage. If you do what I say, at death, your khou will abandon the earth never to return and will join the cortege of the gods of light.

"Now, to enter the land of the dead, you will pass, west of Abydos, through a fissure that opens in the mountain. The boat of the sun glides, every evening, with its cortege of gods, into the mouth of that fissure, and enters into what our blindness calls night. Your soul will glide there behind it under the protection of Osiris, life, health, strength.

"But first, you will have appeared before Osiris, lord of the Occident, and before the forty-two judges. Even good, you will have appeared trembling and you will have feared the evidence of your heart. You will have said: 'O heart, my heart, which comes from my mother, my heart of when I was on earth, do not stand up against me as a witness, do not accuse me before the great god.' Those whose hearts stand up against them as a witness fall into low places; they only find filthy matter there for nourishment and act amid the swarming of snakes and scorpions; after a thousand dolors, they finally encounter oblivion.

"But you, my son, if you listen meekly to my words, will sense your science and your power growing before the judges. Your heart will absolve you. You will take, amid the cortege of the gods, the forms that please you: golden hawk, lotus, phoenix, and swallow. You will combat the crocodile, the hippopotamus, the tortoise and the serpent. You will be aided by

Isis and by Nephthys and you will become Osiris. You will travel the celestial dwellings and you will be, in the fields of Aaru, the mystical laborer. Then you will mingle, for a long time, with the troop of the gods and you will march with them in the adoration of the sun."

In a seemingly multiple stupor Pythagoras listened to these noble dreams and follies, that poetic beauty and infantilism. He did not understand how so many contradictions could rip the fabric of the discourse without the orator perceiving them.

He thought:

A thousand generations of priests, geniuses and imbeciles, have heaped up that crumbling mass. I can hear the ancient words of a myriad of years and suddenly, words that have the ring of fragile novelty, but those who pronounce them believe them to be all of the same age. Several races have been superimposed and mingled on this soil of Egypt; their religions have also overlain one another, and ancient summits emerge amid the dusts of yesterday. Commentaries spread like a stucco over the most obtrusive contradictions are confounded with the solid stone.

He wondered: *Was Pherecydes right to send me here?*

He reread secretly the Orphic poem that Protogenes, his Athenian host, had given to him. And every evening, before going to sleep, he recited *The Lair with Seven Coverts.*

He found in his master's rhythms an increasingly rich meaning, and said, tentatively. "Perhaps I had heard all the Word with my ears from the start, but it required numerous words to deploy it before my mind. Pherecydes was the rolled-up volume; the mysteries and the priests are the hands that display it."

Sometimes, Oinuphis recounted a dolorous drama: Osiris torn apart by Typhon, and the anxious search and tears of Isis. Pythagoras then thought about the shreds of Zagreus dispersed by the Titans, or Cora vanished, for whom Demeter searches with a torch in each hand. Without words, or with the vague words that do not come as far as the lips, he thought about the

Substance that is called Strength, when the sterile season seems a definitive death. But she will rediscover the husband or son; he is not lost, he is not dead; he is only hidden and folded up in sleep. And the sadness of winter believes that it is weeping but is singing, without knowing it, the approach of spring.

One day, on a column, the young philosopher read an inscription:

I am King Osiris, life, health, strength. At the head of an expedition I traveled the earth as far as the inhabited places of India and the mysterious regions that incline toward the She-Bear. I drank from the sources if the Ister and, resuming my course, went as far as the Ocean. There is no place on earth I have not visited, and I went everywhere doing good. I have not conquered men by means of arms, but instruction and gentle persuasion. I have not conquered men in order to be their tyrant, but in order that they might become their own masters.

And Pythagoras took a bath of hope and comfort. Later, soon, he too would go to conquer men by means of truth and mildness, conquer them for Osiris or Zagreus—which is to say, for themselves.

In the night he sometimes pronounced enthusiastic words:

"O my brothers, I want to become and to teach you to become. Let us strip away that which palpitates within us without being our heart. Let us be what the Titans spared of Zagreus, and, over that quivering remnant, the fixed and fecundating eye of Zeus. Let us be the intelligence inclining everything toward the heart; let us be, in the calm light, the man who is reformed in his entirety around the heart. Let us be, in the peaceful clarity, hearts enlarged, triumphantly."

When, among the beautiful thoughts that he heard or read, Pythagoras had been listening to Oinuphis for long years and studying the books of Thoth, he received letters from Eunomus, his elder brother. His mother Parthenis, who was ill, desired to see him again before she died. His father

Mnesarchus, very old, also hoped to embrace him in the increasingly burdensome weakness of his arms.

Pythgoras therefore said his goodbyes to his master the prophet, and he left Heliopolis.

Amasis was dead. Psamtik III, his son, was struggling desperately against Cambyses, the son of Cyrus. While Pythagoras was going down the Nile, the Pharaoh suffered an irremediable defeat. The invading Persians ravaged the country, and they seized not only Egyptian soldiers but travelers, whom they accused of spying and conspiring.

Pythagoras captured by the Persians, was sent to Babylon.[38]

---

[38] It is Iamblichus' "biography" of Pythagoras that contains the assertion that Pythagoras was captured in Egypt by the invading forces of Cambyses II and sent to Babylon, where he made contact with the Magi.

Book Four: BABYLON

During the voyage to Babylon, Pythagoras thought about the sudden ruination of powerful Egypt. He listened to the soldiers or his companions in captivity talking about the recent fall of the kingdom of Lydia and the empires of Assur and Chaldea. The Egyptians kept quiet, overwhelmed by the weight of their heart. The Greeks boasted, because of those collapses, of the strength and thunderbolts of irritated Zeus. The Hebrews clamored hatefully about the power of Yahveh and the inevitable blows with which he strikes the persecutors of his people. But Hadabab, a young Chaldean priest who was accompanying soldiers of his race, imposing silence on the others, affirmed: "Everything that happens in the world is the work of Marduk."

An Israelite protested: "Marduk is a false god. He could not even protect his city. Yahveh alone is powerful; Yahveh alone is faithful."

"Jerusalem," the Chaldean remarked, "fell before Babylon. But in the fall of Babylon more than anything else it is appropriate to admire the strength of Marduk. King Nabunahid, the one that the ignorant Jews calls Balthazar, was impious. That is why the master of the gods, profoundly afflicted, and all the gods inhabiting the temples of Babel abandoned their sanctuaries.

"In those dark days, Marduk and the divinities allied with him were no longer seen in the processions of Kalanna; they took refuge in other cities that did not refuse them respect. However, the race of Sumer and Akkad, all in mourning, begged him to return. To accede to that request and satisfy the people, Marduk chose a master who would govern according to his will. He will proclaim Cyrus and those who will descend from him kings of the entire world, and he has announced that title to all the nations. He invited Cyrus to march against Babylon, his own city. He guided the Persian army as a friend and a benefactor.

"The troops of Cyrus, which you cannot number any more than the waves of the Euphrates, and their swords and bows and clubs, were only a vain ornament. For Marduk led them, without combat or resistance, all the way to Kalanna; then he surrounded and conquered his own city. Marduk delivered King Nabunahid, because he had scorned Marduk, into the hands of Cyrus.

"The people of Babel, and many among those of the race of Sumer and Akkad, and the nobles and the priests had risen up against the impious one and they refused to kiss his feet. They transported their oath of fealty and rejoiced in their new master. For the God who brings the dead to life and is helpful in all misfortune and all anguish had, long before the birth of Cyrus, called Cyrus by his name, and now he has granted him his full favor."

Pythagoras laughed internally. And he said to himself, silent words:

It is not the gods who overthrow empires or the enemies of empires. Empires overthrow themselves. Whatever the poets sing, when the Titans heaped mountains on mountains, Zeus did not seize his thunderbolts. Zeus the geometer watched and laughed. At the sound of his laughter, the disproportionate mass collapsed, crushing the lunatic non-geometers who had established them.

Pharaohs, Assur, Babylon, O imprudent tyrants who pile provinces upon provinces and who rejoice when the monstrous mass increases, neither Zeus nor Yahveh nor Marduk has any need to intervene for your mountains with overly narrow bases to collapse. Now the Persians are recommencing the folly of pride and accumulation; in their turn they will erect, by means of great effort, their imminent ruination and sonorous collapse.

For men know how to construct a pyramid: they give it a broad base, and the edifice narrows as it rises. But one man believes that he can become the basis of an empire, and the edifice broadens as it grows, and the conqueror is insane who poses the pyramid on its tip.

The Chaldean priest, having observed the beauty of the philosopher and his silence interrogated him in these terms:

"Who are you, who take no part in the quarrels but remain as mute as the Egyptians with heavy hearts, although your face says that you are not a son of Misraim, and your lips and gaze sing a song exempt from sadness?"

"I am the Son of Silence," Pythagoras replied. "Often, my speech has caused me to lose something; always, my silence has enabled me to gain something. Permit me, then, to bear a closed mouth and ears that listen."

"Where do you come from and what were you doing in Egypt? For you seem as foreign to this land as to mine?"

"I come from a distant island. But for years I have been living in Heliopolis, listening to the words of priests and reading the secret books."

"The priests of Egypt know very little, and it is not in the Occident that it is necessary to search for the source of light. Misraim does not know the true magic words and the efficacious signs. My heart is drawn to you and I want to make you a present that all the Egyptians combined could not procure you. Take this, always wear it on your person, and you will be fortunate."

Pythagoras thanked him ardently, as if he had, indeed, received a treasure. Meanwhile, he considered the Chaldean's gift. It was a fragment of bitumen, ornamented with mysterious characters.

"That asphalt," the priest explained, "comes from Mount Gordyaens in Armenia. It covered the remains of the ark of Xisuthrus, whom the ignorant Jews call Noah.[39] Conserve

---

[39] The version of the story of the Deluge in which the ark-builder was named Xistuthrus, or Sisithrus, is contained in the *Babyloniaka* of Berossus, written in Greek in the third century B.C. The Babylonian cosmogony narrated by Hadabab is

preciously what I have given you, not only in memory of a friend, but for its own value. You hold between your hands the most powerful of talismans. It is a boundary-marker that cannot be removed, a boundary-marker of the sky and the earth, which cannot be displaced and which no god can uproot. Disposed against maleficence, it is a barrier that cannot be passed, and which you can oppose victoriously to all your enemies."

"Would you care," asked Pythagoras, to teach me to read the characters traced on that inestimable shield? And would you care to tell me the story of Xisuthrus, whom the ignorant Jews call Noah."

The young Chaldean embraced the young Greek.

"O my brother in age," he exclaimed, "of generous heart and prudent thought, you aspire to become my brother in the certain knowledge that no one outside the priests of Babel possess in their original purity. If, as the wisdom of your words seems to announce, you are worthy of knowing, I will inform you of what you ask and other marvels that you cannot even imagine. But tell me first what you have learned about our first masters."

Pythagoras exposed what he had the right to reveal among the teachings of Pherecydes, the spectacle of the mysteries, the words of Epimenides, the rhythms of the Orphic poem, and finally, among the Egyptian profundities swarming with a combat of light and darkness.

Often, his new friend interrupted him with laughter, but the philosopher did not laugh with him. He devoted himself entirely to remaining silent about what he had promised to keep silent, and reforming, from the remaining shreds, an ingenious fabric that did not manifest any lesions. The priest believed that the Greek was making great efforts of memory and was not astonished by his taut physiognomy.

Eventually, he exclaimed: "What a heap of poverties you have just erected before me. Hellenes and Egyptians are mere

---

based on the same source, whose reliability as an account of actual Babylonian beliefs must be considered highly suspect.

children. Prepare yourself, for you are going to hear the word of a man for the first time.

"You, who are my brother by age, but in whom I already love the son of my mind, first forget the ignorant chatter that misfortune has led you to encounter before me. Open to my riches an intelligence empty of all error and ears that are unencumbered by vain memories. As a temple is cleared on the morning of a festival, throw away the ordure of human reveries; purify your soul in order to welcome the teachings of a god. Oannes himself will speak to you through my mouth. Receive, therefore, and piously preserve, the unique treasure:

"In the time when what is above was not yet called the sky, and what was below was not yet called the earth, the limitless Abyss espoused the sea of Chaos. They procreated beings such as your frightened eyes have never encountered: warriors with the bodies of the bird of the desert, humans with the faces of crows, bulls with human heads, dogs with four bodies and the tails of fish. But the generous effort of the gods destroyed that monstrous offspring, and the world you know was created in seven days. Earth, firmament, stars, plants, animals—everything that surrounds us—emerged from the hands of Ea, the supreme god. But it is Marduk, son of Ea, who modeled a man with mud after he had mingled is own blood with it, and he enclosed him in a garden of delights between the four great rivers, Euphrates, Tigris, Pishon and Gihon.

"Now, Tiamat, the sea in rebellion, to whom Ea said 'You shall go no further!' and who was gnawing his bit noisily and, always vanquished, was still struggling against Ea and his works, wanted to conquer the favorite child of Ea, the son of the blood of the gods. And Tiamat was the serpent of the darkness, and he said to the man: 'Revolt against Ea, in order that you might be greater than him.' And the man revolted. That is why the irritated gods expelled him from the garden of delights, and he descended, weeping, to the plains of Chaldea and populated them with his children. The Chaldeans are the most ancient of men.

"But those distant ancestors lived in the fashion of animals. In spite of the sin of their first father, the gods took pity on us, and the savior Oannes emerged from the Red Sea at the place where it neighbors the land of Babylon.

"Oannes had the body of a fish; but above the head of a fish he had the head of a man, and from his fish's tail a man's feet emerged. He had a human voice. He spent the day in the midst of our ancestors and did not take any aliment. He taught them writing and all knowledge. From him came the rules for founding cities and constructing temples, and the principles of the laws, the art of measuring the earth and the art of cultivating it. Since the time of Oannes, nothing excellent has been invented. In the evening he returned to the sea and emerged again in the morning.

"Oannes wrote a book about the origin of the world and the commencement of civilized life and he gave that book to humans. But the Book said things summarily, in such a way that, after a few generations, the word of Oannes being deformed, humans no longer understood the book. Then the second Annedotus emerged from the sea, similar in every respect to Oannes.

"Later the mystical Oannes emerge from the sea, and later still the fourth Annedotus and the finally Anodaphus. Now these gods resembled in all respects the first Oannes, and they developed point by point what the first Oannes had exposed summarily. And this is what Oannes had exposed summarily and what the second Annedotus, the mystical Oannes, the fourth Annedotus and finally Anodaphus, the last of those who informed humans, developed:

"The earth, the abode of men, is like an upturned boat. I do not mean one of those absurd long boats that the Egyptians use, but one of the round and beautiful boats that you see floating on the Euphrates. And the underside of the earth is hollow. Ea enclosed the Abyss, the abode of darkness and death. Now, the portion of the earth that the living inhabit is surrounded by the coils of the serpent Tiamat, and the serpent

Tiamat continually launches the waves to assault the land, but Ea has imposed limits that his rage and efforts cannot surpass.

"Babylon, the city of Ea, is at the center of the world. On the other side of the Tigris stands the mountain of the land, the holy mountain, the mountain of the gods; for the gods love the earth as a husband loves his wife.

"The sky is half of a hollow sphere, and we see the hollow of the demi-sphere. The bottom of the sky is supported all around the extremities of the terrestrial boat, beyond the Ocean and the rages of Tiamat. The top of the sky is supported on the mountain of the Orient as on a pivot, and it rotates in its entirety around the mountain of the gods, and the stars rotate with it.

"But there are planets, and they are not stars. They are not the sky, nor are the sun and the moon. But the sun, the moon and the planets are not as high as the summit of the mountain of the gods. They are birds of light, seven in number, always flying between the earth and the sky. Between the sky and the earth, there are also innumerable children of Tiamat, but which, tamed by the force of Ea, have become servants of Ea, to wit, the winds, the clouds, the lightning and the rain.

"Now, humans, after the time of Anodaphus, were tempted again by Tiamat. They allowed the revolt and bitterness of the sea to enter their hearts, and they forgot the teachings of the gods, and rose up against Ea. The world had existed then for many years, and it was six hundred and ninety-one thousand years since Ea had created the world.

"Ea saw, therefore, that the world had become evil and he repented of having created it. He said: 'This world, which is evil, I shall deliver to Tiamat, in order that Tiamat can destroy it.' But there was one just man, and that just man was named Xisuthrus. And a voice said to him: 'Ea wants to destroy the world, which is evil, but he wants to save you, because you are good; and he wants to save with you the seeds of all life, so construct a large vessel.

"Then Xisuthrus constructed a large vessel.

"When Xisuthrus had constructed a large vessel, the voice spoke to him for a second time, saying: 'Take the books that contain the commencement, the middle and the end; take the books of Oannes and bury them in the city of Sippara.

"When he had buried in the city of Sippara the books that contained the commencement, the middle and the end, the voice said again: 'Take into the great vessel all the seeds of the earth—which is to say, a couple of animals of every species, a male and a female.'

"And he took into the vessel all the seeds of life, and asked: 'Now, where shall I go?' And the voice replied: 'Toward the gods.' Then the voice spoke these final words: 'In the evening, destruction will rain down, Enter the vessel, therefore, with your wife and children, and close the door behind them.

"When evening came, the earth was delivered to Tiamat and the sons of Tiamat for forty days and forty nights. The clouds caused such a quantity of rain to fall for forty days and forty nights that the water surpassed by fifteen cubits the highest mountains of the earth of men; but they did not rise as high as the sky, and even the base of the sky on the far side of Tiamat was not moistened, nor the summit of the mountain of the Orient which the gods inhabit, nor the summit of the mountain of the Occident, behind which the sun sets.

"But I shall tell you another day how all the living beings were destroyed except for those in the great vessel; how those, emerging from the vessel after the deluge, repopulated the earth; how, for a long time after that there was only one people and one language. So I shall tell you the story of the wicked men who forgot the deluge and the force of Ea and the anger of Ea.

"Seeing their immense number, they allowed their hearts to be inflated by pride, rebellion and the bitterness of the sea and wanted to build a tower whose stages would rise as high as the mountain of the gods. Some said: 'We shall inhabit the sky with the gods.' And others, more wicked said: 'We shall expel the gods on to the earth and we alone shall inhabit the sky.' But Ea humiliated them and he confused their language, in such a way that some spoke one language, others another, and they were all obliged to disperse without having completed the work—and that was the commencement of the different peoples.

"But all those marvels I shall relate to you at leisure.

"Listen now, however, to the teaching of Oannes relating to death. You are not only, my son, the body that I see; you are also a soul that my eyes cannot see. Your body will die but not your soul. When your body falls into dust your soul will fly away through the air all the way to beyond Tiamat, and it will attain the great mountain of the Occident behind which the sun sets.

"Then it will enter into the immutable country, into the region from which there is no return; the dwelling that one can penetrate but from which one cannot emerge; the road by which one can descend but not ascend again; the subterrain into which one always plunges deeper; the prison in which there is only dust to appease one's hunger and only mud to slakes one's thirst; where one can no longer see light but where one wanders in darkness; and the shades, like birds fill all of space as far as the vault.

"There, no different exists between the rich and the poor, between what you call good and what you call evil. For what you call good has received its recompense on this earth and what you call evil has received its punishment on this earth. But between the first and the second, the distance is not great enough for the gods to remember it after we are dead.

"However, there is in a hollow of the Abyss the source of life, and the genii of the underworld hide it from the souls. When an entirely excellent man dies, however, the gods guide him secretly to the source of life, and he drinks deep draughts and returns to the earth if the living.

"Be then, my son, not what you call good, but what I call entirely excellent; only then will you return to life for the works of life.

"In order that you should be an entirely excellent man, however, to whom it will be given to return to life, it is necessary that you conserve in your heart the things I am going to tell you. And even the things that I am going to tell you, it is necessary that you know that already, in order that you should be the good man who will resemble the wicked once fallen into the Abyss, but who is happy today while he is doing for the first and last time the works of life.

"Listen, therefore, to my words. Retain them strongly in your mind and your heart. And be good. And, if you can, be entirely excellent.

"There are many gods that you ought to honor; but it is not given to men to know the names of all the gods. That is why you ought to honor them by calling them gods, or God—for they are many and they are one, for He is one and he is many.

"Hear, however, the names of the gods that you are to honor in particular.

"There is first of all Anu, and Anu is the sky, the oldest of the old, the father of the gods, the lord of the world below and the world above, the master of darkness and hidden treasures. In Babylon, you will see in the temples a man with an eagle's tail, and on his head that man wears, like a miter, the enormous head of a fish; and the body of the fish falls over his shoulder and down his back. When you see that image in a temple you will know that it is the image of Anu, and you will adore Anu.

"The second god that you will adore is Bel, the Lord of the world, the master of all the countries, the sovereign of spirits. And he is seated on a throne.

"The third god is Ea, the intelligent guide, the lord of the visible world, the master of sciences, of glory and of life, the spirit borne over the waters. He has wings, which number four, and are always deployed.

"Those three gods are equals. They are three and they are one; and He is one and He is three.

"When you honor one of those gods, you honor all three, and in particular you honor each of the two others. When you name one of those gods, you name the other two, and each name signifies all three. And when you say the three names together, it is as if you were pronouncing the name of the One, the first of numbers, the father of numbers; it is as if you were pronouncing the name of the One, the first of beings, the only Being who really is.

"And you will honor with them the goddesses that emerge from them and reenter into them; for their daughters are their wives and their wives are themselves, and you will name them Anat, Belit and Davkina.

"And the six are one, and each is the six.

"And ordinarily, when you speak of the six, you will name Ea, because that is the name that they took to create the sky, the earth and all visible things, except man.

"But they are too great to hear prayers, and there is between them and us a mediator, and the mediator is named Marduk, son of Ea. He it is who disposes of welfare for humans; he it is who publishes the decrees of Ea; he it is who will reveal to you, if you merit it, the great name, the mysterious and efficacious name that puts demons to flight. He is the Son and he is the merciful; he it is to whom you must pray if you want to be heard, and provided that you are pure, he will hear you, and he will plead for you with the other gods.

"But if you are ill, if you are impure, if you have committed a great sin, you will be too far from Marduk and he will not hear you. Then you will pray to Gibil, the god of fire, as the intercessor after Marduk, the merciful Son, who, in his turn, will intercede with Ea, king of the Ocean. And you will offer Gibil an onion and a date, and he will consume them, and will judge you with mercy.

"Marduk inhabits the planet that you call Zeus, and the other gods inhabit the other planets, to wit, Ninip, Nergal, Ishtar and Nabu. But there is one god whose name I cannot pronounce. Marduk will inform you of that name, if you become worthy of it. The One whose name I cannot say is above the other gods as the other gods are above men. That one alone is God. The others are, however, also gods, because they are Him and because he is all, and each, of them.

"Now you know what it is necessary to know. Be worthy of what you know. Be good. Be better every day than the one before. Never do any evil that you know to be evil. Never do anything if you do not know whether it is good or evil. Always do what you know to be good. Thus you will advance in science and piety, and Marduk, the merciful Son, will reveal to you one day what it is necessary for you to learn before becoming entirely excellent. He will tell you how you can break the spur of death and discover in the darkness the source of life. If you become as I say, if you obtain the mercy of Marduk, every time your body dies, you will drink the water of the gods and you will come back to life for the works of life. Meanwhile, work, pray and do good, in trembling, because many are called but few are chosen."

Pythagoras carried Hadabab's words away with him. He compared them with the poems of Pherecydes and Orpheus, the revelations of the Hierophants, the reveries of Epimenides and the Egyptian dogmas. And he did not know which words contained more wisdom and which contained more folly.

For a doubt had come to him touching the *Lair with the Seven Coverts* and the Orphic rhymes.

There, he said to himself, *and in the mysteries of Zagreus, I believe I sense more beauty and find a purer truth; but perhaps, in spite of my effort to make myself a human mind I retain the mind of a Hellene; perhaps my intelligence remains hostile to barbarians and partly closed to whatever comes from them. Perhaps I understand them less completely, and even to what I understand of them, I remain unjust.*

Every evening he resumed the examination of his ancient and recent acquisitions; he strove to distinguish between full words and empty words. Every time he said to himself: *I have not yet heard enough words. I cannot yet choose wisely.*

And he recommended himself: *O Pythagoras, do not speak yet, even to your soul. Continue to listen to words. You are not yet there; you do not yet have the strength to be your-self. Pythagoras, Son of Silence, the hour of your birth has not yet come.*

At other times, comparing the various doctrines, he shook his head and he thought: *There is wine in all these mixing-bowls, but there is water in all these mixing-bowls too. Will I ever be able to separate the water and the wine? For I fear that I might always encounter, in my thirst for wine, fur-ther mixing-bowls, but never the amphora in which the pure and generous wine is contained.*

Hadabab taught him to read the characters in the form of cones that are Chaldean writing. The Greek spent his days thereafter in the library of Babylon.

Often, when he went in, he reread the inscription:

Palace of Nabopolassar, king of the world, king of Baby-lon, of whom Ea guides he intelligence and to whom Davkina, the daughter and spouse of Ea has given ears to hear and open eyes to see what the commencement of government is. They have revealed to the kings my predecessors this cunei-form writing, manifestation of the god Ea, master of science; I have written it on tablets; I have signed it; I have arranged it; I have placed it in my palace for the instruction of men.

The philosopher admired the order of the library. It was composed of terracotta tablets, flat, thin and square. Over both faces ran a fine, compact, abundant writing. Each book was formed of numbered tablets that were piled one on top of an-other in a separate case.

First Pythagoras studied an interminable grammar in which the difficulties of the writing and the language were examined and resolved in a fortunate order. He read dictionar-ies, collections of laws, books of chronology, veritable manu-als of history, geography and statistics, collections of hymns, works of theology and magic. The majority of the books in question seemed less full than the books of Thoth.

Chaldean arithmetic impassioned him, however. He committed to memory several remarks and reasonings un-known in Misraim. He admired the ingenious table in which figures were multiplied by one another without any mental effort. He spent joyful hours directing a finger of his right hand along vertical columns; in the meantime a finger of his left hand followed the horizontal columns, and he was delighted by the infallibility with which their encounter gave the product sought.

The zodiac of the books of astronomy brought him an even richer and more perfumed bouquet of joys. How many things he learned! The moon is extinguished for our eyes every time that the opacity of the earth is interposed between its poor silver and the golden radiance of the sun. The flight of the birds of light revolves in a complex but constant order, and the two hundred and twenty-third lunaison closes a cycle that immediately resumes in exactly the same fashion. As the grateful lover stammers the name of his beloved at dawn, Pythagoras, his eyes illuminated, repeated in ardent piety the word that named that period.

"Saros! Saros!" he cried. "O light, O circle, O Saros, are you not thus far the most beautiful name that I can give to God?"

He also rejoiced in finally knowing the cause of eclipses of the sun. But no god is perfect and the saros was not sufficient to foresee their precise dates. Thanks to countless observations, the magi predicted the occultations of the King-Star, but only approximately. What remained in their calculations of imprecision and uncertainty saddened Pythagoras, who strove for a long time to complete and perfect the Chaldean science, but did not succeed.

After a day spent in the library he went to find Hadabab. With him he climbed the length of the beautiful dentellate and polychromatic staircases to the highest terrace of the tower of Borsippa. In the unfailing purity of a sky innocent of clouds, which delivers itself to gazes like a fully-clad and sinless woman, they observed the stars. In a powerful intoxication, Pythagoras believed that he could distinguish with his ears the harmony of their movements and their music.

"Finally, finally," he sometimes exclaimed, "I have found for my thirst amphorae in which the wine has retained its purity and its strength." And without being aware of it he made gestures similar to those of a glorious madman or a man who has drunk too much. Was he listening to Hadabab explain to him for the twentieth time the planetary colors of the first stages of the edifice: white, black, red, blue and orange? And the sixth was clad in silver sheets in honor of the moon, but the seventh was gilded like the rays of the sun.

Soon, alas, the loquacity of the priest ceased celebrating the colossal harmony of Chaldea symbols. It was no longer anything but the drool of hated and bitter invectives.

"The son of Tiamat," he grated, "the monstrous Zarathustra has penetrated into Babylon; and he is prowling around the city, a lion seeking souls to devour. You, whom I love like a brother for your age similar to mine, and whom I love like a son because I have given birth in you to science and salvation, avoid with care the leader of the wicked."

Pythagoras, entirely given over to his astronomical and mathematical intoxication, shook himself at first under these words, to which he paid no heed, as a preoccupied man shakes himself under the bite of unperceived gnats—but if the gnats return to frequently to pose on the same part of the face, the preoccupied man ends up perceiving them; and if the same words resonate too frequently around ears that are paying no attention, the ears end up hearing them.

Thus Pythagoras learned the name of Zarathustra, and Hadabab's insults told him that Zarathustra was the master of a new religion.[40] Then he said to himself: *When I have ex-*

---

[40] The "official" accounts of the Zoroastrian religion place the life of its founder in the second millennium B.C., but modern historical accounts estimate the era of its foundation to be the seventh century B.C. That is still too early for Pythagoras to have encountered its founded in Babylon in 525 B.C. or thereabouts, but Ryner can probably be granted a certain chronological license in the interests of filling out his schema.

hausted the amphora that renders my mouth joyful, I shall search out this man and examine the mixture in his bowl.

He had no need to search. An old man of tall stature and authoritarian appearance stopped him at the door of the palace of books. In the old man's eyes, contrasting with his dominating manner, there was a freshness of bounty. In the arid rock that thought had made of his visage, the eyes were as bright and good as the limpid clarity of a spring when you are thirsty. As soon as the old man saw Pythagoras, his lips, previously bitter, molded in a rude scowl and hostile in affirmation, formed an amiable smile as hesitant as a child's.

The old man put a strong but gentle hand on Pythagoras' shoulder, like the hand of a father finding his son again, and he asked: "Are you not the Greek encountered often with Hadabab?"

Pythagoras replied with a gesture, and the old man went on, in a flattering manner: "I addressed an unnecessary question to you; for there are not two young men in the world as handsome as you, and there are no other eyes that see as far as yours, and the silence of your lips is more eloquent than the words of others, and more strength is deployed in your immobility than in the efforts of others."

Pythagoras smiled, saying: "My father, you are as indulgent and caressant as a father."

"Do not think," said Zarathustra, "that I speak in the same way to all men. For there are the wicked, to whom one only speaks in order to insult them, although it is better to kill them, and there are many who would be good is they knew, but their slumber is so heavy that to awaken them to knowledge requires them to be shaken by an irritated hand."

While speaking thus, Zarathustra's lips were the lips of hatred or brutal scorn, and his eyes blazed like a fire long hidden beneath a thin white crust, which suddenly flares up, erupting in flame.

"As for you," the old man went on, "you are the morning sleeper who is stirring and trying to wake up. If Ormuzd permitted a man of today to open his eyes without the help of

Zarathustra, you would wake up on your own. That is why I am summoning you not with an abrupt shake but with a hand that caresses.

"Listen, then, most savant and best among the men to whom I have not indicated the way to the truth. Listen, in order that you become, after me, the most savant and best of all men.

"But it is necessary first that you learn who the man is who is speaking to you, and that you are not hearing an ordinary voice, to which one listens with ordinary ears.

"First, I shall tell you what Zarathustra is.

"Zarathustra was not a child similar to the children you know; God was manifest in him as soon as he was born. The children you know weep and cry on seeing the light. He started to laugh on seeing the light, and he took the sun's rays in his childish hands, and then opened those hands, and they let golden rules fall.

"That is why the child was named Zarathustra—which is to say, splendor of gold.

"Those prodigies were reported to the prince of the magi. He knew therefore, that the child of destiny had appeared, the one who, when grown, would triumph over all magicians and annihilate their power. He had him brought and, seizing a terrible weapon, tried to cut him in two. But the child laughed at the flash of light that the movement of the weapon made, and the prince of the magi felt his hand stiffen. Then he had me thrown in the fire; there was no longer any fire in the hearth where I had been thrown, but I was laughing in a bath of roses. I was thrown under the feet of wild bulls. A bull of extraordinary size and strength defended me and put the wild bulls to flight. I was thrown to the wolves; the wolves went to fetch two ewes, which offered me their teats. But I would never finish if it were necessary to relate all the marvels by which the child announce my future glory.

"When I was twenty years old, I withdrew to the desert in order to find Ormuzd there, the master of the creation of good. First, I encountered Ahriman, the master of the creation of evil, and he tempted me, saying: 'Do not make my creation perish, holy Zarathustra, but abjure the good law of Ormuzd and you will obtain the favor that I accord to the greatest of kings.' But I, Zarathustra Spitama, replied: 'I will not abjure the good law of Ormuzd, for body or life, even if my breath is taken away.'

"The master of the creation of evil went on: 'By what weapon can the beings of the good creation vanquish my creation, that of Ahriman?' But I, Zarathustra Spitama, replied to him: 'The mortar in which the haoma is ground, and the cups from which the haoma is drunk, and the haoma, and the words revealed by Ormuzd, are my excellent arms; by the mortar, the cup, the haoma and the word I shall strike you.'[41]

"Then the master of the creation of evil fled, vanquished by my speech and the strength of my heart, and, an angel having transported me to the foot of the throne of Ormuzd, Ormuzd revealed the words to me. Then, six times, the master of the creation of good send me visions to instruct me. For, every time I stopped at a crossroads of my thought and did not know which one was to direct the paces of my speech, Ormuzd sent me a vision and I knew thereafter how to direct the paces of my speech.

"When I was thirty years old, Ormuzd ordered me to reveal to men the words that he had revealed to me, and I obeyed him. In order to test the strength of my heart and the patience of my heart, however, he would not permit anyone to listen to me. And for ten years, only Maidhyoi Maonha, who was my relative, listened to me. But after ten years when I had announced the good without anyone wanting to believe me, Ormuzd sent me to King Hystaspes and said to me: 'Go to King Hystaspes and, by the force of prodigies for the eyes and the impact of words that will be prodigies for the ears, you will shake his ignorance and will overturn his ignorance.'

---

[41] Haoma, a plant and a beverage made therefrom, featured importantly in Zoroastrian rites; the name is equivalent to that of the Vedic soma.

"I therefore entered via the ceiling into the palace of the king; and in my hand I held a cube of fire with which I played without coming to any harm. But Hystaspes said to me: 'Give me another sign and I will believe in you.'

"Then I caused a cedar to grow before his door, so large that no rope could encircle it, and so high that no rope could reach its summit, and at the top of the cedar I put a room to which no man could climb. And Hystaspes believed in me.

"I shall not relate the other prodigies I wrought for Hystaspes, for you know them already, or will soon know them, for they are a familiar story on the lips of the people. Nevertheless, also hear this concerning Zarathustra, in order that you honor in Zarathustra the father of the future.

"Zarathustra has had two wives who died, and his third wife, who is alive, is named Hvogvi. And I approached her three times, and every time my semen fell on the ground. But it was collected by the angel Neryoseng, and he deposited it in Lake Kasava in the land of Sistan, where it is guarded by djinn numbering ninety-nine thousand nine hundred and ninety-nine. When the first times are accomplished, a virgin will come to bathe in the waters of the lake and she will be fecundated by the semen of Zarathustra and will give birth to a son she will name Ukhshyat-Ereta, and that son will be a great prophet for the salvation of many. The first times will be accomplished when a thousand years have elapsed after the death of Zarathustra.

"When the second times are accomplished, a virgin will go to bathe in the waters of Kasava, and she will be fecundated by the semen of Zarathustra, and she will give birth to a son she will name Ukhshyat-Nemah, and he will be a great prophet for the salvation of many. The second times will be accomplished when Zarathustra has been dead for two thousand years.

"When three thousand years have elapsed after the death of Zarathustra, the third times will be accomplished. A virgin will come to bathe in the lake and will be fecundated by the semen of Zarathustra and will give birth to a son she will name Saoshyant. And it is Saoshyant who will accomplish the Resurrection."[42]

Thus—and not otherwise—spoke Zarathustra.[43]

Pythagoras listened, astonished, and said with the words of silence:

O charlatan worse than Epimenides, you are a mixing-bowl in which there is no wine, but only dirty water that troubles the tempest of your pride. And you have only poured the water of lies and folly into my silence.

Zarathustra had fallen silent for some time. He was looking at Pythagoras with a penetrating gaze. Abruptly, he said: "Do you possess great wealth?"

The prudent Greek replied: "I am a poor man who asks for alms everywhere. Do not turn away from me, though, for the alms for which I ask do not impoverish those who grant them. I ask for the wealth that is communicated without diminution; I ask for the only wealth, wisdom."

"Zarathustra can give you wisdom, and no one else can give you wisdom. But do not forget that the man who rejoices Zarathustra Spitama with his presents also rejoices Ormuzd, the master of the creation of good."

---

[42] The data in the previous passage are taken from the *Zend-Avesta*, which was translated into French in 1893, but Ryner probably found the names (which are slightly misrendered in his text) in excerpts published the previous year in the *Annales* of the Musée Guimet.

[43] The repetition of this formula obviously has in mind the publication in the 1880s of Friedrich Nietzsche's *Also Sprach Zarathustra* (*Thus Spake Zarathustra* in its first English translation; *Ainsi parlait Zarathtoustra* in Henri Albert's 1903 French translation), in which Nietzsche employs the travels and sayings of his fictitious Zarathustra as a mouthpiece for his own philosophical ideas—very different from Ryner's—in much the same way that Ryner employed Psychodorus.

Thus—and not otherwise—spoke Zarathustra. And he went on: "Give me ten full mares and a camel, and I will offer the sacrifice for you, and Ormuzd will love you."

Then he lamented because, since the death of Hystaspes, he no longer had a protector. "Who can I find to protect my flocks and myself, except for Ormuzd and his angels? Is not the duty of a prince and the duty of a rich man to acquire from the wicked by war or usury, and to give to the priest the wealth acquired from the wicked? In acting thus, one diminishes the force of the creation of evil, one increases the force of the creation of good, one saddens the heart of Ahriman, master of the creation of evil, and one rejoices the heart of Ormuzd, master of the creation of good."

Thus—and not otherwise—spoke Zarathustra. Then he fell silent for some time, in order that Pythagoras would be forced to reply to him.

"O Zarathustra Spitama," Pythagoras finally replied, "it is appropriate to speak to everyone according to his condition. Do not instruct me, then, as to the duties of the prince or the rich man, but inform me of the duty of the man poor in money, who desires to remain poor in money, and inform me of the duties of the man poor in science who desires to be rich in science."

"Let the man who can give nothing to the priest engage the rich to give to the priest. Let the man who has not the strength to protect the priest engage the powerful to protect the priest. Now you know your duty, man skillful by silence and by speech. You are not the cloud that pours rain over the thirst of the earth; you are not the river that provides abundant waters; be the hand that digs the channel and directs the water of the river toward the good earth. Then you will reap the crop of doctrine."

Thus—and not otherwise—spoke Zarathustra. Then he quit Pythagoras without adding another word.

For several days he crossed paths with the Greek and pretended not to see him, waiting for Pythagoras to come to him—but Pythagoras did not go to him. He therefore pretended, suddenly, to see the Greek and, approaching him with a broad smile, said:

"O my son, I am the vase overflowing with doctrine, and I want everyone to draw abundantly from the vase. To those who cannot pay, I give my wealth gratuitously. Listen, then and retain."

The Son of Silence listened, for he desired to know whether, at the bottom of the mixing-bowl that had thus far only yielded troubled water, there might be a little wine for his thirst.

Thus spoke Zarathustra:

"In the beginning they were three. And the first of the three is Ormuzd, the lord of all wisdom, who has a further nineteen sacred names and twenty-two other names; and if I said all those names I would have told you the entire truth. However, there is one of these names that has been true, and will be true, but is not true, and that name is Omnipotent, for today, Ormuzd is not omnipotent, but Ahriman holds a portion of power.

"And there was Ahriman and there was Zurvan; but Zurvan is also called Boundless Time, and that name has been true, and will be true, but is not true. For time was boundless before the double creation and it will be boundless after the victory of Ormuzd, but today there are limits in order that the combat of Ormuzd and Ahriman can finish and in order that the power of Ahriman can be ended. And time is Ormuzd's weapon, of which he makes use to destroy that which must perish.

"Before the creation your eyes see, there had been a first creation that your eyes cannot see, but which your mind will see when I have spoken; for the speech of Zarathustra is a hand that tears away a veil.

"Ormuzd had created first the Immortal Saints, and they number seven, and they stand at Ormuzd's sides, three to his left, three to his right and the last lower down, in front of him.

"The first Immortal Saint, the beloved Son, is named Good Thought, and he is the first-born, the infallible wisdom and the infallible good. He is clad in white and ornamented with jasmine. He welcomes and introduces the souls of the just. He it is that Ormuzd sent to me to bring me alive before his throne when Ormuzd wanted to reveal the Holy Law to me; and he it is who watches over the beasts of the creation of good in order to ensure their health and their multiplication; he has for auxiliaries the moon and the bull, and the cock is his sacred bird.

"The second Immortal Saint is named Excellent Rectitude. He is the Rule that Ormuzd makes the creation observe, and it is the Rule that men must observe. He is Equilibrium and he is Justice. He is powerful even in the underworld, and he prevents the demons, who are wicked and unjust, from torturing the damned more than they deserve. For he holds a balance, and there is crime in one pan of the balance and there is punishment in the other, and Excellent Rectitude does not permit one pan to rise and the other to descend. When Ormuzd had created the Holy Immortals he raised his voice, asking, 'Who has created you?' And the seven stood before him in silence, not knowing what to respond; but Excellent Rectitude replied: 'It is you who has created us.'

"The third Immortal Saint is named Good Reign, and he is the envoy of the power of Ormuzd to princes; for the power of princes ought to aid the power of Ormuzd in the destruction of evil and the triumph of good. To Ormuzd alone, glory, majesty and independence properly belong. He is the only one who glories in making the law for kings and giving them, when necessary, great and terrible lessons. For the powerful ought to protect the weak, and if the powerful oppress the weak, Ormuzd sends Good Reign to protect the weak against the great. Good Reign is strength, he is armed, and he is metal. When you cause metal to rejoice in striking the wicked, you cause Good Reign to rejoice; but if you afflict metal by striking the good, you afflict Good Reign.

"The fourth Immortal Saint is female, and has the face of a woman; her name is Piety. The earth is her domain, and she defends the land against pollution, and is aided in her work by the Waters and by Religion.

"But Piety has a sister who is the fifth Immortal Saint, and that sister is called Health. She gives vigor and growth; she watches over the waters that make all things grow, and because the growth of plants is enclosed by the cycle of the year, Health sees that the days and the months each come in their order.

"The sixth Saint, who is called Immortality, makes the plants grow, the healthy plants that cure all the ills of the body; and he makes the haoma grow, the king of plants, which prevents the gods from dying and will prevent humans from dying.

"And those Immortal Saints are the Archangels; and there are seven counting Ormuzd; but when one does not count Ormuzd, one includes with them, in order that they remain seven, Obedience, the foremost of the Angels.

"And the angels, the faithful executors of the orders and the messengers of Ormuzd, are infinite in number.

"But the foremost of the angels, after Obedience, is Fire, the Son of God, the first ally of man in the struggle against the demons and the magicians, the friend who, well-nourished renders a hundredfold what is given to it. Now the word Friend is similar to the word Priest, and the gaze of Fire is similar to the gaze of the Priest. Fire looks at the hands of all those who pass, and says: 'What is it that a friend brings to a friend? What is it that the man who comes and goes brings to the man who cannot walk?' If you bring him wood, piously offered, a sheaf of twigs piously bound, then the Fire of Ormuzd, satisfied, rendered propitious, well sated, blesses you. Let him who has ears to hear, hear.

"And immediately after Fire, among the angels of Ormuzd, you will honor Water. You will not pollute it, for that is a great sin. You will not make it battle with fire, for if, by your fault, two gods battle together, you have committed the greatest of all sins. That is why, every time you put a vase over the fire, you should not fill it beyond two-thirds and must be careful that the water does not overflow.

"Before the creation you see with your bodily eyes, but nevertheless after the creation of archangels and angels, Ormuzd created the fravashis. And know this, man: in the present creation, you seem one, but you are five; for you are body, you are life, you are form, you are soul and you are fravashi. When you die, the body returns to the earth from which it came, life returns to the wind from which it came, form dissolves in the sunlight from which it came, the soul attaches itself to the fravashi, which is immortal, and likewise becomes immortal.

"Your fravashi is more ancient than your form, your life, your body and your soul. When Ormuzd created it he said to it: 'Would you like to remain forever in the spirit world, happily, with the other angels; or, when I have created the world of matter, would you like, as one takes a weapon in order to strike and in order to be struck, to take a body and combat the power of Ahriman?'

"The fravashi was valiant, and it replied: 'When the time comes, O Ormuzd, give me a body as one gives a weapon to a warrior, and send me into combat. I choose combat, Ormuzd. Nevertheless, Ormuzd, let your will be done and not mine.'

"When your fravashi and the other fravashis responded thus, Ahriman heard it from the depths of the abyss and he ground his teeth in rage, and came to attack Ormuzd and his angels. Ormuzd, always merciful, offered him peace, but the mercy of the good encourages the evil, for the wicked are ignorant of the source of mercy and that it flows from an elevated heart, but believe that it flows from a base and cowardly heart that senses its weakness. That is why Ahriman replied that he would not cease to attack. Then Ormuzd asked him if he wanted to combat for nine thousand years, and Ahriman accepted. And time, which had no limits and will no longer have limits after the combat, was limited to nine thousand years. And there was a division in things, and there were numbers, in order that things could be numbered and time and its division could be numbered.

"Then Ormuzd, in order to halt Ahriman's attacks, built the earth, the boulevard of the sky; and the earth, the boulevard of the sky, is the battlefield. The fravashis who had asked to combat therefore descended to the earth. They were healthy and vigorous men; but Ahriman afflicted them with maladies. They had come pious and valiant, but Ahriman unleashed upon them the host of sins and vices. Ormuzd had given them, to nourish them and assist them in their labor, good plants and good beasts, but Ahriman sowed poisons and propagated evil beasts.

"And all the things I have described have lasted for a long time, for Ormuzd had created the archangels, angels and fravashis three thousand years before Ahriman came to attack him. And Ormuzd, in order to create the earth and everything it bears, took six days, but each of those days was five hundred years long, and man only arrived at the end of those three thousand years. During those six days, each of five hundred years, Ormuzd recited the prayer of twenty-one words, and Ahriman was rendered powerless by the prayer of twenty-one words. But when Ormuzd had sent humans into combat instead of the prayer of twenty-one words, Ahriman woke up from his torpor and he made the creation of evil. And for three thousand years Ahriman had been the master of the creation of evil when Ormuzd summoned the greatest of the fravashis and said to him: 'You will go to earth and you will commence my victory, and your name will be Zarathustra.'

"The victory that is commencing will last three thousand years. It will be directed, when my memory is effaced in the hearts of men, by the three sons that I shall have of the three virgins, in accordance with what I have told you. And the last of my three sons will render the victory definitive. Then Ahriman will return to his darkness and the blissful Light will no longer know eclipse.

"I will tell you another time about the creation of the good beasts and good plants, the creation of evil plants and evil beasts. Listen now, however, to the creation of man.

"Ormuzd began to sweat. In the time it takes to say a prayer, he made it into the body of a young man of fifteen years, brilliant and tall of stature. He named him Gayomard. But Ahriman raised against him the demons of pain, hunger and malady, with the consequence that Gayomard withered, became thin and died. In dying, he let his semen fall. The angels collected it, and they purified it in the light of the sun, and sowed it in the earth. After forty years the first human couple emerged from the earth, and had the form of two bushes with fifteen leaves, and the two newborns were fifteen years of age. They came together and they had two children, a son and a daughter, and they devoured them. But afterwards they had seven other sons and seven other daughters, whom they did not devour, and from whom the entire race of humans emerged.

Ormuzd had said to the male and female mortals: 'You are humans, you are the masters of the world; I have created you the foremost of beings, visible by the perfection of your thought. Think good thoughts; say good words; do good deeds. But above all, do not adore demons.'

"Their first thought and their first words were: 'That one is God.' In their second thought and their second speech, they rejoiced on the subject of one another, saying: 'This is a human being.' Their first action was to walk. In their second action they rejoiced on the subject of nourishment and they ate. Then they said: 'It is Ormuzd who has created water, the earth, trees, oxen, the stars, the moon, the sun and all the other creations of good, fruit and root.'

"But that was the end of the day. When darkness came, it lay for the first time over their eyes and their mind, and Ahriman inspired evil words in them, and they said: 'It is Ahriman who has created water, the earth, trees, oxen, the stars, the moon, the sun and all the other creations of good, fruit and root.' They said that, and that lie was Ahriman's first joy; and the mortals became demons, and their souls will remain in the underworld until the final Resurrection.

"Beware, my son, of thinking as the first mortals thought in the darkness; for the word is the daughter of thought and the deed is the son of thought; and the evil word or dead will make you a demon, and precipitate you into the underworld until the final Resurrection.

"Do, therefore, the deeds that are good and pronounce the words that are good; and let the only mother of your actions and your words be good thinking. Now, the mother of your words and actions will be good thinking if you say: 'It is Ormuzd who created the water, the earth, trees, oxen, the stars, the moon, the sun and all the other creations of good, fruit and root.' And those holy words will always be within you like a lighted lamp, if you take care, four times a day, as one pours oil into a lamp that does not go out, to repeat piously: 'It is Zarathustra who has created my science, my heart, my thought, my words and my deeds.' But it is necessary that your heart overflow with gratitude for your two benefactors, to wit, Ormuzd, master of the creation of good, and Zarathustra, the master of your thought; and it is necessary that you offer sacrifices to Ormuzd and presents to Zarathustra."

Thus—and not otherwise—spoke Zarathustra.

Pythagoras, having heard him, thought: *I have done well to persevere and to extend to that man, several times, the vase of my silence; for after troubled water, the man has poured a mixture into me in which there is the water of folly and the wine of wisdom.*

Since the instruction of Oinuphis, Prophet of Egypt, however, Pythagoras no longer saw his silence merely as a mixing-bowl into which many people poured the wine and water of speech. His silence also took other forms in his mind's eyes. That is why he also said to himself:

Before that sculptor, who initially seemed maladroit to me, I have raised up once again the block of my silence. The chisel of his speech has often slipped without biting into the block, but the chisel of his speech has sometimes sculpted a few parts of the block fortunately. And he rejoiced: *The more numerous are the words of which I am the son, the more I am the glad Son of Silence.*

He wandered at random and, mingling the words of Zarathustra with the words he had heard successively, he agitated them all together. And his silence appeared to him to be similar to a mystical winnowing-basket. Many words flew far away from him, light and empty, but those that were full and heavy with nourishment remained enclosed in the winnowing-basket of his silence.

As he was going abroad thus, joyful and pensive, he met the priest Hadabab, who said to him:

"Come with me."

Pythagoras having followed him, the priest made him walk for a long time; and the Son of Silence asked: "Why are you taking me so far?"

"I am taking you," Hadabab replied, "to a place where you will hear the folly and see the abjection of those who do not listen piously to the priests of Chaldea.

They finally arrived in a quarter named Halalat, which was the quarter inhabited by those of the house of Israel.

The philosopher asked: "Explain to me the thought of these men, if you know it."

"These men," replied Hadabad, scornfully, "have no thought. They repeat, without understanding it, the speech of other peoples. Some among them reproach their brothers for repeating the other speech, but the mind of those who pronounce such reproaches is a dark lair in which a single beast agitates, and that beast is the hatred of all other men.

"When we conquered them, they had polished stones for gods, like the most vulgar of barbarians, and in the valleys, under blocks of stone, they cut the throats of their first-born. Some of them, however, had struggled against the stupid cruelty of the crowd, and, amid the insults of the Egyptians, taught a gentler religion borrowed from Egypt. Today they agitate mixed doctrines loudly; they steal the lies of Egypt, the lies of Zarathustra and tear a few sheds from the magnificence of Chaldean truth. Each of their prophets affirms that Ea—although they name him Yahveh—had spoken to him, and accuses the other prophets of repeating the words of Egypt and Chaldea. And those who listen to us, or those who listen to Misraim, the insulting prophet compares to women who prostitute themselves to foreigners."

The two men stopped near a numerous group and gazed with those of the crowd. An emaciated old man, with bristling hair and beard and crazed eyes, was eating human excrement on barley cakes. In the meantime, his lips, dripping filth, cried: "Israel, you shall eat your bread among the nations, and your bread shall be soiled by the ordure of the nations."

He leaned on two drunken courtesans and he cried again:

"Word of Yahveh. Yahveh has said to me: 'Son of Man, you shall eat your bread covered with ordure in order that Israel shall know the fate that awaits it. And you shall espouse two courtesans, for I, Yahveh, have espoused Samaria and I have espoused Jerusalem. But Jerusalem and Samaria are prostituted to Misraim and are prostituted to the Chaldeans who wear the sash around the hips and wear colored cloth upon their heads."

And the old toothless mouth from which the mixture of excrement and insults flowed kissed the drunken courtesans.

Now, the people were powerfully excited by the words and gestures of the fanatic.

"Let's flee this sickening spectacle," said Pythagoras. He added, speaking to himself: *As one raises palaces for a queen, it is necessary to build in thought the nobility of symbols. But the thought that allows itself to be buried without resistance in ignominy and ugliness is not true thought.*

He turned toward Hadabad: "O Chaldean priest, thought is true in several ways. First of all it is true merely because it lives in a mind in the same way that a woman is true merely because she lives in a country. However, if you encounter a hunch-backed, rickety, one-eyed woman with her face ravaged by a cancer, you turn away, saying: 'That is not a woman.' For myself, I stand before all thoughts like the young man who

147

does not like to stand before all women. I accept the kiss of any thought, provided that it is not ugly. When I know myself better, I shall espouse a single doctrine and a single wife. My amour will choose them among the most beautiful in order to find united within them all the beauties that, along my route, have announced themselves to me and promised themselves to me. But as you turn away from the hunchbacked, rickety woman whose flesh and one eye have been eaten away, I turn away from that infamous Jew. As you say: 'That is not a woman,' I say, 'That is not a thought.'"

He added: "Zarathustra is right: daughters resemble their mothers, and when the word or the deed is ignoble, it is because the thought is base. If you tilt an amphora full of generous wine, it is not ordure that flows into the cups."

Nothing alerted Pythagoras to the power of the scorned Jew. Nothing informed him that the seed germinating in the sickening Ezekiel was a mustard-seed in a rich dung-heap.[44] A few centuries more and it would grow; it would spread large branches over the generations; birds would sing in its boughs, peoples and doctrines would die shivering with cold in its shade.

Nothing said to him: "The god of love that you summon, the Zagreus by whom you desire to see the tyranny of Zeus dethroned, this Jew that you scorn foresees better than you the form that he will take in the minds of the future. His Son of Man will triumph, not Marduk son of Ea or Dionysus-Zagreus son of Zeus."

But if a hand of clarity had unfurled the centuries before the eyes of Pythagoras, with what increasing horror the harmonious Greek would have looked at Ezekiel. And he would have shed tears. Only concern for his serenity and eurhythmia

---

[44] As with Zarathustra, Ryner bends orthodox chronology is order to allow Pythagoras to encounter Ezekiel, who is generally supposed to have died in Babylon in c570 B.C., considerably earlier than Pythagoras' supposed captivity there, in 520 B.C. or thereabouts.

would have prevented him from wringing his hands in despair; and he would have groaned: "What ugliness and what ordure over the centuries!"

Then the valiant Greek would have shaken off the nightmare, and he would have proclaimed: "Behind that future, there is the Future. Our evening is descending toward night. But during the night, will not the Beautiful Thought indicate the subterranean sun, Osiris, hastening? He has been seen to set in the Occident. Turned toward the region of his fall, the owls insult his death, which they affirm to be definitive, and praise the eternal night. But look. Armed with his arrows of light, over there, on the other side of the sky, in the direction of his ancient rise, in the Orient at which the owls are not gazing, there, preceded by the white promises of first light, he is rising, he is laughing, and he is surging forth."

Book Five: THE PYTHAGOREANS

Why, before the Chaldean priest, had Pythagoras dispended with his silence, the obstinate mask that many took for a face?

It was not a momentary weakness; it was a new resolution, a direction determined permanently. It was also a particular calculation and a means toward a precise end.

Pythagoras had said to himself:

I have remained enveloped in the warmth of silence like an infant not yet formed in his mother's womb. Now, what others can give me, I have received. It is necessary that I emerge into a life that is my life. The Son of Silence is born, and the Son of Silence is a Word.

But the choice of the moment in which his first free gesture spread was, in the prudent and ingenious Greek, a detail of a plan of material deliverance.

He had studied the character of Hadabab. He knew how much puerility and vanity there is in the pride of a priest. A few unorthodox words would drive the doctor away for days, like a woman wounded in her pretentions who is sulking, and waiting for the offender to come back to beg her pardon.

But Pythagoras did not come back, Hadabab was no longer anything to him but a hindrance and an obstacle.

With the aid of the Crotonian Gillos, encountered a month before in the library of Nabopolassar, the Son of Silence prepared his flight.

The two escapees had anticipated everything that it is possible to anticipate. Their furtive journey was bristling with danger, fatigue and suffering: suffering, fatigue and danger studied with care, and accepted with courage.

In the desert, after the torrid day, the cold fell upon them, a crushing mantle. Pressed against one another, enveloped by anything that could protect their warmth, they told one another stories about the past, or revealed their dreams about their own future, the future of humankind and the future of the earth. Often, too, their eyes turned to the sky and they spoke to the stars; their voices and their gestures trembled then, almost singing, like the hands and accents of your men when they talk to women.

Sometimes, the thirst and lassitude of the day became opportunities for voluptuousness. An oasis rejoiced them with its freshness, its profound well, and the sugary sweetness of its dates. Then they lingered, tracing figures in the sand.

Once, after a long application, after numerous lines effaced, almost with annoyance or discouragement, with the back of the hand and traced again with a hesitant finger, Pythagoras exclaimed:

"A hecatomb! A hecatomb! If it were permitted to kill and I had a hundred oxen, I would offer a hecatomb!"

"To what god would you sacrifice?" interrogated Gillos, sardonically.

"To the Lord of Science, whatever his name might be. But that name, unknown to Zarathustra, Hadabab, Oinuphis, Epimenides, the hierophant, Orpheus, Hesiod and Homer, it seems to me that my amour has finally revealed to me. My hecatomb, I shall sacrifice to God the Geometer."

On the sand next to the figure that he was contemplating passionately, he traced other lines. They represented an ox. In the new design, Pythagoras wrote the signs that expressed the number one hundred. Then he erased the ox and the number, declaring: "The sacrifice is consummated. God the Geometer demands no more."

"God the Geometer," said Gillos, astonished. "Yet another new god...."

"No—the most ancient, although the most unknown: the one for whom everyone seeks with words, but whom it is perhaps necessary to seek with numbers and lines. Be quiet, Gillos. It seems to me that I'm about to find a name even more beautiful that suits him better. O God, would you not prefer me to call you One, or to call you World? One, O ancient and ever-new Monad, sole Eternity, sole Immensity; you who suppress dispersion and death; you who, in a flap of your robe, amass time and space...."

His forehead plunged in the sand, Pythagoras had the most emotional and the most respectful of attitudes observed among the Orientals.

When he got up, he said: "One, you are, and yet, for what you are, it is necessary that you become. You were in darkness; you have created light, and light appeared to kill you, and yet is great enough to create you more beautiful. You have given birth to the mind that divides things, but the parricidal mind will bring together the dispersed limbs of his father and render his a more harmonious life."

"Stop!" exclaimed Gillos. "Stop on the slope of madness."

"Be quiet, my brother, let me descend into the ineffable mystery. Yes, the One is first; but he does not know himself, and wants to know himself. He detaches things from himself as one draws away from mirrors in order to look at oneself within them. But now, his first gesture creates Appearance and seems to kill the Real. As soon as his first effort to make that in which he can gaze at himself, there are Two. And One, believing that he is no longer One, is afraid of himself and his son. Two, you are Appearance, you are Evil, you are the Fall, the Loss of self, the Infinite. But One and Two embrace one another and combat one another. Their struggles, like their kisses, create innumerable things, poor opaque things in which One no longer sees himself.

"Finally, after a thousand gropings of love and hatred, now the unanimous effort produces Man, magnificent mirror of life, wave that is a soul. One, Two and all the gods are afraid before the mirror that flees, quivers and laughs. They want to break the Ephemeron. But one of them—what is he called? Prometheus, if we heed the poets—sees the future. He knows that springs return to the Ocean, and that a dolor, regarded for a long time in the mirror, becomes a joy again. He knows. That is why he protects us....

"Poor mirror, saved by Prometheus, how many hostilities you reflect, how much hatred, how much ugliness, and how easy it is to believe that you are nothing except for the discordant images you reflect! However, you are something else; you are the will to reflect everything and, in consequence, no longer the struggle but the harmony, no longer the Many but the One. Oh, how long it will be....

"Poets, sages and priests seek the road toward the One enriched by self-knowledge, No one knows it. They take all the pathways of dream or affirmation—but is affirmation even a path? Affirmation, is your name not Immobility? You, dream, are a beautiful road, and the most florid; but those who follow you do not perceive that you turn back on yourself. They pass continually where they have already passed and do not recognize places seen a thousand times before, because you, Dream, more prodigal than all springs, cover yourself with flowers that are not yet picked.

"Dream, you are, in a perfumed wind, the flotation of all lilies, all roses, all narcissi, all asphodels; but in the mirror, you efface yourself as soon as you appear. O Dream, not the same face, but the same smile, which flees and comes back, always seductive, always changed. Dream, although marvelously more beautiful, too similar to myself and my surface and my flight, you are not the path I want; my road is called Knowledge. I want the solid route that does not turn back on itself and does not take back what it has given.

"Knowledge, Knowledge, you offer permanent acquisitions, and the presents you make are not worthwhile only in themselves, but are the reliable promises of rich rewards. You alone, O Knowledge, you alone are stable.

"However, O Knowledge, your brother is named Doubt and you only march leaning on that smiling and lame individual—and is it not him who breathes the first word that you speak?

"Your first word, stable Knowledge, is that nothing is stable, that things flow as rapidly as dreams. But your first word has not discouraged me. I have continued to follow you

153

and you have taught me to pay attention not only to the things that flow, but to what there is beneath the flux.

"How could they flow if they did not have a slope? Knowledge, you do not stop the flow of things, but you enable penetration as far as their slope. Oh, the river is deep. While I dive, the water suffocates my mouth and my nostrils, the water blinds my eyes; however, my groping hands seek the Slope. Slope, I want to give you a glorious name and I shall call you Law. Slope, I want to give you other names too and my amour will call you Number, and the music within me will call you Harmony.

"Gillos, my brother, let us seek the Number of everything, let us seek the Harmony in everything. Afterwards, what does it matter if the thing slips through the fingers of our body? It will no longer flee the subtle fingers of our mind.

"Gillos, my brother, look amorously upon these few lines in the sand; you will see the most recent figure of God, the latest design of the Slope. Look, Gillos, at the glory of his hour. Tomorrow will rise for more beautiful glories, but they will be daughters of this one."

"I can only see a triangle," said Gillos, "and squares around the triangle, and other lines which, for me, are confusing and unclear."

"But Pythagoras said: "This triangle has a right angle. It has a number, which, better than the angles, unites the long side with the other two sides. That number, yesterday, humans did not know. Today, the Son of Silence has discovered it. If I die, it is necessary that that number should not be lost. I am going to tell it to you, Gillos, and if I cannot repeat it to others, you will repeat it to them. Humble and small as this discovery seems to you, it will teach them the Slope and God better than anything that Zarathustra and Orpheus combined can tell them."

Gillos listened to the demonstration. It moved him, but not in the same way as Pythagoras. To begin with, he admired the ingenuity and the oblique cunning that led to the truth. Then his voice, anxious, as if groping, said:

"Is not justice a geometry, Pythagoras? Why will you not be the geometer and architect of justice? O Pythagoras, with exact numbers and ingenious lines, pure men and square laws, let us build the veritable city, one which, once constructed, will be, like that figure in the sand, a face of God and an acquisition forever.

"Soon, the winds will efface that figure in the sand, but not in your mind, nor in mine, nor in the minds of those to whom we will show it, renewed, and to whom we shall explain it."

"You're right," said Pythagoras. "Let us construct the city of justice. Doubtless, the crowd will come, a wind of wrath and folly, to sweep away our work in the sand of the present; but some will perhaps remember. Certainly, we shall not have carved righteousness in marble and built justice on indestructible foundations, but perhaps we shall have created, by the example of a day, the eternal idea of righteousness and justice. It is not given to us to engender our distant descendants, or even to know them. In order that, insofar as it depends on us, the future shall live, let us create our children and our works. All that we make will be destroyed, but let us nevertheless throw as much beauty as we can upon the fatal slope, and let our works be fleeting harmonies in the light."

In Heliopolis, Pythagoras found in the hands of Oinuphis letters that were already old. Eunomus announced to him the death of Parthenis, and then that of Mnesarchus. He also indicated that Polycrates, by tortuous roads, was heading toward tyranny, and that the blind citizens were not opposing his designs. Pherecydes, desolate, had retired to the little island of Skyros.

Your master, Eunomus added, *was impotent among us because he is not a citizen. In any case, his arrogant manner indisposed people toward him. But the good hope for much of you; they deplore your prolonged absence and their wishes summon you. O my brother, the immortal gods have not permitted you to collect the last sigh of our father and our moth-*

*er. I pray that they will allow you to arrive in time to redeem
things that are almost fallen, and not to receive the last sigh of
liberty.*

Oinuphis did not have the ideas of a Greek about liberty.
He strove to retain Pythagoras.

"You can change your name," he told him. "You can live
among us, similar to one of us. The Persians will never suspect
that you are not a priest of Egypt. Stay with me, my beloved
son, since you no longer have any other father. Don't abandon
an old man leaning toward Osiris."

The Son of Silence refused to stay any longer than the
time required to prepare the next stage of the voyage. For
those few days he made himself the master of his former master, teaching him the arithmetical and astronomical verities of
which Chaldea had made him a present. He also told him his
own inventions in geometry. It was the old prophet's last joy.

"O my son, O my glory," he exclaimed, "little time remains to me before the summons of Osiris, but I hope those
hours will be sufficient for me to transmit to a few young men
the treasures that you have just given me. O my son, are you
really the Pythagoras whose silence was enriched by my
speech? Or has Thoth, lord of sciences, taken your pleasant
form to recompense me in my decline for a life employed in
knowing, loving and serving him?"

The moment of departure arrived; and Oinuphis, his eyes
full of tears said: "My son, you are too great and too pure to
deceive. Let me bless you with my imposed hands and my
words. Then, even though it will break my heart, go where
your own heart summons you."

As the vessel approached Samos, Pythagoras, full of joyful memories of his childhood, said to Gillos: "Today is the
first day of the hierogamy." And he told him about the last
festival there, and repeated the words of Pherecydes....

Suddenly, he interrupted his story. His astonished eyes
gazed, and his mouth, mute, remained open in amazement. In
the noisy agitation of the winds, a sudden curtain of flames

rose up over the high harbor wall, reddening the verdure of the mountains.

"What?" said Gillos. "Are they lighting the torches before nightfall?" Then he fell silent, ashamed. He sensed that he had just pronounced absurdly petty words before some vast and inexplicable spectacle.

A ship left the port, as if fleeing rapidly, but no one was pursuing it, and its speed diminished.

The men manning the ship in question perceived Pythagoras' vessel. They seemed to want to avoid it; then, remarking that it was a Phoenician ship, they headed toward it.

As soon as they were within range, one of them shouted: "Men, flee Samos, conflagration and death."

"What do your words signify?" the philosopher asked. "And what is that flame that is rising up higher than the harbor wall?"

A voice replied: "That fire is the work of my brother Polycrates.[45] His cruelty has transformed the festival of Hera into a triumph of Ares and Hephaistos. Everywhere in the vanity of the temple, death and fire reign. The good citizens are

---

[45] This episode is not consistent with the version of Pythagoras' life given by Iamblichus, which implies that Pythagoras was in Babylon until a date that can now be identified as 520 B.C., two years after the death of Polycrates in 522 B.C. That account conflicts with Porphyry's version, however, which claims, like the present story, that Polycrates was still ruling Samos when Pythagoras eventually returned there, although it also claims that Pythagoras remained there for some time, even though the island fell under Persian control after Polycrates' death. According to Iamblichus, Pythagoras founded a school in Samos, although he lived in a cave. Some other accounts suggest that Pythagoras arrived in Croton, where he ended his life, considerably earlier than 520 B.C., although the assertion by Diodorus Siculus (writing in the first century B.C.) that Milo of Croton was one of his followers is more consonant with the latter date.

dead. The few who remain are on this ship. We are fleeing while the blind people acclaim the tyrant."

"Is Eunomus about that ship?"

"Eunomus was one of the first to fall, if it is necessary to tell all. For Syloson, banished by a brother's crime, recognizes you, O Pythagoras, deprived of the most virtuous of your brothers."

"I no longer have anything to do in Samos," said the Son of Silence.

Meanwhile, the master of the vessel said: "I cannot land in the midst of flames and war. Where do you want me to take you?"

The philosopher reflected momentarily, then said: "Are the Olympic games not being celebrated soon?"

"Only a month separates us from the Olympic games."

Pythagoras asked to be taken to Cyllene, the port nearest to Pisa.

"At the hour when your brother has just died?" exclaimed Gillos. "The spectacles of Olympia are not funeral games."

"My brother, having died for justice, orders that I found the city of justice."

"You doubtless hope to find soldiers and arms among the assembled Greeks?"

"Neither arms nor soldiers. The sword is not a trowel, nor blood a mortar. The house of justice cannot stand upright on the foundations of constraint, or the house of peace on a base of war. The city that I want to build will not know the soldier and the priest. Armaments are the enemy of thought, as the speech that affirms is the enemy of the truth that seeks."

Pythagoras therefore came to Olympia. Before the assembled people he spoke about justice amorously. His gestures created light and sowed flame. Those who saw him and listened to him believed that they were hearing a god, and they acclaimed him with the same enthusiasm as an athlete or a tyrant.

When he asked: "Who would like to come with me to build the house of justice?" all the people stood up, their arms extended, and cried: "Me! Me! Me!" But the Son of Silence had a doubtful smile on his lips. His hand calmed the unanimous enthusiasm, and he continued:

"I am not the orator or the courtesan who intoxicates men and takes advantage of a temporary intoxication to extract oaths that will be regretted. No constraint accompanies justice, the liberator. It bears neither arms nor tablets. It does not inscribe what men say. It wants our heart always to beat with its rhythm. The arms that are enchained today will work poorly tomorrow. Let us wait for the end of the games. The blind impulse of this moment will have become determination and enlightenment in a few; those will company me, awakened forever. The others will have had a heroic dream and will remember this day as a glory. Thus you will remember having heard the aede sing the virtues for which, as long as the song lasted, your heart seemed great enough."

"We will all, all, go with you...."

When the games were over, of the multitude that had cried "Me! Me! Me!" the multitude that cried "We will all, all, go with you." fifteen men remained faithful to the initial resolution.

Those fifteen were named Gillos of Croton, Lysis, Clinias, Eurytus, Callicratides, Charondas of Catania, Zaleucus of Locri, Hippodamus of Thurium, Euryphames, Hipparchus, Telauges, Metopus, Damasippus, Hermippus and Polos the Lucanian.[46]

---

[46] This list seems to be almost entirely improvised, although it includes some names of known Pythagoreans from the "brotherhood" that the philosopher is said to have founded in Magna Graecia [i.e. southern Italy] near Croton, including Lysis of Taras and Clinias. The English Platonist Thomas Taylor compiled a much fuller list of Pythagoreans from various sources for his own compilation of the life of Pythagoras, but the over-

Three women departed with them, including Phyntis, daughter of Callicratides, and the learned Perictione; but the third is celebrated under the name of Theano. She became the wife of Pythagoras and she gave him, in addition to two sons, Telauges and Mamereus, a daughter named after her mother, whom those who write things sometimes confuse with her.

The nineteen sailed toward the setting sun. The stories of Gillos and other reports made them consider Magna Graecia as the region most suitable to their design.

In vast Hesperia, the cities were volcanoes growling under a layer of snow. Everywhere, under the icy heaviness of despotic government, the people, obscurely as yet, were beginning to agitate.

The companions of Pythagoras lived for a short time in Croton. They spoke to all those they met, explaining ardently what they wanted to realize. Many laughed at their words; others drew away without saying anything; several insulted them, and children threw stones at them.

But the physician Alcmeon, having heard Pythagoras, came to him with these words: "Twenty stadia from the city I possess an estate and a dwelling too large for me. Will you permit me to give them to you?"

"I will accept them," the master replied, "if it is your heart and your mind that are speaking to me."

"It is my heart that is speaking to you, and I love what you are doing. It is my mind that is speaking to you, O healer of evils with which men charge themselves by virtue of their folly."

"I do not want your gesture to be the son of an error. My remedy will act slowly, and I do not know when the generation that I might perhaps cure will be born."

"If I did not fear that my second present might spoil the first," said Alcmeon, "I would say to you: And me, do you want me?"

---

lap between that list and this one is very limited and Ryner is unlikely to have had that source available to him.

"Your second present is a myriad times more precious to me than the first."

Alcmeon took the nineteen to the portal of his domain. He had brought paint and a brush. He wrote over the entrance:

EVERYTHING IS COMMON BETWEEN FRIENDS

Then he went in, in the midst of the disciples.

The slaves who worked the terrain came running. The new Pythagorean said to them:

"Listen, not so much with your ears as with your hearts. Those among you who want to be my brothers as all men are my brothers, let them go freely go wherever they please. But if there are any among you who desire to be dearer to me than the sons of my father and my mother, who desire to penetrate my heart as profoundly as the other sons of Pythagoras, those should stay here, free and our equals."

The slaves cried that they would never abandon such a good master. As their acclamations were prolonged, Pythagoras obtained silence with a gesture of his hand and he said:

"The error that passes by is as noisy as a torrent, but the durable truth makes heard a murmur of a spring."

All the slaves remained for a few days. Soon, quarrels rose up among them. Pythagoras and Alcmeon appeased them with gentle and slightly ironic words. But each slave believed that his adversary had done him great wrong, and was irritated that the injustice went unpunished. In a short time, the majority went away.

Pythagoras said to them:

"The dream of your long servitude was the life of the ordinary free man, not the existence of the philosopher. Go and live your ideal."

Three of Alcmeon's former slaves still remained, however, and they were the best of disciples; their names were Meron, Mnesagorus and Aristoxenus.[47]

In the community, everyone lived freely, working the hours that suited him, taking what he wanted from the common wealth. But all strove actively to love their brothers and to be detached from the vulgar appeal of property.

Their common love for Pythagoras was the strongest of bonds. They asked him for advice, they attempted to resemble him. Their effort toward a common ideal rapidly established customs that made strangers imagine a severe written rule.

The "friends" were clad in white tunics retained by a linen cord. They avoided the cruel use of leather and abstained from all meat. They did not drink wine and did not cut their hair.

In the morning, they ate bread and honey; the evening meal consisted of fruits or boiled vegetables. Before going to bed, they sang hymns.

Their hands were pure of blood, and, as that which is to the right is the symbol of good and that to the left is the symbol of evil, they avoided crossing the left leg over the right.

They gladly received among them young men who wanted to live without stain, but Pythagoras said to them:

"Be silent for a long time. A young man is a vase and his speech the sonorous lid with which he closes himself; but his silence is the opening by which that with nourishes the seed of his soul penetrates."

He also said:

---

[47] These names are fictitious, but it is undoubtedly not a mere coincidence that it was from a later Aristoxenus, a pupil of Aristotle, that much information is derived about the later history of the Pythagoreans, including the story of the burning of the brotherhood's house by a mob instigated by Cylon, although Ryner only takes a few details from that account in order to built his much more elaborate and imaginative narrative of the community and its fate.

"The seed will become the tree, provided that it plunges into the subterranean darkness; the child will become the man in the pensive warmth of silence. The oak is the son of the acorn and of the earth; become the son of the unknown seed that you bear within you and become a son of silence."

Those who were not made for the noble and calm life did not take long to become bored in the calm and noble atmosphere; they went away of their own accord. The others were authorized to bring their property to the community when they had been subject to five years of "silence." As it was necessary to protect themselves against the stupid hatred of the people and accusations of impiety, none was admitted to the free conversations of the elders until he had been subjected to proofs and initiations.

The solemn initiations conserved the form of the mysteries taught at Eleusis, but the words were fuller and easier to understand. After two years, a candidate was admitted to the first initiation; it was necessary, before obtaining the second, to let a further three years go by.

The two years were called "the Great Silence," the three years were called "the Little Silence." However, the absolute repose and what was called "the purification of the voice" only lasted a month. Afterwards, under the conduct of an elder, the young man read aloud. With his eyes closed, he repeated without exterior sound the things read and the commentaries of the master, and he studied the stir produced in him by the new knowledge and the new doubts.

If it happened that a novice spoke in spite of the advice, no one was astonished and no one criticized him. Silence was an absolute name that designated something relative. It was the passive name of the internal activity. Pythagoras sometimes defined it as "the body of meditation."

The man who was forming himself under the warm wings of the Great Silence was recommended never to ask any question. Sometimes, however, during the readings, the imitations or the lessons of the elders, a surprise extracted some exclamation or interrogation from him, akin to the reactive movement that one makes involuntarily before encountering an impact. He obtained no response, but was not criticized; it seemed that no one had heard him.

"In the beginning," Pythagoras said, "do not interrogate either men or nature. Be the vase that collects the waters and is not agitated, for fear of its contents being spilled. One does not confide to tottering infants the care of carrying the vases one fills."

He also affirmed:

"It requires more science than you possess in order to interrogate appropriately. The maladroit question of the ignorant man dictates the response. Instead of being the warm breath that will make one flower more bloom on the rose-bush of science, it is the awkward gesture that breaks a branch."

During the two years of the Great Silence, you studied in addition to your own heart and mind, numbers, the heart of things, figures, the gnomon and sounds, with their intervals and harmonies. You did not write, in order that your memory obtained strength like a child who exercises, and in order that your memory became as faithful as a spouse.

During the three years of the Little Silence, you looked at visible things, you learned what number is the soul of each of them, you understood how figures are numbers, you saw all movements drawing away and approaching according to the intervals of musical sounds; your eyes became ears that heard at a greater distance; your mind became an ear that enjoyed the total harmony of the universe. You were knowledgeable enough to ask questions usefully; your sure memory permitted you to write without doing yourself any harm.

However, you still remained too ignorant and too anxious to speak anywhere other than to the masters; and you never said words that affirmed, but expressed, quivering with dread and hope, the uncertainties that the words of books and the ancients had caused to vacillate in your soul.

Already you were initiated into the Petty Mysteries, and as first light marches toward sunrise, you were marching toward the clarity of the Great Mysteries.

At your first initiation you had heard Gillos, the hierophant and Lysis the dadoukhos, but at the final initiation you heard, along with the dadoukhos Lysis, the hierophant Pythagoras.

On emerging from the Great Mysteries you sang, with the other initiates, the hymn of combat and hope:

"When spring replaces winter, when the orgiastic season has come, Zagreus, who is heart, will liberate hearts; Zeus and the tyrants will be dethroned; Zeus and his laws will be abolished.

"Zagreus will reign, not as tyrant, not as law, but as liberty. Order will no longer come from outside, constraint and conflict; it will spring forth alive, the flower of harmony and love. You will change without effort, and change will no longer summon death. You will look into yourself and ahead of you without fear, and you will see nothing but light; but you will not turn around to look behind you.

"Die, Zeus, and live, Zagreus! Zeus, oppressive law and heavy royalty, your order, hindrance and servitude, encloses life in pain and ugliness. But you, Zagreus, is your order not delight in life that bursts forth radiant? Zeus, vast forehead and furrowed brow; Zeus, implacable as your master Destiny; it is from outside that you govern things while wounding them, wounded yourself, and governed yourself from outside. But you, Zagreus, beating heart, laughing mouth, future heart of things and beings, you govern from within and are not governed. You will confound yourself with things and with beings, O victorious heart of Zeus and Destiny.

"Death to Zeus! Everywhere that there is god, he aspires to die. Death to Zeus, who wants to die in order to become Life! Death to Zeus, who wants to die in order to have a heart!

"O Zagreus-bull, O sun of spring, you who release the earth, you who release hearts! Man, be Zagreus, in order that Zagreus may live. Be similar to God, to God who is not yet. God is not yet, for the perfect is not at the beginning; the tree will emerge from the seed.

"Whoever you are, you are not yet. Liberate yourself, liberate yourself. Spring forth from the ground, plant; spring forth from the beast, man. Whoever you are, be similar to the Liberator who is not yet, but is seeking to liberate himself in order to liberate all things. Do not live according to the law you read or hear; live according to the law that is within you. More profoundly, search more profoundly. Do not listen to your mind; it sees things from without. Listen to your heart; it knows everything; it is everything. Live according to your heart. March to the rhythm of your heart.

"Zagreus is the god who forms himself around a heart. Be, around a heart, a man who forms himself. Man, no longer be a child; man, reject the swaddling clothes with which your heart has been surrounded.

"No, Zagreus is not a god around a heart. He is a Heart that radiates a god. You, be a heart that radiates a man."

The success of Pythagorism: the lightning that illuminates the sky with a single quiver. Every day, numerous young men came to ask for admission. The house of Alcmeon was a narrow nest for so many amours. Throughout Magna Graecia, and throughout Sicily, colonies grew, trees populated with wings and songs, whose shade and music summoned people.

The Son of Silence enclosed himself for months in solitude, not seeing anyone, not pronouncing a word, enveloped in his dreams and his research. His vast hypotheses led him to precise discoveries, but every discovery was an impulsion toward even vaster hypotheses.

For a long time he observed the morning star and the evening star. He eventually realized that they were not two but only one. In a great assembly of disciples he imparted the new truth. His heart and his mind were the flame and the light sprung from the same sun. By the bonds of gold and analogy he attached together what he knew and what he wanted.

"Evening and morning," he proclaimed, "identical light. When I look at the sky or when I look at a man, I sing: O evening and morning, O birth and death, eternal balance around an immutable center, different masks over a face that does not change! Behind the visible sky, beyond space, beyond time, I look at God; and I say: O good and evil, O pure and impure, united in the monad. Each of you, in order to purify himself and realize himself, detaches and realizes his opposite. O good, by the mere fact of being born, you give birth to evil, your twin brother. Uneven, when with perfect wings, you fly toward the Orient, you cause to spring from the same nest the heavy and ugly wings that the Even drags toward the Occident. God and Evil, Life and Death, Finite and Infinite, I know the marvelous country where divine knots enchain you; I also know the banal region where you are separated, contrary and necessitated one by the other, equilibrium of love and hate.

"But do not believe, my beloved sons, that your actions, your words and your thoughts remain indifferent. Yes, there is a place beyond good and evil, but we do not inhabit that peaceful place, and each of us is a battlefield. Good and Evil, identical and different, identical in substance, different in rhythm. O God, your name is harmony. O Evil, you are called Discord. Be musicians, my sons.

"It is a lack of art, my beloved, that does evil even with good. Never marry the uneven with the uneven; you will recoil in horror before the even their brother. Do not confide your lyre to the ignorant; your lyre will wound your ear and perhaps the strings will be broken. Lend your lyre to the man who knows better than you and listen to the sounds he draws from it, and watch the movement of his hands.

"But do you know what I mean by your lyre? It is your heart that I mean by your lyre.

"It is an art, my sons, that sometimes achieves good even with evil. Learn how you can add your unity to the even, and you will love the uneven, your son.

"O identical evening and morning, orient and occident; O sky! O birth and death, two blossomings: human being! O good and evil inextricably entangled and mixed, O caduceus: O Monad! O evil that proclaims yourself god, O constraint that takes the name of order, organization of violence that you believe to be law: O Zeus! But you, fully emerged from dolor, uneven produced by the heart that adds to the abominable even, harmony, liberty, O Zagreus! I look at you, Zeus, evening star, messenger of darkness, and I smile, and I salute you, and I say: In a few hours, will you not be Zagreus, messenger of light?"

After periods of solitude and powerful interior life, Pythagoras traveled from one to another house of Friends. He informed the most advanced of what he had just discovered; he examined and interrogated the novices; he presided over initiations. His activity was such and legend was so easily born around him that people glorified him with the power to be in several places at once. Had not the disciples of Metapontum, which is in Italy, and the disciples of Tauremenium, which is in Sicily, seen and touched him on the same day, at the same hour?

He did not only rejoice in his direct work, communities that were multiplying, agitating their appeals of light on the summits of justice and amour. He was also glad, albeit not without some mixture of anxiety, of the radiation of his work. Everywhere, people crushed by tyrants were rising against them. And the enemies of tyrants, whether or not they had heard Pythagoras, acclaimed him as the Master, declaring themselves to be Pythagorists. In Croton, those friends of liberty ended up comprising the entire people. When the tyrant gave an order, those who had once gloried in being his guards or servants were content to laugh. Without a drop of blood being shed, the frightened tyrant fled.

Thus, Milo, the most powerful of athletes, came with the principal citizens to ask Pythagoras for laws.

The Son of Silence replied: "Tomorrow, assemble the people on the agora. At the fourth hour I will come, and I will speak to the people.

The agora had never contained such a crowd. The sick were carried to the square. The news having spread far and wide, no one knew how, people had walked all night in order to come to hear Pythagoras.

The agora: a vase full of water, agitated and overflowing. Perhaps wisdom can move the vulgar, then? Can it be true that the music of sages attracts and appeases wild animals and gives wings to the inertia of stones? No, strength alone excites peoples; but about strength, as about all things, the people have infantile ideas. To the majority of those who were there, Pythagoras appeared as a Milo infinitely more redoubtable, his speech an energy of the same nature as the athlete's muscles, and which exercised, multiplied, the same power of things devoid of ears.

In conversations, the two names were mingled strangely.

"Milo can carry an ox on his shoulders, but in Tarentum, a word spoken by Pythagoras chased away a bull spoiling a field of beans."

"Milo can wrestle a bar, and choke it in his arms, but in Daunia, Pythagoras changed a monstrously malevolent bear into a gentle being. The bear became a disciple. Now it lives in the woods, nourishing itself on fruits and honey, and it is careful not to beak a branch or crush a bee. The squirrels and the birds know it and come to play with it every day as with a big brother."

"Milo's arms cannot stop an eagle in mid-air; a word from Pythagoras has stopped an eagle in mid-air."

"What could Milo do, surrounded by serpents? One day, Pythagoras found himself in a grotto where vipers and asps were sliding and hissing in thousands. One powerful word, which the priests of Chaldea taught him, killed all the snakes."

"Milo can swim across the widest rivers, but the River Nessus greeted Pythagoras by name and said to him: 'Master, walk where you will; beneath your foot my waves will be as solid as a rock.'"

"Milo is as strong as Heracles, and his beauty, like that of Heracles, frightens enemies. But the word of Pythagoras is as powerful as Hermes or the bow of Apollo, and he is also as handsome as Apollo."

"He is Apollo himself, come from the hyperborean regions."

"That is a sacrilegious lie. Pythagoras is not one of the great gods; he is one of the powerful daemons that ordinarily inhabit the moon."

"He is more than a daemon. He's an Olympian god, perhaps Dionysus, or perhaps Hermes. He has made himself human for a few years. He will reform the mores of people, spread light and salvation over the earth, and then he will disappear, and no one will know what has become of him.

"I don't know what he is, but this is what I know: he has predicted earthquakes with exactitude, eclipses of the sun and moon. He stopped a plague that was desolating the cities of Phrygia. A word from him is sufficient to calm the winds, to deflect hail and appease the waves."

"Don't boast before me, for you know very little. Pythagoras has done myriads of truly divine things and far more marvelous than those of which you speak."

"Listen. He has a golden thigh. Several disciples have seen it, and before them, all the Greeks assembled for the Olympic games."

"This is what I have seen with my own eyes. He changed boiled beans into blood. With that blood he traced magical characters on a convex mirror. He turned the mirror, thus prepared, toward the moon, and he read on the moon what was happening at that moment in all the countries of the world. After that he read the future."

Over the entire agora, such rumors were being exchanged. Toward the tribune of speeches, still empty, but where expectation and hope were already looming like a dominating statue, praise rose up, as the sea rises toward the invisible moon, and the praise made a rumor similar to the round of the rising tide.

He appeared, and there was suddenly a yawning silence. Eyes admired his beauty, ears yearned for his speech.

He began:

"Men of Croton, I will speak to you with love. For every old man is a father to me, every man of my own age is my brother, every child is my son. But you, women, I will speak to you with a more profound emotion. The old man is venerable who has seen many things and suffered numerous evils. But his wife, what has she not seen, leaning over her children; what has she not suffered by virtue of their dolors and the imprudence of their joys? The man of my age is a friend to me and a brother; he has encountered the same events as me; he has been subject to the same shocks and the same emotions. Zeus weighs a common yoke upon all the necks of each generation. But the woman of my age has seen events with several pairs of eyes, she has felt them with several hearts dilated by the same hopes, contracted by the same fears. The child excites my compassion, for whom we must labor to construct the house of justice. But the little girl excites my compassion multiply, who will enjoy our work realized multiply, through her brothers, her husband and her sons, or suffer from our failure. O woman, in being all those whom you love, you are many, and you live the sufferings and joys of several existences."

They listened with an emotional astonishment to these words, so different from voices heard previously. A benediction of light descended from the tribune of speeches where furious tempests had previously formed, amid the rage and thunder of cries; where lies had previously accumulated, and the clouds from which, in collision, lightning had sprung.

"Listen with love to one who speaks to you with love. Love me, in order that I can do good to you. If you hate me or fear me, if you believe me to be the possessor of a power other than your power, capable of fighting against you and capable of commanding you, I can no longer do anything for you. Perhaps you would obey me, trembling, but then, why would you have expelled the tyrant? You might ask me for laws; but then, why would you have expelled the tyrant?"

There was, in the great silence, a suspension of amazement.

"I sense that my words astonish you, men of Croton. You are accustomed to opposing the tyrant and the law. But I say this to you: What is a tyrant but the law made man? What is the law but the tyrant made writing? If I cannot go where I want, what does it matter whether I am retained by hands or by chains?"

The astonishment became restless. Many made an effort not to cry out. A single word from one of the listeners and all would have unleashed themselves in speech and there would have been the war of voices that often precedes the brawl of fists.

Pythagoras understood the danger. The philosopher's forceful gesture quelled the cries before they emerged and the silence became heavy. But immediately, his lips and eyes, and even his hands, were like a vast smile. All of Pythagoras appeared to be saying: *Don't speak. There's no need. What you're going to say, I'll say myself.*

Meanwhile, the noble voice resumed, with a penetrating softness:

"You are right, men of Croton, in whom attitude sings a hymn to law. Nothing is finer, nothing is more profound than the law, and the man who names it liberty is perhaps pronouncing the most glorious of the names that the law can bear. Hear, then, why I speak well of the law, and why I speak ill of the law."

The agora was an immense standing curiosity, a vast living silence

"The laws that I sing are more ancient than men, or as ancient as men, and that is why men have no need to write laws. You have no need to write on a stone tablet: *When a stone is thrown into the air, I order it to fall, and if it does not fall, soldiers will break it.* You have no need to write: *When I confide a seed to the earth, I order that it fructify.* Nor have you any need to write: *When men live together, I order that they live in accordance with justice and love.* Does everyone not feel justice inside him, and does not everyone feel love inside him?

172

"But the laws that you write fix the rules of justice, and by that token, they kill love. You become accustomed to applying the letter of the written law, which deforms and impoverishes what the gods desire to sing in your heart. And the written law is a blind entity that is ignorant of many things, but your heart is knowledgeable. And the written law is one, but life is multiple, with the consequence that the written law harms life.

"Mother, if one of your twin children is taller than the other, do you take a knife in order to cut him down to the same size as the other? That is what the written law does.

"Men, who is it that writes the law? It is men. They do not know the future, and they pretend to regulate the future. Men, let us strive to know the present and live in the present. When the future comes, we shall live in it. You do not say in advance: *Every year, the harvest will be made on this particular day.* You watch the wheat and you harvest it when it is ripe. Do you think you know better what will happen in hearts than what will happen in the earth?

"Men, there are unwritten laws that the earth obeys, and the wheat, and hearts. Strive to discover them. Do not write them with the design of forcing hearts or the earth to follow them. What you write is perhaps not entirely true. And if you call what you write law, what will you then call Law? Do not write laws, if you respect the Law.

"Man, when you write laws, you offend the gods. You invade the domain of the gods in saying: *This domain is mine.* When you do that, the gods avenge themselves.

"Man, you leave the wheat to develop freely. Leave your heart and its gestures to develop freely.

"Man, the laws of the gods and nature are the same thing. But the laws that you write and nature are two different things. That is why the laws you write are bad, enemies of the gods and you.

"Man, do not write laws, in order that you can obey the gods."

Priests, grouped toward the center of the agora, approved loudly. They clapped their hands and they cried: "Men, listen to Pythagoras. Pythagoras is Apollo himself come from the land of the Hyperboreans to teach you the truth."

As a fire spreads and burns all the fuel around it, a unanimous clamor invaded the whole square. The crowd crackled, all aflame: "Glory to Pythagoras-Apollo."

But the philosopher raised both hands in a gesture of protest and refusal, and as soon as silence was reestablished he cried:

"My friends, you do not love me yet as I want you to love me, in order that I can do you good. Pythagoras is not a god. Pythagoras is a man. It is good to be a man."

Then, he took up the thread of his discourse:

"My friends, if you write laws, you will have judges, and the judges will be tyrants.

"My friends, there is no need to write the laws of the gods touching men and justice. Do not ask some among you to fabricate them and to have them observed. But it is necessary that everyone, in every circumstance, interrogates his heart and that he does what Love tells him to do. Do not listen to foreign words touching the laws of justice.

"But can I understand the laws of pity differently? What the gods want me to do to honor them, do they not tell me that also? Are the gods impotent to speak to me without mouths and without noise? It is an impiety to believe the gods to be impotent; what they want to say to me, they are able to say to me, without summoning a priest to aid them. The gods want my heart to be pure and not for me to offer numerous sacrifices. The gods want me to listen to my heart, and not for me to listen to priests.

"Until now you have had laws, judges and priests, and you have been unhappy. See how we live in the house of Friends; see how people live in all the communities of those who listen to me for an hour and listen to their hearts all their lives. There is no written law, there are no judges, there are no priests, and we are happy.

"Let there no longer be among you, then, either written laws or judges. And if the priests continue to make sacrifices according to the rites, let the priests do so, but do not forget that the gods love pure hearts, not sacrifices. A pure heart, whether it beats in the breast of a priest or not, hears the word of the gods; but an impure heart, whether it is rotting in the breast of a priest or not, is ignorant of the word of the gods.

"When you were a child, you saw men sow seed in the ground; and then you saw them harvest more than they had sown. Having grown up, you wanted wheat, and you did as your forefathers had done.

"Look therefore at how we sow justice and love and how we harvest happiness. If you want the same crop, sow the same seeds.

"Look. There was a house with a master and slaves. Now there is a house of Friends. There was a city with a tyrant and subjects; make it a city of Friends.

"Look. In the house of Friends there are not several masters instead of one; there are no judges and no priests. In the city of Friends, let there not be several masters instead of one. Do not have judges, and do not permit priests to become masters."

Slowly, through the people who pressed toward him in order to embrace him, to shake his hands or touch his garments, Pythagoras returned to the house of Friends. And all day long, in Croton, people repeated his words:

"Let us not write laws; let us not appoint magistrates; let us close our ears to the words of priests. I will make my heart pure, and it will speak to me better than the priest. If, one day, I hear its voice poorly, I will go and interrogate Pythagoras. Thus, instead of the sentence of a judge or the order of a priest, I will hear the counsel of a man who loves me."

In the house of Friends, the poet Lysis, the most loving and most beloved of disciples was waiting for Pythagoras.

"Master, my heart is overflowing, and I have so many things to tell you."

175

"Speak then, my son."

"The poem in which I am attempting to put your thought, I finished this morning on the road to Croton. I would like to sing it to you."

"I am listening with my ears and with my heart."

"O Master, O Pythagoras, O you who my thought names Golden-Thigh...."

The philosopher was saddened. "If Lysis speaks like the people, then who will understand me?"

"O Master, the amphora that the people carry and the amphora that I carry are similar, but perhaps they do not contain the same wine. Listen. When I saw you for the first time, on the day that my silence calls the day of my birth, it was in Olympia, and I had arrived from Eleusis. I bore within me coffers that I did not know how to open, the discourse of the hierophant and the mute spectacle of the mysteries.

"You spoke. You believed that you were only speaking about justice, but the words of others contain less than they believe and your words contain more than you believe. While you were speaking, the coffers opened in a dream of light to show me treasures and marvels. But that light was fleeing lightning, not durable sunlight. The coffers and the darkness closed inexorably, and my impoverished eyes retained a regret rather than a memory.

"The treasures that were in me, you alone, I understood, could give me. That is why I followed you; that is why I have loved you with hope, and I love you with gratitude.

"Now, that first day, while I gazed at you and while I listened to you, my thought was a confused emotion, a joyous intoxication and a dancing chorus. I thought about the vulgar Dionysus who, after the death of Semele, Zeus, a strange mother, carried in his thigh. I also thought about the Dionysus of the mysteries, the child folded in the pure human heart, who will one day surge forth in the triumph of justice and love. I thought about his reign, the golden age that the lying poets have placed in the past, but which our hopes and our desires create in the future. That future, more that all other men combined, you bore within you. A ray of sunlight that played, like living gold, over your right thigh, came to mingle with the golden dance of my thoughts. To revive by a single word the multiple emotion of that moment, Master, my silence often calls you Pythagoras of the golden thigh."

"I desire to hear your poem, not the praises of a pious son who sees his father more handsome than a man."

"O Golden-Thigh, do you think that my poem does not direct any praise toward you? Do you think that one can speak the truth without naming it Pythagoras, of justice without naming it Pythagoras, of love without naming it Pythagoras?"

Then, without leaving time for a criticism, the malicious Lysis made his lyre resonate, and his voice rose:

"I sing the truth that Pythagoras, the greatest of men, taught me. And I sing Pythagoras, who taught me the truth.

"Hermes, among his sons, loved Aethalides particularly. He promised to grant him his desire, no matter what it might be, provided that the child did not ask for immortality.

"Aethalides replied: 'O my father, allow me to remember everything that will happen to me henceforth.'

"A long time after the death of Aethalides, there was Euphorbus; and Euphorbus remembered having been Aethalides.

"A long time after the death of Euphorbus, there was Hermotimus who came to Branchide, to the temple of Apollo. And Hermotimus recognized the buckler that Menelaus, on his return from Troy, has suspended in the presence of Euphorbus.

"A long time after the death of Hermotimus, there was Pyrrhus, a fisherman of Delos. And Pyrrhus remembered having been Hermotimus.

"A long time after the death of Pyrrhus, the fisherman of Delos, there was Pythagoras. And Pythagoras, the greatest of men, remembered having been Aethalides, Euphorbus, Hermotimus and Pyrrhus."[48]

---

[48] This account of previous incarnations claimed by Pythagoras is based on an assertion made by Diogenes Laertius, who

"What does that tale signify?" asked the Son of Silence, anxiously.

"Master," said Lysis, blushing, "it is a symbol from which the song of metempsychosis such as you teach it."

"It's necessary, then, before verses in which the truth is enveloped by lies, to sing lines that advertise how the words are lies and how the words are true?"

"Master, it's difficult...."

"Give it to me, that I might try."

And, taking the lyre from his disciple's hand, Pythagoras improvised this song:

"Man, if you have need of water or your house, you transport it in a vase. Thus the poet, to bring you the fluid truth, encloses it with the ingenious precision of his lies. Man who is thirsty, learn where the water is found, and where the truth is found.

"The vase is alabaster. Its color is a song of freshness and limpidity However, the vase of limpid freshness is not the water for which you are thirsty.

"On the alabaster vase the ingenious artist has sculpted a river; and the river flows before your eyes, but it does not flow into your mouth and toward your thirst.

"In a wild dance, the artist has strung light nymphs around the vase in order that they give you water, but open the vase, and you will drink."

---

claimed to be quoting Heraclides of Pontus. Nothing is known about Diogenes Laertius except that a collection of the lives and opinions of the Greek philosophers attributed to him has survived, but he probably lived in the third century A.D. and his account of Pythagoras might well have been roughly contemporary with Porphyry's. Heraclides of Pontus lived in the fourth century B.C., and is nowadays remembered as an important advocate of the thesis that the earth rotates on its axis every 24 hours, thus causing the apparent motion of the heavens, but none of his writings survive and everything known about him is hearsay.

"O Master, I shall inscribe those verses before mine. By virtue of those verses, my poem will be worth something."

The Pythagoras of the poem, the one who remembered having been Aethalides, Euphorbus, Hermotimus and Pyrrhus, sang his successive lives. Then came a beautiful metaphysical surge:

"Man, listen to the sentence of necessity, the ancient decree of the gods, the eternal pact sealed by vast oaths: when a daemon, one of the beings destined to immortal life has soiled his body by the error of his soul; when led stray by evil, he has committed a perjury, it is necessary that for three myriad years he wanders far from the blissful, animated one after another by all kinds of perishable beings and traveling the changing routes of a painful existence. The air chases him into the waves of the sea, the sea casts him up on the earth, the earth hurls him into the rays of the indefatigable sun, which precipitates him once again into the turbulence of the air. Each element expels him toward another, for he is an object of scorn and hatred for them all.

"Man, you and I are of those exiles wandering far from God, because we have listened to furious Discord, because we have loved the Many, because we have wanted, proudly, to make ourselves a closed life; now, instead of remaining the happy wave in the unfathomable Ocean, we have become the isolated drop on the sand, which is drying out."

After the song of Metempsychosis, after the marvelous voyages in a thousand animal and human existences, Pythagoras, a new Orpheus, descended into the Underworld. He saw the tortures of the wicked there. The poets who have lied about the gods were subjected to harsh punishments. Hesiod was grinding his teeth, attached to a column; Homer was hanging from a tree, surrounded by serpents.

"What position will you inflict on Lysis?" asked Pythagoras, smiling.

But the poet, with the lightest and most youthful of laughter, relied: "Prudently, I have made you descend into the

Underworld before my death. Thus, posterity will not know the torture of Lysis."

The Pythagoras of the poem encountered Chthonian Dionysus, who taught him the salutary truths. In order that men would have confidence, the god touched the philosopher's right thigh, and he returned to the surface with a golden thigh.

Golden-Thigh went to the Olympic games, and before the assembled Greeks he said:

"I will sing the double law of things. Sometimes many form One, sometimes One is divided into many. Double is the birth of mortal beings, double their disappearance. By the dispersion of elements, forms weaken and dissipate; but the elements only divorce for new unions, and birth is always mingled with destruction. The circle is closed and that vicissitude never ends. Sometimes Love brings elements into Unity, sometimes the hateful action of Discord separates them and takes them in different directions. Because the multiple gives birth to the one, because the one is resolved in its turn into the multiple, beings are born and die, and no form can endure. But because the wheel turns without ever stopping, beings subsist, as fleeting forms, eternal substance, in the indissoluble circle.

"I shall sing now of the gods emerged from the rich monad, whose effort reconstitutes and maintains, with difficulty, a poor unity."

The poem described the generations of the gods such as Pythagorean initiation taught them. Then while the lyre resonated with a more enthusiastic force:

"Man, hear my two words. Man, imitate God. Man, perfection is not at the beginning, and it is necessary that you understand my second word in order that my first word should not be a lie to you.

"For God was Uranus, space without limit and chaos without form. Then there was no number.

"And you, child, were you not incoherence and chaos?

"For God was Cronus, time that only creates to destroy. Then there was number, which cannot be counted, number that flees the more one searches for it.

"Remember: you were the passage of myriads of thoughts that destroyed one another, a river that made wave after wave.

"For God is Zeus, law that governs the world. And there was Zeus and there was the world. There was the dyad. There was number that can be counted. Zeus commands and the world obeys. The world is a well-built house; Zeus is the house.

"Silence. Be quiet. Listen. Hear. When what you are told seems true, obey. When the stone that is placed on another stone is in equilibrium, let the mason work who wants you to grow, O commencement of a house. Be the palace that allows itself to be built.

"Until now I have been singing in a loud voice, in order to be understood by all. Now, initiate, listen to my whisper. Listen not only with your ears but with your mind, which knows the surface of the secret, with your heart, which must divine the profound secret.

"God, who was Uranus, who was Cronus, who is Zeus, will be Zagreus, heart of the world, heart that blossoms in the world. Then the world will find its law in itself and it will destroy the law from outside. And there will, in fact, no longer be any outside. Everything will be interior. The world will be a living being. God will be its life. There will be the number that creates itself and unfurls over itself. There will be the Monad. There will be the Even-Uneven. Initiate, you feel strong enough. Cause all the voices from outside to fall silent. Overthrow Zeus from the throne that he has erected within you, set aside everything that is not your heart. Radiate around you from your liberated house and fold yourself up to brood your heart. The living being that you ought to be will emerge from it, one by virtue of life, multiple by virtue of the actions of life; you will be the sacred number, simultaneously one and many, even and uneven, which creates itself and unfurls within itself."

Thus the poem of Lysis ended in a vast and supple conclusion in which the wisdom that knows and the wisdom that wants were mingled like the serpents of the caduceus. For the poet was not anxious about completing his fable. When the water was drunk, what did the vase matter, and the sculpted river, and the dancing nymphs?

The Son of Silence had heard the end of the poem, when disciples arrived and said to him:

"Master, there is often disorder in the House of Friends. A rule that everyone knows and that could be reread if necessary would remedy that evil. Write the rule, therefore, in order that we many obey it piously."

Pythagoras could not suppress a gesture of astonishment. Nevertheless, he expressed his thought immediately.

"Since you wish it," he said, "announce to all the Friends that tomorrow, at the fourth hour, I will read the rule."

The disciples retired, satisfied, and Lysis went with them. But one young man remained, who had come from Croton a few days before. His name was Cylon.

"Master," he said, impetuously. "I would like it if the justice you honor with your words were also honored by our actions."

"I am the friend of justice and not the just. Tell me, then, in what I have failed, in order that I can correct myself and you will become my benefactor."

"I am not similar to the others that are here, but until today you have committed the fault of treating me like the others. You do not know, however, that I possess immense wealth. If I employed it to create partisans I could, in a few years, become the tyrant of Croton. I am therefore sacrificing great things."

"I congratulate you, for you are sacrificing a great misfortune."

Cylon made a movement of amazement. Nevertheless, he went on: "It matters little to me by what names things are called. Let us call misfortune, if you wish, the tyranny that I am renouncing. But you will confess that it is not a misfortune devoid of glory. That splendid misfortune I love like a troop of beautiful courtesans. It would be cowardly to exchange it for a vulgar happiness. I am setting aside myriads of joys that would come to me in supplication, and yet I am choosing a single joy that I am espousing forever. It is, at least, appropriate that my bride should be beautiful."

"There is no vulgar happiness," said Pythagoras.

"The other Friends give little; I shall give a great deal. You are insulting me if you treat me like the others. Let them be subject to your conditions; I have the right to make my own. I demand that Gillos initiate me at the next initiation, and that I know the Great Mysteries a few months thereafter. What I ask, remark, Master, is not only necessary to my glory but to my heart, which loves you. I am in haste to bring you all my wealth—to wit, a third of the houses in Croton and a quarter of the fields surrounding the city—in order that we can forge together irresistible means of conquest."

"O my son, each of your words is a soiling. You are inferior to all the others, and long proofs will be necessary to raise you to their level. Your bath in the great silence will last three years instead of two."

"I am not patient and I do not like to be mocked."

"For myself, I am patient, and I am not accustomed to mock. If the physician who touches your burning skin says that you have a fever, he is not mocking. If you cry: *I am hungry*, but he, for your salvation, orders you to diet, you would be a poor fool if you said: *That man is mocking me*, and became irritated against him."

"I am irritated against whoever does not want what I want."

"So are the insensates that are called tyrants."

"You know the sole conditions on which I will consent to stay. Refuse again and I shall leave immediately."

"I do not want to do you harm, and I do not know whether I will ever be able to do you good."

"You are scorning me—me, Cylon, the richest, and, if I wish to be, the most powerful of Crotonians. Adieu. You will soon find, imprudent, that you have made an enemy more powerful than you."

"Poor enemy of yourself, with what pity I love you."

Cylon drew away amid furious cries. His obsequies were celebrated that same day. That was the custom of the Friends every time someone abandoned the community to return to banal life. A statue crudely reproducing Cylon's features was laid in a coffin among myrtle, olive and black poplar leaves, and the whole was buried.

Then leaning over the freshly-moved earth, Pythagoras said:

"Ordinarily, O Deo, when we confide one of ours to you, we incline toward you as the sower inclines toward the furrow, and we know that the seed will live in your darkness, and then spring forth in the light to bar new fruits. Today, forgive us Deo; we are throwing into your bosom an empty husk, of which the beasts and the passions have eaten away the seed."

The next day, the disciples came to request the promised rule.

"Let each of you take his tablet," Pythagoras said, "and write." Then he dictated:

"The Rule is God.

"Rules are the enemies of the True and God.

"God is one. He is the fire, the hearth and the altar. The first shadow is called Two.

"Rules are the shadows of the Rule.

"One is the only virtue. Two is the first lie.

"Your heart is One. The rule that you read anywhere but in your heart is Two.

"If you say: 'I am doing this because I love,' you are One.

"If you say: 'I am doing this because it is written,' you are Two.

"Always say to yourself: 'I am doing this because I love,'

184

"Always say to your friend: "Do out of love for yourself the thing that will do you good.'

"Act in such a way that your friend will love you because he loves himself.

"When I speak, listen to your heart.

"When he looks at time, a man only sees behind him. The old man has passed where I am passing. The old man who loves wisdom has seen the road on which I am walking in reverse. The old man who does not love wisdom will always be blind.

"That which you have given without love, you no longer have, and the person to whom you have given it does not have it yet.

"The slave possesses nothing; the master possesses nothing. The man who is a friend possesses everything.

"The child does not obey his mother's word; the child obeys his mother's smile.

"But what is a mother's smile? It is a light coming from the child's heart. That is why the child is glad; he is obeying his heart.

"Always obey your heart.

"The great science is to love yourself. So long as you do not love others, you will not divine what it is to love oneself.

"Love all men who consent to be loved. Few men consent to be loved.

"A man is a house; the heart is the door; love is the key. Many men are plain rock and have no door.

"Seek the door on all sides; but do not remain with hands full of presents before rocks. Few houses expect your arrival.

"When you open a heart, be a light that enters.

"Imitate God. What does God do? He seeks. Where can God be sought? In all the beings to which he can gives himself.

"Be a music. Music is a mathematics that sings, loves and opens hearts.

"Be a mathematics. The mathematics that does not sing, which does not love and which does not open hearts is nothing but a shadow."

Only a few days had gone by since Pythagoras had cast that light and that flame toward his disciples who had asked for shadow and a rule when the Crotonians came to appeal to him.

"Master, disorder, quarrels and brawls are breaking out all over the city. Come, in order that you can appease the quarrels, the brawls and the disorder. Come in order that the people can tell you what is needed."

Pythagoras, therefore, went to the agora. Several disciples accompanied him. Among them were Charondas, who later gave laws to Catania, and Zaleucos, who later gave laws to Locri.[49]

When the philosopher arrived, Milo spoke on behalf of all the people.

"O Pythagoras, since we have had no law or magistrates, there is disorder in the city, quarrels and brawls."

"Are there more of them than when you had laws and magistrates?"

The rich cried: "There are many more of them."

The poor cried: "There are slightly fewer."

When the double clamor had died down. Milo went on:

"An unjust magistrate is to men what hail is to wheat. But is not a just magistrate to men what the sun that makes it ripen is to the wheat? We have expelled the unjust tyrant. We

---

[49] Charondas, who established laws in Catania in Sicily was said by some to have been a pupil of Pythagoras, although it is not known when he lived. Zaleucus, who allegedly drew up the Locrian Code, almost certainly lived much earlier, in the seventh century B.C. The two are, however, linked, in that a similar anecdote (which Ryner would undoubtedly have judged to be a parable) is told about them in which they killed themselves after violating one of their own laws.

want a just magistrate. We implore Pythagoras to be our master, in order that the justice of Pythagoras becomes the justice of Croton."

"Have I not given each of you a chief and a magistrate?"

"You have not given us either a chief or a magistrate."

"You did not hear me, then, when I said to each of you: 'Man, obey your heart.'"

"Be our master, in order to force us to obey that one."

"The man who obeys force is not obeying his heart. And the man who commands has forgotten the word of his heart.

"But all the people cried: "Long live Pythagoras, tyrant of Croton. We shall all obey Pythagoras."

"Pythagoras has only one order to give: 'Obey your heart.'"

But Milo said: "The acclamation of the people is not sufficient to your scruples. Very well; we shall vote according to the ancient laws—but not a single bean will fall anywhere but in our urn."

"The priests of Egypt," said Pythagoras, smiling, "have taught me to avoid beans. A bean is bad for the man who casts it, and bad for the man who receives it. If you are incapable of obeying your hearts, you will be unhappy with or without magistrates. But if you have magistrates, you will never be capable of obeying your hearts."

He explained these things, which are difficult for people to comprehend, at length. Finally, the people thought that they had understood and cried:

"Be content, O Pythagoras; we shall not have magistrates."

A soon as the philosopher had gone, however, they all cried to Milo: "We will obey you as if you were a magistrate. Act in order that there will be no more disorder in the city."

Now, the words of Pythagoras against laws and magistrates were not only difficult for the people. The majority of his disciples were troubled by not having any written rule and not having any leader in command.

Charondas of Catania and Zaleucus of Locri were among the number of the faint hearts. On the agora, as soon as Pythagoras had spoken about the beans, they had stopped listening to the Master's words. But they had reflected about the abstention from beans.

Charondas, who was later to give laws to Catania, said to himself: *It is necessary not to eat beans because beans weigh down the spirit. In any case, beans are impure and their name is infamous.*

But Zaleucos, who was later to give laws to Locri, thought: *Abstain from beans; that dictum is a symbol. Alone among all those that are sown, broad beans have no membrane that divides them. That is why they are the symbol of immediate and rectilinear generation. Their name serves to designate the souls of brutal desire that precipitate themselves avidly toward a new life, whatever it might be. But other souls name themselves bees; they only desire generation if the life offered by the Moirae permits being just. After they have accomplished on this earth works agreeable to the gods, they return joyfully to their first abode. For the bee returns gladly to the hive from which it departed, and loves justice, and is sober. That is why the priests call libations made with honey "sober."*

Since there are only those two kinds of souls, when Pythagoras curses beans, it is because he wants me to be a bee. I shall always obey him. I shall never precipitate myself blindly toward the objects of my desire but I shall make a tour of them while buzzing the praises of the gods. When the bee that I am finally penetrates into the flower, it will neither break it not wither it, but will collect the honey without doing the flower any harm.

Thus those two men of good will, but already blinded by the legislative folly, believed they were penetrating the thought of Pythagoras profoundly, and yet their subtle commentary took them a long way from the thought of Pythagoras. They were two streams, running toward a gulf. An obstacle stood up in their path. They murmured around the obstacle, and then deflected waters to the right and the left, which soon joined up again and continued to fall toward the abyss.

Some time after these things, several citizens of Sybaris, wanting to live free, rose up against Telys, the tyrant of their city. They were vanquished, and took refuge in Croton. Telys demanded them, with promising words and threats, but the Crotonians were not so cowardly as to surrender the fugitives. The tyrant therefore marched on Croton. Milo came out to meet him, vanquished him and returned with abundant booty.

Quarrels broke out on the subject of that booty. Milo and his friends wanted to sell it in order to buy land that would be common, and they hoped to make all wealth, gradually, common between the inhabitants of Croton. But many of the people, excited by Cylon, wanted the booty to be shared out immediately. Almost all the young men were with Cylon, for they hoped with their share to buy wine and courtesans.

Several times already, Milo's party and Cylon's party had come to blows.

One day, when Pythagoras and the majority of his disciples were in Milo's house. Cylon roused the people with money, promises, wine and violent words, and came with a large armed crowd to attack the house. Milo and his friends immediately barricaded the entrances; but Pythagoras said: "Let me talk to them."

He opened a window and, standing up, unarmed, presented himself to the furious mob. He spoke uplifting words. several among the nearest began to wake up and look upwards, and the majority of those who heard Pythagoras felt their malevolent courage declining, no longer knowing what to do. But Cylon, seeing these things, excited those who were too distant to hear the uplifting words, and they began to cry out and launch darts.

The arrows and spears, launched by drunken men who were too closely packed together, did not reach Pythagoras, and some became frightened because of the marvels that were reported with regard to his powerful magic.

An awkwardly fired arrow passed close to the philosopher, in an uncertain and oblique flight, and his rapid hand seized it. Then, showing it to the people, his voice dominating the clamors, he shouted:

"The man who loves does not send back the darts that are aimed at him, but he breaks them." And he broke the arrow.

Many were struck with amazement, and they said: "Not only do our arrows miss him, but if he wants an arrow for a symbol, one of our arrows flies meekly into his hand without doing him any harm."

And Pythagoras continued, before the hesitant people:

"Hatred," he proclaimed, "is a powerful shock. For the effect of the shock to continue and be transmitted, it is necessary that it always encounter hard and hateful objects. But I am the space empty of hatred that nullifies the hatred and the shock. Hatred is a great fire; it burns as long as it encounters obstacles that it consumes as fuel. But I am the empty space where the fire dies out."

Horrible triumphant laughter replied to him, and from all sides a cry went up as joyful and ignoble as a victory of soldiers.

"Let's see if the fire will go out!"

At four different points, Cylon and a few among the most malevolent had set fire to the house. The flames were already rising, agitated and howling like hateful follies.

The disciples shouted to Pythagoras: "Flee, beloved Master!"

But, turning toward them a loving smile as profound and as beautiful as the sky, he said: "I shall flee last."

Then all those who were in the house made haste to flee, some because they were afraid for themselves, the majority because they loved Pythagoras. They dared not do him any violence in order to drag him away with them, and made haste in order that he would not depart too late.

The Son of Silence looked to see which way his beloved were fleeing. They were all fleeing toward the Orient, across open country, in order to go back to Alcmeon's house. Having seen the direction of their flight, Pythagoras hastened toward the Occident, and he attracted all the effort of the enemies to him.

He was old, although vigorous. Clouds that encounter cold lose their light beauty and fall as rain. Several of his floating hopes had fallen that day, on encountering hateful and stupid vulgarity, and he did not know whether he wanted to live or if he wanted to die.

He fled in order to make the pursuit last, in order to give his friends the time to save themselves, in order that the drunkenness of the people would diminish and that a single murder would serve to dissipate it..

The hazard of his course took him to a field of broad beans. The enemy was approaching and he had no other passage for his flight but the field of beans. The memory came to Pythagoras of what he had said about beans some time before, and he smiled as he went into the field.

But he perceived an old woman who was beginning to gather them. She was poor, thin and utterly worn out.

"Oh, the poor woman," said the philosopher, in a low voice. "How she needs her meager beans."

He took pity on the field, which would have been devastated by the passage of the crowd. He took pity on the old woman, who would doubtless have been knocked down and trampled beneath the mad rush. And he thought that his friends were now out of danger.

He therefore stopped on the edge of the bean-field to wait death. His eyes turned toward the sky, his arms slightly raised and rounded like the arms of a lyre, he sang:

"O death, O vain appearance. Always the work of the Titans remains futile and their victory is a defeat. Always the living heart of Zagreus escapes them. And around the heart, life gathers again to recommence his springtime glory."

Turning toward the murderers he summoned them with these words:

"Come and change me into myself. Come and deliver from perishable heaviness that which is in me that is immortal."

Cylon arrived first. His sword transpierced the noble old man, who fell to the ground.

Pythagoras died holding out toward his assassin arms of pity and love. While his eyes closed forever, he said:

"I love you, Cylon, for the good you are doing me. I pity you, Cylon, for the harm that you are doing to yourself."

CYNIC PARABLES

Preface

The truth, a multiple cloud with capricious metamorpho-ses, is seen by the dogmatist as a system of blocks that his hands can seize. Floating lights and dancing shadows, the en-tire joyous flow, he imagines disposing in an immutable order and seating in a construction of eternity and necessity. To lis-ten to him, he has never left behind him the slightest disequi-librium, the slightest instability, but his mortar of logic binds together solid stones, on which disciples and successors may climb without danger, and build further.

Without difficulty, the critic shows one of the pretended stones that it is mist or void: a distant symbol of the intangible and ineffable Reality, or an unhealthy dream with the avid weight of the nightmare. The pretentious edifice does not even have sufficient consistency to crumble; no ruin encumbers the place where it was thought to stand and nothing hinders any attempt to construct successive monuments there; and the wind that carries them away one after another is not always weighed down by a memory. A philosopher has said: "Noth-ing is easier and nothing more futile than refuting a philoso-phy."

Thus, dogmatism appears at first to be naivety and affir-mation. On looking at it more closely, does it not become ne-gation and poverty? The line, in order to purify itself of all breadth, vanishes there; the surface, in order to liberate itself from all thickness, disperses there; thought, in order to flee all contradiction, loses all life there. Oh, the truly rich know bet-ter how to enjoy the changing Reality. They do not choose between the marvelous dreams of things. Several, for our joy, cause their wonderstruck voyagers and alternating smiles to float in the flux and reflux of dialogue.

But here come the sages. The mirage that attracts them today excites them with the same laughter as the mirages with which the past believed it might refresh itself. To the same extent as the obsolete scholasticism, they scorn the new scholasticism, the one to which their time gives a name of confidence and glory: gnosis, revelation, orthodoxy, doctrine or science. If the logical armor that cedes to every proof, and which Don Quixote is obstinate in patching up and putting on again, stops their gaze momentarily, it is only as a museum specimen good for amusing the eyes. But under one or other of its innumerable aspects, they perceive within themselves, undeniable save for philosophical amusement, the mountain of Being that is affirmed. For them, nature, wisdom, love, virtue, detachment, liberty and harmony are not, as for other men, dazzling names or vain sounds; they are fingers, excitedly extended, which indicate the slopes of Wellbeing.

Too certain of remaining impotent in the land of pretentious follies, their mercy turns away from professional deformities that, in a glory of mocking light, bear their tumors of doctrine, their humps of erudition, their docile calluses and their goiters of poorly-digested memories. Turned toward the vulgar, whose ignorance, so long as it is not raised in a tempest by the hatred of officials, remains hesitant, less aggressive, sometimes confident, and whose stupidity, in matinal grace, seems curable, the sages speak. Their great—but how rare!— victory is to make a simple individual rise to self-knowledge, to the noble Socratic science that, with a catchphrase, sets aside the futile and inaccessible outside: "All that I know is that I know nothing."

Either to affirm his practical certainties or to sing the flotation of dreams that clergy and universities will make ugly and paralyze into systems tomorrow, the sage willingly relates parables: an action as precise as a beautiful woman's body but a thought whose features, where the eyes glitter and the smile is indefinite, are blurred by a veil.

In whatever century or whatever region the sage lives, it seems that perfume always emanates from him.

Of numerous writings by cynic philosophers, only the titles remain; several clearly indicate collections of parables. What are the cynic deeds that legend has transmitted to us except parables in action? And the cynic sayings that have reached us, as soon as one considers them as the conclusions of parables, are illuminated by a new and fortunate light. His comic genius inspired Diogenes with symbols as striking and almost as crude as those inspired in Ezekiel by Yahveh.

Criticized for frequenting fishermen and publicans, Jesus responds, in the Gospel: "It is not those who are well but the sick who are in need of physicians." To the same reproach Antisthenes had replied, according to Diogenes Laertius: "It is among the sick that physicians go." In a similar case, Diogenes of Sinope riposted: "Sunlight enters latrines, and is not sullied thereby."

It would be temeritous to affirm that one or other of these three responses was made directly to adversaries in the circumstances that credulous biographers report. For the audacity of such a certainty, it would be necessary to forget the laws of legend and the familiar directions of its transformative power. Legend is a poetry that dramatizes. It gladly plays with words and actions; according to its books or speeches it imagines the deeds and attitudes of the writer and the orator. Any story, emerging from the mouth of a speaker of parables, becomes for him an anecdote he has lived; are not the accounts of the fabulist Aesop an amusing collection of fables? Each of the responses that you have just read might perhaps be, not a projectile launched at an enemy present and attacking, but the sudden light of a conclusion or a crown, on a tale that smiles and proceeds harmoniously.

Undoubtedly, other words, presented nakedly in Matthew, Luke or the sixth book of Diogenes Laertius[50] were originally the center and the body of parables whose variegated vestments, before eyes that were amused and which remembered, slowly fell away. Among the written works, even setting aside forty significant titles by Antisthenes and Diogenes, does it not seem that parables live in the *Amusing Letters* in which Menander "introduced the gods as characters"? And what, if not parables, could those collections of works by Monimus be in which "pleasant inventions envelop a serious meaning"?[51]

The Christians who, sometimes by indifference, and sometimes systematically, destroyed such a vast number of ancient books, have not left standing any monument to cynic wisdom. A bold and continuous apology for nature and individualism, derision of the City, of Religion and all the docilities that make the herd walk with heads owed, that literature must have wounded in the heart the holders/tenants of Antiphysis,[52] the organizers of authority, the professors of

---

[50] Chapter 2 of Book VI of the *Lives of the Eminent Philosophers* credited to Diogenes Laertius, is devoted to Diogenes of Sinope (c404-323 B.C.), the most famous pupil of Antisthenes, the alleged initiator of the cynic school of philosophy. It contains much if what is "known" about the philosopher, although it is merely a loosely connected series of dubious anecdotes, most of which were surely invented, as scandalous abuse if not as parables.

[51] Monimus of Syracuse was, according to Diogenes Laertius, a pupil of Diogenes of Sinope; his writings have not survived, but various sayings attributed to him are quoted by other writers—most famously "All is vanity" and "Wealth is the vomit of fortune"—and strongly imply that he was an enthusiastic employer of *spoudaiogeloion*.

[52] *Antiphysie*, or *Antiphysis* [against nature] was a borrowed term lent gravitas by Rabelais, which has long had a certain fashionability in French left-wing rhetoric; it has extended far

196

respect. But the basis is not the only scandal here and more than one fanatic was irritated by the fact that, five centuries before the Gospel, so many parables had been pronounced with a significance too evangelical to be orthodox.

At any rate, when I have attempted to restore the nobility of cynic thought, one form has been imposed upon me, and Psychodorus, disciple of Diogenes, has appeared to me only to be able to speak in parables.

---

beyond nineteenth century Anarchists to its employment by such recent scholars as Jean-Paul Sartre ad Roland Barthes.

I. The Spring

In his old age, the hazard of his travels brought Psychodorus the Cynic back to Greek soil. Now, renown having spread rumor of his travels and proclaimed his wisdom, men flocked around him. A few accompanied him everywhere, becoming, somewhat against his will, his disciples. Others listened, curiously, for an hour, a day or a week, and then drew away, shaking their heads in pity or admiration.

The majority, having returned home, declared the words of Psychodorus to be as incomprehensible as oracles and, that, even more than Phoebus, the philosopher merited the name of the Tortuous. And the ingenious Greeks, who liked enigmas, came running to hear the sage and to try to open up his closed words.

For he did not speak directly advice as to conduct or physical verities; but like a poet or an old man leaning toward children, he related fables and myths. More often than not, he neglected to strip the lesson of its ingenious envelope and many only heard the tales that amused them. And if he was interrogated, his response almost always commenced with the recommendation:

"Hear a parable."

One day, among his auditors there was another old philosopher. Seated very close to Psychodorus, Lycon,[53] his head tilted, listened gravely, and yet the tip of his staff traced mysterious signs. At the center of the lines there was a figure that

---

[53] The reference is to the Pythagorean Lycon of Iasos, whose lost book *On the Pythagorean Life* apparently praised temperance, rather than the later peripatetic philosopher Lycon of Troas. Ryner's Lycon, unsurprisingly, is deeply respectful of "the son of silence."

resembled the orator, but it was holding a finger over sealed lips.

When Psychodorus fell silent, Lycon, the old sage who many thought to be mute, asked:

"Why are you talking?" Without waiting for a response, however, he continued: "Nothing is as futile as speech. And sometimes, nothing is as armful. The words you pronounce are, to nearby ears, vain and strange sounds. The sage talks to men with the words of their own language, a language they do not understand. The words have a full and noble meaning on the lips, but the mind of the majority of men, a vase with a narrow neck, only lets the sounds penetrate, which are like envelopes emptied of their contents. And in the infamous vase fetidities ferment, such that whatever falls into it becomes putrescent. More than once, Psychodorus, I have heard the maxims that you have pronounced nobly repeated to excuse or glorify vile actions. And I tremble at having dared to venture a few words myself, for perhaps the noble precept has contributed to determine a vile action."

"In the same way, the ray of sunlight and the drop of dew, nourishment and honey in the veins of the fig-tree, become poison in the flowers of the hemlock. Numerous rays and numerous drops also fall uselessly into mud or on to rock. However, O Lycon, you are not convinced that the sun will go out or that the dew will dry up forever."

"Believe me, O Psychodorus. Come into my solitude, where thoughts imitate the followers of the blossoming silence. We shall gaze, together or one by one, at the same things. When our eyes meet, each of us will love the beauty of a friendly gaze. But our tongues will remain immobile in the fortunate dampness of the mouth; and if the emotion becomes too strong, our right hands will clench."

"I will not go into your solitude today," said Psychodorus.

Lycon therefore got up in order to depart alone; but Psychodorus stopped him with a gesture and the words: "Before you go, O very wise Lycon, hear a parable:"

I stopped next to a clear and abundant spring, which was singing like a little girl. A few paces further away, the ground fell away rapidly before the stream, but the cascade was a leap of joy.

I had come from lower land and I told the spring, which I had seen from below that the avidity of men had divided the noble stream into rectilinear channels, and had made of its light limpidity an ugliness in which it dragged itself along muddily and heavily. I do not know whether the spring heard my saddened warning, but it did not reply, continuing its generous movement and its song.

A few years later, I passed through the region again, and saw a new spectacle down below. I went up to tell the spring what I had seen.

"Stop, O spring," I exclaimed. "Cease a futile labor; you no longer pass."

The sound of the spring over the pebbles seemed to be laughing at me.

"Stop, O spring. Foolish men have made of your flowing life an immobile death. In the middle of the valley your river, running into a thick and high dyke, spreads out into a pestilential marsh. Stop, O spring, for you have been transformed, dear vivifier, into a sower of malady and death."

The spring continued to flow, with the same mocking song.

"Stop, O spring. For one day, by virtue of the accumulation of your waters, you will carry away the dyke that men have built with stones and folly. When the obstacle is toppled by your weight you will be impotent to retain your muddy fall and, instead of a fecund river, you will launch on to the plain inundation and ravage. O spring, you whose waters are a laughter, stop the laughter of your waters, which will end up making the poor Ephemerae weep."

Without responding, the stream continued to flow.

I drew away, saddened by its obstinacy, and the folly of men.

Many years later, I passed that way again. The region had changed its aspect again. The dyke had disappeared. A city was bathing its feet in the magnificent and supple river, and the people were drinking the water, which bore, as women wear jewelry, sparkling and metallic colors. And the men were dying numerously, as in a battle, for higher than the city, among tanneries, there were I know not what other factories, which were charging with barbaric dyes and poisons the waters that had previously been healthy and clear.

I went up one last time, and I cried, in a desperate tones: "O spring, O injured innocence, know that the folly and avidity of men have made a poisoner of you."

But the spring continued to flow, amid joyful sounds.

Psychodorus fell silent. Without saying a word, Lycon took a step to draw away. But Eubulus,[54] the favorite and best of the disciples said: "It depended on the spring to provide the water that vivifies. What was done with its gifts no longer depended on the spring."

"Listen," cried Psychodorus. "You hear, Lycon: it sometimes happens that a word is understood by someone. You see: it sometimes happens that a man goes up to the spring to drink freshness and purity; but those to whom my waters do harm, other waters would kill instead of mine. Those who are content to live down below are destined to be poisoned."

---

[54] Although the reference is to a fictitious character, it is probably not a coincidence that there was a fourth-century Athenian comic poet and playwright named Eubulus, only fragments of whose work have survived, who apparently employed mythological themes to attack contemporary tyrants in a manner of which Psychodorus and Ryner would have approved,

II. The Bleating Flock

Among the disciples, many seemed mute as long as Psychodorus was there; but among those who spoke, two stood out, from the earliest days.

Eubulus of Andros was skillful in following the floating meaning of parables. He often continued the master's thought. Some affirmed that he resembled Psychodorus as a son resembles his father. Blond and mild, however, the young man had in his smile and mind more tenderness than Psychodorus ever had, and less malice.

Excycle of Megara,[55] however, was a passionate individual and singularly changeable. He passed with a puerile facility from tears to sonorous laughter. Sometimes he exaggerated the master's thought to the point of rendering it repulsive even to the master, and only then did he like the thought in question. Ordinarily, he stubbornly opposed what had been said, and he had a mania for disputing everything, as a young dog with toothache bites all objects. Vain and obstinate, he strove to make people admire the ingenuity and independence of his mind. His eyes sparkled when he thought that he had embarrassed the aged philosopher by means of a captious question. But he detested parables and all responses that smile and undulate like light. He wanted to be confronted with precise for-

---

[55] I have left this name, which does not appear to exist anywhere outside the present text, as Ryner renders it, rather than adjusting it to bear more resemblance to an Anglicized version of a Greek name. Excycle's place of origin, however, might be intended to link him with Euclid of Megara—not the great geometer but a pupil of Socrates, who appears to have been something of a dogmatist, although he was a precursor of the Stoics.

mulae, rigid affirmations and negations that the mind can seize like an irritated hand in order to break them or tear them apart.

The day after Lycon's departure, Excycle interrogated in these terms:

"O Psychodorus, does money produce fewer evils than the poisoned spring you mentioned yesterday?"

He received this response:

"Money produces more evils alone than all the torrents that fall from the mountains."

"But," Excycle added, "the man who invented it only thought about certain advantages that it would realize. He wanted it to be a benefactor of men. He wanted to facilitate exchanges that bargaining rendered difficult and uncertain. I suppose, therefore, that you absolve him as you absolve the spring—or rather, you love and admire him."

Psychodorus shrugged his shoulders.

Excycle's words became bitter. "If I understand correctly, Master, the imprecise response with which you deign to honor me, you are committing an injustice at present; of two similar actions, you are condemning one but approving the other."

"The inventor of money, my son, does not resemble the high spring. It required, in order to conclude such an invention, thought singularly applied to base concerns. He has given nothing that corresponds to healthy human needs. Has he produced anything that can satisfy hunger or protect against cold or elevate you above dread and desire? He is, rather, the poisoner who has interposed factories between the spring and the city; and who soils the waters that come to our mouth with metallic and fetid reflections."

Psychodorus fell silent momentarily and his lips, twisted a moment before as if by nausea, soon broadened into a smile.

"Nature," he continued, "determines that fruits, meat and other necessary things cannot be conserved for long. That sage anticipation had established a fraternity between men and a kind of necessity of reciprocal benefits. Once, the man who had too much nourishment gave some to his neighbor, even if the neighbor possessed nothing that could be an object of trade. Generosity was the sole remedy for the suffering of seeing the good rot uselessly."

The philosopher's eyes seemed to be gazing at a distant and joyous horizon. However, a sadness almost closed them as he finished his discourse:

"Today, alas, money permits that which will perish to be exchanged for a durable material, devoid of use and value in itself, but which our folly accepts as real wealth. In a form as hard as the heart of a rich man, the man who has too much heaps up what others lack, and he builds, with the hunger of the poor, the edifice of his power and their servitude. The inventor of money has perfected something: he has perfected tyranny and slavery; he has rendered durable, solid and increasing the inequality that was previously precarious, light and uncertain. He is the father of myriads of murders, myriads of lies and myriads of base actions. Did he foresee some of his crimes and did he desire them, a brigand laughing behind a mask? I don't believe so. He was, rather, an individual whose vile thought harms when it wants to serve, one who has only given his ordure and who spreads his excrement at hazard, on the bread that has just been baked as well as on the field that is to be fertilized...."

"However," Excycle objected, "People praise him, and always will."

"A noble argument for a philosopher!" exclaimed Eubulus.

But Psychodorus said: "Hear this parable:"

A man said to a flock of sheep: "Love me, for I have sharpened in an artful fashion the knife with which you throats will be cut. Acclaim your benefactor, therefore."

Now, the sheep all bleated in unison, but I could not divine whether the bleating was approving. The bleating of flocks and people almost always acclaim butchers and sharpeners of knives. Sometimes, however, its meaning remains uncertain, equivocal and obscure.

Some affirm that the voice of the people is the voice of the gods. Perhaps they are right, and—until a priest or an orator translates them in a fashion to please tyrants—the rumble of thunder, the flight of birds, the bleating of sheep and the discordant cries of the people signify absolutely nothing.

III. The Lamp

"Master," said Eubulus, what evil do you see in the fact that, just as the lame support their steps with crutches, my infirmity supports its poor gestures on the opinions I have of the gods? Is it not, on the contrary, a means of giving my life unity, nobility and poetry?

"The crutches of the lame," said Psychodorus, "are not made with mist and the words of priests." After a pause, he added: "You are speaking, my son, of a dangerous folly, a folly that I sometimes call, in the secrecy of my mind, the double blindness and the double fall. For the sage avoids, with equal prudence, affirmation in a dream and hesitation in conduct."

Numerous disciples came forward, and the old philosopher went on: "Hear a parable:"

A lamp was alight on a table. In the agitated light of the lamp, three men were sitting, chatting together.

The first, who was a priest, said: "There is darkness, and there is light. In the same way, there is truth and there is error. All that is not light or truth is necessarily darkness and error. Thus, any man who is not Greek is a Barbarian, and the frontiers that surround Greece or reason are precise."

But the second man was named Diogenes and he came from Sinope. He replied:

"Frontiers are human imaginations. In reality, there are gradual transitions between things, or rather, things in their entirety are only transitions. The crude distinctions we make are always conventional and arbitrary limits, but some of them are necessary in order for you to be able to speak or act. Words and deeds transform into discontinuity what is really continuous. It is necessary that you know these things in order that you are not intoxicated by your thought like a diviner and do not become irritated like a judge against the thought of others. But it is necessary that you forget them partially when you speak, and even more so when you act; if not, you risk becoming mute and paralyzed."

He went on: "Look more closely about what arises from that lamp. Between the shadow and the light floats a circle of uncertainty that you do not call shadow or light but penumbra. And that region is not uniform throughout, being almost darkness here and almost light there. And the luminous dance is not uniformly bright, nor the immobility of the darkness uniformly dense and deep. No one, not even a god, can determine the precise point at which the light becomes penumbra or the penumbra becomes darkness."

The man who had not yet spoken remarked: "So neither one of you can determine where darkness commences or light ends. Now, what cannot be defined has no reality, and when you say 'darkness' or 'light' you are pronouncing vain words. But the duty of the wise man is to keep quiet, unless he can explain to futile talkers the duty of keeping quiet."

The other two laughed.

"Laughter," said the sophist, bitterly, is a response almost akin to the step you took, Diogenes, when my master Zeno[56] demonstrated to you the impossibility of all movement. Your laughter today, Diogenes, and today's step, are ignorant agitations. I can compare them without injustice to the shove or the punch with which a soldier would believe he was refuting me."

"Does warmth differ from cold?" asked the cynic.

Zeno's disciple laughed. "When you can demarcate their limits with a precise lined, I will see a difference between them."

---

[56] Like many of the Cynics, the fifth-century philosopher Zeno of Elea is mostly known via the account of him given by Diogenes Laertius, which is probably fictitious, although his widely-cited paradoxes secured his notoriety long before that.

Diogenes took one of the man's fingers and drew it gradually closer to the flame. The astonished sophist let him do it without resistance. A moment came when, after a warmth that was mild to begin with, then increasingly intense, the finger felt pain. Then the hand recoiled, fleering the burn.

And Diogenes asked, with an amiable smile: "Explain to us the movement you just made, O negator of movement and heat."

Then, for a long time, Diogenes laughed, while the other spoke.

IV. The Treasure

When Psychodorus had described the ingenious gesture of Diogenes, after the ingenious words of the three men around the lamp, a listener stood up. None of the disciples knew him yet, for he had only arrived a few hours ago, but they discovered subsequently that his name was Theomanes.

Irritated against the aged philosopher, Theomanes said:

"I am scornful of your words, having heard higher and richer ones, but I cannot repeat them because I have been sworn to silence. Psychodorus, instead of spreading your ignorance, sterile dust, you ought to have yourself initiated and inseminated at Eleusis. Perhaps, Psychodorus, your mind is a noble torch, but no torch can be ignited by itself, and the man who is initiated is the only Prometheus who holds the fire of minds."

Theomanes had half-closed eyes and a strange smile on his lips, for he was seeing again, trembling anew, the gesture of the hierophant drawing away the veils, and his soul was repeating, like a dazzled echo, the formulae that a voice of certainty had planted like torches in the gold empty of fables.

"I mistrust lights that hide," said Psychodorus, negligently. "Helios lights the bald summits of mountains for longer than the woods and valleys, but he does not enter the caverns where brigands and the priests of secret cults go to earth."

"O wicked man! Brigands assemble to do evil, but initiates assemble to do good."

"What good are you talking about?"

"All that I have the right to say is that I have been promised, after my death, delightful, intense and never-ending joys. In order to merit that marvelous and inexhaustible treasure, I conduct myself piously."

"You conduct yourself foolishly, who, instead of seeking yourself, seek what perhaps does not exist."

"Even if the promise were a lie," cried the initiate, "O noble lie that gives me hope...."

"Hope today, disappointment tomorrow."

"And it keeps me upright, the useful hope, and it alone conducts me toward the good."

"You love a phantom that steals the real from you. You love a dream that prevents you from accomplishing your work. You are driving your plow among the clouds, instead of sowing your field and harvesting it."

"Your words are obscure to me."

But Psychodorus addressed everyone: "Hear a parable:"

An old man who was about to die thought:

My three sons are ordinary men. I should like to make valiant and dogged laborers of them. By what means can I inform them usefully that labor is a treasure?

He reflected momentarily. Then he smiled, for he thought he had found the answer.

Having summoned his children, he spoke to them with a mysterious air:

"Don't repeat this secret to anyone. In the field that I am leaving you for a sole heritage a treasure is hidden, buried deeply but enormous. I don't know the exact spot, but you're strong enough to dig everywhere."

Having said that, the old man died, tranquilly. He hoped that the land, better dug, would give his sons a triple yield.

Now the youngest of the brothers believed himself to be a poet. He spent days lying in the field. With a joyful emotion he said to himself: *Perhaps I'm on top of the treasure!* He dreamed of the voluptuous pleasures that his share would give him, and sometimes, taking his tablets from his bosom, he wrote a bad epigram in honor of Aphrodite or Dionysus.

The two older brothers dug the ground fervently. When they arrived at the corner where the versifier was dreaming, they shouted at him: "Get up, good-for-nothing. You're doubtless on top of the treasure." He took his body further away, and the banality dazzled his dreams, and they dug in the place where their hope was buried.

But their hope was a root without a stem, which fled before effort, and which the hand never grasped. They continued to dig deeper, and found nothing.

When the time for sowing came, the eldest said: "Why should we sow? The value of a harvest is negligible, if you compare it to the treasure that we shall discover tomorrow."

The second had a different opinion. "Let's sow anyway. I like benefits that accumulate. You wouldn't throw away even a small part of the treasure; why, then, should we lose what we can gain further?"

He sowed the entire field; but with the same ill-humor or the same indifference with which he shoved his young brother out of the way, he dug over the wheat that was growing when, instead of thinking that the treasure was in the poor place where his brother as dreaming, he imagined that it was in the rich place where the plants were sprouting.

In the end, the crop enriched others and the three brothers harvested nothing. Their fearful poverty dug the ground with trembling hands. Even the poet started digging as avidly as his elders. But soon, creditors came, who took possession of the field. The domain being too small to pay all the debts that the riches of tomorrow had permitted, the seekers of treasure were sold themselves as slaves.

V. The Generous Acorn

"Who needs philosophers?" said Theomanes. "The entire law is summarized in one word: Love."

"Love whom?" interrogated Eubulus.

"Love everything. Love first and foremost, above people and things, the God who created humans, who built the earth to serve as their dwelling; who deployed the glorious tent of the sky over their heads; who ripens fruits to nourish them and causes lively waters to flow to refresh them. Then love his creatures, and particularly other men in whom we can, as a emotional brother believes that he can see the smile of absent parents and his own smile in his brother's face, recognize the image of the Creator and ours own. For it is permitted to proclaim this information of the mysteries before all, that we are made in the resemblance of God."

Eubulus smiled, seduced. But Theomanes continued:

"He has given us everything. And as he is everything, at every moment, he gives himself by means of myriads of presents offered in myriads of luminous hands. He is the sole virtue and the sole happiness."

Theomanes could no longer speak, and, as if under a joy that was too powerful, stammered: "To give oneself, oh, to give oneself…"

"Master," said Eubulus, "Theomanes is great."

"There is no human grandeur greater than wisdom," objected Psychodorus, and Theomanes is not wise if he does not know the hour and manner of giving oneself."

"Always, always," affirmed the initiate's stammer. "It's always that it is necessary to give oneself, and it is in all manners…."

But the old philosopher interrupted him, saying: "O my impatient sons, hear a parable:"

An acorn, fallen from an oak tree, sang a hectic canticle on the ground:

"I love, I love, and I want to give myself."

"Poor child," said the oak, "later you will have a great deal to give, provided that you refuse yourself now. For the duty of an acorn is not to give itself, but to realize itself. Slide silently toward solitude. Along your path, hide yourself under leaves, in the grass and between stones, for fear that you will be perceived by some hungry animal.

"When you have found your desert, bury yourself deeply in the soil. Let everyone remain ignorant for a long time of your work upon yourself, and that your roots are slipping like serpents, seeking the juices dormant in the earth in order to make life of them. Stand up gradually, grow and develop. Don't worry about the solitude that surrounds you and do not summon enemies to that protector of your weakness.

"Later, your beauty will be the powerful summons that populates a country. Then the fingers of the wind will make each of your branches quiver like a melodious spring and you will be a vast lyre, a crossroads of singing life. You will be shelter and shade. As chorists know the choirmaster and dance in harmony with his steps, the birds will know you and their wings and throats will vibrate to the rhythm of your branches. Young people whom amour has persecuted will learn the road that leads to your broad trunk and they will lean against you to exchange kisses.

"Thus you will display yourself under cascades of light, a world charged with twittering nests and trembling thoughts."

But the obstinate acorn did not listen and still clamored; "To give myself! To give myself!"

He did not remain hidden, offered as prey. He made an effort, however. He wanted to avoid importunate advice or, as he thought, the nonsense of old men. He therefore applied himself to rolling toward the nearby road in order to increase his chances of being perceived and giving himself.

He succeeded.

A herd of pigs was just passing by, amid grunts. The generous acorn had the joy he summoned. He was crushed between splendid teeth. Thus he became a little excrement and a little meat dipped in mud.

"O my sons," Psychodorus included, "strive to be powerful and harmonious. By that means you will give yourselves and you will give a great deal. But the impatient individual, who wants to give himself instead of realizing himself, commits a multiple crime: he destroys the vast future of shade and songs, he gives little, and he gives poorly, to those who are worth less than him."

VI. The Reflections in the Water

One of those who were following Psychodorus out of vain curiosity addressed himself to Eubulus.

"For several days, I haven't understood anything he's said. Let's leave."

Eubulus replied: "Certainly, I don't understand everything he says. But I also like the words I don't understand. It seems that they help me to become better and more capable of truth."

Then Excycle sniggered: "How can what you don't understand produce that effect on you?"

But Psychodorus, who was passing, stopped and said: "Hear a parable:"

After an abrupt climb, a vast plateau was encountered, the greater part of which was occupied by a lake.

As soon as a stranger arrived in the area, he was taken to the mountain, placed in a standing position on the edge of the lake and the order was given to him: "Speak!"

Now, while the stranger was speaking, the indigenes did not listen to him, but they looked. They looked at the lake. It seemed that the words, taking on a form, launched forth toward the other shore, and strange reflections were seen gliding over the surface or in the depths of the water.

More often than not, they were the shadows of serpents that were crawling in the water, or the shadows of toads hopping heavily, or other ugly things, too monstrous and grimacing to have a name, agitating in vile gestures.

Then the people, becoming irritated, insulted the stranger, shoved him and chased him over the frontier.

But one day, the man taken to the mountain happened to be a sage—I believe that it was my master Diogenes. When he spoke, the rapid flight of swallows was seen in the water, and the reflection of blackbirds hopping lightly, like mocking quips, and the reflection of soaring eagles seemed motionless in the calm depths.

The indigenes did not weary of looking; they also listened that day, with their ears, and their tongues attempted to repeat the words they heard.

When they repeated them with servile exactitude, the variegated reflection of a magpie mocked them; but if their words were different and of equal beauty, they too caused flocks of swallows to be reflected, or, when they mocked, with a liberated heart, the foolish slaves that comprise the multitude, reflections of hopping blackbirds opening their beaks like a whistling joy. Nevertheless, in spite of repeated effort, none of them could cause the reflection of an eagle with wings outspread and seemingly immobile to soar in the depths.

"Master," said Eubulus, "that parable is truly too difficult. I sense that it will torment me during long days and nights. I beg you, love me enough to explain it to me."

His voice was so soft, so affectionate and so avid, that Psychodorus could not resist him.

"Perhaps," he said, "if the stranger was my master, the lake was my soul."

"And the inhabitants who repeated the words of Diogenes?"

"Perhaps my thoughts, without yet understanding the words of the sage, at least imitating their manner and the nobility of their light."

"Why do you say: 'Perhaps,' O Psychodorus, dear to my heart? There is in your words, as there often is, an uncertainty and a hint of mockery. What if you were to speak today entirely seriously?"

But Psychodorus smiled, and his eyes were two moving smiles that seemed, like playing children, to flee and pursue one another.

"If I knew what you are asking at present," he replied, "I probably would not tell you."

VII. The Conspirators

"The other day," said Excycle, "you were speaking against slavery. Now, an event has occurred that will bring joy to your heart. The slaves of Sicily, having revolted, have declared war on their masters."

"You are reporting news interesting to a historian, but indifferent to a sage; for I doubt that the slaves, if they triumph, will be any less wicked than the masters."

"They have, at least, begun by taking a few by surprise, whose throats they have cut. I rejoice when ferocious beasts are destroyed...."

"By other ferocious beasts, I fear."

"I thought," said Excycle, "that you would persuade us to assist the soldiers of justice, and that you might even come with us."

"If two dogs are fighting over a bone, the sage does not take sides between them."

"And if a dog bites a man that beats him, whose side would you take?"

"That," said Psychodorus, laughing, "depends on the dog's reasons—but I haven't known many dogs who were philosophers." He added: "Hear a parable:"

In a solitary clump of trees at the edge of a vast estate, three slaves were talking.

The first was as strong as Heracles and his name was Simon. In a low voice, in which one could almost hear the effort he was making not to howl, he said:

"It's ridiculous that I, the equal of ten men put together, am condemned to serve a master with a puny body. According to natural law, he should be my slave. I hope in future, if you support me, to put things and people in their proper place.

But Elaphus, as clever and subtly as Odysseus himself, bore in a pointed head like that of a fox, all the cunning that the vulgar and the poets call wisdom.

"The foolish," he affirmed, "are born to obey the wise. Nature has made me a leader. It has given me, along with the art of sudden ruses that surprise victory like a prey, the slow suppleness that makes domination last. I despise and hate the master with the coarse and brutal mind. That is why I have allied my prudence with your strength, O Simon-Heracles. Nothing can resist those combined powers. And I assure that I shall be able to make better use of the conquered riches than their present possessor—for voluptuousness is a mistress who only gives herself to the most ingenious of her worshipers, to those who show themselves fertile in both malice and pleasant inventions."

The third slave remained silent. He listened to the words of his companions with indifference, or perhaps with scorn. His name was Neocles. Because of his short stature, his snub nose and his bold and forceful speech, however, he was often called Little Socrates.

The one whose mind was subtle and avid eventually questioned him:

"More than once, O Neocles, I have heard you speak ill of masters, and I disapproved of you secretly because your words were dangerous, without opportunity and without utility. But many people listen to you with respect and, seeing that you are with us, would know that justice is with us. That is why we have asked you to come, in order that you can become our brother in labor and in glory."

Neocles shook his head and shoulders in a negative gesture.

"Undoubtedly," Elaphus went on, "you don't understand what we're proposing to you—or you're brave in words but cowardly as soon as it's necessary to act. We're proposing that you become a master who commands numerous slaves and numerous pleasures."

"I'm unworthy," said Little Socrates, "not because I'm a slave, but because there are slaves."

Neither Elaphus nor Simon replied. They were listening anxiously to a noise that was drawing nearer. Soon, they saw their master approaching. They exchanged a glance. The one who was subtle recognized that the one who was strong was ready for anything. Andocidus was on his own, and he had already seen them. The three men therefore waited, unmoving.

"I'm glad to find the favorite members of my household together," said the master, "for I like and admire your strength, Simon equal of Heracles, and I like and admire the subtlety of your mind, Elaphus rival of Odysseus. As for you, Neocles, or, as they call you, Little Socrates, I ought to hate you since I approve of the judges who condemned the true Socrates, an enemy of the gods and the laws. In spite of myself, however, and I don't know why, I like you too. Or rather I would, although I see you rarely, if you liked me and praised me."

Little Socrates had a malicious smile on his lips. The other two drank the master's words as one drinks hope.

"This," the master continued, "is what I have decided. I shall make three friends, in order that you, Heracles, will be my strength, you, Odysseus, my intelligence and cunning, and you, Little Socrates, the malicious tongue that stings my enemies."

"I hear a fool talking," said Neocles.

Simon raised a fist at him that could have felled a bull with a single blow, but the man he was threatening measured the vast body with his eyes and then shook his head, saying: "You are a beast with a hearty appetite."

Andocidus stopped Simon's gesture.

"I am the sole judge here," he said, in a firm tone, "and I forbid you to strike."

"I obey you, as I would Zeus himself," growled the inept and terrible individual, "but I'd rather give you pleasure by striking than by not striking."

"I shall free all three of you," the master went on. "In addition, I'll give each of you a fine domain, with thirty slaves to work it."

Simon and Elaphus, forgetting the puny body and coarse mind of the man, fell to their knees before him, and with raised arms, proclaimed: "O great, O magnificent, O beneficent...in truth, Andocidus is the name of a god who is visiting the earth."

Little Socrates remained silent. He gazed with pity are the abasement of the two and the arrogant pride of the other.

"What about you?" said the master. "Can you not find words appropriate to the circumstance? I thought gratitude a philosophical virtue."

"What should I say, insensate who gives what does not belong to him?"

"I don't understand."

"A man only belongs to himself. Whoever, under the visage of a man, has a nature so bestial and servile to believe himself a master or recognize himself as a slave, I despise."

Elaphus trembled that Andocidus might go back on his decision. He went to Neocles and advised him rapidly, in a low voice: "Accept and free the thirty who are given to you; that way you will have done good."

"Every man is free, in spite of appearances, if he knows human dignity. But the man is truly a slave who proclaims himself a master. I had thought that there was only one slave here; I see that there are three."

"I'll prove to you," cried Andocidus, "that only one will remain. What I promised, I will maintain for these, whose grateful heart renders them worthy of liberty. As for you, ingrate, you'll be better on the cross."

Neocles, therefore, was crucified, and then ten thousand slaves of the domain insulted him, for they had been told: "He could have liberated several of our companions with a word, but he refused, cruelly, and has shown himself to be, against you, the worst of tyrants."

220

The master, however, ordered them to be silent, and de-clared; "I am as good as a god. If he recognizes my power and my generosity, I will have him taken down from that ignomin-ious tree. But let him beware; the water and freshness are ex-hausted, and the inverted clepsydra will let flow the burning hour of justice and vengeance."

Little Socrates looked upwards, and did not even deign to recognize that those people were there. Instead of replying, he began to sing. And his song said:

"Always I have remained upstanding as a man, deaf to the plaintive yapping or menacing growls of those whose souls walk on four feet. That is why I have obtained the recompense of dying higher than I have lived, launched toward the sky."

The master shrugged his shoulders and went away.

Then the slaves, picking up stones, began to throw them at the victim of torture, amid laughter and jeers.

But the subtle Elaphus remarked: "There ought to be or-der even in games."

He arranged the slaves. Those who wanted to do so came, each in his turn, to place himself at the distance appro-priate for throwing a stone. Thus it was a day of celebration and laughter for everyone, and there were prizes for the most adroit.

VIII. *The Sculptors of Mountains*

Men were leaving to found a colony. They encountered Psychodorus and, surrounding him, listened to him speak. They remained with him and his disciples for several days, but sometimes they spoke among themselves secretly.

Finally, the one who seemed to be their leader said: "O Psychodorus, we do not know any wisdom equal to yours. Come with us, then, and when we have built our city, you shall give us its laws.

"Hear a parable," replied Psychodorus:

A sculptor said to Alexander:

"Give me Mount Athos, in order that I can make a statue to your glory. In its wide open right hand, it will carry a city, and its left hand will clutch the urn from which a river will pour."

When Alexander was not drunk on Roman wine like a poor man, or on incense like an imbecile who thinks himself the son of Zeus, he had the wisdom common to many madmen of recognizing foreign follies. He mocked the ambition of the man and refused his request.

The leader of the colonists remarked:

"O sage, you have not spoken in accordance with your wisdom, and you have taught us nothing. We know the story you have just told us, and it does not respond to the request that we have just made of you."

"Some people," said Psychodorus, "would like to reform all men and sculpt them according to their dream of humanity. Those I compare to the insensate worker who strives to make, with the earth that we inhabit, an immense statue of Demeter. Others apply themselves only to modeling a city, and those I call, appropriately, the sculptors of mountains."

"So you're refusing a labor and a glory beyond your courage?"

"Beyond the power of a man, O man! But even the certainty of failure would not stop me making the attempt, if the attempt in question were not a crime."

The colonists burst out laughing. "A crime!" one of them exclaimed. "Against whom?"

"Against the mountain and against the sculptor. The mountain and the crowd have a certain grim beauty; but the sculpted mountain or the civilized people...what ridiculous ugliness! O Lacedaemon, grimacing caricature of Lycurgus. O government of Athens, drooling grimace of Solon.... For myself, I shall never render myself culpable of such uglifications. By what right would I, who do not obey anyone, command anyone? By what right would I, who consider constraint to be the only evil and who is scornful of all constraint, constrain others? But I scarcely dare, sometimes, when I am asked, to give advice that causes hands to stir. I am not the enemy of tyranny with the intention of becoming a tyrant. I know that a citizen is no longer anything more than the cadaver of a man, and a legislator the cadaver of a sage."

"Plato, however...."

"I am indignant against Plato when, in the book of the *Laws*, he advises a magistrate to arrange marriages by trickery, ruses and lies. I am indignant every time he forgets the great dictum of Socrates: 'All order that is supported by constraint and not on persuasion I call tyranny, and I do not call it law.' I am indignant when he surrounds his decrees with threats, judges, punishments and armed men. Can you not see it? The dream of the sculptor of mountains is a mephitic atmosphere in itself, and, as one emerges feverish from a marshy region, Plato emerges from his legislative dreams a liar and violent. Thus, every time, even in thought alone, a philosopher becomes a king or a magistrate, there is one tyrant more and one sage fewer."

Psychodorus fell silent momentarily. Then he resumed, in an even firmer tone:

"No, Plato's adventure is not a singular accident. You're not unaware of the ferocious beast into which tyranny transformed the sage Periander,[57] but perhaps you don't know the story of Niobe."

"I've often heard it told."

"You've heard it told poorly. Niobe, as skillful and strong as Phidias, but crazed with pride, wanted to sculpt a mountain. The mountain was stronger than her and it was Niobe who was transformed into a rock. Thus Alexander took barbarian peoples in his strong hands and strove to mold them into Greeks, but it was him who became a barbarian in his vestments, his mores, his capricious folly, his irritability, his impotence to remain master of himself, and throughout his fleeing soul."

With the air of a prophetic threat, Psychodorus added: "Be careful, O man. The mind of the sculptor is, in large measure, the work of his statues. I am not talking only about those he has realized. Those in which he fails, either because is dream is too broad and diffuse or because his hands are applied to a material that is immune and fugitive, also fabricate the sculptor, a poor dolorous statue so easy to deform."

---

[57] Periander, named as one of the Seven Sages of Greece, became tyrant of Corinth. Accounts of his reign range from complaints about his harshness to hymn of praise to his administrative skills. Diogenes Laertius was ambiguous in his judgment.

IX. The Pilot

Eubulus had lost his father a long time ago. The death of his mother put him in possession of a rich inheritance. Secretly, he sought advice from Psychodorus.

"If I considered riches as goods I would weep bitterly at gaining them by the loss of my mother; but I know, thanks to you, that riches are indifferent, or rather harmful, and that under the fingers of the sculptor Wellbeing, the life of a rich man is less plastic than the life of a poor one. Tell me, what ought I to do with that which the unjust law has given to me?"

"I cannot lift your legs with my hands to make you walk. It is up to you to act, in accordance with what you are and what you can be."

"You haven't always refused me your advice. To do something because it is good is a joy to me. To do something because you have recommended it, you whom I love and admire above all, is the greatest of my joys. Why do refuse me, while my heart is overflowing with mourning, what would be my most precious consolation?"

"An infantile and docile joy ought not to count for anything, my son, in an action that ought to be entirely virile and entirely free. For myself, if I did as you ask, I would be surpassing my rights. I can sometimes stop a hand that is about to sow repentance, but I never permit myself to push anyone toward action. Certainly, nothing is finer than being poor, but on condition that one loves poverty. The voluntary pauper, if he experiences regret, becomes inferior to the man who remains rich. He resembles the weak man who has tried to climb too high on a difficult mountain. He is out of breath, fatigued; he looks down; his heart lights up with desire for the valley and his head reels with vertigo; finally, his ill-assured foot slips on a stone that shifts, and the presumptuous individual falls down, bruised, lower than the companions who are sitting down half way up the slope. It is up to you to know who you are, and then, without asking whether others have the strength to go further or stop sooner, to walk on your own feet. Know thyself."

Having heard these words, Eubulus ran to the city, sold his heritage and distributed the money to the poor. Nevertheless, he kept, in addition to a donkey and its two baskets, various coins whose collective value was one talent.

After that, every time they went through a town, Eubulus went into shop and loaded the donkey with a few provisions. In the country, those who were hungry came to take bread from the right-hand basket, and figs or olives from the left. But the donkey never carried unnecessary beverages; Psychodorus and his companions liked to drink from the hollows of springs or from the drinking-fountains that herdsmen make with a reed similar to a flute, which pours out the sonorous freshness of water as other reeds allow a thin continuous thread of music to fall, drop by drop.

Excycle, who was miserly, disapproved in his heart of what Eubulus had done. He thought that Psychodorus had counseled those things and sometimes said to himself: *How dangerous that old man is to those who believe what he says....* When he spoke to others, he dared not proclaim a direct criticism, but he mocked Eubulus under the name Crates and Psychodorus under the name Diogenes.

"Crates of Thebes, the rich hunchback, was mad: he deprived himself of his wealth to obey a man who could not even get rid of his hump for him. He could not see that Diogenes of Sinope, poor and jealous, resembled the dog in the fable, which, tethered to a manger, could neither eat the hay not tolerate the horse eating it. But the horse, less inept than Crates, paid no heed to its envious barking."

Excycle added: "For myself I think one can philosophize very cheaply."

"You," said Eubulus, "load yourself with useless stones in the hope of rising more lightly to the summits."

And Psychodorus, smiling at his favorite disciple, said: "I read this parable somewhere:"

For two days a tempest had been shaking a vessel angrily. They passengers were weeping and crying. Only the pilot remained calm.

Lamentable voices rose up around that man as if around a god. Arms were extended toward him as if in prayer; anxiety and panic agitated. Now, the arms, the attitudes and the movements, as well as the words, all cried: "Save us! Save us!"

The pilot said: "The vessel is doomed. Let those who want to save their lives prepare themselves, like me, for the inevitable shipwreck."

He took off his clothes, and everyone imitated him.

The, not far from the high and rocky coast, a skillful maneuver threw the vessel on to a sandbank. The prow stuck, while an abrupt wave carried away the poop, fleeing with it like a thief.

The pilot ordered those who knew how to swim to throw themselves into the waves and reach the shore. He distributed planks and various debris to the others, which sustained them. To all of them he indicated the mouth of a river which, hidden among the rocks, was the only place where it was possible to land.

He got down last and he swam toward the weakest, sustaining them and guiding them.

When he reached the shore he saw that the majority of the passengers were weeping, naked in the cold wind, and turning regretful gazes toward the ship.

At that moment, the vessel sank entirely.

Then, those that the skill and devotion of the pilot had saved began to abuse him because, they said, he had caused them to lose all the abundant wealth that the ship was carrying.

But the pilot had known for a long time the unjust folly of men, and his strength was exhausted. Without saying a word, he passed through the middle of those who were shouting at him and, reaching a hollow in the rock that was sheltered from the wind, he lay down in order to go to sleep.

X. Those Who Walk

"O Psychodorus," said Excycle, "I have reflected, and nothing is as vain as wisdom. What I will do shortly depends on what I have done thus far and what the universe has done thus far. My second gesture depended on my first, which did not depend on me. Thus, from before my birth a road was traced out for me in its entirety and I cannot deviate from it by an inch, with the consequence that my knowledge remains useless to my actions."

"You think it indifferent whether you advance in light or in darkness?"

"It is fortunate, in any case, that things march like an army in which no soldier quits his rank. Otherwise, there would be, in that which we see, disorder without remedy and eternal chaos. There would be, in the observer, an ignorance over which nothing could triumph, bewilderment and fear. If the events that succeed one another or are manifest simultaneously were not linked by the inflexible and brilliant gold of the Law, no one could know anything, not even the gods.

"To know is to know the Law. The man who says 'the Law' says 'the facts.' It is the hand that holds the seed because it holds the ear, which holds the crop because it holds the seed, which holds the seed of yesterday and the tree of tomorrow in the fruit of today. There are burning winds that open the ears, disperse the seeds, reader the harvest impossible. There is, O joy, no whim or caprice that can undo the Law and disperse the facts.

"Otherwise, if nature were impotent like the city, if its orders could be eluded like those of tyrants, I would weep, like a general whose soldiers were in mutiny; for the past, the future and all of the vast present that my eye cannot see would escape my mind, sniggering. Enclosed in the despairing silence of the vanquished, I would not even dare say: "The sun will rise tomorrow."

Excycle fell silent momentarily. Then, with a victorious laugh, he resumed:

"Your thought, O vain Psychodorus, is no more free than the sun. What you call, superbly, your revolt, is an obedience to the Law that you do not know and a product of that Law. Or, if you do not want to admit it, dare to affirm that something comes from nothing, that the son has no father and the event no cause."

Psychodorus replied:

"Go tell the conductor of the chariot, when he goes around the boundary marker: 'Spare all effort and all futile attention. Anterior events necessitate the present direction of the horses and you can do nothing for your salvation or your crash.'

"Go tell the sculptor: 'You believe in vain that you are directing your chisel toward the disengagement of beauty. Each of your gestures is determined by the state of your body and the state of the universe.'

"Or tell yourself, savant Excycle: 'Why strive to tame thoughts, to contain them within the narrow path of logic and modify them slightly in order that they will accord with one another and sustain one another? Are you unaware, then, that each of your thoughts is determined in its slightest detail by the ensemble of things. Each of your thoughts and each of your dreams, whatever effort you make, is an actor that exists for all eternity and cannot appear before its hour or miss its entrance in the passive theater that you are.'

"And also tell yourself, O Excycle: 'Don't preoccupy yourself with looking at some object that you want to examine as a physicist,[58] for even the direction of your gaze does not depend on you.'"

---

[58] I have translated Ryner's *physicien*, here and elsewhere, as "physicist," although he means something more akin to "natural scientist" than what we would nowadays mean by the term.

"But...."

"Ah! In spite of the ineluctable fatalities that surround you, in spite of the Law, you try to see that which can inform you and strive to give your mind a scientific education. In a certain measure, you make logical determinism, which is intellectual liberty, triumph over the determinisms of mechanics and life, which are your servitudes. And sometimes, your obedience to the nature of things is a domination over things. Why do you not want me to give my character a strong education, that I may bring about the triumph, in my thoughts and actions, of the determinism of wisdom, which is my moral liberty, over the will of things and my body, which are my slavery? Knowledge of the laws of the world permits you to dominate the world while obeying its laws. Knowledge of myself permits me to utilize the laws of my nature in order to dominate my nature.

"However...."

"Shut up, Excycle. For, since you accord the laborer the power to sow the future, the sculptor the power to realize beauty, the physicist to choose the object of his study and the dialectician the power to direct his thought, if you then refuse the sage the liberty to direct his own conduct and create his wisdom as the savant creates his science, you are speaking with injustice and you resemble the madman of the parable:"

On the agora, with skillful arguments, Zeno the Eleat denied movement, as you denied liberty just now. Several people were taken in, naively, by the tight mesh of his fragile net. Others sensed the error, but could not discover how it arose, and they remained astonished, like the traveler who wants to divide, beginning with the first thread, the spider-web extended across his path. Whether he has seen the web or not, how-

His employment is deliberate, reflecting the Aristotelian significance of that which metaphysics—a term that Psychodorus, as in the next parable, refuses to use—lies beyond

ever, the lion passes through, and carries away the shreds, while other threads hang down ridiculously from the bushes. So Diogenes, a man of practical wisdom, did not seek with vain words to oppose the vanity of the words that denied movement, but simply started walking.

Excycle said:

"You have had a mania, for several days, of telling the most banally familiar tales, and you risk having lost all power of invention."

"There are," said Psychodorus, laughing, "things that you know, of which you are unaware. There are others of which you are unaware, to the point of believing that you know them. But I announced to you just now that there was a madman in the parable. Others before me have told you, without you hearing them, what the sage Diogenes did. Has someone already told you what the madman did?"

"No," admitted Excycle.

"Listen, then, and this time, if you can listen:"

Diogenes headed toward the right-hand edge of the agora. But the madman I mentioned seized him by the arm and shouted:

"Come with me, to the left, to the left, I tell you. Have you not understood Zeno, the teller of truths? Have you not understood his irrefutable demonstration, and that, in the direction in which you are striving to go, all movement is impossible?"

XI. The Brigand Termeros

"O Psychodorus, I have heard you proclaim universal necessity many times, but just now, you affirmed that man is free."

"There are two wisdoms, Excycle. One wisdom tries to dream of divine things. Men designate that by hesitant words. Some call it "that which comes after physics." Often it is what I think when I say "philosophy." But there is also a wisdom of human actions. Now, that which concerns the divine things or the utmost profundities of nature remains uncertain, and it is appropriate to talk about it while smiling with joy and doubt, as when you recite the verses of Homer. For that wisdom is poetry, but the beauty it creates bears a singular and glorious name; it is called Unity. Each system is a song or poem; and I love all those who dream nobly of Unity. I have no need to know, and you cannot know any more than I do, whether Helen was in Troy, as Homer sings, or in Egypt, as Euripides says. I do not torment myself with that matter as one torments oneself with a verity. If I usually speak like Homer it is because the *Iliad* is more beautiful than the tragic fable. Thus, Plato is a better philosopher than Aristotle because his dream of Unity is more harmonious, more supple and more seductive."

"Tell us about the other wisdom," asked Eubulus.

"You are interested, Eubulus, in that which Socrates and my master Diogenes called simply 'wisdom.' That is what says: 'Know thyself,' and afterwards falls silent, in order that you might listen. As for the dreamer that I praised just now with a smile, as one praises a woman of promising words and fleeting movements. Socrates and Diogenes scorned him as futile. They made philosophy descend from the heavens to the earth. They only affirmed human movement and, when we have lit the torch near the ground, the freedom to walk behind it.

"When I walk, it is also over resistant ground, and, having arrived at the edge of the cliff, I do not place a reckless foot on the cloud that seems to continue it. But I do not dare, with Diogenes, to criticize Plato because he has wings. Except that I never forget that in the air, the bird, if it is not to fall, must flap its wings; and in the thoughts that are beyond physics, the philosopher must move his mind continuously. It is necessary that he smile on the lips and that the seemingly malicious ecstasy of the gaze lifts the words, annulling their weight of affirmative folly. But as regards human conduct, I do not seek rules in the dream, for I'm not a sleepwalker."

"So," mutter Excycle, "sometimes you say yes and sometimes no."

"Sometimes I recite verses on Barbarians; but if a city makes war on Barbarians, its strategy forces it to know the enemy other than through verses, even harmonious ones."

"You generously give yourself the right to contradict yourself. However, contradiction is the mark of the false."

"No, child, but the mark of falsity of mind is the spirit of contradiction."

"You're playing ingeniously with words."

"As for contradiction, it's the sign that all reality bears. And that is why no reality is eternal. Nature ought to be called That-which-contradicts-itself."

"What are you saying?"

"Do you not know the doctrine of old Empedocles that all things are daughters of Eros and Discord?"

"I know it, but I don't know whether I approve of it."

"It's necessary to approve of it, since it's beautiful, as you approve of a tragedy by Sophocles."

"You make strange comparisons.

"The philosopher who spends his life repeating: 'Being is; Non-Being isn't, and adds nothing more, probably does not contradict himself, but he risks saying nothing—or, I fear, even repeats a lie."

"A lie?"

"For nature employs eternity in creating and destroying—which is to say, in affirming that Non-Being is the denial of what Being is. Every birth whispers to Parmenides: 'You lie,' and every birth cries out to him: 'You're mistaken!'"

"However...."

"The disciple of Parmenides and Xenophanes, Zeno the Eleat, showed the contradiction in all things that our minds grasp and our eyes see. That ambitious individual claimed to have penetrated as far as the Being that does not tear and does not deny itself, and all our realities he called vain appearances. But I say: "If you speak of the One, the Truth and Being in a ponderous fashion, supporting yourself on them, you will fall, with your support broken. For it is the multiple that denies the one; it is realities that hinder the truth. Appearances, an eternal bacchanal, rip up Being and carry away its fragments as the Maenads carried away the bloody shreds of Orpheus.""

"Something remained of Orpheus."

"Yes, a voice and a harmony. Zeno believed movement to be impossible. Now, everything is movement. Immobility is a lie of the eyes or a conception of the mind. The phenomenon, of its myriad sniggers that pass and recommence, eternally denies substance."

"You frighten me."

"Sometimes, however, avid for beauty, I name Substance what there is in common to all phenomena. But that is unknowable. And my ear, which listens, believes that it can grasp harmonies; it is its obstinate attention and its imperious desire that creates them. And I call immobility the equilibrium of all the movements, And what I name One is the very possibility of Many. But the words, of which each one seems a hymn, Being, Immobility and Unity, who then could sing them and who could understand them, if there were not the eternal chorus of phenomena, of movement and the multiple?"

"But...."

"And believe me, life, such as we can know it, is not condensed at the center and in the thymele; it is dispersed all around and it belongs, fragmented, to each chorist."

"Oh, how many difficult things you say...!"

"And as soon as I try to speak beyond what we can see, I consent joyfully to the necessity of contradicting myself. For no word is a vase large enough and deep enough to contain all the truth. I am, with the thoughts that germinate within me and the florid words that attempt to agitate my perfumes around me, not the container but a minuscule part of the contents. Each idea and each word are murmurs that surround and cover the negative cries of the infinite.

"O insensate who talks about his house and thinks he says the city; he talks about the city and thinks he says the earth; he talks about the earth and thinks he says our universe; he whispers our universe and thinks he is singing powerfully the All. But the man who, joyfully and anxiously, squeezes between his hands and his breast what he can grasp of the All, oh, how he senses the narrow weakness of his arms, and how he hears, around his thought, the sonorous collapse of all Thought.

"With the gold of straw or the gold of a formula, one can tie a handful of ears of wheat or a large sheaf, but what madman would try to surround with a tie all the wheat that Demeter gives to men during the month of Hekatombaion, or collect in a single basket the rain of fruits that Metageitnion shakes from all the trees?[59]

"That is why, when I approach certain regions of dream or desire, I only speak while smiling, as befits a mortal, or even a god. For the gods, when they speak, are subject to the power of words, and according to what words demand, they separate things that hold together or confound things that are distinct. And they do not know much better than we do whether all things hold together and how they are held, since Phoe-

---

[59] In the Attic calendar, Hekatombeion overlapped our July and August, and was directly followed by Metageitnion.

236

bus has the insolent naivety not to be Zeus and Zeus the infantilism to flee Hera or marry her."

The disciples listened, a few standing up, the majority sitting on stones or on the edge of the ditch. Among the latter was Eubulus, his elbows on his knees, his face between his hands. He finally raised his head and he said:

"Those words are beautiful and disquieting."

"Enrich with them, my son, the true treasure of thought, the treasure of anxieties. But when it is a matter of those dreams that float beyond physics, never imitate Excycle of Megara or Zeno of Elea. Except for priests and other impudent individuals who affirm without smiling, and surround their affirmations not only with puerile proofs but also with threats and promises, don't reproach anyone who contradicts themselves. For you also, if you father a son one day, your son will be mortal. But the Eleat seeker of contradictions is the impotent individual who kills the children of others. And his fashion of saying 'No' to all doctrines resembles that in which eunuchs say 'No' to all women."

Psychodorus fell silent momentarily. Then he went on: "Hear a parable:"

The brigand Termeros had a head as hard as a rock, and he killed passers-by by bumping their heads against his own.

"Little children tell that story," Excycle interrupted, "and the people even have a saying that affirms that a man who has a splitting headache is suffering from "Termerian sickness."

"Tell us, then, O Excycle, how Termeros died."

One day, the passers-by—his names was Heracles—had a head harder than the brigand's. And the brigand died in the same fashion as his victims....

After a pause, Excycle added:

237

"That, at least, is what they say. But I don't see any connection between that fable and what we were saying about contradiction."

"That's because you understand fables with your ears. And as you have a tongue, you can repeat them. But your mind has not understood."

"Master," said Eubulus, "the man who kills by means of the Termerian sickness will perish by the Termerian sickness. In the same way, if, one day, Zeno said something...."

"Favor us with your silence," recommended Psychodorus, swiftly. "Your mind knows the story, but don't talk about it anymore, for the men to whom one tells all never know anything."

XII. The Smoke of Incense

Psychodorus had just been talking at length in one of those lyrical surges in which he sometimes indulged; and he had around him spectators rather than listeners. Their eyes were looking at him curiously and their charmed ears were doubtless receiving the valiant music flying from his lips; but their minds were disinterested in sounds that remained too opaque for them and might be empty.

Eventually, the philosopher fell silent.

"Master," said Eubulus, "when you started speaking, it seems to us that we were going to understand. But your discourse, in which we sensed a quivering and rising beauty, became less clear to us, and seemingly more distant, with every sentence."

"That is perhaps," replied Psychodorus, "because my discourse, departing from too high, never ceased to rise. It is not useless to you, however, in spite of initial appearances, if it has made you look up."

Excycle was wounded in his vanity, and he sniggered. "Master, can you not cause the discourse to descend, in such a way that it remains for a few moments at our level. The eagle, in spite of the power of its flight, can walk on the ground like a dog."

"The eagle," Eubulus remarked, "which walks on the plain, can no longer take off again, but it strikes the dust of a road with too broad a wing, which wounds it, and drives it to despair."

"Hear a parable," said Psychodore:

At the summit of an old tower whose staircase had collapsed, there were—I know not how—a few grains of incense.

Lightning set fire to that incense, which burned slowly, causing a blue and odorous smoke to rise toward the sky.

Men were watching from below, and the smallest of them said: "What does that smoke mean to us, which is trembling over the immobile tower like the plume of a marching warrior? The fire of heaven has doubtless set fire to some ordure. Let us congratulate ourselves on being down here, able to escape the stink."

Meanwhile, the smoke continued rising, and it said to itself: "The humans cannot sense my exquisite odor, but the gods will rejoice in it."

"That smoke was a theologian," sniggered Excycle.

But Psychodorus, who had not heard, went on:

It continued: "Perhaps the sky is uninhabited and I shall plunge uselessly into the vain heights. But I'm not something that can descend. I'm a light smoke and it's necessary that I rise."

Excycle drew away, murmuring:

"If someone, in order to attempt the conquest of the smoke, breaks his legs on the ruined stairway, it won't be me."

Meanwhile, Psychodorus finished the parable:

The smallest of the men exclaimed:

"What is a smoke for you to remain like that in an awkward attitude, looking up? Rather turn toward me. I'm palpable, and I don't give stiff necks to those who want to look at me."

The other men did not even know which of them was making an unwelcome noise down below, and they did not see the small companion agitating, at first, and soon going away. But with a dolorous aspiration, like a commencing nobility, they continued to watch the smoke, which continued to rise.

XIII. The Sleeper and the Dryads

Excycle and Theomanes were quarreling about the subject of the future life. The former denied that there is any other existence after this one, and, he declared, it was necessary to be mad not to see death as the denouement of the tragic or comic fable enacted by humans. But Theomanes praised death as the portal that, beneath our obscure groping, opened a sudden blaze of light and the entry to inexpressible joys:

"O death, O threshold of the true life, if humans were just they would call you life. But what they call life, they would name an overlong death and a tomb from which one emerges very belatedly...."

Then, without hearing the insulting laughter of Excycle, he described the marvelous Elysian Fields with which the hierophant had intoxicated him.

Psychodorus said:

"I am not accustomed, Excycle, to believe that the horizon is the limit of the world. The horizon is a wall to the weakness of my eyes, but which, opens up to my footfalls or beneath the wind of my thought."

"Your comparison," Excycle sniggered, "is singularly poor. The horizon is a coward that recoils when you advance. Death waits. No rapid runner has ever reached the horizon, but the slowest man will arrive at death."

"To our right," said Psychodorus, the view is closed by a mountain that, if we walk toward it, will wait for us. Do you believe that there is nothing on the other side of that mountain? In a few hours, whether you like it or not, night will arrive. Do you believe that there is no day on the far side of the night?"

"I remember having traversed mountains and nights. I don't remember ever having traversed death."

"Nor can you recall the first things that followed the crossing and cannot say, except by repeating tales told to you, what you did when you were a few months, or even a year old. I cannot explain to you, because I don't know, of what darkness that stupor is made, and of what darkness that forgetfulness is made, but you are constrained to admit that you were stupid and devoid of memory for a while and cannot know how long that period lasted."

"You reason nobly," approved Theomanes.

"However," Psychodorus went on, smiling, "I do not believe, like you, initiate, that there are beyond the horizon things very different from those I see here. It is always in my dreams that I have encountered marvelous spectacles, never in reality. Realities are poor and monotonous, like a forest or a miser's coffer; the forest produces many trees but few species; the treasure contains many coins but no great number of metals. Of countries that few people have visited prodigious tales are told, but seen at close range, the prodigies vanish or are reduced to simple things. On the other side of the mountain, I suppose the same elements as on this side are in conflict and harmony. Only their disposition varies, and their relative quantities. The river enjoys in its meanders a few differences, but always between solid banks, and its strangeness is limited by the same laws of nature as the agitations we see.

"Have no fear, however, that I shall imitate you, courageous Theomanes and draw the map of countries I have not seen, saying: 'Here runs a river, there stands a hill, there, under the subtle fingers of the wind, a forest sings.' No, I shall not even say such words, let alone dare to affirm that this river flows with milk and honey, that hill is a mass of gold larger and more brilliant than the sun, and that from those trees, by way of fruits, hang birds ready plucked that one only has to cook.

"I shall not talk gladly with precision about things of which I have no knowledge. I am content to say: That which I cannot see exists, like that I see. That which I cannot see doubtless resembles, in great measure, what I see. If I add a few vague probabilities, it is while smiling, and making fun of myself to some extent."

He fell silent momentarily, and then said:

"When it is a matter of unknown things, it seems to me to be appropriate to cast over our involuntary lies the modesty of a little mist and darkness. Tomorrow's sun will enlighten us tomorrow; in the meantime, let us talk about tomorrow, if you wish to do so, in hesitant and uncertain parables:"

A man penetrated into a forest that no one had ever entered. He walked for a long time among the quivering wonderment of the population of dryads. Then, feeling weary, he lay down on the ground and went to sleep.

The nymphs leaned over curiously toward the alarming spectacle and exchanged comments and anxieties.

"Alas," said one, "that admirable being, that walking tree, that god, rather—for that is how I imagine the gods—has fallen forever. The tree that is extended on the ground does not get up again."

"You're mistaken," replied the svelte inhabitant of a cypress. "Look more closely at that compact form, the form of a seed and not a tree. The seed is going to sink into the earth. Soon, its realization will emerge, fully grown, and it will become a myriad things nobler than its promise. In truth, that one will reemerge as superior to itself as the oak is superior to the acorn."

The dryads spoke for hours. Ingeniously and abundantly, they opposed argument against argument, comparison against comparison. Some erected the future of the sleeper like a tree of dreams, but the mouths of others, exhaling the cold wind of negation, tore apart the branches made of clouds of intoxicated hopes.

Eventually, the man woke up.

Amazed, they saw him stand up, entirely similar to himself, and walk away unchanged.

The dreamers and the deniers remained speechless for a long time, and they were saddened by an equal disappointment.

XIV. The Sculptor and the Ape

Excycle was subject to crises of zeal. For three days and three nights he deprived himself of food and drink, or, from dawn to dusk, he remained as motionless as an inanimate being; and he believed himself superior to all men.

He boasted, in these periods, of having attained an insensibility that he called divine, and scorned as cowardice the most natural emotions.

Excycle was undergoing one of these fevers when the tender Eubulus lost his mother. Excycle, having seen Eubulus weeping, was overcome with outrage. Like a refrain among insulting iambi, the same words often returned to his story and disdainful lips:

"Oh, what a poor philosopher...."

"Well," said Eubulus, finally, "I'd rather never become a philosopher than cease to be a human being."

But Psychodorus, who was passing, said: "A philosopher, for from destroying or deforming his humanity, is the only one who knows how to sculpt his humanity."

"A philosopher," Excycle defined, "is a man who annihilates his passions."

Psychodorus shook his head negatively. "It is necessary," he said, "to suppress the excess and the baseness of the passions—everything that forms, if I might put it thus, their animality. Wisdom does not consist of no longer enjoying and no longer suffering, no longer hating and no longer loving, but always sensing oneself to be human, never a ferocious or cowardly beast."

"Such distinctions," protested Excycle, "are subtleties and weaknesses. How can you distinguish between that which is human and that which is excessive or base? Will not the measure change with each individual? It is simpler to destroy everything, and also surer and more heroic, and that is more philosophical."

"O ape of philosophy, but no philosopher!" exclaimed Psychodorus. And he added: "Hear a parable:"

A sculptor was working in marble. His attentive, slow and prudent chisel disengaged a marvelously beautiful statue.

Not far away, an ape, also armed with a chisel and mallet, was striking another stone. His blows were much more vigorous than those of the sculptor. Soon, the entire block that the ape was attacking was nothing but debris.

Now Excycle, having seen these things, reproached the sculptor for the laxity of his effort.

"Take as an example," he said, "that valiant ape. See how in less than an hour, he has destroyed all the heaviness of the stone. Blush, then, you who have been timidly scratching at the same marble for days on end, as if you were afraid of harming it. Look and blush, for there remains before you almost as much matter as there was before your cowardly and hesitant hand undertook that task."

Excycle continued his speech for a long time, praising the courage of the ape and scorning the idleness and awkwardness of the sculptor.

Psychodorus fell silent. With a bitter laugh, Excycle said:

"I don't remember having passed the place you mention, or having seen the spectacle you describe, or having pronounced the words you claim to be repeating. Nevertheless, since you like that scarcely ingenious fiction and that insulting lie, tell me: What can the sculptor reply to the absurd but embarrassing speech that you credit to me as a sophist?"

The sculptor, having heard Excycle' words, shook his head and smiled. Then he declared, amiably:

"Your judgment, young man, dos not astonish me. You are not even alone in your opinion, and my donkey agrees with you. When I listen to you, I can hear in advance the complaints of the day when he transports the statue: 'O gods,' he will cry, 'why have you not given me for a master the ape, whose valor would have diminished, or rather annihilated, my burden...?'"

XV. The Child and the Lizard

"Hear a parable," said Psychodorus:

I was lying by the roadside. A child passed by with a bold expression. His right shoulder bore one of those iron implements with a handle, which serves to dig in the earth and can become, if necessary, a formidable weapon.

The child stopped, lifted his pick-ax to strike and said:

"Get out of the way, in order that I can kill this lizard, which was about to sting you."

I drew nearer to the reptile in order to protect it, but it slid away and was lost in the grass.

"Why did you save that malevolent beast?" the child reproached me,

"Lizards are not malevolent."

The child shook his head. "Not malevolent?" he said, astonished. "But yesterday, I killed one...."

As Psychodorus fell silent, Eubulus interrogated: "Had you no reply to make to the child?"

"There is no point in replying to judges," remarked Psychodorus, smiling. "Nevertheless I said this to him:

"If the lizard had killed you, the lizard would have been malevolent. Since you killed the lizard, it is you who are malevolent."

"What did the child reply?" asked Eubulus.

"The child did not reply in words. He had not been taught, I suppose, that it is customary to reply on such occasions, and the word paradox was unknown to the young peasant. But he shrugged his shoulders, and it was a naïve and sincere gesture.

"Then he looked at me. My face was serious and my critical eyes frightened him. He thought that I was the stronger and, wanting to give me pleasure, he laughed very loudly at what I had said, which was surely a joke.

Then—for the child was brave—without apparent haste, he drew away from the dangerous madman I might have been.

An hour later, Psychodorus heard the end of a conversation between two of his disciples:

"I assure you that Carystus is a bad man; the judges have condemned him several times."

No one ever knew why Psychodorus, who had been walking in silence for an hour, suddenly burst out laughing.

XVI. The Paradox

Psychodorus had just spoken one of those verities whose very simplicity renders them astonishing and repulsive to superficial minds.

"O ingenious paradox!" exclaimed Eubulus.

But the old philosopher said: "Hear a parable:"

I know a country whose inhabitants are always clothed. Next to a woman in labor the priest and the magistrate wait, and as soon as the child appears, grabbing hold of it, they wrap it up completely, hands and face included, in an elastic fabric that follows the contours of the body and will grow with it. Perhaps, in spite of its elasticity, the fabric resists, opposing the growth, for the people of the country in question remain singularly small.

The strange garment has openings that correspond to the eyes, the nostrils and the mouth, but it folds over slightly, stuck to the rim of the natural openings, and nowhere can that indecency, the skin, be perceived. It is even stuck over the eyelids. The lashes, joined by that artifice, almost as the feet of swimming birds are joined, give the gaze I know not what expression of stupidity and baseness.

During the growth of the child, and even later, because of wear and tear or some accident, the vestment sometimes splits. The victim of such a misfortune often succeeds in hiding it and remedying it in secret. In the contrary case he receives five strokes of the whip and then kneels down, and amid ceremonies and prayers, and the magistrates stick two superimposed patches of modest cloth over the rip.

I passed through that country in an epoch when hostile men had deprived me of my cloak. I walked innocent and nude among that religious people.

The women and young men soon assembled around me. A numerous troop followed me, praising the color of my vestment and its supple delicacy. After a time, however, priests arrived who abused the crowd with cries accompanied with gestures of execration. Then armed men dispersed them with blows of cudgels.

Seizing me, they took me before the supreme magistrate. There, an accuser got up and said: "This man is guilty of not wearing the garment that the city orders and of introducing an extravagant costume. He is guilty of corrupting women and young men by that means. Punishment: death."

"What have you to oppose for the defense?" the judged interrogated.

Naively, I replied: "I'm a stranger and I don't know your laws. However, I'm certain of not wearing the garments they condemn, since I'm as naked as a child emerging from his mother's body."

Now, those men affirmed that they liked urbanity, mental finesse and ingenious surprises of speech. They looked at one another therefore, smiling with their lips and their eyes; and the judge proclaimed:

"This is a stranger of an intelligence too pleasantly paradoxical for me to have the courage to condemn him."

The audience approved; and the accuser declared:

"More than anyone else, I admire grace and wit that is put into speech. That is why I withdraw my accusation against this man. There is also a profound meaning and useful information in his jest. The knowledge of the laws forms around the citizen a garment that warms him and an armor that protects him, with the consequence that this man, ignorant of our laws, the only natural and reasonable ones, is indeed as naked and poor as a new-born."

The little man was applauded warmly, whose gaze beneath his united lashes shone like agitated water beneath the feet of a duck. I sensed that the desire for that applause had contributed to my salvation, and I exchanged long felicitations with my unexpected defender.

The judge asked me whether my plan was to establish myself in the country or merely to pass through it. Before replying, I wanted to know what treatment I would receive in either case. My prudence was praised and it was explained to me that if I were to remain in the country, my unnatural vestment would first be removed, after which I would be dressed like everyone else. But if I were only passing through, they would assume that the paradoxical clothes that I was wearing were legal and noble in my own city and they would be content, for the time of my passage, to cover the local impiety with a long tunic similar to the one worn in winter to defend against the cold.

All those present surrounded me, exalting their country as the mildest of fatherlands and making efforts to retain me that certainly flattered me. Nevertheless, I preferred to protect, by means of a prompt departure, the integrity of what they called my paradoxical vestment.

XVII. The Shepherdesses of the Night

Excycle and Theomanes were quarreling. The other disciples formed an attentive circle around the disputants.

Excycle was lamenting the iron necessity that drives men, and which, from one falls to the next, rolls them down the hill all the way to the abyss of death.

But Theomanes was praising the golden necessity that draws men toward the immortality that is disengaged and revealed; in an almost animal life, it guides them to a divine life.

Each of them frequently pronounced the word Necessity. Sometimes, however, Excycle insulted the Fatality of things, while Theomanes praised the Providence of the gods.

When they fell silent, Psychodorus expressed a doubt: "Perhaps," he said, "you are not speaking about the same shepherdess." Then he went on: "Hear a parable:"

On an arid road that sloped downwards like a torrent of stones, I encountered innumerable blind men whose necks were trapped in carcans. Dogs were running along the two sides of the road and, amid barking, bit the blind men, who tottered. Behind the harassed troop, a woman armed with a prod struck those who lagged behind. Often, one of them fell, and other falls covered his as it was extended and prolonged. Then the dogs barked more loudly, bit more deeply, and the prod was agitated more actively. The blind men got up, wounded and groaning, to resume the groping march, fearful and jostled, but soon fell down again. Sometimes, in a song that mourned incessantly, they detested, under the name of Necessity, the Shepherdess who jabbed them with the prod, who had them bitten by the dogs and precipitated them down the rapid slope over the wounding stones.

At the end of the road that the innumerable troop was descending, an abyss abruptly swallowed the frightened blind men, but new sightless heads kept coming to maintain, and even increase, their number.

I fled far away from that terrible spectacle.

On another road that was scarcely less sad, shaded here and there by a few talkative oaks, I saw a second troop of blind men. Like a bacchante, a woman was pouring drink into cups and drawing them into her own intoxication with her mad song and the disordered racket of her dance. Those blind men were praising the gods in a canticle that reeked of baseness and wine. They were scornful of the road and its harshness, boasting of the implacable steepness of the slope, and looking forward to the voracious abyss. They called that slope Necessity, and the drunken woman who intoxicated them they called Religion or Initiation. They loved her wine of hope and her madness of promises.

She affirmed that the final fall would hurl them, eyes suddenly open, into a bottomless happiness. However, she said, it was necessary not to be deceived; it was necessary to fall to the right of the gulf and not to the left. When she declaimed regarding the gulf sinister and its infernal horrors, the dogs bounded, growing rapidly, at her head, her howling mouth, her agitated breast and her belt, which seemed like a circle of fire. But the drunkenness of the men praised the bites as benefits. The evils of today, said their chorus, are eggs soon hatched, from which living joys emerge. And like a miserly peasant-woman slipping one egg more under the brooding hen, they struck their bodies with whips and were ingenious in creating other sufferings in order to enrich the imminent treasure of their immortality.

I watched those madmen and the madwoman who was directing them for a while, and then I drew away.

It was hazard that had conducted me over the two steep roads toward the blind troops. My will and a light summoned me toward a third region.

The men who were walking there in a grave joy had open eyes. But over them and around them the darkness of a forest was stagnating, through which no paths cut, each of them was laboriously opening and upward route. A woman was marching ahead of them; she turned round frequently and the torch she was holding in her hand illuminated a smile and an encouraging gaze. The light and her face were visible, but the route along which she was guiding them, alas, was not. It seemed that, behind the light and behind the men, hasty brambles were growing, closing the passages.

The labor here was joyful, and the singer grave. The song said:

"O Necessity, whose other name is Light. O Light, whose other name is Reason. O Reason, whose other name is Liberty."

And the chorus repeated: "O Necessity-Liberty."

The hymn then said:

"No one is evil voluntarily. How can someone want to harm himself? But the man who falls has not seen the obstacle over which his foot has tripped, and alas, almost all men are blind."

"Where are you going," I asked, "behind the torch, through the obstacles?"

"We're marching behind our thought. We're traversing life, since we're mortal, climbing toward death, into which so many others are descending."

"What does the road matter, and what does it matter whether you climb or descend, if the end remains the same?"

"O insensate," cried one of the men, "sleep will soon weigh upon your eyelids, and for you the illuminated torches will be extinct. Is that any reason to crouch down in despair, close your eyes and refuse to see, while you can, the marvels that surround you? You eat today, and tomorrow you will be hungry again, but you do not say: 'What is the point of eating, since I will be hungry again?' Look at this blooming rose. This evening it will be faded. Does that foresight prevent you from loving its present color and its temporary perfume?"

The men were singing in chorus. Each one was saying his own words to his own rhythm, and yet, as a thousand gleams make one great light, I only heard one vast voice.

The strophe said:

"O Light, it is you that I name Necessity; for I know of necessity that which is good and that which is beautiful."

But the antistrophe responded:

"With all my strength, I march toward the good I sense, toward the beauty I see. With all my strength, I climb toward myself. For you are me, noble rising flame, and the poor animal slowness with which I am charged follows your joyful effort."

Then the epode of mildness and firmness suspended these words in the air, like a swaying dance:

"The hour that aspires me is the hour of apparent repose. I do not know what reality is hidden and is agitating beneath the immobile surface. I am on the brink of inevitable death, ignorant of what death is; but the gleams speak and you have told me, O torch, that life is neither a good nor an evil. That is why I, who understand you, will not die a coward. For whether my fate is better or worse than that of the men who still live, I cannot say, and only fools would dare to decide."

XVIII. Oedipus

"I do not attack anyone, but if my enemy raises his hand against me, I will raise my hand against him. Provided that my strength equals my courage, the aggressor will regret his error, and having mistaken a free and brave man for a cowardly slave."

Thus spoke Excycle, and he struck his chest sonorously.

The mild Eubulus, however, shook his head as a sign of disapproval.

But Psychodorus said: "Hear a parable:"

A king whose wife was pregnant sent someone to consult the oracle.

Phoebus the Tortuous replied: "The child that the queen bears in her womb is marked by the Moirae to kill his father and marry his mother. He will be the brother of his sons....

"That's the story of Oedipus you're telling us," remarked Excycle, disdainfully. "Do you imagine that we don't know that fable, as all children do?"

"You do, indeed, know it as a child does; and you have not understood it. No one has understood it, in fact, not even the harmonious Sophocles."

"O jealous man! O blasphemer!"

"And," Psychodorus continued, as if he had not heard, "there are in these illustrious adventures certain things un-· known to all, of which I want to inform you. Let him who is capable of understanding listen."

Left for dead on Mount Kitheron, Laius, his strength exhausted, saw the murderer draw away as if in triumph. Then two women appeared before him. And they both said:

"The man who has struck you mortally is your son. Watch him march gloriously toward the pomp of an incestuous marriage and the remainder of his destiny."

Laius, raising his dolorous body feebly, said: "Who are you and what do you want with me?"

Now, the visage of one of the women was as hard as iron; but she wrung her hands as if in impotence, and she made no reply to the dying man's question.

The other was as beautiful as Athene herself, and as serious and as regally calm. She spoke.

"The one that you see beside me," she said, "is named Violence. She has fallen silent at present because you no longer have the strength for the follies she counsels, but she has spoken to you before and you have listened to her. That is why you are dying wretchedly. Look—you'll recognize her."

"I recognize her," murmured Laius. "But she has changed her name. Once, I sometimes called her Prudence and sometimes Justice."

The apparition who bore, on a face similar to that of Athene, an even nobler calm, went on:

"As for me, you do not recognize either my voice or my features. However, I am never separated from this bad adviser. Every time she came to you, I accompanied her, but you only had eyes and ears for her, and when I tried to speak, you forced me to shut up, ignominiously.

The old man interrogated: "Tell me your name, you who are accusing me."

"My name is Abstention."

"That's the name of a slave, and I was a king."

"Fools believe, in fact, when I am named, that the reference is to a trembling slave, but few sages are unaware that my name is nobler than Olympus. And I am not only more powerful than Zeus, but more powerful than the destiny that curbs Zeus and the rest of the living."

Abstention continued:

"If you had listened to me, your son would not have struck you. He would not be hastening now toward the maternal bed, the infamous source from which, perhaps, ineradicable evils will flow for him and for others. Every action, O man, has its cause and produces its effect. Every action is a link in the circle of folly and iron that blind men and the cruel Moirae forge. The evil that you fear makes you commit an evil from which precisely what you fear will emerge.

"All violence is fecund, and its daughters, who bear the same name, are furies turned against the man who espouses their mother. All cunning is fecund, and its daughters are named deceits. But the wise man who refuses violence and lies is freed from the circle of iron and, climbing to the serene temple, is higher than destiny and freer than Zeus.

"If wise men were numerous, many links would fall and the Moirae would weep, unable to reforge the chain. But destiny has no fear of losing one day the quivering stool formed under its feet by the heads of men, and the yokes and necklaces with which they charge themselves, for wise men are always rare."

"What do these things matter to me?" said Laius, "at the moment when I am about to die."

"Presumptuous man!" groaned Abstention, "you speak as if you knew what death is."

Excycle remarked: "Abstention would not have been able to make such a speech to Oedipus, for Oedipus was subject to a fate that he had not created."

But Psychodorus continued:

Abstention made all the dying hear analogous words. She said to Agamemnon under the fatal net:

"If you had not sacrificed Iphigenia...."

She said to Clytemnestra under her son's dagger:

"If you had spared Agamemnon...."

She said to Orestes:

"O shame! It was necessary, for the circle to be broken, that the gods show themselves less wicked than men...."

"I asked you what she could say to Oedipus," the hostile disciple persisted.

The one that the trembling gods name Abstention and the stammering of mortals sometimes calls Wisdom said to Oedipus, when he remained alone in the wood of Colonna:

"If you had not killed, you would not have killed your father."

Oedipus had a bitter curl at each corner of his mouth, and he replied, as violent as with Tiresias, as harshly mocking as with Creon:

"O speaker of futile naiveties...."

But Abstention cried:

"It is you who made a naïve and futile gesture on the day when, gripping the golden claps of Iocasta's garments, you punctured your eyes! How naïve and futile that gesture was! For you were always blind, you who could not see a relative in every man you encountered, you who did not recognize a brother in every Ephemeron of your era, a son in every child and a father in every old man!"

XIX. Boreas and Auster

Excycle, amid loud cries, was waving his arms desperately. And tears, running down his cheeks, were suspended like dew in the hairs of his nascent beard.

Psychodorus asked him: "Is it for the treason of a woman or the bite of a tarantula that you're dancing all alone an entire tragic chorus?"

"Alas! Alas! Alas!" replied Excycle.

"But you're dancing an ugly and disordered chorus," the philosopher went on. "You ought to have picked up your lyre first."

The young man quivered and trembled all over, under the pins and needles of a thousandfold impatience. Then, in a voice that was already irritated while still weeping, he said:

"I have no need of a lyre or advice. This isn't a game. This is an agony, an irremediable agony. My dolor, my powerful than me, more powerful than the universe...."

"Excessive and impotent being, whom the superficial tide of things always tosses from one folly to another! Today you're groaning like a child who has broken his toy; morrow you'll be laughing and bounding like the child who has been given knucklebones. However, if you wish, hear a parable...."

"I don't want to hear anything. Your voice reaches me as insignificant and vain as the unconscious song of a bird amid the din of a storm. My heart is a vast sea entirely uplifted by the blackest of tempests."

Psychodorus smiled, and said, approvingly:

"O my son, how right you were to close your ears to my futile parable, for your lips have said it before mine."

Excycle, moved by curiosity, said: "I don't believe I've said any parable."

"Let me, then, open before you the parable that you have given me regarding the blackest of tempests. Perhaps that coffer, which seems banal to you, contains an unexpected treasure:

Boreas said one day to Auster:

"Your power is feeble. Under your breath the sea scarcely changes color; it remains green-tinted or dark blue. But if it's me who penetrates it and raises it, the astonished waves rear up suddenly as a herd of black mares."

"That's true," replied Auster, "but the black mares you whip up, whinnying, all the way to the clouds, disappear as soon as you cease to blow, like a deceptive herd of dreams, and, in no time, the surface of the sea, which no longer remembers, extends evenly like a mirror. But if my less abrupt impetuosity has overturned the ocean, a long time after my kisses and violence have gone to sleep, you can still perceive a fermentation in the waves, which cannot forget me, and a disturbance that is not appeased."

Glorious and mocking, Auster went on:

"O Boreas, similar to an amorous caprice or the savage dolor that howls and that a sight will calm down, I change initial appearances less than you, and my impact appears at first to be felt less, but I am like the amour that endures. Or, if you prefer, the dolor that resembles me plunges deeply and hides, and gnaws away at the heart with unperceived and tenacious teeth."

As soon as Psychodorus had drawn away, Excycle resumed his lamentations. And he protested that after such an event, his life would be a cup forever overflowing with bitterness.

An hour later, however, among numerous companions, he was speaking with animation, and his face radiated a foolish pleasure. His mouth, previously twisted with dolor and sobs, was wide open to let through the harmonious laughter that shakes the entire body as it bursts forth.

XX. The Sea

The gentle Eubulus had a fiancée. She also came to listen to Psychodorus, but she did not understand anything he said. She was, therefore, astonished by and jealous of the young man's affection for the philosopher.

She said: "If you love me, how can you savor joys that I do not share?"

And then she said: "I want the heart that loves me to do so entirely. I cannot tolerate that the man who speaks to me of love can listen happily to a voice that is not mine."

Finally, she said: "Choose between me and that old fool."

"Alas," groaned Eubulus, "it's you who have chosen. You call folly what I call wisdom. I cannot associate my fate with the fate of a stranger who does not understand my language and who, instead of trying to climb my path, proud of her unintelligence and baseness, mocks the summits to which I aspire."

"Since that is your wish," exclaimed the young woman, "I'm leaving forever, and you'll weep for a long time."

"If I weep," relied Eubulus, mildly, "at least you won't know it."

When he was alone, the abandoned individual at first insulted the one who had left, but soon, in fact, he wept.

Several uncertain days and nights went by. Sometimes the young man uttered the valiant speeches that rise up, and which one tries to follow. Sometimes he hid from everyone in order to dissolve in tears. What rendered him more unhappy than anything else was that he blushed at his tears and would have liked to hide them from himself.

Finally, he came to ask for consolation from Psychodorus. He told him about his dolor and the cause of his dolor. He explained the combats that he was sustaining, and his frequent defeats, and how he got up only to be subject once again to the battle, the laceration and the fall.

"I'm ashamed," he sighed. "For, among noble and fragile aspirations, my suffering agitates vile sentiments of which I did not think myself capable. I'm ashamed, for, at times, I feel and think as basely as the most cowardly of men."

"The coward," said Psychodorus, "is not the man who falls, but the man who does not get up again." He went on, while embracing Eubulus:

"Oh my son, hear this parable:"

The sea lamented in these terms:

"In vain I lift my waves and launch them toward the inaccessible sky. Always, O sadness, they fall back. Always, O shame, they fall back heavily to the level of the most noxious pools."

The wind replied to the sea:

"You are an earthly thing. You wear the universal yoke, weight, and it is necessary for every surge that you support on the earth to fall back there. But you are the strongest, the largest and the most vivifying of earthly things. Do not insult your dancing waves by comparing them to the leprous and stupid waters of marshes. Pools never whip up the magnificent pride of tempests and never send a purifying breeze to the land. Rejoice, profound and robust sea, for you are the most beautiful thing I know; you are a struggle that does not yield, a heroism that gets up again, a defeat that, since it recommences combat, remains unvanquished. You are, O noble sea, a rising harmony of hymns, efforts and aspirations."

XXI. Childbirth

The disciples came to Psychodorus and said to him: "Several of the parables that we have heard from you remain obscure. Can you not reveal their secret to us?"

"No," replied Psychodorus.

"Why not?"

"In order that you can retain some chance of understanding them."

"Now you're speaking an enigma. Will you, at least, consent to give us the key to that?"

"So be it," said Psychodorus. "But it will be a parable:"

In the dolors of a first childbirth, a young woman was crying out in a cowardly fashion. Amid her screams and sobs, she reproached the man who was about to become a father:

"Since you had the whim of seeing a child in our house, you might have done well, instead of imposing on me the long inconvenience that I have traversed and the suffering that I shall perhaps escape in death, to adopt an orphan."

While she was weeping and crying, the husband consoled her with vague exhortations. But when she repeated the criticism he made no reply. Once, she even became irritated because she thought she saw him smile.

When the child had come, the servants took the little body away to wash it. Then they came back and placed it, crying and bursting with life, in the maternal arms,

The young woman emerged from the exhaustion that had followed her agitation and her cries. She looked at the child, and her face radiated a great joy.

Then the husband, breaking a long silence, asked: "If I had brought into the house a child already formed, would you have loved him like that one, and would you have adopted him, like that one, with a glad enthusiasm?"

It was the young woman's turn not to respond, and to smile.

XXXII. The Couple

Psychodorus was walking pensively, fully occupied with interlacing the harmony of yesterday and today, the weave of memory of thought, the caduceus of life in which joys and regrets twist to the same rhythm and are coupled.

In a low voice, separated by long intervals, he pronounced a few words.

Eubulus collected them in the emotional cup of his mind, as a herdsman receives patiently in his hands, united like a kiss, the water of a spring that was flowing generously yesterday but is falling one drop at a time today.

Now Psychodore, amid long silences, said to himself:

All the thoughts that visit me and all the joys to which I open my heart still bear the name and visage of the beloved.

Or, sometimes, he exclaimed: "Oh, beloved, disappeared so long ago, with the naïve eyes that only looked outwards…!"

And he asked himself:

Do you know, Psychodorus, whether Psychodorus is anything but the visible form of the memory of Athenatime?

He also said:

"My thought—or, so at least, it seems—grows and is colored like a fruit in autumn. But the growing and increasingly gilded globe encloses the same nucleus around which its green and light youth hugged so tightly."

Then he fell silent for a long time. Meanwhile, Eubulus admired the light of ecstasy that glided, quivering, over his entire face: the light of ecstasy that sprang from his eyes like the nearby springs.

Finally, he young man could not contain his love, and he said, with a tremor of indefinable emotion:

"O Master, all the wisdom that I have heard resounding on lips, or that I have read in books, offered weaknesses, and also all the joys that I have known by way of my heart or the words of men. But you, your infallible wisdom and your infallible joy...."

"I love," said Psychodorus, "and I am loved."

Excycle, who had approached, told Eubulus; "It's to himself that he is speaking, not to us. The words that you have addressed to him have not reached his consciousness."

Psychodorus looked at Excycle with a mischievous smile, and Eubulus with a smile of affection; and he said: "Hear a parable:"

A tempest had cast up a number of men on Circe's island. Thanks to her beverages, which translated into material forms the stupidity of minds or the baseness of hearts, the enchantress had augmented her herds of donkeys and pigs.

One man and one woman remained unchanged, however. They went forth holding hands, frequently putting their lips together, which seemed not to be able to pull apart thereafter. They bit into the same fruits and drank from the same springs.

Circe presented them with the most energetic of philters, a philter powerful enough to metamorphose Phoebus into a peacock, Hermes into a fox or Ares into a tiger.

Without realizing it, they took the beverage that was offered, and they drank from the broad cup together, like two doves' breaks plunging into the same hollow in the rock after the rain.

When the cup was empty, they let it fall negligently on to the grass and drew away.

They did not go away in the debased form of animals. They were still walking upright and svelte, gazing into one another's eyes. They sometimes stopped, lips joined. They walked and they paused, still a man and still a woman.

Circe, furious, followed them covertly, and she wondered: *What, then, has destroyed the redoubtable strength of the philter?*

They did not know that anyone was behind them, or the question with which the enchantress was lacerating herself furiously; but Circe was soon mourning her irremediable impotence, for a slight internal disturbance had caused the lovers to speak.

The beloved man had said to the beloved woman: "I have reason to be a man, O life of my life, since you are a woman."

And she had replied: "Since you are a man, O heart of my heart, it's necessary that I am a woman."

The other disciples were walking in a dreamlike glow, and they felt charged with a joyful interior weight, as if after a satisfying meal.

But Excycle sniggered. "Athenatime has been dead for a long time, Psychodorus, and you are alone now."

The old philosopher looked at Excycle as one looks at a madman.

"Are you sure," he asked, "that one can be alone when one loves, and that one can be dead when one is beloved?"

No one replied, and Psychodorus was silent for a long time.

XXIII. The Conjugal Bond

"Marriage," proclaimed Theomanes, "is a sacred thing. When religion has united a man and a woman, I deem it criminal if they draw apart from one another and separate."

"When a stupidity," said Psychodorus, "is too absurd and tyrannical for men to admit it, they make it a sacred thing, and that is the purpose the gods serve. The follies for which Law, shameless as it is, dares not make itself responsible, are thrown back to its sister, Religion."

"Will you, who wear your unbound fidelity like a belt woven of gold and crimson, so many years after the death of Athenatime, deny the nobility of the unique union and the bond that nothing can dissolve?"

"No foreign bond attached us to one another. No magistrate's stupidity was between us, and no priest's lie. But hear instead a parable:"

On the agora of I know not what city, a dog and a bitch where exhausting themselves in efforts to peel themselves apart. Children were laughing at their grotesque and vain movements. The most malevolent were even throwing stones at them.

The animals—the dog and the bitch, that is—seemed to become increasingly irritated with one another. Their desire had been satisfied for a long time, and had mutated into disgust some time ago. Now it was as if they were enchained by a folly of hatred, and that hatred was exasperated further by the fact that before the spectators and under the stones, they dared not howl and bite.

A physicist tapped me on the shoulder and said: "The poor animals! How cruel nature is to them. In truth, the mechanism of their pleasure is the mechanism of a trap. Imagine it. The dog's member contains a hollow bone that allows passage to the channel of the future; but around that bone, flesh is dormant that desire awakens and sensuality hardens and swells. The dog's joyous extremity becomes as enormous, during the sacrifice to Aphrodite, as a triumphant tyranny. The sacrifice complete, the poor swollen priest remains inside the sealed door, attached to the altar. Recall the child in the fable: he had seized hazelnuts in an urn with a narrow entrance, and could not withdraw his full closed hand; but it only required the child, provided that he thought of it or was instructed, to open his hand and pull it out. The dog is obliged to wait for a long time, and its efforts before that time, entangle it further."

The physicist went on:

"Let us thank Nature; she has not made humans on the model of the dog, and permits us to flee at the moment when sensuality is saddened."

But a woman was standing behind us, who murmured: "Alas, when she has forgotten a cruelty, how Religion and the City are able to substitute for Nature!"

I turned round, and I saw tears in the eyes of the speaker.

Although the physicist was from the locale and appeared to know the woman, I did not think it necessary to ask him whether she was married.

XXIV. The Tree

"Only logic produces truth," said Excycle.

But Theomanes, in a scornful tone, said: "Logic is that which I call appropriately the Sterile, or even, on days when I am not generous to my enemies, the Impoverisher. A syllogism only renders in its conclusion a portion of what is given to it by its premises. If the end of your discourse is richer than the commencement, you have been illogical. Now, you have emerged from the narrow and desert circle to go toward the true or the false in accordance with whether you are heading in the direction of the One, which is Being, or the direction of the Multiple, which is Appearance."

"Where will I find, then, according to you, the fecund mother who gives birth to verities?"

"I don't know whether she has a name among the philosophers, but for myself I call her Esctasy; for she enables me to emerge from myself and lose myself, an intoxicated drop, in the divine ocean."

"What do you bring back from such voyages?"

"Truth, I tell you. But it isn't thought and words; it's sentiment and emotion. When my amorous and stammering folly attempts to name it, I call it, trembling, That-Which-Has-No-Name. O Ineffable...."

Theomanes was, in fact, trembling, and his eyes seemed to be gazing at a glare that no one could see.

"Now he's as drunk as a bacchante!" remarked Excycle; and with both hands he shook the initiate, as one wakes a sleeper.

"Would you like us," he said, "to obtain the advice of Psychodorus."

Vague and weary, Theomanes' voice was that of a diver coming up, breathless from the depths of water or slumber.

"Psychodorus," he said, with a fatigued gesture of semi-repulsion, "charms me and desolates me. That sage shows me the emptiness of wisdom, the weakness of Antaeus when he was no longer supported by his mother Gaia, the weakness of man when he refuses to support himself on God.

The philosopher went by, one hand on Eubulus's shoulder. The disciples who had been listening to the quarrel summoned him, and, sometimes several speaking at once, they explained the subject of the dispute confusedly.

"Logic," Psychodorus declared, "is a necessity of intelligence. The reduction of the multiple to unity is another human need. The satisfactions that intelligence gives itself, here as there, come from within, not from things or being. Now, between the fullness of things and the avidity of thought, is there concordance, and does the water with which we fill it have, before entering the vase, the form of the vase? That is a question that I always leave without response, a poor blind thing, with only my eyes to see my eyes and only my mind to judge my mind."

"To the blindness of which you speak," remarked Theomanes, "the gods would be subject as well as men. The gods themselves, if it is not necessary to reject your words as an impiety and a despair, could not affirm that they know the reality of things."

Psychodorus shook his head, smiling.

"Euclid can tell the truth about the circle, because his thought has created the circle, and he is not naïve enough to worry about whether there are, outside of his thought, perfect circles and equal radii. Perhaps the thought of the gods creates things as the thought of Euclid invents figures. Perhaps, too, I am a god and I create my universe. But if you regard the mind of the gods as a receptivity that knows a world composed, outside of them, of I know not what realities, then they too as are ignorant as the man who, instead of boldly projecting his universe, wants to become, timid and servile, the science of I know not what foreign universe. In that case you believe that there are large mirrors, but you are a small mirror. And it is not being large that will permit the mirror to know whether it is distorting objects. And what a strange and active mirror it is necessary for you already to be, if you know that you know nothing, if you perceive, in a somersault, that only one thing is certain, knowing that the image is not the object."

The philosopher fell silent momentarily. Then he added, softly: "However, the quarrel of Theomanes and Excycle was perhaps agitating other thoughts a little while ago. Hear then, concerning unity, a parable:"

In one of my voyages or one of my dreams—what does it matter?—I saw a tree as large and as bushy on its own as an entire forest. It was populated by an innumerable multitude of tiny humans. They had exactly the same form as us but their size was that of the red-headed ants that are as brutal and mad as soldiers, who make war on other ants and have slaves.

The occupations of the minuscule beings who lived in the tree resembled those of Greeks and Barbarians. The inhabitants of one branch fought battles against those of other branches. They contracted alliances like those uniting two bands of brigands or two peoples for a dangerous and difficult expedition. They agreed truces or wrote peace treaties on the debris of leaves, which they tore up as soon as they thought they were the stronger.

Toward the middle of each branch, a leaf was set up that was called the agora. At times that were perhaps regularly fixed they gathered there to talk, sometimes bombastically, sometimes amid discordant cries, about certain trivia designated by the name of public affairs. Those little people held trials, made speeches and delivered judgments in order to decide whether the third vein of the fifth leaf of the seventh branch to the right belonged to the owner of the second vein or reverted to that of the fourth.

Amid the agitation of these poor creatures, the grave appearance of certain individuals was noted. They bore four hairs on the chin, which were known as the philosophical beard, and their mouths opened readily to insult the folly of others; but they were often less mad than the others.

Some of the little philosophers traveled from branch to branch or, as their murmur put it, from fatherland to fatherland. One of them, while I was watching, descended as far as the trunk. He went around it two or three times, at various heights, astonished and rejoicing no longer to find the multiplicity of branches. However, the odor of damp grass reached his height and intoxicated his little brain. Soon he started singing to a slow and religious rhythm, and this is what his hymn said:

"O Unity, O You who created us and supports the branches and the multiple, O Unity, nothing is more profound than you...."

He climbed back up to the inhabited regions, and he went about clamoring his discovery everywhere, but the other sons of the branches, occupied in fighting, making speeches, judging and negotiating for the debris of dead leaves, did not listen.

"Now, an animal, arrived during the night, had scratched the foot of the tree. I saw that little people of the same species were also living on the roots. I noticed one of them who had the philosophical beard. He was searching for I know not what, in a hope that was groping, dubious and anxious. A fortunate hazard or wise conduct guided him to the trunk. When he had recognized it, he went back down again precipitately. While protecting with his tiny hands eyes that had been wounded by too much light, he sang, that individual ignorant of the branches, much as the individual ignorant of the roots had sung.

"O Unity," his enthusiastic ode said, "O You who dominate the multitude, nothing rises above you, Altitude. Nothing, no nothing, rises up any higher in the dazzling cataracts of light."

XXV. The Moles

Several disciples were talking animatedly. They finally headed toward Psychodorus, and Eubulus said:

"Master, we have made sincere efforts to understand your attitude concerning divine things and the utmost human depths. But all those thoughts that are beyond physics, it seems to us that you sometimes scorn and detest them as hindrances to action, and sometimes love them as rare and precious things.

"If you can," said Excycle, supportively, "explain to us the contradiction that Eubulus has just brought to light."

But Eubulus protested: "you're exaggerating and deforming my thought, malevolently. What is an amorous anxiety, you're making into a hostile accusation. Sometimes, Psychodorus, I think, in a flash or a dream, that I perceive the unity of thought concerning these things. But I can't succeed in gripping it strongly enough to enclose it in narrow words that would render it sensible to others and permit me to conserve, of that broad but fleeing joy, a perhaps diminished but durable pleasure.

"Hear a parable," said Psychodorus:

Moles are blind nowadays. If someone examines them superficially, he might think that no mole's head has ever known light. However, by lifting up the hair as compact as a fabric, one perceives their eyes, shrunken and devoid of gaze, as sad as dispossessed kings. And one thinks that the head in question has not been deprived by the dictate of nature, but by the slowly obstinate crime of ancestral habit.

This, then, my sons, is the Pythagorean dream that I had one melancholy day, as I gazed at one of those impoverished heads.

A myriad years ago, I lived in the body of a mole. Similar in all other respects to the moles of today, we still enjoyed the light. Many among us went abroad preaching: "Never open the eyes. The eye is not an organ, it is a trap that receives dust and dolor during labor."

The people listened to that cowardly wisdom. Those who initially rejected it with a generous indignation ended up, after having suffered several times in their eyes, by submitting to the necessity. Some, however, were obstinate, proclaiming scornfully the folly of their generation and courageously keeping their eyes open. Alas, the earth, which wounded their weeping irises continually, blinded them more rapidly than the others.

Instructed by their misfortune, I made myself a rule of conduct and I explained it to anyone who cared to listen. But it was criticized for being subtle, unequal and difficult to understand. You would find it easy, my sons, by virtue of the part of your mind that does not resemble the mind of a mole.

While, in the groping search for nourishment, I hollowed out my subterranean tunnels, I kept my useless and dolorous eyes closed; but I gave as little time as possible to that labor of digging, and all my leisure I occupied in going above ground, in order to drink joy and light with my expanded gaze.

XXVI. The Dimensions

"Geometry," affirmed Excycle, "is a system of certainties that is imposed upon the gods as well as mortals. I defy anyone who has a knowledge of space to conceive it in any other way than with its three dimensions."

"Even when it is a matter of geometry," remarked Psychodorus, "I think it dangerous to be dogmatic and intolerant. But listen, on that subject, to a memory of a voyage. Perhaps it includes, for those who want to hear it, a parable:"

I had arrived on a large island off the far coast of vast Asia. The inhabitants were small, yellow in color, with anxious faces, and hooded eyes that, descending from the root of the nose toward the apples of the cheeks, would resemble, if they were not too narrow, the openings of certain tragic masks. They appeared to me at first to be intermediate beings between children and apes. When I learned their language I was struck by some of their thoughts and I knew what I ought to have divined—to wit, that their eyes, different from our eyes, do not see all that we see, but see numerous things that we do not see.

I remained in their country, trying to enrich myself with the universe of their eyes.

I became the friend of an old sage who was followed by a large number of disciples. I listened, hiding myself in that attentive crowd. But when the old sage had said enough he searched for me with his gaze and ordered:

"Speak in your turn, Psychodorus."

I would have liked to remain silent, fully occupied in classifying my new riches with a jealous care; but he said: "You are too rich and too just to receive without giving. In exchange for my coin, pay us with the drachmas and mines of our homeland."

"Our money is not worth as much as ours."

"Give anyway, in order that these should know that it is different and equal. Give in order that they can make progress toward the knowledge of the only universal currency."

And if a disciple asked: "What is the universal currency?" the old sage with the hooded eyes replied: "Perhaps the scorn for all local currencies."

One day, when we were in his house, he took from various cages ten or twelve little animals quite similar to our mice. As soon as they were free they formed a ridiculous circle, each putting its nose to the tail of the preceding one, and then, in that singular order, began to turn in a rapid and hectic round.

While we were considering the alarming spectacle, the master said: "One of my mice having died this evening, I shall show you something."

He opened the head of the dead mouse. Behind the interior part of the ear he directed our attention to two minuscule bony conduits, which he called, by virtue of their form, the semicircular canals.

Then he explained: "This is the part of the animal that knows the dimensions of space.[60] Humans—I will show you as soon as I can procure the cadaver of a victim of execution—had three pairs of these canals, and that is why human space has three dimensions. The mouse of our country only has two pairs, and it manifests, by its fashion of running, that its space is reduced to two dimensions."

He added:

"The elongated fish that we call a lamprey only has a single pair of semicircular canals, and so its space as only one dimension. But it is a calm animal, and it does not manifest its opinions in a fashion as tumultuous as our mice."

Someone asked:

---

[60] This fundamental proposal was first put forward by the pioneering neuroanatomist Pierre Flourens (1794-1867), although Ryner's elaboration of it is idiosyncratic, especially its extension to speculations regarding the dimensions of time.

"What if a child—for the gods sometimes produce monsters—were born with four pairs of semicircular canals?"

"He would discern four dimensions in space," affirmed the sage with the hooded eyes, without hesitation.

Then he said, seeming at first to be speaking to himself:

"What organ gives us the knowledge of time? I don't know. But it is as poor in us as the organ of space is in the lamprey. Among the inferior gods it is doubtless double or triple, with the consequence that their chronology does not elongate like our poverty-stricken and linear chronology, but is displayed in breadth, and rises and plunges like our geometry. Some of them are released in the abyss of time like our birds in the abyss of air; they open vast wings in order to flutter or soar there. Oh, the marvelous voyages they enjoy! Be jealous, O voyager Psychodorus! Through what is the past for our ignorance and our heaviness, they travel when they want to, all the way to the birth of worlds. But if they desire tragic spectacles they launch themselves toward the collapse of the universe, future and hidden from our immobility. Sometimes, also, their flight traverses these ruins to reach renaissances so distant and indecisive that our thought names them in a vertigo."

My lips smiled during this enthusiastic discourse. The sage perceived my smile.

"You don't believe the gods I describe to be possible?" he asked, with astonishment.

"I don't know the limits of the possible, but I find you bold because you affirm it."

"That is because I know the art of affirming one thing without denying others," he said. "Wisdom, when it occupies itself with such questions, is an audacious woman who destroys the limits initially perceived and then goes everywhere, seeking boundary-markers to tear up and barriers to knock down. Believe me, Psychodorus, the world is not as small as you. All of the beings that you can imagine exist, and all of those that those beings can imagine. Go as far as the forces in increasing circles. There all boldnesses remain timidities and all prodigalities are poor. The world is myriads times richer than the thought of the gods before whom the gods you honor bow down trembling."

"You are saying a great deal, my generous host."

"No, I am saying very little, or rather I am saying nothing, since I am trying, stammering with impotence, terror and love, to say everything."

XXVII. The Sons of the Centauress

Eubulus said, in a plaintive tone: "In spite of my efforts, I cannot arrive at unity. I sense noble ideas germinating and quivering within me trying to rise up, but heavy idea that fall and almost drag me down with them also emerge from me. It's as if I were not only thinking with my head but also with my belly."

"Strike the thoughts in your belly," ordered Excycle, "until they die."

"They don't want to die. Sometimes, it seems to me that it would require very little to make them thoughts of the head, with the consequence that I hesitate to strike them, expel them, or even to dislike them."

"Lighten them," said Psychodorus, "and sustain them, in order that they might rise to the dignity of the others."

"How shall I do that?"

"Only nourish yourself with humanity and desires from above. Then you will have nothing heavy to give to your offspring."

"It seems to me that I almost understand, but...."

But Psychodorus, extending his hand, said: "Hear a parable:"

A widowed centauress had two sons. She was often seen lying on the grass, her rump extended over the ground, with her upper body propped up on her elbow. She stretched out her hind feet but tucked up the front ones, curbing one and bracing the other on the ground like a horse about to get to its feet. She leaned sideways slightly in order to give milk to her sons. One, carried in her arms, drank from her human breasts; the other trailed in the meadow, hanging from her mare's teats.

She was a centauress admirable in her strength and in her double beauty. Half her body was that of one of the spirited mares of Thessaly that have not yet been domesticated, and the other half that of the most beautiful woman in the world, except that her ears were straight and pointed, like those of satyrs in paintings. All those who saw her thought that she was happy, but a chagrin was afflicting her heart.

She came to consult the oracle, saying: "O Apollo Loxias, one of my sons, as you know, is a meadow in which nothing but joy grows, but the other is a field of stones and dolors. He hits his brother brutally and his piercing teeth bite my teats if I move, or even if I shiver in the wind. Tell me how I can put a stop to his malevolence and my suffering."

"It would be sufficient," said the oracle, "to strike him with your hooves to kill him."

"I love him, alas," said the centauress. "I love him as much as the other."

"Nourish him, too, on your human milk."

"I've tried. He refuses it."

"Make your animal teats dry up."

"By what means?"

"No longer eat, even when no one can see you, anything but human nourishment, and disdain, as if there were not a mare beneath your upper body, the raw grass of the meadow."

The centauress asked other questions, but the god made no reply.

XXVIII. The Blind People

Eubulus, emerging from long reflections, asked: "Do you see the fable that you told us yesterday in all its astonishing richness?"

Psychodorus expressed a doubt. "Perhaps you are enriching it with some poverty of which I was not thinking. Speak, then, in order that we know."

His voice sounding like the voice of a man who has drunk too much, amid enthusiastic gestures, which rendered a suddenly unsteady gait strange, Eubulus exclaimed: "I shall go to my city. I shall tell the shivering citizens the parable of the centauress and her sons. My fatherland, having understood, will become noble and god, which will render noble and good those of its children of whom it complains.

Psychodorus shook his head.

"I only speak to men that I encounter," he said, "or who come to me, because it happens that a man has ears. But a fatherland, my son, never has ears, even straight and pointed ones, and is not made for hearing parables, but for abusing as a fool a man who tries to tell them, and, if he tries to explain them, for exiling or killing him.

Eubulus stopped, and groaned.

"I believe I hear Anaxagoras, and Socrates, and a whole chorus of sages singing that you are right. For myself, I am saddened and do not understand. Why do men treat as enemies the best among them, those who would bring them happiness and justice if they listened to them? Why do they deprive themselves of words that could cure their ills? Why do they exile the orators of those words to barbaric lands, or all the way to the regions of death? That problem seems despairing to me not only for the benevolent individual who only feels happy amid the happiness of all, but also for the less ambitious individual who would simply like to understand. What would a Euclid say about that who applied himself, not to knowing the properties of triangles and circles, but to distinguishing the nature of human beings?"

Psychodorus replied: "Hear a parable:"

There is a land in which the light is kinder than in Greece itself. The climate is so benign that people there have no need of garments or hoses. Wild berries grow there abundantly, more flavorsome than the best-cultivated of our fruits. A plant ten times as large as our wheat, which bears delicious loaves of bread instead of ears, ornaments the sides of all the roads of its own accord.

But aristocrats and priests are jealous by nature; goods that are not privileges and superiorities lose all value for them. They have organized the city in such a way as to be the only ones to enjoy the advantages of the region freely. They forbid other men to collect the bread and the fruits, and allow an enormous quantity of nourishment to rot. They distribute insufficient food to the poor. For themselves, they have the art of making themselves vomit and eating again immediately thereafter. They are, however, unhappy, always weighed down and afflicted by painful indigestion, always worried by the idea that is some poorly monitored corner of the land, someone is doubtless stealing a little of what they affirm to be theirs.

After several centuries, however, they have found a means of being partly assured. As soon as a child of the people comes into the world, his eyelids are sealed with a glue that the priests and certain servants of the rich, known as savants, know how to make. Thus, only the aristocrats, the priests and the savants enjoy the light. They often strike the other men, who, knowing their inferiority, curb their heads. But the poor are terribly brutal to one another.

Gold seems to be useless in such a country, but it is nevertheless highly esteemed. Sometimes, the groping and questing hands of a blind man find a treasure. Then the magistrates assemble. Some examine the circumstances that preceded or accompanied the discovery. Those circumstances seem futile and irrelevant to anyone who has not studied their laws, but the magistrates discover there what they call justice and they proclaim that the inventor of the treasure ought be put to death, or that it is necessary that he be raised to the class of the sighted. Then, with a solvent of which the priests keep the secret, the eyelids are unsealed.

The aristocrats, the priests and the savants, however, tell the people that the country is terrible to behold and that, without their wise administration, famine would be a continuous scourge. They lament, in loud voices, the necessity of conserving their eyes in order to guide their more fortunate brethren through the horrors of the region. The people praise their devotion and the benefits of living with sealed eyes, without having the trouble of guiding themselves. In any case, death, it is affirmed, opens the eyes of the poor to a beautiful country as pleasant as a kiss, which never ends.

Among all their worries, the rich, the priests and the scientists have one terrible anguish. Sometimes, in fact, a man of the people feels his eyes opening. The accident can happen in two ways.

Sometimes, for an entire day, a wretch escapes the jealous surveillance and, through closed eyelids, attempts to see some object. The eyelids gradually seem to become transparently thin and the object slowly becomes distinct. When dusk sets fore to the sky, the patently observed object finally takes on precise lines, and the eyes open. The man, who suddenly enjoys the ensemble of things, agitates in too violent a joy, and utters cries of wonderment.

Sometimes, too, a poor man says: "Personally, I accept my condition, since I have the strength to bear it, but why do the gods charge so many weak individuals with that excessive burden, whom I hear moaning and falling?" If that pity is strong enough to make tears flow, the merciful individual feels his eyelids lift up freely, and he sees the people and things agitating around him, in a tremor in which love and desolation are mingled.

Now, if the newly-sighted keep quiet before the people, or if they consent to praise the condition of the blind, they are tolerated. Often, they are even allowed to enter a college of priests or savants. If one of them has the imprudence to praise the light publicly, however, his mouth is sealed with a gag and he is forced into exile.

If he takes hatred of his fatherland and its social organization to the extent of trying to explain the means by which the eyes can be opened, then the aristocrats, the priests and the savants drown his voice with their cries. They accuse him of deceiving the people, and have the consolation of seeing the crowd, with a magnificently unanimous impulse, throw themselves upon the liar and kill him.

XXIX. The Wisdom of Heracles

On the subject of the powerful, Psychodorus was making scornful and mocking remarks. Excycle interrupted him.

"Pardon me if I speak before you have finished your discourse, but strangers are among us who have arrived today, whose ears and tongues are perhaps not reliable."

"Their ears do not depend on me, nor their tongues."

"What depends on you is that their ears do not hear words that their tongues might repeat to your misfortune. Mistrust, O Psychodorus, is an aspect of wisdom."

"I know better than cowards what wisdom is in its entirety. For myself, I call wisdom that which renders mistrust unnecessary; for I read this parable somewhere:"

The huge Heracles was walking in the country, and his son Hyllos was running to keep up with him. They came to a stream, which Heracles traversed with a stride. Then he waited on the other bank, looking at his son and smiling. On his lips and in his eyes there was a mischief and a sort of question: *What are you going to do?* But there was also a pride and a sort of affirmation: *Of course you can do it, being the son of Heracles.*

Hyllos with the aid of a sharp stone, detached a large branch from a bush. Then he took a run-up, and, supporting the extremity of the branch on the edge of the stream, he leapt, lifted up by his effort and the pole.

Under his weight, the branch snapped.

A centaur who was in the vicinity heard the splash of his fall.

Having fallen in the water, the child was not frightened and, without astonishment, he began to swim vigorously.

When the centaur arrived, Hyllos, soaking wet, was climbing up to join his father.

On the other bank, his head lowered toward the two pieces of wood, the monster sniffed. He soon straightened up and said: "O Father, it's necessary to teach your son to look inside people and things. He would have seen that this wood is elder and that its interior, lacking firmness, contains a soft and limp marrow. Let this accident be a warning to you, that you might teach your son henceforth—and, if I dare say so, your-self—the wisdom whose familiar name is mistrust."

In a voice that resounded like thunder and like laughter, Heracles replied: "If, for you, wisdom is called mistrust, I call it strength. The education that I have given myself, and am giving to my son, is to put ourselves beyond dread. I am teach-ing him to look inside, not things and other people, but him-self. It is not on circumstances or people that he should rely, but on himself alone, on his energy, on his ability never to be afraid, and on an intelligence that is never astonished, and does not abandon him even when his body suffers an unex-pected fall."

The centaur whinnied toward the setting sun, and he said, as if in a prophetic intoxication: "O Heracles, so proud of your strength, soon you will be a dusk of flame, blood and screams, and you will die because you have had confidence."

But Heracles shook his head. "Have you seen, then, O centaur, the winter sun that hides in a cowardly fashion behind the thickness of clouds enjoy a longer day than the one that boldly sails in the summer sky like a heroic ship?"

And he added:

"You are mistaken, O demi-beast, when you say that I shall die because I have had confidence. I shall die as you will die, because we are mortal."

XXX. The Defeat of the Gods

"Men and gods," proclaimed Psychodorus, "are equally impotent against the sage."

"Men, perhaps," consented Theomanes, "but the gods...."

Several others shook their heads, thinking that the philosopher, out of pride, was blaspheming.

"Hear a parable," said Psychodorus:

In the country of Laconia, old Pantlas lived in an isolated house that was almost falling down. He was very poor. He sometimes went without nourishment for two or three days. Nevertheless no one ever heard him complain; the words that emerged from him were as calm and joyful as light.

Now, Athenian soldiers came, who burned Pantlas' house and took away the old man, along with other prisoners. They were sold as slaves on the agora. His companions moaned, cried out and agitated. He remained motionless. In ordinary eyes, he was like an item of merchandise. But for a sage he stood up, like a masterpiece by Phidias, draped in silence, nobility and liberty. If my master Diogenes had passed that way, he would have had no need to light his lantern to know that he was in the presence of that rare spectacle, a man.

A peasant bought Pantlas for a few obols, and struck him with his stick, saying: "Try to walk as quickly as my donkey, old man."

The Laconian looked up at the sky and murmured: "I thank the gods because they have always protected me from all harm and all servitude."

The Attic laughed. "I believe I've bought a madman. Your house has been burned; you're the slave of a master who, I promise you, will be harsh. You've just felt the weight of my hand and my stick. How can you pretend to be exempt from all evil and all servitude?"

The old man remained silent. But his master, becoming irritated, struck him again and exclaimed: "I order you to reply. What is it that you call harm or servitude?"

"I would call it harm and servitude," Pantlas said, softly, "if I were to lose my temper or strike someone."

At that moment, Zeus was looking toward Athens. He was astonished by that strength of soul. He summoned Hermes and ordered: "Go liberate that man, but make him confess, if you can, the power of the gods."

Hermes went, therefore, and lifted Pantlas up into the air. Proud of the strength of his flight he boasted: "Men are impotent against you; but the gods, if they wished, could do you harm and make you confess your servitude."

Pantlas declared: "One can only do harm to oneself, and one only ever obeys interior tyrants."

"However," Hermes growled, "I'm taking you to Tartarus and toward long suffering."

The sage, as he was dealing with a god, did him the honor of joking: "Thank you for carrying me, when you could have dragged me."

Swooping like an eagle, Herms let himself fall on to rocky and uneven terrain. He gripped the old man by both feet, and he dragged him bloodily over the stones.

"Impious man," he demanded, in a tone of angry triumph, "is anything more required for you to admit that you are unhappy?"

"It would, in fact, require something more," said Pantlas.

"What?" said Hermes, astonished.

"It would require that I support it without patience. But that, I am certain, depends on no other god but me."

Hermes was ashamed of what he had done. And, letting Pantlas get up as best he could, he fled without looking back, his head sunk between his shoulders, like a vanquished malefactor who has committed an unnecessary crime.

"Your Hermes is not a very obstinate or ingenious combatant," said Excycle. "In his place, I would have rendered my enemy mad."

"He could also have killed him," Psychodorus remarked, softly. "And those would have been two slightly more shameful ways of admitting the defeat of the gods."

XXXI. Phryné's Choice

Eubulus declared:

"That doctrine of indifferent things is as high and steep as the thought of a god. But in certain human sentiments a gentler beauty appeals to me and charms me. My health might become indifferent to me, or the grace of my smile, my face and my body, the rude and prideful attitude of an athlete might replace the simple and natural gait of a man walking; but if you want me also to count as nothing the lives of those I love and their affection, if you require, O Psychodorus, that I be ready not to weep on the day when you cease to love me or the day when you cease to live…no, I do not feel that I have that inhuman strength. In fact, my heart, merely by hearing you talk thus, overflows with bitterness."

"O my son, many hear the doctrine you mention poorly, and they repeat it as if through a tragic mask, making their voice loud and raising clenched fists toward the sky in which no storm is gathering. I love you, and your love, and your confidence. And I love above all extraneous things—such as my health, my external beauty and my life—Athenatime. However, I would not have wanted, when she died, to have howled the cries of a wounded beast or made some great inharmonious gesture unworthy of her or of me.

"Even under the impact of grief, my hands did not merit the mockery of the sage directed at those who believe alopecia to be a remedy against mourning and death. If I had departed before her, I would have said to her, as my last words: 'Do not forget, O beloved, that the dolor one bears poorly becomes a shame. But the dolor of the one I love will remain valiant and will not roll on the ground like a coward with colic." Or rather, I would not have said that, or anything like it, knowing that it was unnecessary, and Athenatime did not make me any insulting recommendations. But I heard in her silence, and

293

sensed in the grip of her hand, read in the smile of her lips and her eyes they joy of knowing that they were unnecessary."

The voice of Psychodorus was emotional, but remained valiant.

"You do not imagine that Socrates," he continued, "because he died with firmness, loved his children less than the man who cries: 'What will become of my children when I am gone?' He had an equal and more beautiful affection for them; he loved them like a man, whereas the man who moans loves them as a bitch loves her pups."

The valiant and emotional voice fell silent momentarily. Then it resumed:

"Hear a parable:"

Praxiteles desired Phryné madly. The latter, in exchange for one night, demanded a statue. The sculptor, agreeing, said to her: "You may choose it yourself."

Phryné hesitated between too many works, all of which seemed beautiful to her, and she did not have confidence in her own eyes. But she devised a ruse.

While the sensualist was trembling in the courtesan's cold arms, a slave, secretly bribed by her, came with a desperate expression to say that the studio was on fire and that many statues had already....

Praxiteles did not let him finish. Forgetting the woman who was there and the kiss he had bought, and everything except for his most perfect works, he got up and ran out, semi-naked, and cried: "Let's save Eros and the Satyr; for the rest, I'll console myself."

In comparison to those two masterpieces, the other statues, at the moment of danger, became indifferent to Praxiteles, as, at the critical moment that will lead to victory or defeat, the death of some obscure soldier is indifferent to the quivering general.

And Psychodorus said:

"O my son, when the hatred of men or the injustice of the gods sets fire to the studio that is within each of us, let us always save Eros and the Satyr."

XXXII. The Music

"For several days the sun has not shown itself. The clouds weigh over our heads heaped up like funereal veils. The cold earth is as sad as a widow. Each of us can hear in the depths of his hear someone weeping. But if we look at you, O Psychodorus, we always see you in the colors and attitudes of joy...."

"O my sons, hear a parable:"

A very savant painter wanted to make a portrait of joy. He chose for a model a young woman of a grave and serene beauty, all of whose visage sang like the smile of a mother when leaning over to look at her infant.

Now the painter worked slowly, with a glad application, but he was careful, for fear that his model might get bored, to have music as delicate as light played to her. When the musicians fell silent, he pronounced some of the words with which the wind caresses and refreshes.

One day, I don't know why, the musicians neglected to come. But the painter talked as he worked, and the young woman did not notice their absence.

When the ingenious talker got up to leave, she looked in all directions and said, astonished: "It's strange—there are no musicians."

"They couldn't come. Tomorrow, if they're still unable, I'll hire others."

"But we didn't miss them," said the woman, increasingly amazed.

The painter replied with an amiable lie: "Are you not the sweetest music yourself?"

"What would the painter have said if he hadn't lied?" asked Excycle.

"I can't answer that question. Only know this: I have no need of the sunlight and the song the earth sings when the magnificent mantle envelopes it with warmth and caresses; I always find enough light and music in you and in me."

XXXIII. *The Garden and the Citadel*

In front of several disciples, Eubulus said:

"Master, I sometimes try, following your advice, to en-close myself in my center. Alas, I often find sadness and ennui there. Once, I dispersed myself in numerous enjoyments. None of my pleasures was culpable. However, they enveloped me with misfortune and anxiety; they rendered me similar to a beast caught in a flowery bush, which fears being unable to flee if the hunter comes."

Psychodorus replied: "Hear a parable:"

A man had built an impregnable citadel and he remained fearfully enclosed within it. No enemy ever approached the high walls, but their inhabitant died of boredom.

Another man lived in a garden of innocent delights; but an enemy came, who killed him.

A third, having seen these things, built in the middle of his garden a reliable citadel. He enjoyed himself and worked in the shade of his trees, to the fresh song of his stream. If an enemy appeared, he retreated into his citadel, where he laughed, invincible. The garden invaded the walls of the for-tress; they rose up green with ivy, colored with wild flowers and valiant thoughts, animated by the wings of butterflies, birds and dreams. Those who went past in the plain mistook the refuge from afar for an immense tree in which spring was seated. And in moments of peace, the man who lived in the garden sometimes wondered:

Is my citadel made of stones or flowers? Is it built with strength or smiles?

XXXIV. The Corinthienne

A young man came to listen to Psychodorus. He was pale and depressed. He seemed to have been exhausted by a long journey, privations and debaucheries.

"Tell me your name, if you please," asked the philosopher, "and why you are wearing that sad expression, and what fatigue is overwhelming you."

"My name is Cleobis, and I've come from far away."

"He's doubtless arrived from Corinth," said the malicious Excycle.

"It is, indeed, in Corinth that I live. A proverb denies that it is given to everyone to land in its port. The proverb would do better to warn people to flee the city." And Cleobis added: "I loved a courtesan."

"You don't know what it is to love," said Psychodorus, shrugging his shoulders.

But the Corinthian lamented: "I was rich; I'm ruined. I had the strength of a pentathlete and the pride of a conqueror; now I'm feeble, weary and humiliated, like the beaten athlete whose blood is flowing from numerous wounds. The people proclaimed me eloquent and my friends recited my verses; today I'm incapable of an ingenious thought or a phrase that marches to the rhythm of beauty. That is why I've come here, in the vengeful hope of hearing the noble Psychodorus speak ill of women abundantly."

"You won't obtain the words for which you hope from me. Woman is man's equal. But you've never seen a woman, poor inhabitant of deserts. Learn that woman and man are rare beings, and the lantern of Diogenes could travel throughout Corinth without discovering a single one of either."

The young man burst out laughing. "These philosophers," he exclaimed, "are admirable. You are right, O

Psychodorus, and Corinth lacks women as the sea lacks water."

"O naïve Cleobis, you have wanted to appease your thirst with sea-water and what Corinth calls amour, and you're astonished at being thirstier than you were before...."

In a voice that was suddenly grave, Psychodorus continued:

"A sage does not accuse anyone, since there is no more evil for him. The man who climbs toward wisdom only accuses himself, since he understands that he is the sole author of his woes. You appear to me to be incapable of the slightest commencement of intelligence; insult the outside, then, if you wish, but don't take insolent absurdity so far as to insult woman; she is too far above you. If you find some pleasure in it, insult the female."

"What difference are you making?"

"I call man and woman the noble realizations that you cannot know. But I see you both with the lantern of Diogenes and I refuse, O Cleobis, to call you a man and he person for whom you mourn a woman. If it is absolutely necessary to give you a name, I will call you male, or Priapus. And her I shall call female."

"What evil shall I speak of the female?"

"You may say, if you wish: 'Priapus is a folly of prodigality; the female a folly of avidity. Priapus is the present that expends itself; the female is the future that devours the present, the dung-heap that rots whatever is offered to it in order better to nourish the possible seed.'

"Cleobis, I have observed the mores of insects for a long time, for I gladly watch animals in order to know, with less humiliation, those that dare to call themselves humans. Among the insects, the female is generally stronger than the male. Is it not the same with the slaves of instinct and cunning? In telling you the verities of the physicist, therefore, I shall perhaps be a philosopher who is telling you one or several parables."

Having looked down into the grass, Psychodorus smiled.

"Aphrodite wants to recompense Cleobis for the numerous sacrifices he has offered to her. She is going to show us, I believe, one of the parables I just mentioned. Apply yourselves, my friends, to looking attentively, patiently and discreetly:"

Look at this insect, pale green all over, whose underside sometimes tends toward white. Its body is elongated, with a beauty that seems noble. The majority of insects have the ugliness and the inconvenience of their head being joined directly to the thorax, but admire the gracious neck of this one, which is flexible in all directions.

The slender creature can stand upright, like a man, and carries in front, higher than the two long feathery antennae that are agitating on its head, two curved feet that almost meet up.

"It's a mantis," said Eubulus.
Psychodorus continued:

Because of that pious and solemn gesture, which seems to promise words coming from the top of the head, the Greeks do indeed call it a mantis, which means "One who Prophesies," and I know a barbaric people who call it "the one who prays in the grass."

Our children threaten it, saying: "Prophesy, O Prophetess," but the children of the barbaric country say to it, with threats: "Pray to the gods for us."

Now, the children are mistaken here as there, and the people with them. The attitude they remark is not one of prayer or prophecy, it is one of mistrust and war. Observe more closely the curved part of the foot; it is a powerful toothed scythe, ready to unfurl with an abrupt release, and strike.

Now look, half a pace behind the large mantis, at that small mantis. The large one is the female, the small one the male. It is approaching, intoxicated by Aphrodite. Watch what happens carefully.

Psychodorus fell silent. The disciples observed silently, motionless and excited, lying in ambush for a secret of nature.

The male advanced slowly toward the female, which waited. When he was close enough, he threw itself upon her and penetrated her. She looked back, examined the assailant briefly, and then, with an abrupt thrust of the little toothed scythe, cut off his head. The male wedged himself, deployed himself, and made love as if he were still a complete being.

"That's singular," said Cleobis.
"Do you have need of your head?" asked Psychodorus.

Meanwhile, the female, having devoured the head, partially turned round, and ate the male. He, continuing what he was doing without being disconcerted until, finally, his abdomen having been attacked, what remained of the lover was detached and fell away.

Cleobis picked up a stone. He wanted to crush the female, who was serenely continuing the nuptial feast. Psychodorus stopped him.
"Spare the shadow and the symbol from a futile gesture. It is necessary to kill folly in oneself and not strike externally at an opportunity for folly—for everything is an opportunity for folly."
Then Psychodorus and his disciples walked slowly along the road, which twisted like a river of dust and sunlight. Rocks bordered it to the right and grass, blanched by desiccation, to the left. Grasshoppers launched themselves numerously under the feet of the walkers. They opened their gray wings, which confounded their repose with that of the rocks, the dust and the dried plants and displayed beneath their prudent costume, the sudden beauty of blue or red silken wings. They fled at hazard. Several took bounding refuge in Psychodorus' beard, which seemed to them to be a clump of burned grass.

Cleobis, his eyes and mind lingering behind, directed insults at the mantis by the roadside and the Corinthian courtesan. He mourned the devoured male and admired the heroic persistence of his amour.

Meanwhile, Psychodorus went on:

What you have seen is not a singular case. Many insects have analogous mores. Female spiders, for example, willingly devour their males. You are certainly familiar by sight with the species that physicists call the garden spider.[61] Ugly hairy feet support a large red-tinted body, but the back is ornamented by an inverted white cross that seems pretty to me.

Among the spiders of that species there are large ones, which are the females, and much smaller ones, which are the males. Males and females hang their webs on bushes and live for a considerable time without encountering one another. A time comes when instinct speaks to the inept Cleobis as the spur speaks to the horse. Cleobis becomes anxious and the succulence of flies is no longer sufficient to the needs of his heart. He sets forth, abandoning the dwelling he has constructed. Will he ever see it again, the dear tent that his both his shelter and food-supplier?

The lover whose favors he seeks is an ogress. More farsighted than ours, this Cleobis prepares a retreat. From the female's web to a nearby branch, he extends a thread, a bridge that might perhaps permit him to return. He arrives, fearfully.

The beloved is waiting for him. She hopes for his caresses first, and his flesh thereafter. A poorly nourished housekeeper, divided between multiple cares, she does not give all her attention to the bagatelle. She is waiting for that visit but also lying in wait for her ordinary prey, that which is only nourishment. And she knows that it is necessary to pounce on them occasionally, sometimes so prompt to tear the web and flee. The web has trembled, announcing a presence. The large

---

[61] The reference is to the orb-weaving spider *Araneus diadematus*.

spider launches forward gluttonously, bites, enlaces, devours. In mid-meal, she sees what she has done and regrets not having obtained of the circumstance all that the circumstance offered.

She consoles herself, for a second male presents himself, this one recognized. The female, monstrously stronger and larger, goes toward the second visitor, coquettishly letting herself slide along a thread. Oh, the charm of the foreplay—do you remember that, Cleobis? The male, pursuing her, descends behind her; she climbs up again, he climbs up again. Finally, she allows him to reach her. The two lovers feel one another, stroke one another. Smile, Cleobis, at the joy of those preludes. But they cannot be sufficient. Aphrodite orders you to complete the sacrifice. You obey. It is a rapid, anxious mating. The male remains alert, ready to flee at the first movement of the enemy. The enemy, calmer, savors the voluptuousness. Satisfied, she turns around, bounding, and devours the lover in the same place as the amours.

It sometimes happens, however, that the male succeeds in fleeing. As quick as lightning striking a tree, he slides along his thread and disappears. But he will come back, and before or after the new caress, he will be an exquisite prey.

Excycle had a cruel smile on his lips. Several sensed around them an atmosphere of folly and storm, a quasi-religious horror. They were all walking silently.

Soon, however, Psychodorus spoke about other insects and their conjugal habits.

The argyronete spider constructs its dwelling underwater.[62] There too the female willingly eats the male, but the ingenious male builds his house alongside the lodging of the one he desires. He watches for a propitious moment, breaks down the intermediate wall, and enters with an abruptness that is

---

[62] *Argyroneta aquatica*, sometimes known as the diving-bell spider.

often victorious. Before the female has recovered from her surprise, the male, rapid and ruthless, has collected his joy and fled.

Psychodorus had scarcely finished that last tale when he exclaimed:

"Aphrodite is definitely favoring us today."

He invited his disciples to observe the mating of a grasshopper, the one that taxonomists would late call an analote:[63]

The little male was overturned on his back. The enormous female, covering him, received his caress. Prudently, she immobilized the upper part of his body, in order that he could not get away shortly. When the caress was finished, she maintained him with her claws. Another male offered himself now, which she accepted without delay, and during the second intercourse, she ate the first lover in joyful little mouthfuls.

"This time," said Cleobis, "I recognize her." He asked: "Have physicists given a name to that species of grasshopper?"

"I don't believe so," declared Psychodorus.

"So much the better," concluded Cleobis, with a bitter laugh, "for I shall call it from now on the *Corinthienne*."

---

[63] i.e., a member of the genus *Anonconotus*, which includes locusts.

XXXV. *The Two Brothers*

"Aristotle was right," said Excycle, "when he composed happiness by associating virtue and voluptuousness."

"Who, then" said Psychodorus, "told me this parable:"

Two brothers were walking toward a high mountain. Intending to reach the summit toward the end of the night, they wanted to see, before the glory of the rising sun, first light, a smile of pallor parting the darkness.

The elder of the two was twenty years old. Like the light, his words were simply, joyful and grave. His stride was even and never weary, but his brother sometimes scolded him for his slowness.

The younger was eighteen. He proclaimed aloud a few words of a song, and then murmured a few lines of an ode. He often ran, jumped and danced. At other times, his feet dragged wearily, or he asked that they stop and he sat down on the grass.

Thus they traversed the flat country and arrived in the evening at the foot of the mountain.

The elder took a piece of bread from his knapsack and drank water from a nearby spring. Then he lay down in his cloak and went to sleep.

The other had not inconvenienced himself with a knapsack. He refused the provisions that he brother offered him. "I'll go to the hostelry that you can see over there. I'll eat at my ease and sleep for a few hours, and I'll be beside you, slowcoach, well before you wake up.

Now, as he was eating in the main room of the hostelry, the sound of instruments came from atoner part of the house. He ran to see what it was. Ephebes and courtesans were beginning to dance, laugh, drink and sing. He stayed with them, did likewise, and got drunk. The middle of the night had passed when it was necessary to carry him to a bed.

His brother, having woken up, came to the hostelry and summoned him; but the other, opening his dazed eyed, moaned: "I'm ill. Let me sleep."

That is why the elder brother climbed the mountain alone. Alone, he saw the beauty of the dawn, the terrible beauty of Helios struggling below against the serpent of mist, the splendid and pacified beauty of the sun finally master of space. He also saw a vast extent of country, as pretty as a childhood and a promise in the glimmers of the tremulous and hesitant early morning, and as noble as a life of certainty and courage in the streaming and joyful vertigo of bright light.

He went back down with his eyes glad and rich. He sensed the philosophical dawn rising and growing within him. He sensed that the sun of wisdom would soon emerge triumphantly and illuminate the immense calm landscape of his soul.

When he returned to the hostelry, his brother, his head in his hands, his eyes heavy, his mouth nervous and twisted, complained of aching throughout his body. The elder said to him, gently: "Rest, my brother. I'll sit down beside you; and tomorrow, we'll go up tomorrow to a spectacle with which one is not sated."

The other sniggered. "I'm more philosophical than you. I can't be content with spectacles that cost no effort." He added: "I want to go home."

The elder took him in his arms, supporting the weak hesitations of his tread. But he turned away in order not to see his face and his exhaustion, almost causing him to fall. He enclosed himself in his thoughts and memories; for he strove not to hear the moaning debauchee, who affirmed that he too was a philosopher, lamented the human condition, and praised the pleasures of the entrails as the sole consolation of unfortunate mortals.

XXXVI. *The Lyre of Orpheus*

"Aristippus often employed the same words as his master Socrates."[64]

"Yes, but he asked for payment for his words. If a tyrant did not hear him because he spoke standing up, he threw himself to his knees as if before a god. When the tempest shook his vessel, he went pale with terror. Aristippus spoke the words of Socrates, and yet I laugh, as if I saw Thersites dragging himself along, crushed by the arms of Achilles. When his maxims are not in harmony with his life, a philosopher merits being mocked, like the musician whose voice is not in harmony with the lyre. Displayed against a background of shameful conduct, beautiful sentences resemble the glittering armor of the coward who is running away; they render shame shiny. Or perhaps you think, Excycle, that victory belongs to the beauty of the weapons, not the courage of the combatant, and that the art is in the implement, not the hand of the workman. Dionysius the Tyrant bought at a great price the tablets that the poet Aeschylus had used, and wrote on them in his turn. Doubtless Excycle approves and admires the verses of the Syracusan tyrant as much as *Prometheus Unbound.*[65]

As Psychodorus fell silent, Excycle said, laughing: "You can't think of a parable on the subject?"

"A parable?" the old philosopher went on. "It's you, Excycle, who can tell us that. But perhaps you haven't heard

---

[64] Aristippus of Cyrene adopted a philosophical outlook very different from his former teacher Socrates, advocating that the goal of life is to seek pleasure and to maximize it by adapting both oneself and one's surroundings to that purpose.

[65] Only small fragments of Aeschylus' *Prometheus Unbound* survive, but there are second-hand descriptions detailing its plot.

it. Would you care to tell us what you know about the lyre of Orpheus?"

"I know the fable that everybody knows."

"Tell is, and we'll be grateful to you."

When the women of Thrace had torn apart the singer who, out of fidelity to a dead woman, scorned the living, it is claimed that his head, thrown into the Hebrus, floated, giving voice to the harmonies of mourning and glory. The lyre floated too, and, touched by the subtle hand of the winds, it accompanied the marvelous threnody. They descended thus to the mouth of the river and traversed the sea as far as the isle of Lesbos. The inhabitants of Methymna placed the head in a sepulcher at the place where the temple of Dionysus now stands, but they suspended the lyre in the temple of Apollo.

"That, at least," Excycle concluded, "is what was told to me in my childhood, and what nurses still repeat to all children."

"Have you not learned anything more on the subject of the lyre, or do you believe that it is still asleep in the temple of Apollo."

It is no longer there. And this, according to the popular tale, is how it disappeared. Neanthus, the son of Pittacus, having heard tell that it played of its own accord and that it had charmed the trees and the rocks, desired it with the ardor that others put into desiring a courtesan. He gave several silver talents to an employee of the temple, who gave it to him one night in secret. He fled, as glad and trembling as a man who is abducting a beautiful slave; he thinks of the imminent sweetness of the kiss, but he fears being discovered by the master and dragged before the judges. As soon as the thief thought he was sufficiently far away, he unwrapped the envelope in which he was hiding the melodious treasure, and, in marvelous expectation, touched the strings with his fingers. But what sprang forth from the unworthy instrument was a racket that brought dogs running, who tore the impudent fellow apart.

The young man fell silent. Psychodorus did not add any commentary—and Excycle took some time to realize why the other disciples were looking at him with malicious smiles.

XXXVII. The Gardener

Psychodorus stopped, and his disciples stopped with him. Then, turning to Eubulus, he interrogated him with these words:

"What's wrong with you, my son? For several days, you have been dragging I know not what languor, like an ill-defined and capricious burden that catches on the obstacles in the path. And at this moment your face is pale."

Eubulus's pallor reddened girlishly, and in a voice that tried to be valiant, the disciple replied: "Nothing's wrong, Master, save for insignificant physical pains—banal suffering that isn't worth talking about."

The old philosopher smiled, and said, in a gentle tone: "You'll talk to me about it, though, not as a sage and a master but as a loving father."

When he replied, there was in Eubulus's expression the palpitation of a glimmer of joy and the palpitation of a shadow of shame.

"Listen, then," he said, O powerful tyrant of my heart. For five days, a pain has been agitating, like a beast or an army, half of my face. Claws tremble and dig in around my left eye, and numerous teeth gnaw my temple, my ear and the edge of my jaw."

"How have you greeted this visitor?"

"In a virile fashion, I think, since I haven't mentioned it to anyone."

"I congratulate you on your modesty…but what do you say to yourself and what do you say to your pain?"

"At first I declared to it: 'You are not an evil.' And at first I declared to myself: 'It is not an evil.'"

"Why do you say: *at first?*"

"Afterwards, I doubted," Eubulus admitted, whose face was suddenly redder, and his smile paler.

311

"Explain your doubt to us."

"I've often said to the malevolent beast: 'I don't reproach you for biting my flesh, but I think it unjust that you're gnawing my mind.' Because, Master, and this seems to me to be an evil, I can no longer think or read. Sometimes, in fact—how can I not be irritated against it?—you speak, O Psychodorus, and the pain prevents me from listening and understanding."

"Is your pain, then, my son, a jealous woman who wants you to belong to her alone? Thank her for embracing you with such a fervent amour and yield to her demands."

"You're doubtless making fun of me, for it seems to me that you're counseling a cowardice."

"What does it matter, my son, what you think, provided that the rhythm of your thought remains noble and personal? We are not among those poor fools who, having an objective external to themselves, risk encountering obstacles without or within. The other day, you remember, a troop of merchants seemed to be following the same road as us. Sometimes, like us, they addressed cheerful remarks to the surroundings or to one another. But a mountain barred the common route. Then they cursed the mountain. They demanded feverishly of the local people the way to a gorge, and they agitated like ants whose hole has been blocked. We, however, marched ahead. We went up, amid the increasing light, into the new beauty. That is what the sage does. He always says to the unexpected: *Greetings, you whom I might have taken for an obstacle, in whom I recognize my road and my joyous necessity.*"

"You advise, then, that I think about my dolor?"

"Yes. But I want it to always be you who is thinking, and that, whether caressing an object bright or dark, the light always remains vivid and dancing. Occupy yourself with your pain, my Eubulus, converse with it as with a foreigner whose visit is prolonged. Interrogate it in order to learn what it knows. Interrogate it, too—do you hear me, my son?—in order to distract yourself from it."

"Now you're becoming obscure to me."

"I like torches whose flame laughs in the irony of the smoke and the wind. Look closely, my son, for I'm lighting a parable:"

Philopardes was a gardener as Sophocles was a poet. Flowers that astonished the first glance, as new and strange and follies, but which soon retained the satisfied eye and the mind, as beautiful and harmonious as revealed necessities, made his house a multicolored enclosure where shadow and sunlight played like two children, sometimes running, sometimes lingering, charmed. But more than his flowers, more than the freshness of the moving shadows and the flowing water, more than the fecundity of the sun, the father of flowers, fruits, clouds, springs and shade, Philopardes loved his daughter, with the love of a father and a widower.

Now, that child died, and the orphaned father was like a madman. He shut himself away in the tenebrous silence of his dwelling. Or, without distinguishing day and night, he remained on the tomb, as motionless as a desiccated tree that does not feel the winds. He refused the nourishment that was offered to him with a gesture, and did not worry at all about the languor, the agony and the death of his garden.

His friends said: "He's doomed. He no longer looks at flowers."

But one of them took Philopardes by the arm and addressed vehement reproaches to him.

"Why," he demanded, "does your daughter's tomb resemble all tombs? Why are you not ashamed of its banal poverty? If I were Philopardes, oh, what marvelous living adornments would embroider the earthen robe of the dead woman I loved!"

Philopardes heard those words with his ears and his heart. He began to plant and sow on the tomb. Having kept grimly silent until then, he soon wept and groaned; and he took nourishment in order to have the strength to care for the dead woman's flowers.

Because the gardener had remained a gardener in his grief, Philopardes was saved. He lived for many years, causing to flourish in the earth and in his soul melancholies with noble stems, perfect forms and soft colors.

If, therefore, you are a gardener, let the tombs that you carry within you become gardens.

Psychodorus having stopped speaking, Eubulus sat down to one side. He took tablets from his bosom and began to write. Throughout the time that his suffering lasted he composed a dialogue every day in which a sage conversed with dolor. He read what he had written to the master. Psychodorus approved of some words, and asked that others be corrected.

Thus Eubulus, who believe himself completely given over to his dolor, belonged in reality to the harmony of his thought, to the choice of words that his hesitation caused to shine and smile in the light, to the rhythm of phrases that fell like wounded soldiers, and stood up like proud conquerors, or canephora marching, supple and grave. He was the artist that models clay; his eyes watched the earth worked by his hands, but, spurred as they were by desire or joy, they did not see the vile matter so much as the beautiful form, not such much what nature gives us as what the worker is going to make of it, or has just made.

XXXVIII. The Nettles

"Ordinarily," said Excycle, "I feel a malevolent joy, perhaps more joyful and youthful than wicked, and my heart, my lips and my eyes smile, if my words sting like a nettle or if, like a bramble, it clings with numerous thorns, and becomes embarrassing in the unexpectedness of its interlacements. Today, I don't know why, my thought, which seems to me, however, to be stronger and richer than ever, has no malevolence, no piquancy, no desire to torment or bring down.

"Perhaps," said Psychodorus "it's because your mind is in flower." And he added: "Hear a parable:"

A father and his son were walking in the country. They were wearing short mantles, and their feet and legs were bare.

There was a place where they left the torrid road in order to walk in the freshness of the grass. Soon, however, they were opposed ahead of them by a passage bristling with nettles.

The father marched on, and did not appear to notice the sly hostilities that were awaiting him. The son warned him: "Be careful, Father; there are nettles."

But the father, without turning round or replying, continued walking at the same pace as before.

The son touched a plant timidly. He touched it with the tip of a finger, then the palm of his hand, and then the back. He was astonished not to feel any pain.

Finally, he also entered that alarming patch. He ran after his father. When he caught up with him, he said: "A few days ago, these nettles covered my legs with sudden bumps and stings. Today they're undulating in the wind with innocent smiles and we're traversing them without suffering any offense. If you can, Father, explain this mystery to me."

"Don't you see, my son, that they're in flower today? All quivering with joy and generous amour, they forget to hate. They stand up, beautiful and happy, to give off honeyed perfumes, and think of the seeds with which they'll inseminate the future, a limitless garden. They have no jealousy today to appease with spiteful gestures or the pain they create."

XXXIX. The Broken Statue

"Why do you not write down your thoughts?"

"Perhaps to be more certain of continuing to think."

"What does that mean?"

But instead of replying, Psychodorus wondered: "Where have I read this parable:"

A pupil of Phidias had made a statue of Aphrodite that the master thought worthy of praise. From that day on the young man ceased to study, and spent his time looking at his work and praising it.

When his master said to him: "Work, my son," the pupil replied: "I don't know of what the others are capable. For myself, when I examine my Aphrodite, I find no fault with it, and I don't feel that I can do any better. Why would I consent to do less well, or even as well?"

Phidias did not reply.

One morning, however, as the young sculptor came, as was his custom, to make the sacrifice of his time to the goddess—or, rather, to his own vanity—he found that his masterpiece was broken.

"What jealous person," he cried, has committed such a crime against me? What impious person has insulted a great goddess thus? What barbarian has had the courage to destroy such perfect beauty? O Aphrodite, you who know him, strike him in his eyes, even more guilty than his hands, and, since he is already as blind as a beast, render him as blind as a blind man."

Phidias said, softly: "You are pronouncing imprecations against your master. Fortunately, the only gods in which I believe are those that emerge from my hands, and those majestic but motionless sons respect their father."

"What are you saying?" stammered the young man, strangled by astonishment. "It was you?"

"I want you to do better than you have done. Take up your chisel again, my son, and surpass yourself. To surpass yourself is the law of man. But if today cannot surpass yesterday, at least it can renew it freely."

"Is it, then, necessary to destroy anything beautiful that has been made?" said the pupil, sardonically. "Are you going to order me to break your Zeus or your Athene?"

"Your gesture would be futile, for I have broken those works in my mind—I mean that I have forgotten them, in order to be able to make new ones, with an intelligence as free as my hands."

Phidias continued: "You do not work by holding in your hands a statue already made. The mind of a sculptor is like his hand; it cannot both caress yesterday and labor today—but many sculptors do not know these things."

XL. The Plague

"Certainly," said Eubulus, "there is something infantile about loving glory for itself; but sometimes, glory can be useful to others. Do you not think that your words, for example, O Psychodorus, if they were spread and if they endured, would be good for the men of today and for those to come, for centuries?"

"The wheat that the poor man produces and the iron he extracts from the ground are stolen by the powerful. The metal that the miner dreams of transforming into a plowshare, they use to forge weapons, and the pacific nourishment they use to fortify the cruel soldier. Words are also stolen by inept or cunning echoes, and they become empty or harmful noises. I have heard the most liberal words of Socrates deformed into counsels or servitude or civic duty."

Psychodorus was pensive for a moment. Then he went on: "Hear a parable:"

A skillful physician lived in a land that was desolated by the plague. The majority of the sick people that cared for, he cured. He saved the richest man in the country. Now the son of that man, disappointed in his hope of soon becoming the master of great wealth, became secretly irritated against the physician and, having waited for him by night in a deserted place, he killed him.

At the place where the crime was committed, the people erected a rustic sanctuary. The cadaver was laid out on a crimson bed; people came to kneel before it and said: "Continue your benefits, O Benefactor. Heal me, O Healer, Save me, O Savior."

Even people who were not suffering in their bodies brought offerings and prayers, for the continuation of their health and the salvation of the sick that they loved.

On the sumptuous bed, however, the god that everyone was imploring rotted, and around him, through the clouds of incense, the germs of the plague spread.

The people were astonished that, in spite of their great piety and their kneeling before the Physician, the evil was like a lion whose fury was increasing and exasperating.

And Psychodorus, having finished the parable, exclaimed: "O my sons, protect yourself against the maleficent being that death will make of me. Hastily throw a little earth upon my body, and forgetfulness upon my words."

XLI. The Crowns

"Alas," said Excycle, amid the approbations, "we live in the saddest and most inglorious of centuries...."

Eubulus, however, remarked: "My grandfather had the custom of lamenting the inferiority of the times in which he lived, and I have read such complaints in books of all epochs." After a moment's reflection he added: "Perhaps glory is made of distance. Excycle, who loves definitions and formulae, might cry: 'O Glory, you who are an effect of perspective...'"

But Psychodorus said: "Hear a parable:"

In a garden there were crowned women. Each of them said, jealously:

"My sisters wear noble crowns, but I am devoid of glory."

For, as Momus noted one day when he was passing that way, none of them had eyes placed in such a fashion as to be able to see above her head.

"Do you believe, then," asked Excycle, "that all epochs are equal?"

"Have I said that all the women were the same height, or all the crowns of the same value? Hear the end of the parable, though."

The gold of crowns is heavy, and it digs into the bruised head. What is below is always wounded by that which is on top.

And each woman groaned: "Alas, alas! Not only am I deprived of the brilliant crown that honors my sisters, but the Moirae have charged my head with I know not what burden and I know not what wound."

With ardent fingers, the stupid women strove to remove the burden and to throw it on the ground. The majority succeeded, and they kicked the fallen crowns with furious feet, and broke them. Their trampling turned the ground into a mud that soon surrounded the gold and hid it.

But some did not succeed in tearing away the tenaciously living gold. Those remained, in spite of their folly, glorious and envied.

XLII. The Tree-Frog

"The sage says, according to the times: Long live the King, long live the City, long live Philip, long live Demosthenes."

"No, my son. The sage scorns, in all times, the City and the King, those two tyrannies; and Philip and Demosthenes, those two follies. Diogenes mocked the agitation of the besieged Corinthians, and he mocked Alexander when Alexander thought he could do something for Diogenes, as for an Aristotle...."

"However...."

"O my son, will you always call philosophy the cunning that goes toward indifferent things, twisting and leaning like an old woman over a poor fire? Will you always praise, then, the unquiet suppleness of Odysseus and his cowardly disguises, or those of the chameleon, or those of the tree-frog whose eyes have not been put out?"

"What tree-frog?"

"The one of which I speak as a physicist, and simultaneously as a man who is relating a parable that is easy to understand:"

That tree-frog changes color according to the place in which it finds itself. Ordinarily, it is green, but it ordinarily lives among the leaves of trees. If it descends on to the trunk, it becomes brown, like the bark. In the same way, Alcibiades became in soft Asia more voluptuous than a satrap, and showed himself in Sparta more sober and temperate than a Lacedaemonian citizen.

But if, capturing a tree-frog of the species I am talking about, you pluck out its two eyes, it always remains green henceforth, as Socrates and Diogenes always remained themselves.

323

"So, what you are saying is that the wisdom of Socrates and Diogenes was made blindly?"

"I know, my son, a fortunate blindness that is the noble companion of disdain. You don't worry about that which concerns a troop of gossiping women, but you pass by without seeing what it is that excites them. You don't perceive either the carrion over which the crow is flying or the little bird after which the excited child is running. But perhaps there are things within that you can already see a little, of which the child is unaware."

And Psychodorus added:

"When, then, Excycle, will you strangle the ape that lives within you, to create the man that you will be? When will you put out within you the cowardly and docile eyes of the tree-frog, in order finally to open, upon the spectacle that every gaze embellishes, human eyes, wise and fortunate eyes?"

XLIII. The Blind Man

Excycle had put a large stone in Psychodorus' path. When he approached the danger, he asked him a difficult question. Thus, the old philosopher did not pay any heed to the obstacle, but his foot stumbled over it and he was on the brink of falling—but Excycle was careful to lend him his arm, and sustained him forcefully.

Then he burst out laughing, and said:

"In truth, it's me who is guiding my guide. I fear having taken a blind man to guide me, and to prevent me from falling, someone who can't stand on his own feet."

"O my friends," exclaimed Psychodorus, "listen with some grace to the philosopher Excycle mock philosophy. He speaks to me as the old woman of Thrace spoke to the sage Thales, for he likes the prudence of curbed and groping old women, and believes that wisdom is a matter of always looking down."

"The stones are down there, and also the pitfalls."

"Go then announce the truth to those who are worthy of it. Your truth seems to me to be interesting for wolves, foxes and the other beasts for which shepherds and farm-workers set traps. But your eyes of a wolf, a fox, or perhaps a lynx, remain blind to human things. Whoever looks uniquely at what is there, looks with the eyes of a beast, not with human eyes."

"What do you mean?"

"That which is there is a particular thing devoid of interest. But a human being likes to see the general and universal, which are not there for the eye attentive to prey or traps. That is perhaps what I mean. Perhaps I mean other things too. But instead, hear a parable:"

A blind man, sitting in the middle of a plain, felt the sunlight streaming over his face, joyfully. Picking up his lyre, he encouraged himself in a soft voice:

"Let us sing the light and its beauty."

But an old woman who was passing by heard him. I shall not tell you whether the old woman was from Thrace, or whether she was an ancestress of the clear-sighted Excycle, for, in truth, I don't know. She mocked the blind man, saying:

"Sing, if you wish, the voices of assembled men, or the sound of the wind in the forests, or the tempest that growls over the sea. Sing the things that are seen, if I might put it like that, with the ears. As for the light, truly, if anyone ought to celebrate it, it isn't you."

"The only man who really sees," affirmed the blind man, "is one who, having looked outwards yesterday, looks inside himself today. But I suspect, woman, that your open eyes remain poor beneath the moving opulence of light." He added: "What is your name?"

"What does it matter? You're not from this country, and my name would mean nothing to you."

"I'm not from this country, but perhaps you know the name that is given to me in my homeland and a few other homelands. I am called Homer."

The blind man did not add a single word with his speaking voice; but, accompanying himself on the lyre, he praised light and its beauty with his singing voice."

When he fell silent, the woman exclaimed: "O Homer, I don't know what engaged me to close my eyes while your voice and your lyre were vibrating, but I did, and the marvel was accomplished in me that with my eyes closed, for the first time, I began to see the light."

XLIV. The Inconstancy of the Trees

Cleobis said, insultingly:

"For a week I've been following you and listening to you. The first day, when, by talking about insect female, you made me think about the women of Corinth, you interested me. Since then, I've heard nothing but boring things. And often what I hear irritates me because your manifest thought is as fleeting, fickle and faithless as a courtesan."

"Thought," replied Psychodorus, "is a life or a world. Its fecund unity produces a thousand children and presents a thousand aspects. If the face that was serious this morning smiles in the midday sun, would your eyes refuse to recognize it? But I know minds more naïve than the eyes of a child and more unjust than the eyes of a rival. To those it is not given to perceive the unity in the richness, and the continuity in that which moves. However, hear a parable:"

Somewhere in the barbaric lands stands a singular city built, in the middle of the sea, on narrow tongues of land and minuscule islands. Its streets are canals and its chariots are boats. The ground is entirely occupied by houses, porticos and rare paved passages, with the result that one dies not encounter a single garden there. Many of the inhabitants die without ever having seen a tree.

A slave who had never left the strange city was maltreated by his master and fled. When he abandoned the boat that had brought him to the shore he plunged at hazard into a country where everything astonished him. As he feared being pursued he hid in the depths of a forest.

It was winter. The solitary man ate roots that he dug up and animals that he killed with stones or caught in ingenious traps. He looked at the trees with amazement, but gradually, he learned to love them. The vigorous unity of the trunk struck him with a quasi-religious respect. The divergent multiplicity of the branches amused his gaze and his mind, and even more so the rich subdivision of the branches into twigs. The new shoots, yellow or pink, moved him like young smiles.

Soon, on all the branches, sub-branches, twigs and shoots, there was a blond dust of buds and leaflets striving to emerge.

"My dear trees are falling ill," the slave sighed.

That dust was extended and transformed, becoming an increasingly forceful foliage, darkening the fugitive's retreat with green shade, covering it with a green roof in which every tile seemed to be alive. He shook his head, but said nothing more.

He quit the disquieting refuge and wandered in open country for some days. As everyone looked at him suspiciously he became frightened and returned to the forest.

The trees had changed again. Unexpected gems mounted in green metal, they displayed the intoxicated colors of flowers everywhere among the leaves.

Trembling, the slave thought about the evil power of the gods

He saw calices and petals falling. Every fall seemed to him to be a divine threat directed at him. He knelt down and raised his arms desperately.

Then fruits hung down, which became heavier every day.

One night, a tempest shook the forest and the slave fled, pursued by the furious crashing fall of acorns, beech-nuts and all sorts of hard fruits.

He returned to his master, imploring his mercy.

"What is it that has made you aware of your crime?" the master asked him, with condescension.

"I took refuge among trees," the slave explained, still shivering. "As soon as I got used to their aspect, the implacable gods took them away and replaced them with others, quite different, I ended up understanding the will of heaven, and I came back."

Those to whom the slave related his confused adventure believed, like him, that the gods had multiplied prodigies around his revolt. The master, who was pious and grateful, erected a little temple in the middle of the forest.

XLV. The Cothurnes

"What a pity it is," said Eubulus, "that you didn't hear Excycle. He spoke magnificently for some two hours about the equality of the soul and the moderation of the sage."

"The subject he had chosen," said Psychodorus, smiling, "might have engaged him to a little more discretion."

"For several days," remarked Theomanes, "Excycle has been thrown, for the most futile of reasons, into the most violent fits of anger, but after the racket and seething of his fury, like a river after a waterfall, he expands himself at length in discourses on mildness and vast eulogies to calm, with the consequence that I'm astonished...."

"You're always easily astonished, Theomanes. However, my sons, hear a parable:"

I know a satrap of a great king who is extraordinarily vain, even for a satrap. Once, in a military expedition, he was obliged to walk for a long time through the snow, and his feet were frozen.

Since then, having previously been glad to stay in his palace lying on cushions, one encounters him every day in the streets of the city, supported by two robust slaves, putting on a semblance of walking. His dead feet, useless weight, are still weighed down and shackled by magnificent cothurnes. Made of a golden fabric and ornamented by pearls and gems, those items of footwear, whose soles are doubly lined with the most beautiful crimson, are the richest part of his rich costume. Once his long robes hid his feet; now, raised up by a belt and clasps, they allow the splendid cothurnes to be seen, like two glories.

XLVI. The Macedonian

"As long as you are attached to something foreign, which you call your property, you remain exiled from yourself."

"I'm distracted from myself," admitted Excycle, "until I've conquered wealth. When I finally possess what I need to satisfy all my whims, I shall feel the mot liberated of men and I'll be able, without anxiety, to occupy myself uniquely with myself and philosophy. Then, Psychodorus—if you're sincere, you'll admit it—I shall enjoy your wellbeing, as well as the sensualities, honors and independence of the rich. You're shaking your head, O cynic, doubtless to say that the wealth of which I speak is a small matter. I grant you that, but follow my reasoning, I beg you, and concede its exactitude. If to a great deal I add a little more, I shall necessarily become richer. A myriad increased by a unity becomes greater than the myriad that does not change."

"The day when you achieve the object of your desire, you will be the Macedonian who has caught up with the other Macedonian, but is not permitted thereby to return home."

"What are you saying?"

"A brief story, which you may understand, if you wish, as a parable:"

Philip had shed a great deal of blood in battles. During the peace he began show himself to be more economical.

One day he judged two men who, according to the law, merited death. But the king, not being drunk that day, was less foolish than the law. He contented himself with exiling the first of the accused. When the turn of the second came—your turn, my poor Excycle—Philip said, laughing:

"I forbid you to return to Macedonia unless you bring back the man I've just condemned."

Having reflected momentarily, Excycle declared: "More ingenious than the king, I would have killed the exile and come back carrying the cadaver over my shoulders."

"Act in accordance with the advice you have given, then," said Psychodorus.

"I didn't believe," said Excycle, astounded, "that your thinking could approve of murder."

The old philosopher shook his head, laughing.

Eubulus said: "Have you not understood, quibbler, who the Macedonian is that Psychodorus is persuading you to kill?"

Excycle did not reply, but his face was covered by a blush.

XLVII. The Hermaphrodites

A few disciples cheered up their march by making wishes.

Eubulus had said, while blushing: "If The Moirae gave me a choice between human fates, I would take, in order to know the love of Psychodorus, the lot of a woman; I would take the lot of Athenatime."

Having laughed uproariously, Excycle had declared: "My dream is more philosophical. A rare merit, it would be approved by Plato and also by Diogenes. I would like to be an individual who really is self-sufficient, an individual who has nothing to desire outside himself. I would like, grouping within me powers, joys and vertigoes, to become a complete being. Oh, to be duplicate, in soul, intellect and body, simultaneously man and woman, as is said of the son of Hermes and Aphrodite."

"Your wish is my wish," sighed Cleobis.

Psychodorus arrived, and heard the end of Excycle's discourse and Cleobis' approval.

"Children!" he exclaimed, "the game you're playing is not exempt from ugliness."

"Why is that?"

"Be careful of thinking that a wish is an ordinary dream. It's similar to an egg that will end up breaking its shell of impossibility; and from it will emerge, like a serpent that crawls and bites the heart, desire."

Excycle protested: "I spoke words that are scarcely original, and when you think you are criticizing me, perhaps you're criticizing Plato; for the myth that he sings in the *Symposium* does not seem to me very far from murmuring a wish or, if you prefer, mourning a regret."

"Wish or regret," remarked Theomanes, "makes no difference for Plato, since he knows that learning is remembering."

Psychodorus smiled in a seemingly-distant fashion. Then he said: "Hear a parable:"

Did I ever know the name of the strange country in which I learned of the death of Plato? In a bleak and seemingly unhealthy landscape, a passer-by clad in a short mantle, armed with a staff and carrying a knapsack, gave me the news.

I saw to my right a shallow sea, pale, weary and dying. Flat pointed boats, weighed down by an abundant catch of oysters, were cutting like plows through a little water and a little mud.

On the other side of the road, in the melancholy stagnancy of a marsh, a naked man was walking. In order to put them into an amphora that he was holding under his arm, his hand was collecting from along his legs leeches that were biting him.

Between those almost equally sad and dead waters, snails were trailing sticky mucus on the gray and arid earth.

For my limbs, the words of the cynic I had encountered were like a crippling and debilitating blow. I sat down on the burning ground between the marsh and the muddy sea. Soon, a bad slumber weighed upon me and it brought me a dream, which was this:

Hermes was walking, followed by a shadow, and, addressing the shadow, he said:

"O Plato, you have insulted Zeus and myself, accusing us of having broken, out of jealousy, the joy and strength of ancient humans who, according to the song of your folly, possessed both sexes. We did nothing similar. But if my hand had delivered human beings from such an ugliness, with what gratitude you, a lover of the Beautiful, ought to have praised me and glorified me.

"O Plato, I have had a son with Aphrodite in conformity with your dream, and ever since I have been sickened by androgynous gestures. Look, in any case, and you shall see."

And then, on the muddy shore, oysters opened their shells. But Plato, having seen what was happening inside the open oysters, turned away in disgust.

"It's before your dream," said Hermes, "that you're recoiling. The sophist of the *Symposium* ought not to be scornful, he ought to be jealous of these animals, which are hermaphrodites. From the month of Metageitnion to that of Mounichion,[66] during the period when you find them good to eat, oysters have male organs and they elaborate, with an enjoyment that you know, the male liquid. But from Thargelion to Hekatombaion, when you abstain from heir unhealthy flesh, they are female, with ovaries that ferment, bud and populate numerous eggs; and those eggs become white as they mature. Oysters of Hekatombaion are open before our eyes. How can you turn away from the mystery of their fecundation? Look, therefore, with intoxicated eyes, O singer of androgynous amour: all the fervent life that is formed during the male period is now laying siege to the eggs and penetrating them. Each of those oysters is a swarm of joys, a vast fête, a maritime city in which numerous matelots are seizing numerous women and fecundating them.

Hermes continued the ironic and nauseating strophe, implacably, for a long time. Then he added:

"Perhaps other hermaphrodites realize your desire of amour and unity more fully. Look to see whether that happy marsh is not the fatherland of your ideal."

In the marsh, still ignoble and green-tinted but transparent to my eyes, leeches were coupling. In each of them, from a crevice situated near the mouth, the male organ surged forth, while the female organ was sunk above the anus. The double kiss formed a head-to-tail that mingled, in I know not what

---

[66] i.e. from August/September to April/May; or, in terms of the English proverb, the months that have an r in them.

infamous friction, the drool of the mouth and the drool of the anus.

Plato's gaze and mine turned away from the sickening vision.

Hermes sniggered. "That doesn't satisfy you? You're difficult to please. But I can show you something even better."

The dream had stripped my body of the mantle. It had covered me with snails, which were coupling, in abundantly flowing mucus. I wanted to shake myself and cast those nauseating things far away, but the nightmare immobilized me, terrified, constraining me to suffer the sight and contact. And this was what I saw as I looked at myself involuntarily:

On the edge of a kind hollow or vestibule, opening narrowly at first and then gradually more widely, the organs have just made contact. Oh, the infamous richness....

In addition to the instrument of active lust and that of passive lust, my horror-saturated eyes saw a third organ, with no analogue in other animals. I soon understood that it was an organ of excitation, something like a trickling finger or the darting tongue of a courtesan. Or rather, one might have thought it a dirty sword, half-emerging hesitantly from a viscous scabbard and going back in only to emerge again.

The ignoble preludes lasted, interminably, for entire days. I can still see and feel stickily upon me the ignominy of endless viscous frictions and pressures. Finally, the lovers were decided. The swords emerged clearly from the scabbards and sank into the excited and oozing flesh. Then the male organs, crowned with gray foam, surged forth like two triumphs and, in a flood of mucus, the double union was accomplished.

When the dream permitted me to look at Plato, he was closing his eyes desperately, but tears, raising the determined heaviness of his eyelids, were running down his cheeks.

XLVIII. The Dipsads

"What is a pleasure?" said Excycle. "The sentiment of a need that has been satisfied. If, therefore, I multiple my needs ingeniously, by the same token, I enlarge my capacity for pleasures."

"Find a tarantula," said Psychodorus, laughing. "It will enrich your need to dance. Or, since we're on the bank of a river, have yourself bitten by a dipsad."[67]

"What is a dipsad?" asked Eubulus.

"I believe," sniggered Excycle, "that without warning us, Psychodorus is commencing a parable."

"A parable? If you wish. It's facile, but perhaps Excycle will be ingenious enough not to understand it."

As I was going from Libya to Egypt, while I was traversing the rocks known as the Grand Syrte, I encountered a tomb built in the waves of the sea, and I looked with astonishment at the statues that surmounted it.

In the center of the group was a man lying face down. A snake the size of a viper was coiled around his foot. The man seemed to be drinking avidly, and was surrounded by women who were pouring water over him.

The epitaph explained the strange composition. It said: *Passer-by, beware the dipsad of the sands. A dipsad bit this man; while he drinks avidly and the nymphs of the seven rivers*

---

[67] The *Dipsadidae* constitute a large genus of snakes in modern taxonomy, only found in the New World, but the mythological dipsad of Libya, described here, is best known from two poems by the Roman poet Lucan in the first century A.D. and the satirist Lucian a hundred years later, both elaborating an account given by Nicander of Colophon in the second century B.C.

337

pout all the freshness of their urns over him, he is dying of thirst and heat.

And I was told by an indigene that a dipsad is a snake that lives in the deserts of southern Libya. A person bitten by one feels a thirst that is not disagreeable at first, but as he drinks, his thirst increases and is exasperated. Every mouthful causes a great ardent fire to run through his mouth and throat into his breast and his entrails. If he bathes, as oil nourishes a blaze, the water burns him with a violence that becomes more intolerable every second. The unfortunate eventually dies as if in the flames of a pyre.

Once, the Libyan added, the requests of the sick man, murmured at first but soon roared, were obeyed. He was given something to drink, and abundant water was poured over his body, as over a burning house. Sometimes he was even plunged into a river. Today, instructed by experience, the physicians shut him away him for nine days and refuse any beverage to his pleas and cries. Those who have not drunk anything between the moment when they were bitten and the moment when they are imprisoned are cured, but those whose misfortune leads them to encounter the slightest drop of water die in the most frightful torment.

XLIX. The Two Nightingales

"Aristippus," affirmed Excycle, "had more intelligence and grace than Diogenes."

"Tyrants and slaves," remarked Psychodorus, "call graces of intelligence I know not what sinuous and crawling suppleness. Personally, I scorn Aristippus and admire Diogenes, for what I call graces and surprises of intelligence are unexpected wing-beats.

"But rather hear a parable:"

An inhabitant of the country came to Syracuse and went into the palace of the tyrant. The latter had a bird in a gilded cage. The peasant listened to it and said:

"Poor creature. Its dolorous song, which is striving impotently to imitate joy, is racking the nerves. However, it seems that if it were free it would have a rather beautiful voice." With a more vivid and joyful smile he added: "But last night, I heard a nightingale."

The courtiers burst out laughing.

"O rustic," one of them asked, "are you deaf and blind? Can't you see, even if you're incapable of hearing, that the bird to which you're listening is a nightingale?"

The peasant made a broad gesture of astonishment. He drew nearer and considered the bird for some time in silence. Then he declared:

"I see, in fact the form and plumage of a nightingale, but I hear the voice of a caged bird."

"They doubtless sing better in the vicinity of your cottage!"

The peasant's ecstatic eyes seemed to be gazing at and absent landscape, and his ear listening to a melody from the past. "Oh," he exclaimed, "the song of the nightingale who is my neighbor is a rain of wellbeing that penetrates you, for it is made of amour and liberty."

He drew away without looking back, pursued by the jeers of courtiers and slaves. The slaves and courtiers believed that one sings better in a palace than in the country, and that, for rendering a voice more beautiful, nothing can compare with a gilded cage.

L. The Slope

"Oh," moaned Excycle, "the horror of descending ineluctably toward death, the horror of being unable to pause in the shelter of a joy, or, when the slope of life rolls us further down, of not being able to climb back up to that freshness and sweetness...."

But Psychodorus said: "Hear, my son, the facile mystery of joy and dolor. There are elements in each of our emotions that depend on space, which you can renew, but there are others that time carries away, and those, fortunately, escape the will.

"Yesterday, while you were eating a few olives and chatting with Theomanes, I saw your face suddenly light up with radiance, as limpid and softly singing as the spring next to which you were lying. Do you want us to return to that spring? We can be there at the same hour when you were joyful. In the same play of shadow and light, you can extend your limbs on the same grass. You can eat olives again and repeat the same quips that you were making to Theomanes.

"You're shaking your head, Excycle, in a gesture of refusal. You know very well that you won't find yesterday again; the flower has faded and the perfume vanished.

"Remember, now, the thorns that scratched you the other day and made you cry out. Ah! Your lips are parting, Excycle, in order not to cry out. The thorns of the other day are desiccated and devoid of force; they can no longer scratch you, but they're tickling you to the point of laughter."

Now, what you know today you felt vaguely yesterday and the other day. That sentiment gave flavor to your joy and your pain, as the salt we mix with it gives flavor to our bread.

"O Excycle, it is passing through them and being unable to return that makes pleasures so agreeable; it is passing through them and being unable to return that makes pains so light.

"When the moment presents you with a cup of sweetness, it pours the bitterness into it of the sentiment of the temporary and the unique; but only that bitterness prevents the sweetness of the cup becoming insipid and sickening.

"If, to your lips, which recoil in vain, the hour applies a bitter cup, you know that the chalice will be drained and that you will never encounter the same again. That knowledge is the drop of honey that renders bitterness tolerable to the many, agreeable to a few.

"When I try, Excycle, to dream of eternity, I ordinarily see it twisting upon itself and closing like a crown. Beings have been traveling the circle forever and will never cease to travel it, but they will encounter, in the course of the Great Year, many rivers from which one drinks forgetfulness. And I rejoice, although tomorrow has been yesterday a myriad times over, that it will still be tomorrow, by which I mean the unknown and the inevitable.

"Do you not see, my son, that space, because we believe that we can move through it freely, scarcely interests us, but duration and what we sense as fatal impassion us. For every man who reads a description of the earth, there are a thousand who interrogate oracles and diviners anxiously.

"Even when you return to a familiar place, it is an effort that you are making in order to return to a familiar time; your legs walk because they believe they are transporting your mind and your memory.

"Listen, Excycle. The majority of fools put their happiness in the impenetrable and inevitable future. If they possessed the power you desire, there would no longer be any more happiness for them, even in dreams. For none of those inept seekers places a joy that is prolonged on the mountain he has visited, in the plain that is familiar to him or beside the stream from which he has drunk. Only one form appears beautiful to them, an ungraspable form that no sculptor will ever realize, and which he will always call tomorrow. Only one color intoxicates their soul, a color that painters do not know and which, like the blue of the horizon, flees and vanishes as one approaches it, the color of tomorrow.

"For myself, since the day when I understood the words of Diogenes, my life has been a river of free joy that flows over itself. However, I experience, in the firm certainty of my wellbeing, I know not what amusement in reflecting new and unexpected sights. I have loved the narrow green landscape in which trees close the horizon to me like a shivering and singing wall. I dream with a hopeful emotion about the extents that the privation of winter will expose to me. And my seething waters receive, equal joys that add value to one another, the reflection of the midday sun or the great sky that starry evenings unfurl like a regal tent.

"But instead, Excycle, and all of you, my friends, hear a parable:"

I visited certain people who have legs for time as we have them for space. They slid at will along both directions of their lives, descending toward their mouth or returning to their source. If they desired to pause, they pause. And their pace had exactly the degree of slowness or rapidity that their caprice imprinted upon it.

Some, when I passed that way, were sitting on the slope of their life as we are sitting on the slope of this hill. They were yawning and saying:

"Why elsewhere rather than here? Such a mist of ennui rises from all landscapes, or this quivering heaviness of warmth and fatigue...."

For the Moirae have refused them the shelter and the calm, the restful death of a few hours, that is sleep. Slow or rapid, stagnant or flowing, it is necessary that they bear the intolerable burden of continuity, the tenacious consciousness of their existence.

Some hasten toward the abyss. Their entire duration is a cascade and it falls in fewer hours than what you call a day.

Some, on the brink of death, stop or go back, but there is no valor in those returns. Those people go backwards, sad and discontented with themselves, like the timid bather who recoils before the initial coldness of the water or the effort and peril of swimming.

Here is one thing that my guide to that strange country told me: no one has ever consented, even lying on the softness of grass or remaking the voyage twenty times in either direction, to endure for one of our years. Amid praises addressed to death and the unknown, however, or insults addressed to life and banality, they take, the most belated at the time when our infants are beginning to walk, the last step that you are lamenting.

Psychodorus added: "O Excycle, if, to punish your folly, a cruel god were to open an insurmountable ditch between your imminent thirst and the spring of death...ah! I believe I can see you sitting on the edge of the arid ravine, hands extended like desires toward the forbidden freshness; and you are weeping, Excycle; and only your abundant tears sometimes relieve, momentarily, the burning eternity of your thirst."

LI. Geometry in Conflict

"O Psychodorus," exclaimed Excycle, "you never tell us about anything but dreams...."

"If I could say enough about dreams, perhaps I would have said everything about what you call reality."

"O narrator of dreams," asked Theomanes, bitterly, "what injustice permits you, then, to criticize my thoughts by calling them dreams?"

"I never reproach a thought for having wings and being a dream. I sometimes reproach one for being unaware that other dreams are living and fluttering around it. When you believe that the line that draws an object on a wall or the shadow that it projects on the ground is the same as the object itself, then I criticize you. I criticize you, above all, if you affirm that the dimensions and the direction of the shadow do not vary. But rather listen to a parable:"

On a summer day in my youth I was passing through Megara. I decided to visit old Euclid, a disciple of Socrates and the greatest of geometers.[68]

Euclid had gone out, but his slaves affirmed that he would be back soon. I therefore waited in the courtyard, where the air was more agreeable than in the apartments.

Toward the middle of the courtyard, a large block of marble was expecting a bust of Socrates promised to Euclid by one of his friends, a sculptor. I stared at that marble, and soon my ears thought they could hear sounds emerging from the stone, as is said of the statue of Memnon.

---

[68] Psychodorus is confusing Euclid of Megara, previously cited in the text, with the geometer Euclid, who was active in Alexandria in a later period, around 300 B.C.

Those sounds, indistinct at first, gradually took on a frightening meaning in my mind.

And I realized that the Line, the Surface and the Block were quarreling, because the Surface had just been insolently singing its own praises.

The Block, with a heavy remark, imposed silence on it. "Shut up, O poverty, O absence of thickness, O Nothing!" it said.

The Surface replied: "If I disappeared and one of my sisters consented to replace me, you, poor Block, would be a mist that the sun would disperse. It's you who ought to be silent, you who are nothing but the assembly and sum of my sisters."

But the Line became irritated in its turn.

"I'm tired of your boasting, Surface! If I disappeared and none of my sisters consented to replace me, I ask you, O proud one, what would remain of you?"

"O insolent poverty," exclaimed the Surface, "O absence of breadth, O Nothing!"

The Block affirmed, with the crushing tone of certainty:

"You're dreams of Euclid, but I exist."

They both replied: "You're nothing but a society of what your ingratitude dares to call dreams."

When Euclid arrived, I was still listening. Now, the as-yet-unsculpted Socrates who was to surmount the pedestal spoke to me. His voice was distant and airy, coming from the land of what might be. Nevertheless, I listened to it.

"O my son," it said, "lines and surfaces are thoughts and dreams of men, but the block is a rendezvous of lines and surfaces. The sunlight illuminates some of them. The light of your mind can illuminate successively myriads of others. It would never exhaust, even if it were obstinate in doing so for eternity, the lines agitating in the smallest surface, or the surfaces that intersect and penetrate one another in the smallest volume."

The distant voice, amicable and slightly mocking, continued: "Believe me Psychodorus, what you call reality is, like the block at which you are looking, an intersection of thoughts

346

and dreams. Never affirm one of those thoughts or dreams as the total reality; but never affirm, either, a reality distinct from the ensemble of dreams."

Excycle asked: "Did you repeat to Euclid the various discourses you had heard?"

"I carefully refrained from doing so," replied Psychodorus, smiling. "Euclid, an admirable geometer, was a poor philosopher; he loved to dispute, to demonstrate, to refute, instead of loving to think. He sometimes resembled the obstinate donkey who does not want to go to the other side of the mountain, and the deafening certainty of whose cries denies that which he refuses to go to see."

LII. The Last Parable

For several days, Psychodorus and the most faithful of his disciples had been marching along the frontiers of Greece. They arrived at a mountain and the philosopher said: "This is the place of separation. It's necessary now that I continue my route toward the She-Bear and that you retrace your steps."

"Master," begged Eubulus, permit me to follow you still, and always to follow you."

"What you are asking, my son, would be bad for you and bad for me. Perhaps the words I have said to you thus far will help you to hear the voice of your soul. But believe me, the time has come when it is appropriate for you to sit down in solitude in order to listen jealously to the things that you have to say to yourself."

"In what way would our presence be bad for you?" asked Excycle, wounded and almost aggressive.

"I came to you overflowing with a wisdom that wanted to spread. I've given you my surplus in order for you to make of it what you can. Now, what I had to say, I've said. If I continued to talk to men, it would no longer be my superabundant thought that would create my words. It's my speech that would be projecting in me, as on arid ground, shadows and appearances of thought, and the vain itch to talk, or that folly, the desire to appear wise, would create my words."

Theomanes exclaimed: "If, Psychodorus, instead of expressing and exhausting your thought alone, you related the instruction of the gods, you would never feel the weakness that you confess nobly; you would be a lake that a higher source assisted continuously, and never allowed to dry out."

Psychodorus shook his head. "The work of the morning," he said, "is health and joy. But when the evening and fatigue weigh heavily upon the rumps of the oxen and the shoulder of the laborer, the laborer unhitches the oxen and lies down with them on the grass to go to sleep. Tomorrow they will work again. To give of oneself in a fortunate measure aids in self-formation and self-realization. To give of oneself too obstinately deforms. I have deposited on the shelves of the human hive the honey that I had stored. A fraction of that honey will be useful and nourishing, a fraction will be embittered by the dirty cells. Now, I tell you, the bee ought to bury itself in solitude, visit unknown flowers, penetrate the treasures of virgin calices and amass on its laborious thighs different honey and different wax."

"If I understand correctly," Eubulus said, joyfully, "you're promising to come back."

"I'm not making any promises. But if, thanks to the retreat, I find an excess of strength and thought in me again, then I shall return, certainly not to you, but to other men. It is no longer necessary that the best of you receive, for fear that they might become idle and incapable of any effort. Even you, Eubulus, will only approach for a rapid salutation and a memory. But perhaps others will be hungry and thirsty and they will surround my branches with renewed fertility and bite into the savor of my fruits."

"Master," said Eubulus, "you're breaking my heart, and yet I dare not contradict your wisdom. But it isn't in a valley that we ought to part. Let's go up on to a mountain together. We shall enjoy in common a grandiose spectacle, and it's on the summit, after a valiant effort, that we'll separate. Perhaps also, as one gives a present to a guest who is leaving, you'll tell us one last parable up there, as an adieu."

"Come on, then, my sons. And if the proud mountain or the broad spectacle tells me a tale, I'll repeat it to you."

Now, when they were on the summit, they looked for a long time at the plain and the sky. Then, they sat down on the narrow peak crowded together and they fell silent, waiting emotionally.

Psychodorus was still gazing, as if, in fact, things were accumulating words in the vase of his silence. But a light

349

breeze got up that made him shiver. Then, as a lyre silent for a long time sings under the plectrum, Psychodorus spoke.

He had never had so much enthusiasm in his eyes and his tone, and never more smiles and doubt on his lips.

But before the hectic canticle, he voiced the quiver and the uncertainty of this prelude:

"Rejuvenated by a bath in my own being, I came to you, my sons, with the matinal song of the skylark on my old man's lips. Now, a new evening is descending upon me and my eyes are avid for repose. Hear, then, the crepuscular song. May it, like the setting sun, shine a heroic light toward your souls."

God thought: "I am powerful." And the souls of kings were irradiated.

God wondered: "On what shall I exert my power?" And in space were sown, along with our earth, myriads of earths on which kings carved out kingdoms."

God affirmed: "I am omnipotent." And from the glorious center violent and avid souls sprang forth on all the worlds: Cyruses, Xerxes and Alexanders.

But the Being interrogated himself: ""Am I really omnipotent?" And he replied: "No power exists outside me, and that does not come from me. But am I powerful to the extent that nothing is impossible for me? How would I know? Every thought of mine is creative, with the result that for me, the impossible and the unthinkable are confused. I cannot know what my limits are, nor whether I am limited. O strange weakness!"

"Now, during this reactive meditation, shadows of negation were projected on the worlds alongside the conquering flames previously irradiated. A Thomyris lay in wait for each Cyrus. The road of each Xerxes, previously as broad and luminous as the sea, darkened and shrank into a defile where a Leonidas was waiting. Next to each Alexander, an impotent Porus emerged, and a great cup overflowing with so much life that it would give death.

The Creator looked at the universe delivered to tyrants and the murderers of tyrants. The struggle between those who always said "Yes," to themselves and those who said "No," seemed somber to him.

"Alas," he regretted, "the earths I have created are bad." And that repentance poured out deluges of water and fire.

God wept at having had that maleficent remorse.

And mild and feeble beings, in long moaning processions, wandered over the worlds.

"I am good, though," the Being said to himself. "Bounty is an ever-extended spring, which does not sleep." Great active devotions emanated from him, and God smiled at the Heracles.

Now the Spirit had many other dreams and many other thoughts.

The Unique affirmed: "I am Evidence." And there were the Pythagorases, the Parmenides, the Empedocles, and the Platos, all the mystics, the ecstatics, the seers of the invisible, and the stammerers of the ineffable.

The Immense thought: "Infinite in detail, I am impossible to embrace entirely." And those who, groping in the dark, seized the petty particular verities of their universe, but would never see either the Center or the Circle, appeared, curbed and anxious.

The Creative Thought said: "I am Beauty." And the Homers sung to the lyre; the Phidiases gave harmonious life to marble; the Parrhasiuses and the Apelles made serene canvas smile.

When God had thought a great deal he compared the creations of his thought with himself, and, amazed, he said: "I have given more than I have kept. The ensemble of the worlds has now become greater than me." And that astonishment created the blind souls of atheists and deniers.

Now the Generous perceived that his diminished power was no longer producing any but incomplete, wretched and malevolent beings. Then, like the cynic who could to longer do anything for others or for himself, he held his breath and died, God, in one last movement that made the worlds shiver, dispersed what remained of himself and gave it to the universe.

Now the Creator was no longer outside creations. The waters, wombs of the living, no longer feeling the fecundating power upon them, shivered in sorrow and caused the aridity of the rocks to hear the sad vocalization: "Great Pan is dead."

Multiply, however, on all the earths, the Thought was made flesh. There were strange little infants in cradles. When their mothers followed the direction of their gaze, they believed that they saw new stars lighting up in the sky; and their wailing seemed to collide with echoes to sing: "Peace to men and good will."

Each on his earth, those who were the last effort and, as it were, the last dispersed limbs of God, traversed life doing good. A small number of the poor and weak followed them and loved them. But one day, without comprehending any of their words, the people acclaimed them. The powerful arrested them and put them to death.

Then, heavy with pity, each of those divine beings descended to the earth immediately inferior to his own, the one that his compatriots, divining it vaguely, called Tartarus and populated with crazy tortures. He tried to enable the inhabitants of that slightly more dolorous world to hear words of hope, to tell them that what they dubiously named the Elysian Fields was an earth as real as theirs and that their efforts toward thought and toward good would take them there one day, like wings.

Then each of those last envoys rose up to the earth immediately superior to the one that had seen him suffer and die. He reached that universe, which his compatriots divined vaguely and populated with crazy marvels. He recommenced in that slightly less harsh world, his work of external suffering and joy of ascension. And the one that belonged to the most perfect word returned to the center in order to recommence God.

Uplifted by hope and dolor, the procession of worlds rose slowly toward God, in order to remake him entirely. Everywhere, the Idea of striving Love was combated, and apparently killed, by the Forces of Hatred. Sometimes, clever powerful individuals took possession of it and crowned themselves with it, like a lie of light. But the bleeding Idea that was scarcely perceptible continued its slow and invincible effort. It carried away in its wake the hostile forces that were tearing it apart. And the whole, every myriad of years, rose by the breadth of an infant's finger.

When the times were accomplished, when God was reconstituted entirely by the voluntary death of the universe, he thought, in a miserly first joy:

"Every cycle resembles the previous cycles. The ring of eternity is always the same. What point is there in recommencing the anticipated pleasures and dolors familiar to my dilatation, to which they respond, in centuries of centuries, the sufferings and joys savored thousands and thousands of times of the concentration of worlds?"

But God perceived that that egotistical thought was transformed into evil beings.

He knew his inexorable power, and that each of his dreams had to project crawlings or flights. He exclaimed: "I'm too great not to create!" And admirably resigned beings, Socrates accepting death, Diogenes accepting the world, radiated.

The thought of God continued: "I love you and I want you to be free, O my Necessity. For perhaps this double movement, always the same in appearance, is a little more beautiful each Great Year; perhaps every time, the sacrifice of the God dying for the life of the worlds, and the sacrifice of the worlds dying for the life of God, becomes more conscious and voluntary."

And God continued to extinguish himself in luminous universes and radiant souls.